Praise for
That Summer

"*That Summer* incisively examines the way privilege shapes and shields those who wield it, *and* explores the circuitous path toward healing when justice falls short. Despite the heavy subject matter, Weiner's prose is as warm and inviting as ever."

—*The New York Times*

"Weiner has made a major literary career out of writing engrossing popular novels that take women seriously. One of Weiner's signature strengths as a writer is her ability to realistically depict how people change in body and soul. . . . Weiner writes incisively, yet with restraint. . . . *That Summer* is a compelling, nuanced novel about the long, terrible aftermath of sexual assault and the things that can be stolen from women that can never be fully restored. But, because it's a Jennifer Weiner novel, it's no polemic. It's empowering in its own way. Weiner seems to steadfastly believe in the saving grace of humor, the ability of time to open up possibilities, and the strength of female friendship. Me, too."

—*The Washington Post*

"Weiner's ability to take a complex, painful situation and spin it into an engaging, thoughtful story about women's inner lives is showcased throughout this novel. The beautiful beachside settings and aspirational lifestyles are on full display, but the depth of the story is what shines."

—*Library Journal*

"Like many of Weiner's works, the novel explores themes of femininity and motherhood, but it's the book's tackling of the #MeToo movement through more than one complicit character that sets it apart."

—*Shondaland*

"[Weiner's] legions of fans will applaud this emotionally affecting and often surprising story."

—*Publishers Weekly*

"A classic Weiner heroine who grows wings . . . Weiner's storytelling skill is such that she paints an uncompromising, complicated portrait that is also a lot of fun to read. Weiner's latest is a summer banger with a ripped-from-the-headlines plot, which is sure to garner lots of attention."

—*Booklist* (starred review)

"Fans will enjoy references to the murder plot of Weiner's previous novel, *Big Summer* (2020), and sprinklings of Weiner's signature descriptions of food and cooking."

—*Kirkus Reviews*

That Summer

BOOKS BY JENNIFER WEINER

FICTION

Good in Bed

In Her Shoes

Little Earthquakes

Goodnight Nobody

The Guy Not Taken

Certain Girls

Best Friends Forever

Fly Away Home

Then Came You

The Next Best Thing

All Fall Down

Who Do You Love

Mrs. Everything

Big Summer

NONFICTION

Hungry Heart

FOR YOUNG READERS

The Littlest Bigfoot

Little Bigfoot, Big City

Jennifer Weiner

That Summer

A NOVEL

WASHINGTON
SQUARE PRESS

ATRIA

New York   London   Toronto   Sydney   New Delhi

**WASHINGTON
SQUARE PRESS**

ATRIA

An Imprint of Simon & Schuster, Inc.
1230 Avenue of the Americas
New York, NY 10020

First Washington Square Press/Atria Paperback edition April 2022

WASHINGTON SQUARE PRESS / ATRIA PAPERBACK and colophon are trademarks of Simon & Schuster, Inc.

For information about special discounts for bulk purchases, please contact Simon & Schuster Special Sales at 1-866-506-1949 or business@simonandschuster.com.

The Simon & Schuster Speakers Bureau can bring authors to your live event. For more information or to book an event, contact the Simon & Schuster Speakers Bureau at 1-866-248-3049 or visit our website at www.simonspeakers.com.

Manufactured in the United States of America

3   5   7   9   10   8   6   4

Library of Congress Control Number: 2021932216

ISBN 978-1-5011-3354-1
ISBN 978-1-5011-3355-8 (pbk)
ISBN 978-1-5011-3356-5 (ebook)

In memory of Carolyn Reidy

WILD GEESE

You do not have to be good.
You do not have to walk on your knees
for a hundred miles through the desert, repenting.
You only have to let the soft animal of your body
    love what it loves.
Tell me about despair, yours, and I will tell you mine.
Meanwhile the world goes on.
Meanwhile the sun and the clear pebbles of the rain
are moving across the landscapes,
over the prairies and the deep trees,
the mountains and the rivers.
Meanwhile the wild geese, high in the clean blue air,
are heading home again.
Whoever you are, no matter how lonely,
the world offers itself to your imagination,
calls to you like the wild geese, harsh and exciting—
over and over announcing your place
in the family of things.
        —Mary Oliver

I'm just a girl in the world.
That's all that you'll let me be.
        —Gwen Stefani, "Just a Girl"

Prologue

She is fifteen years old that summer, a thoughtful, book-struck girl with long-lashed hazel eyes and a long-legged body that still doesn't completely feel like her own. She lives in a row house in South Boston with her parents and two sisters, and attends a private school in Cambridge, on a scholarship, where she gets mostly Bs, except for As in English and art. She dreams about falling in love.

One afternoon in May, her mom, who is a secretary for the English department at Boston University, comes home from work with news. One of the professors in her department has two little kids and a house on the Cape. This woman, Dr. Levy, is looking for a mother's helper for the summer, and thinks that Diana sounds perfect for the job.

Her father is against it. "She's too young to spend a whole summer away," he says. "She'll probably meet a pack of spoiled rich kids and come back with her nose in the air."

Together, Diana and her mother go to work on changing his mind. Her mother talks about Diana's college fund, her dreams of the future, how she'll get to spend every day with a real, live writer, and how the fifteen hundred dollars that Dr. Levy's offered to pay will more than cover her expenses for the coming school year. Diana, meanwhile, reads every novel she can find that's set on the Cape, and describes for her father the pristine, golden beaches, sand dunes with cranberry bogs and poets' shacks hidden in their declivities. She conjures the taste of briny oysters and butter-drenched lobsters, fried clams eaten with salt water–pruned fingers, ice-cream cones devoured after a day in the sun. For Christmas she gives him a coffee-table book of photographs, holding her breath when he flips to the pictures of Provincetown, and the drag queens on Commercial Street, six and a half feet tall in their heels and more beautiful than most women, but her dad only shakes his head and chuckles, saying, *You don't see that every day.*

She doesn't tell either of her parents that what she is most looking forward to is what her sisters have told her about their own summer at the beach—how she'll be on her own for the first time in her life, free to enjoy the sun, and the beach bonfires, and the boys.

"And you're going to be in a mansion," Julia says, her freckled nose crinkling at the memory of the cottage in Hyannis where she'd stayed three years before, sharing a bedroom with the kids, and a bathroom with the kids *and* the parents, in a one-story house that had smelled like mold. "Truro," Kara sighs. "You're a lucky duck." For Christmas, Diana's sisters present her with a yellow bikini. It's neither polka-dotted nor especially itsy-bitsy, but it's still enough to make her dad harrumph and her mom give a secretive, tucked-up kind of smile.

In the bathroom, Diana tries on the swimsuit, standing on the lip of the bathtub so that she'll be able to see as much of her body as possible in the mirror over the sink, turning from side to side as she sucks in her stomach and regrets the stretch marks that worm across her thighs. She is fifteen years old and has never been kissed, but she knows that a summer in Cape Cod—*on the Cape,* as people say—will change that.

When her parents finally tell her she can go, she's so happy that she throws her arms around them and says, "Thank you, thank you, thank you!"

Her grandmother gives her a hundred dollars—"you'll need some new things"—and her mother takes Diana shopping. Together, they scour the clearance racks at Nordstrom and Filene's. Diana packs her Christmas bikini, plus a plain blue tank for actual swimming, a denim romper, and a sundress made of white eyelet cotton, with skinny straps that tie in bows on her shoulders. She brings worn copies of *A Wrinkle in Time, A Tree Grows in Brooklyn*, a collection of Stephen King short stories, and *The Mists of Avalon*, thinking that the familiar books will be a comfort, wondering if it will feel different to read them in a new place.

The children are Sam and Sarah, four-year-old twins. Mr. Weinberg, their father, is some kind of attorney. He'll spend his weekdays in Boston, come up to the Cape on Friday afternoons, and leave Monday mornings. Dr. Veronica Levy—"call me Ronnie"—is a real-life novelist, with a doctorate in the Romantic British poets, the subject she teaches at BU. She's written three novels, and, ten years ago, one of them, the story of a woman leaving an unhappy marriage, was turned into a movie—not a hit, but they still show it sometimes on cable. "I still can't believe how well that book sold," Dr. Levy says as they cruise along Route 6, through the Eastham rotary and on toward Provincetown. The road narrows from two lanes into one, a dark ribbon twining its way toward the ends of the earth. "Lots of women out there who want happy endings. I was very lucky." Diana can't help gasping when they crunch up the shell-lined driveway and she sees the house, three stories of glass and silvery cedar. "It's an upside-down house," Dr. Levy says, and tells her to go ahead and look around—"the kids can help me unload."

Diana steps inside, breathing the faintly musty scent of a house that's been closed for the winter. On the ground floor are two bedrooms, each with its own bathroom, and a powder room in between. The larger room, with framed finger paintings and ABC posters on the wall, is for the twins, and the room across the hall, with a queen-sized bed with a blue-and-green-striped comforter, is hers. Her bathroom (her bathroom!) has marble tile floors and a white-tiled shower, and the floors and the towel racks are heated. It's sparkling clean and looks barely used. As she arranges her handful of toiletries on the counter, Diana can feel her cheeks starting to ache from smiling.

There are two more bedrooms on the second level, including the master suite, where the bed and the bathtub both have stunning views of the bay. The top floor is one enormous room, with a kitchen and dining room on one end and a sprawling living room on the other. Floor-to-ceiling windows surround the room, filling it with light, looking out over the sand and the water, making Diana feel like she's standing on the deck of a ship. There are sliding doors with decks everywhere—decks off the kitchen, with a grill and a picnic table, decks off the second-floor bedrooms, and a half-moon deck off the living room. She's brought a camera, the family's Pentax, and she can't wait to ask Dr. Levy to take her picture, to show her sisters and her mom where she's living and how well it's all worked out.

"What do you think?" Dr. Levy calls from the kitchen.

"It's the most beautiful house I've ever seen in my life," she says, and Dr. Levy smiles, looking pleased and flustered.

"When I was about your age, my parents bought this tiny cottage on a dune, a few miles north. They'd rent it out for most of the summer, but every year we'd come and stay for two weeks, all six of us. Some of my happiest memories are in Truro. I always dreamed I'd buy a place here, and bring my kids for the summer." She hums to herself as she unpacks the groceries, smiling, looking younger, and happier, than she did when they left Boston that morning.

Diana quickly falls into the rhythm of the summer days. She's on the clock from eight a.m. to three o'clock in the afternoon, Monday through Friday. She sets an alarm for seven thirty so she'll have time to shower before helping the twins through their morning routines, making sure teeth are brushed and beds are made and breakfasts, which always include fresh fruit, are consumed. Three mornings a week, Dr. Levy drives them to Gull Pond, a freshwater pond at the end of a long, rutted dirt road in Wellfleet, the next town over. The pond, carved out of the earth by a glacier, has clear, fresh water with a white-sand bottom, and it's ringed by lushly leaved trees. A few docks protrude into the water. People paddle canoes or tack back and forth in sailboats. Kids paddle in the shallow end, putting their faces in the water at their instructor's word, blowing bubbles. Teenagers sun themselves on the dock.

Dr. Levy stakes out a spot near one of the scrub pine trees and helps Diana get the twins ready for their lessons. Sam is skinny, and speaks with a lisp. He hates the feeling of sunscreen, and whines and tries to squirm away. His sister's more stoic, patient while Diana dabs the thick white cream on her nose and her cheeks. "Stop being such a baby," she says to her brother, her hands on her hips.

Dr. Levy kicks off her flip-flops and leaves her cover-up hanging from a protruding branch. In her plain black one-piece suit, she wades out until she's waist-deep, then submerges herself, dunking her head, standing up with water streaming down her shoulders and back. Once she's taken the first plunge, she launches herself into the water and swims in a slow, steady freestyle, all the way across the pond and back again.

"What if you get to the middle and you're tired? Or you get a cramp?" Diana asks. Dr. Levy looks thoughtful, and then a little guilty.

"I really should use one of those personal flotation devices," she says, half to herself. Then, brightening, she says, "But I'm a pretty good swimmer. Honestly, the only thing to be afraid of are the snapping turtles. And once, I was right in the middle, and something brushed my leg. It was probably just a fish, or a water weed, but I screamed like I was in a horror movie."

Dr. Levy has the same stretch marks as Diana, plus more on her bosom. There are fine lines around her eyes and dark circles underneath them. She pulls her hair back in a scrunchie most days, and doesn't seem to notice, or mind, that it's frizzy. She has a nice smile and an easy laugh, and Mr. Weinberg still looks at her like she's beautiful. She's a good mother, too, calm and patient, never yelling (although Diana thinks it's probably easy to be calm and patient when you've got someone to help you most of the day).

At Gull Pond, while the kids are at their lessons and Dr. Levy's paddling across the pond, Diana sits on the shore with the other nannies and au pairs and mothers' helpers. Alicia, who's got short, feathered brown hair and wide-set brown eyes, a curvy figure, and golden-brown skin, is with the Dexters. The previous summer, Mrs. Dexter and the three Dexter kids, plus Alicia, had a place in Nantucket. "Ugh, don't get me started about Nantucket," Alicia says, using her fingers to comb her hair back from her face. "Everyone's white and everyone's thin. Like, I don't even think they let fat people off the ferry. They just make you get back on and go back where you came from. I felt hideous!" she says, and the other girls hurry to reassure her that she's not fat. Maeve, who's Irish, tall and pale and freckled, with red hair and knobby knees, takes care of the Donegans' new baby. The previous summer, Maeve worked at Moby Dick's on Route 6, living in a dorm with thirty other Irish girls employed by the restaurants and hotels on the Outer Cape. Maeve still knows the Moby Dick's crew, so she tells the other girls about all their parties and beach bonfires, and makes sure they know they have an open invitation.

Marie-Francoise is the Driscolls' au pair, and Kelly works for the Lathrops, who live in a mansion on the same dune as Dr. Levy. Kelly helps clean, and watches the Lathrop grandchildren when the grandchildren are in residence.

Most days, Diana and Dr. Levy and the kids spend the late mornings and early afternoons by the water, either at the pond or at Corn Hill Beach with its wide stretch of sand and its gentle, lapping waves. Dr. Levy twists an umbrella into the sand, rocking it from side to side to make sure it won't blow over, and Diana plasters the twins with more sunscreen, then gives her own shoulders and back a more modest coating from the bottle of Coppertone she keeps in her tote. Dr. Levy dons a gigantic red-and-white sun hat and sits in a folding canvas chair with an extra-large iced tea and a novel or a *People* magazine (sometimes, Diana notes with amusement, she'll have the *People* folded up inside of the novel). On Fridays, Mr. Weinberg meets them, bringing them a late lunch of sandwiches from Jams, the convenience store in the center of town, or fried oysters and French fries from PJ's in Wellfleet. "Oh, I shouldn't," Dr. Levy says, helping herself to his fries as the kids come out of the water.

"Feed me like a baby bird!" Sam says.

"Feed me like an animal in a zoo!" says Sarah.

Laughing, Diana gives them chunks of icy watermelon or bites of string cheese or pepperoni, dropping the food from her fingers into their eager mouths. Sometimes, after lunch, the Lewis Brothers ice-cream truck shows up. The driver, a young bearded man with an easy smile, emerges from the olive-green truck and blows a single note on a plastic horn, and the kids, screaming with delight, run out of the water to ask their parents for money. Dr. Levy always obliges. "Don't tell Daddy," she says, digging her wallet out of the tote bag and handing Diana a twenty. "If they've got that mint cookie, can you get me a tiny baby scoop in a cup?"

By two o'clock, the kids are tired. Diana and Dr. Levy gather up the blankets and towels, the plastic shovels and the pails full of scallop shells and jingle shells. Diana herds the kids into the outdoor shower, using the handheld attachment to spray their swimsuits and their bodies, making them raise their arms over their heads, then bend and touch their toes so she can rinse away every grain of sand.

After showers comes siesta. Diana gets the kids dressed again and puts them down for a nap. Usually they fall asleep immediately, stuporous from their exertions and the sun. Then she's on her own. "Enjoy!" Dr. Levy says, from her spot on the couch, or behind the kitchen counter. "We'll see you at dinner."

Sometimes she takes a book from the crammed shelves in the living room. Each one, when opened, exudes the smell of sea salt and paper and damp. Sometimes she sits on the deck overlooking the bay and writes in her journal, describing the pond or the bay or the beach, the color of the sky at sunset or the sound of Maeve's accent. Sometimes she paints—she's brought a travel-sized watercolor kit, and a pad of artist's paper, and she's attempted several sunsets and seascapes.

But most days, she puts on her bikini, rubs more sunscreen onto her shoulders, and goes down the six flights of stairs to the beach. For the first two weeks, she strolls back to Corn Hill Beach, where she spreads out a towel and sits in the sun, listening to the cheerful din of kids and parents, the music from a half-dozen portable radios, the sound of instructions, sometimes patient, sometimes exasperated, as a dad tries to teach his kids how to sail a Sunfish or fly a kite. Sometimes one of her nanny friends will be there, and they'll trade bits of gossip about their families. Diana hears all about it when Marie-Francoise almost gets fired after Mrs. Driscoll found a boy in her bedroom, and when, on a Saturday night in P-town, Kelly spots Mr. Lathrop through the window of the Squealing Pig with a woman who is not Mrs. Lathrop on his lap.

"What are you going to do?" Diana asks, wide-eyed, and Kelly says, "He gave me forty dollars to forget I saw anything." She shrugs and says, "Turns out, I have a terrible memory."

One afternoon, Diana rides her bike all the way to Province-town, almost ten miles along the road that hugs the coastline. She passes the Flower Cottages, which are trim and white with green shutters, each one named for a different flower, the two motels, and the cottage colonies that straddle the line between Truro and Provincetown. When she's in town, she locks her bike at the library and walks along Commercial Street. She tries not to gawk at the drag queens, and slips into a store that sells vibra-tors and lubricants and leather harnesses, flavored condoms, and other things, glass dildos and cock rings and anal beads in locked glass cases. She leans over, her breath misting the glass, trying to figure out how each item works, which part goes where, and to what effect. No boy has ever touched her, and at home, with her sister sleeping less than three feet away, she's too nervous to touch herself.

But now, she's got a bedroom to herself, a bedroom with a lock on the door, and her shower has a nozzle that she can slip off its post and hold between her legs, adjusting the flow and the pressure until she's gasping and quivering, limp-limbed and flushed against the tiles, and the water's gone from hot to warm to cold. *Having a wonderful summer*, she writes, in the postcards she sends home. *Really enjoying myself!*

One afternoon, she decides to try to get a look at the Lath-rop mansion from the water, so she descends the stairs and starts walking in the opposite direction, toward Great Hollow Beach. She's wearing her Christmas bikini, with a fine gold chain around her right ankle and her hair spilling loose against her shoulders. The sunshine warms her skin as she splashes through the shal-lows, and a school of minnows goes darting past, the fish flashing like shadows over her feet.

Kelly and Maeve have both told her about Great Hollow Beach. The Irish and English kids who work at the restaurants come there when they're off-shift, along with teenagers on vacation. There's a volleyball net, set up on the sand, and boom boxes blaring competing radio stations, and usually beer, and sometimes pot.

"Over here!" Diana peers along the beach until she sees Maeve's waving hand. Maeve is wearing a green maillot, cut way up on her thighs, and her red hair is in a French braid with tendrils that brush her cheeks. She introduces the boys that she's with: Fitz and Tubbs and Stamper and Poe. "Are those your real names?" Diana asks, and the boys all start laughing.

"We're the men of the Emlen Academy," one of them—Poe?—tells her.

"Ignore them," says Maeve, in her Irish accent. "They're arseholes." She hands Diana a beer, and Diana sips it as one of the boys snaps open a beach towel, letting it unfurl and float down onto the sand. He's wearing blue board shorts and a Red Sox cap over dark, curly hair. His blue T-shirt says EMLEN across the chest. His teeth are straight and very white. There's a patch of hair on his chest and a trail leading down toward his waistband. Diana lifts her eyes to find the boy watching her. She blushes, but he just grins.

"Want to sit?"

She hopes she looks graceful as she eases herself down, feeling his scrutiny, wishing that she'd worn lipstick, or at least a swipe of mascara. Ever since she came to the Cape, she hasn't put anything but sunscreen on her face. But her skin is tanned golden-brown and her hair is as glossy as a chestnut shell. Instead of flinching from his attention, she sits up straighter and toys with one of her bikini's straps.

"Tell me everything about you," he says.

She laughs, even though she isn't exactly sure if he meant to be funny. "Which one are you again?"

"I'm Poe," he says. "Where are you from?"

She tells him that she's from Boston, that she is working as a mother's helper. He says that he just graduated from this Emlen Academy, and that he and a bunch of his classmates have rented two of the Flower Cottages that line the curve of Beach Road, so that they can be together for one last summer, before they all go off to college.

Diana knows, from friends, and from novels, that she is supposed to listen to him, to flatter, to ask him questions and keep him talking. But this guy, Poe, wants to know about her. Does she like living in a city? ("It's noisy," she says, and tells him that she can't get over how quiet it is here at night, how brightly the stars shine against the black of the sky.) What grade is she in? (Tenth, she says, and hopes he'll think that she just finished tenth grade, when, really, it's the grade she will start in September.) What's her favorite subject? (English, of course.) What does she want to do after high school?

"I'll go to college," she says. "Maybe Smith or Mount Holyoke." She'll need a scholarship to attend either one, but Dr. Levy, who went to Smith, tells her it's more than possible, and that she'd be happy to help Diana with her essays when the time comes.

"And how about after that?" asks Poe.

"I think I'd like to be a teacher." This sounds more realistic and less arrogant than telling him she wants to be an artist or a writer. "I like kids." She doesn't—not really—but this seems like the kind of thing a boy would want to hear.

"I believe the children are our future," he tells her, deadpan, and smiles when she laughs. They've both worked their feet into the sand while they've been talking. As she watches, he scoops up a handful of fine sand and lets it spill slowly from his hand onto her ankle. She stares at the trickling grains. Poe isn't even touching her, but still, this feels like the most intimate thing a boy has ever done to her. For a minute, she's sure she's forgotten how to breathe.

When the last of the sand has fallen, he turns, squinting up at the sun. "I should get going."

"Yeah, me too."

"Well, it was nice meeting you."

"Nice meeting you, too." She's dying inside, her insides curling in on themselves like a salted slug at the thought that this is the end, when he says, casually, "Maybe I'll see you here tomorrow?"

She nods. "Tomorrow," she says. She can still feel her ankle tingling. Strolling back, she feels shiny, and beautiful, tall and strong as the breeze blows her hair and sunshine warms her shoulders, and she falls asleep picturing his face.

Every afternoon for the next week, she and Poe meet at Great Hollow Beach. "Ahoy!" he calls when he sees her walking toward him, and she feels her heart rising in her chest, fluttering like a bird. One day he asks if she's thirsty, and passes her a water bottle that says EMLEN on the side when she nods. She puts her lips on the bottle, right where his had been, one step away from kissing, and she can feel his eyes on her mouth and her throat as she swallows.

Most of their talk is banter, teasing and big-brother-y. He asks if she's ever had a boyfriend (no), or if she's learning how to drive (not yet). When she asks him, after taking a day and a half to work up the courage, if he's dating anyone, he tells her that he'd dated the same girl for the winter and spring of his senior year, but that they'd agreed to break up after prom, so that neither of them would be tied down when they went off to college.

"Do you miss her?" she asks. He's piling sand on her again, handful after handful, until her feet are just vague lumps at the end of her legs.

"Sure," he says. Then he looks at her, right into her eyes. "But I can't say I'm sorry to be single right now."

Diana knows she isn't beautiful, not like Marie-Francoise, with her high cheekbones and her gray-blue eyes, not like Tess Finnegan at Boston Latin, who has a perfect hourglass figure and dark-brown hair that falls in ringlets to the small of her back. But when Poe looks at her, she feels radiant, like a sun-warmed berry, with her thin skin pulled taut over the sweet, juicy pulp of her insides.

Sometimes, she'll realize that she doesn't know very much about Poe. She knows that he is handsome and likes to play pranks, and that the other Emlen boys look to him as their leader. She knows, or can intuit, that he comes from money. He wears leather dock shoes, Brooks Brothers shirts, and Lacoste swim trunks, and, when she's close, he smells like good cologne.

She doesn't know what he does at night, when she's back at the house, reading or watching *Masterpiece Theater* and eating ice cream out of a mug. Maybe he's at parties, or at the bars in Provincetown; maybe he's meeting other girls, older ones. She wonders if he thinks about her, if he sees her as a little sister, or as a potential girlfriend, and what will happen as the summer draws to a close.

He occupies her thoughts every minute they're not together. She thinks of him when she's locked her bedroom door, when she's directing the flow of water between her legs, or using her fingertips to touch herself, gently, then more urgently, until she's gasping and trembling. The boys at home all seem like children, like outlines of the people they'll eventually become. Poe is a finished portrait, filled in and vivid, every detail complete. In bed at night, she pictures the way his shoulders pull the fabric of his shirt taut, the dusting of hair on his forearms and the pale hollows behind his knees. She thinks about how it would feel if he were to pull her close, until her head rested on his chest; how it would feel for him to kiss her, how his lips would be firm and warm and knowing, how his touch would be possessive and sure.

I love you, she imagines him whispering, and her stomach flutters and her toes curl, and she falls asleep with a smile on her face.

Too soon, it's the last week of August. In four days, Poe will be going home, to pack up and start college orientation at Dartmouth. On Friday, she and Poe are lounging on his towels at the beach when he sits up straight and whispers, "Look! It's the nudists!" She peers across the sand to where he's pointed and sees an elderly man and woman, in matching white robes, holding hands as they make their way slowly around the curved lip of the beach.

"Oh my goodness," she says. Poe has told her about them— an elderly husband and wife who walk to a deserted inlet and lie naked in the sand—but she's never seen them before.

"They're cute," she says. "They look like matching wallets."

Poe looks at her admiringly. "Good one," he says, and she flushes with pleasure. She hopes he'll bury her feet again, but just then one of the other boys comes trotting across the sand with a volleyball in his hand.

"Hey, lovebirds, wanna play?"

Lovebirds. Diana feels her face get hot, and she ducks to hide her smile.

"What do you think?" Poe asks.

"Sure," she says, and lets him pull her to her feet.

Her gym class did a unit on volleyball the previous year. Over nine weeks, Diana barely managed to get her hands on the ball, but that afternoon, she is unstoppable. They play three games, and win all three. Twice, she sets the ball, and Poe spikes it, sending it rocketing over the net and into the sand. The first time, he high-fives her, but the second time he grabs her in a bear hug, lifting her up, holding her so that they're skin to skin, chest to chest. She thinks that he's going to kiss her, and that it will be perfect, an absolutely perfect first kiss at the end of the day at the very end of summer, but instead he sets her back, gently, on her feet.

When the game is over, he touches her hand and says, "Hey. A bunch of us are getting together tomorrow night. The last bonfire of the year before we all go off to college. Can you come?"

She nods. She has been waiting for this, waiting for him, since the day her sister gave her the yellow bikini; since the first day of that summer, since, maybe, the day she was born.

What to wear, what to wear? Diana's antsy and distracted all day, desperate for the hours to pass. After the beach, she takes an extra-long time in the outdoor shower, shaving her legs and under her arms and at the crease of her thighs, then rubbing oil into the bare skin. Alone in her room, she towel-dries her hair and works mousse through it, from the roots to the ends, then lets it air-dry, touching the curls anxiously, hoping they'll look right, that she'll look right.

At dinner, which is Dr. Levy's famous lobster Cobb salad, she casually says, "Some of the kids I've met are having a bonfire on the beach tonight. Is it okay if I go?"

Dr. Levy and her husband exchange a look across the table. "What would your parents say?" Mr. Weinberg finally asks. "Do you think they'd be okay with it?"

Diana knows the answer is that her parents would probably not be okay. Like her sisters, she won't be allowed to date until she's sixteen, and she knows what they'd have to say about a party with older boys and drinking. She puts on a thoughtful expression and says, "I think they'd tell me to be careful, and not to drink anything, and to be home by midnight."

"That sounds sensible." Dr. Levy gives her a look. "You have to promise, though. I see your mother every day and she'd kill me if anything happens to you on my watch."

Diana nods, her head bobbing up and down eagerly. In her imagination, she's picturing Poe, the line of his back, the way his face lights up when he sees her. She's remembering how it felt to have his arms around her, his whole body pressed against hers, her skin on his skin.

In her bathroom, she swishes mouthwash over her tongue and teeth, brushes her teeth, flosses and rinses again, and looks at herself in the mirror. Her eyes are bright; her cheeks are flushed. The narrow straps of her white sundress set off the gleaming golden-brown crescents of her shoulders.

Good enough, she thinks, and eases open the sliding door and steps out into the night. She takes the steps two at a time, and once she's on the beach she races, fleet-footed, over the sand, toward the glow of the fire, the smell of smoke, the sound of music and raised voices.

Poe is waiting by the bonfire for her, in khaki shorts and a Ballston Beach tee. She feels suddenly awkward, like her legs have gotten too long, and she doesn't know what to do with her hands, but then he puts his arm around her shoulders and pulls her against him, and she feels herself relax. He smells like fabric softener and whiskey, and she can see a tiny dab of shaving cream on his earlobe that he's neglected to wipe off.

"Come on," he says. She follows him to the fire, sits down beside him, and lets him pull himself against her so that her head is leaning on his shoulder. He takes one of her curls between his fingers, pulling it straight, letting it boing back into place before he tucks it behind her ear, and rubs his thumb against her cheek. Her eyes flutter shut. She thinks she might faint, or swoon with the pleasure of it.

"You know what I thought, the first time I saw you, on the beach?"

She shakes her head.

"I thought you looked like summer. Like, if I was going to

paint a picture and call it *Summer*, it would look like you." He gives an embarrassed laugh. "That probably sounded stupid."

"No!" She opens her eyes and looks at him. "It's the nicest thing anyone's ever said to me. It's perfect." *You're perfect.*

Smiling, he takes a red plastic Solo cup from somewhere and wraps her hand around it. "Bottoms up." The moon is full and shining, and the stars are brilliant pinpoints in the sky, and she can hear the wind, the churn of the waves, the heave and toss of the dark water, the endlessness of it. As she raises the cup to her lips, she thinks, *I will never be happier than I am, right now, in this moment.* She thinks, *This is the best night of my life.*

Part
One

~~~~~~~~~~~~~~~~

The Two Dianas

1

~~~

Daisy

2019

Daisy Shoemaker couldn't sleep.

She knew, of course, that she was not alone, awake in the middle of the night. She'd read Facebook posts, magazine articles, entire books written about women her age consumed by anxiety, gnawed by regret, tormented by their hormones, fretful about their marriages, their bodies, their aging parents and their troublesome teenagers and, thus, up all night. In bed, on a Sunday night in March, with her husband's snores audible even through her earplugs, Daisy pictured her tribe, her sleepless sisters, each body stretched on the rack of her own imagination, each face lit by the gently glowing rectangle in her hands.

Picture each worry like a gift. Put them in order, from the mildest to the most intense. Imagine yourself picking up each one and wrapping it with care. Picture yourself placing the gift under a tree, and then walking away.

Daisy had read that technique on some website, or in some magazine. She's tried it along with all the others. She had imagined her worries like leaves, floating down a stream; she pictured them like clouds, drifting past in the sky; like cars, zipping by on the highway. She had practiced progressive muscle relaxation; she played, in her noise-canceling headphones, murmurous podcasts and Spotify mixes of soothing, sleep-inducing sounds—the chiming of Tibetan singing bowls; Gregorian chants, whales moaning to one another across the vast and chambered deep. She had swallowed melatonin and slugged down valerian tea, and trained herself to leave her phone charging in the bathroom instead of right next to her bed, with the ringer turned up in case her daughter, away at boarding school, should need her in the middle of the night.

Thoughts of Beatrice made her sigh, then look guiltily over her shoulder to make sure she hadn't woken Hal. Hal was still sleeping, flat on his back, arms and legs starfished wide. They had a king-sized bed, and most mornings Daisy woke up clinging to the edge of her side. Hal, while not unsympathetic, had been notably short on solutions. "What do you want me to do?" he'd asked, sounding maddeningly reasonable and slightly indulgent. "It's not like I'm pushing you off the bed on purpose. I'm asleep." He'd given her permission to wake him up. "Just give me a poke," he'd said. "Shake my shoulder." Probably because he knew she never would.

Sighing, Daisy rolled over to face the window. It was still dark outside, the sky showing no signs of brightening, which meant it was probably two or three in the morning, the absolute pit of the night. She had a big day coming up, and she needed to try to sleep. *Breathe in, two, three, four*, she coached herself. *Hold, two, three, four. Breathe out.* She exhaled slowly, trying, and failing, not to think about how the dean had sounded when he'd called to inform them of Beatrice's latest transgression, which had involved gathering up the members of the Emlen Feminist Liberation (pronounced Ef-el) and spray-painting the word RAPIST across a male classmate's dorm-room door.

"Unfortunately, this is not Beatrice's first infraction of our honor code," the dean had intoned. "We'll need at least one of Beatrice's parents to come up here to discuss this."

"Okay," Daisy had stammered. "Although—would you mind calling my husband? You have his number, right?" She wanted Hal to handle this. Hal was the Emlen graduate in the house, the one whose own father had attended the school, a loyal alumnus who donated money each year, in addition to paying Bea's tuition. He'd know what to do . . . and, if the dean called, Hal would hear the news from the school and not her.

"Of course," said the dean. Daisy had hung up, her legs watery with relief, thinking, *Hal will fix this. Hal will talk to him. He'll figure it out, and by the time he comes home, everything will be fine.*

But Hal hadn't, and it wasn't. Two hours later her husband had stormed into the house, wearing the blue suit and red-and-gold tie that he'd left in that morning and a thunderous look on his face. "They're probably going to expel her," he said. "We need to be there Monday morning. Don't look so happy about it," he'd snapped before Daisy had even said anything, and Daisy turned away, her face burning. He brushed past her, on his way to the stairs. "I'm very disappointed in her. You should be, too."

"But . . ." He was already halfway up the staircase. When she spoke, he stopped, his hand on the railing, his body telegraphing impatience. "Did the boy do what she said?"

Hal turned around. "What?"

Daisy steeled herself. She hadn't talked to Beatrice yet—her daughter was ignoring her texts, and every phone call she'd made had gone straight to voice mail. "Don't you think we should hear her side of things, too? To find out what really happened?"

Hal shook his head. "Whatever happened, Beatrice isn't judge and jury up there. She vandalized school property, she accused someone, in public, of something he might not have done. And," he concluded, like he was making a closing argument in court, "she'd already been in trouble."

Daisy bent her head. It was true. Even before the incident, Beatrice had been on academic probation for cutting classes. Her daughter ran an Etsy shop on which she sold tiny felt replicas of pets for a hundred dollars apiece. She had made it very clear, to her parents and the school's administrators, that she preferred crafts to academics.

"Maybe Beatrice just wasn't a boarding school kind of kid," Daisy ventured. This was a point she'd made repeatedly when they were deciding whether to send her, a decision that was no decision at all, because, practically from the moment of her birth, Hal had been planning on Bea going to Emlen, which he, and his father, and both of Daisy's brothers, had attended. "You'll carry on the family tradition," he'd said, to which Beatrice had rolled her eyes.

Hal believed the experience of boarding school would make their daughter strong and independent. Daisy thought that Beatrice was too young to be away from home, and that she'd be going to college soon enough, so why rush her out the door? "And Beatrice doesn't even want to go," Daisy argued. She'd tried to explain to her husband the particular tenderness of the fourteen-year-old girl. She remembered being that age and feeling as if she was moving through the world like a snail or a turtle whose shell had been removed: freakish and vulnerable; naked and weird. At least, that was how she'd felt, although she suspected that her daughter was made of sterner stuff. Still, she'd made her case: that girls their daughter's age were especially susceptible to any insult or injury, that even the smallest slight would wound Beatrice terribly, and that she would carry those hurts with her forever, the way Daisy herself did. But Hal hadn't listened.

"It's not up to Beatrice," Hal said, in a tone that was pedantic and ever-so-slightly patronizing. "It's up to us to do what's best for her."

They'd gone around and around, and Hal, as usual, had prevailed. He'd gotten Bea to write an essay through some combination of cajolery and outright bribery, and Daisy suspected that he'd upped his annual gift to the school to an amount that could have ensured the acceptance of a hunk of rock. Beatrice had gotten into the car willingly, had been chatty and even excited on the drive to New Hampshire. But after she'd arrived, her phone calls consisted of one-word answers ("How are your classes?" "Fine." "Do you like your roommate?" "Sure."). On her first-semester report card, she'd gotten straight Cs and a dozen unexcused absences.

Hal continued up the stairs, muttering about how that was the last donation he'd ever be giving Emlen. Daisy waited for the sound of the bedroom door closing before calling her daughter, who finally deigned to pick up. "What happened?" Daisy asked. She wasn't sure if Beatrice would be angry, or sad, or ashamed. Given the vagaries of fourteen-year-old emotions, any of those, singularly or in combination, wouldn't have surprised her. But Beatrice sounded calm, even—could it be?—happy.

"They'll probably kick me out. You and Dad have to come up here." She lowered her voice. "The dean wants to talk to you."

Daisy said, "Do you think there's any chance they'll let you stay?"

"Probably not!" Beatrice didn't just sound pleasant, Daisy realized. She actually sounded cheerful. "It's fine, though. Now I can tell Dad that I tried, but that this isn't for me."

Daisy's mind sped backward to a memory of her daughter at two and a half, in a tiny pair of denim OshKosh overalls, with a striped pink-and-white T-shirt underneath, determinedly trying to climb the garden stairs, falling on her diapered bottom each time. *No, Mumma, I want to do it my OWN self.* They'd called her

Trixie back then, and Daisy could still see her, on her first day at kindergarten, posing proudly with a backpack that looked as big as she was. She could remember the powdery, milky smell of Bea's skin when Daisy would kiss her good night; the weight of her as an infant, like a warm, breathing loaf of bread, when she'd finally fall asleep in Daisy's arms. She could remember, too, getting teary at some Disney movie or another when Beatrice was four or five, and her daughter staring at her curiously, asking why she was crying. "Because it's sad," Daisy had said, gesturing toward the screen. Beatrice had patted her mother's forearm with her plump starfish hand. "Mumma," she'd said kindly, "those are not real people."

Timidly, Beatrice asked, "Is Dad really mad?"

"He's just worried about you, honey," Daisy said. "He wants you to be happy."

There'd been a pause. Then Beatrice, sounding cynical and older than her years, had said, "We both know that's not true."

Picture each worry like a gift.

Daisy began with the biggest one, her daughter. Hal had already decreed that, if they expelled her, Beatrice would attend the Melville School, a private, co-ed institution on the Main Line that had already told Hal they'd be more than happy to take her for the remainder of the year (they'd also been happy, Daisy had noted, to charge them for an entire year's tuition). Beatrice would probably complain about not going to Lower Merion High, with her middle-school friends, but she'd survive.

Of course, Beatrice back home meant another three and a half years living with a daughter who behaved as if she despised her. Daisy hadn't realized how bad it had gotten until Beatrice was at Emlen, and there'd been a lovely calm spell, stretches of nights without fights, without wall-rattling slammed doors or screamed "I hate yous!" She and Hal had enjoyed a few quiet dinners, a few peaceful hours together on the sofa. Several of those evenings had even concluded with a pleasant interlude on the king-sized bed. Hal had commented, frequently, on how pleasant things were, how enjoyable, with Beatrice gone, but to Daisy, the silences seemed to echo more loudly than the shouting ever had. The house felt like a museum, and she felt like a trespasser, sneaking around and trying not to trip the alarms.

Daisy worried about her daughter. She worried about her mom, who'd had two small "cerebral events" the previous year, and had spent six weeks in a rehab facility. Even though her mother's gentleman friend Arnold Mishkin had promised he'd take care of her, Daisy still had fantasies of opening her front door one morning to find Judy Rosen standing in her driveway, surrounded by suitcases and the Lladró figurines she'd recently started collecting. Of course, her brother Danny would help. Danny lived sixty miles away, in Lambertville, with his husband, in a three-bedroom ranch house with plenty of room, but Judy would insist on staying with Daisy. Daisy was the youngest, and the only girl, which, in Judy's world order, made Daisy the one responsible for her care.

In her imagination, Daisy wrapped her mother, and her mother's figurines. She put them away and moved on to the other worries impatiently waiting their turn, jostling for her attention.

There was Lester, their elderly beagle/basset hound, whose heart condition was getting worse. Poor Lester, at twelve, had been diagnosed with congestive heart failure and was on three different medications, and he seemed to be losing his appetite, and Hal was already making noises about how it might be time for Lester to go to that great dog park in the sky.

Which brought her, finally, to Hal. Did he still love her? Had he ever loved her? Was he having an affair? Two years ago, there'd been a summer associate of whom he'd spoken almost endlessly, and, at a Christmas party the year before that, Daisy thought she noticed one of the paralegals staring across the punch bowl. The pretty young woman's gaze had moved from Hal to Daisy back to Hal again, and Daisy could imagine what she was thinking: *I don't get it. What could he possibly see in her?* At fifty, Hal was handsome, even dashing, his shoulders still broad and his belly still flat, the lines on his long face and the gray in his dark curls only adding to his appeal, whereas Daisy, twelve years younger, just looked short and dumpy and, probably, desperate. If Hal wanted extramarital fun and excitement, he'd have ample opportunity. Daisy tried not to think too much about that, or whether she'd care if she learned that Hal was cheating, or if she'd just feel relieved that someone else was tending to what he used to call *my manly needs*. She would have asked her best friend, Hannah, her opinion, whether Hal was being faithful and what she, Daisy, should be doing if he wasn't, except, nine months ago, Hannah had died.

Daisy rolled from her left side onto her right. She sighed again, and made herself close her eyes. She had met her husband when she was twenty years old, and he was almost thirty-three. *Red flag, red flag, red flag*, her friends had chanted, all of them certain that there had to be something wrong with a guy Hal's age who'd never been married, who was interested in a woman almost thirteen years his junior. Hal had clearly been aware of the conventional wisdom, because, on their first date, he'd said, "I should probably tell you how I got to be this old with no wife or kids."

"At least you don't have an ex-wife," said Daisy.

Hal hadn't smiled before clearing his throat. "I was a pretty big drinker, for years."

Daisy said, "Oh." She was thinking about twelve-step programs, about Higher Powers and meetings and sponsors and *You're only as sick as your secrets*. She thought, *At least he's telling me now, before I got really interested* and, then, *Ugh, but I liked him!* She'd liked his confidence, and—shallow, but true—she'd liked his looks. Hal was handsome, with olive-tinted skin that stayed tanned even in the winter and emphatic brows, like dark dash marks over his eyes. He had a way of taking up space that felt like a first cousin of arrogance—the result, Daisy assumed, of his age, the money he'd grown up with, and the success he'd already had as a lawyer. He'd come to her door in a tweed sports coat and a tie with a bouquet of flowers for her mom, apricot-colored roses and lilies. He'd held the car door for her, waiting until she was settled before walking around the car and getting behind the wheel. He drove skillfully, and asked Daisy questions, and seemed to actually listen to what she said.

Daisy had liked that he was older; that he knew who he was, that he already had an advanced degree, a house, a career. A man like that seemed unlikely to announce, the way her roommate's boyfriend recently had, that he wanted to pursue an MFA in poetry instead of an MBA in finance, or to decide, like one of Daisy's previous beaus, that he wanted to try sleeping with men in addition to women.

All of that zipped through her mind as she sat across from Hal in the restaurant she'd picked. Hal must have seen it. Daisy had never been good about keeping her feelings off her face. "Don't worry," he'd said, smiling. "My friends didn't do an intervention. I never went to rehab, and I don't go to meetings. It wasn't anything like that. I liked drinking, but I didn't like who I was when I drank. So I stopped."

"Just like that?" Daisy had asked.

"Just like that. For the last three years, I've had a glass of champagne on New Year's Eve, and that's it." He made a rueful face, those emphatic eyebrows lifting. "I'm not going to tell you that the first few days, or weeks, were pleasant. But I'd never been an every-single-day drinker. I guess I was lucky. But yes. I just stopped."

"And it doesn't bother you if . . ." She'd nodded at the sake that he'd ordered for her.

He shook his head. His voice sounded a little gravelly when he'd said, "I like to see a woman enjoy herself."

She'd kissed him that night, made out with him after their next date, slept with him on the date after that. And it had been good. Better than good. The best sex she'd ever had. Not that she'd had a lot of sex. She'd slept with exactly four boys, two of them just once, and Hal had been the first one with whom she'd had an orgasm. At first, when he'd kissed his way down her belly and gently coaxed her thighs apart, she'd been self-conscious and shy, wondering if she should have waxed, or shaved, or washed herself ahead of time, but then he'd pressed his face right against her, breathing her in, his hands tightening on her hips, pulling her closer, like he couldn't get enough of her. He'd eased her underpants down her legs, and, before she could worry about how she smelled or looked down there, Hal had done something, made some combination of movements with his fingers and his tongue. Daisy had jolted off the bed like she'd been electrified. "Oh," she'd said. "*Oh.*" Hal had laughed, low in his throat, and then Daisy had forgotten to worry, or to think about anything at all. When he raised his face, still wet, to hers, Daisy had kissed him, and she'd tasted herself on his mouth. Hal had still been kissing her when he'd rolled on top of her, pushing inside of her in a single stroke, then pulling out slowly, and doing it again, and Daisy had thought, *So this is what all the fuss is about.*

When it was over, she'd rested against him, catching her breath, and then she'd gone to the kitchen, determined to woo him, to delight him the way he'd delighted her. She'd cracked an egg into semolina flour, running the dough swiftly through her pasta machine while a pot of salted water came to a boil. She'd cooked the ribbons of pasta perfectly al dente and served them with salt and pepper and good Parmesan and a poached egg resting gently on top. Hal had twirled the first strands around his fork and raised them to his mouth, and from the look on his face she thought she was feeling a version of what she'd felt when he'd done that thing with his tongue. "This is amazing," he'd told her. "You're amazing." Daisy had smiled shyly, wondering how long it would take before they could make love again.

Six months later, they'd been married. Her college classmates had been shocked, some of them appalled, others just titillated, at the idea of Daisy dropping out of school and getting married so young. Daisy's mother was unabashedly delighted. "Your father would have been so happy," Judy had sniffled, before lowering the veil over Daisy's eyes. "He would have wanted to pay for it, too. He wanted to give you everything." But Daisy's father, Jack Rosen, who'd spent his whole life being either flush with cash or close to broke, had died of a heart attack when Daisy was fourteen, at the bottom of one of his slumps. There were no savings. He'd left no life insurance, either, and her brothers, twelve and thirteen years older than she was, were just starting lives of their own.

Daisy had abandoned her plan of following her brothers to Emlen, which had gone co-ed just three years before. Instead, she'd moved with her mother to a two-bedroom condominium in a not-great part of West Orange, graduating from public high school, taking out loans to attend Rutgers. After Hal had proposed, she'd told him that, while she knew it was traditional for the bride's family to pay for the wedding, in her case, that wouldn't be happening. Hal had looked at her tenderly, then pulled out a credit card. "This is yours, for anything you need," he'd said. "I'm your family now."

The wedding had been in a hotel in Center City, a raucous affair that had gone until two in the morning with lots of Hal's friends from his law firm and college and prep school. There'd been a three-week honeymoon in Hawaii, and then Daisy had moved into Hal's house, the four-bedroom colonial on the Main Line where he'd grown up, which he'd inherited from his dad, who'd moved into a retirement community after his wife's death. Vernon Shoemaker had taken almost all of the furniture with him, leaving only a pair of towering oak bookcases in the den and a king-sized box spring and mattress in the bedroom. Other than a pair of folding chairs and a very large TV, the house was empty. Hal told Daisy to keep the credit card and get whatever she wanted.

Her plan had been to transfer to Temple or Drexel and finish her degree, but she'd spent that first year shopping and decorating, settling in. For their first anniversary Hal had taken her to Paris, and when she'd come home she'd been pregnant. Instead of a college graduate, she'd become a mom.

Daisy opened her eyes, flipped onto her back, and stared up at the ceiling. *I have everything I want*, she told herself. A stable marriage—or maybe just a marriage that would stay stable as long as she didn't ask questions. A smart, creative, accomplished daughter who was, if not happy, then at least healthy. Financial security. A lovely home. A thriving, if small, business, giving lessons to the cooking-challenged. A husband who didn't yell, and certainly didn't hit; a man who still seemed to desire her. Why, then, did she sometimes feel lonely or trapped or incompetent?

It was true that Hal had been moody lately, quiet and brooding for the last six months. Stress at work, fights with Beatrice, and then, right after they'd finally dropped her off at Emlen, one of Hal's friends had died.

Daisy remembered everything about the morning she'd learned about Brad. At seven o'clock on a Tuesday morning, Daisy had come downstairs, still yawning after another mostly sleepless night. Hal was in the kitchen, in his running clothes, with a spinach-based smoothie in the blender and his phone in his hand. Daisy knew immediately, from his posture, and the untouched smoothie, that something was wrong. "What is it?" she'd asked, placing her hand on his back, against the slippery, high-tech fabric of his shirt.

In a faraway voice, he'd said, "Bubs died."

"Oh, no!" Brad Burlingham, otherwise known as Bubs, was one of Hal's group of Emlen buddies, a heavyset, florid-faced man with an endless supply of dirty jokes. Daisy had never liked him, maybe because she only ever saw him at parties, and he was almost always drunk, but he'd been one of Hal's senior-year roommates. "What happened?" Heart attack, she guessed. The last time she'd seen Bubs he hadn't looked well. But Hal, still sounding distant, his face still grave and shocked, said, "Suicide," before setting his phone down gently on the counter and saying, "I need to call the guys."

Daisy had offered to accompany him to Brad's funeral, but Hal had turned her down, saying, in a clipped voice, "You didn't really know him." *And what I knew, I didn't like*, Daisy thought. She'd never understand why Hal included Brad in his boys' weekends, had never been able to discern any kind of appeal, but she'd just smiled, said, "Travel safe," and made sure there was a fresh toothbrush and a new razor in his shaving kit.

Daisy sat up and swung her legs out of bed, sliding her feet along the floor until she found her slippers with her toes. She moved noiselessly through the darkness with the ease of long practice. From the chaise lounge against the wall, a piece of furniture that existed to be a repository for clothes and for baskets of laundry, she picked up her robe, pulling it around her shoulders as she padded down to her desk just off the kitchen. She pulled her laptop free from its charger and carried it to the living room, opening her email in-box. Saks was having a sale; the local library needed volunteers to run the book drive; and she'd been invited to a fiftieth birthday party in Marin County. *Brad and I hope you'll join us for a glorious weekend of wine, food, and reminiscing!* read the text, beneath the picture of a verdant vineyard in the honeyed glow of a setting sun. Daisy read on, learning that the party would be at the Vintage Wine Estates, that there was a bike ride planned and a spa day for those who didn't want to ride, and that cedar-plank salmon and filet mignon would be served at the Saturday night dinner. She felt a little guilty even looking, because this invitation, of course, was not for her. Daisy's real name was Diana, and she'd used it as part of the email address she'd claimed way back in high school—DianaS at Earthlink. This other woman, the other Diana, was Diana.S at Earthlink. For the last six months, Daisy had been receiving emails that she realized were intended not for her, but for the other Diana.

The other Diana's emails were innocuous things—an invitation to a tennis tournament or a dinner or to grab drinks at a bar. Enough to give Daisy a sense of the contours of the other woman's life, and to realize that, of the two of them, the other Diana seemed to be having a lot more fun.

As Lester navigated the stairs on his stumpy legs and heaved himself effortfully onto the couch beside her, Daisy sent the birthday-party invitation email back with a brief note—*sorry, I'm the wrong Diana.* She was about to open up Facebook and post some obligatory comments—*so cute!*—on her brother's latest photographs of his kids when her in-box pinged. A note from the other Diana, with SORRY!!! in the memo line, had arrived.

Daisy clicked it open. "I'm so sorry you keep getting my emails. I apologize on behalf of my friends."

Daisy stared at the missive, and then, before she could overthink, she wrote back. "No worries," she typed. "I'm enjoying living your life vicariously (in lieu of having my own)." The instant she'd hit "send" she was awash with regret. Had she sounded too flip? Too snobby? Did anyone say "in lieu" anymore? Should she have included an emoji, or at least written "LOL"?

She'd been on the verge of panic when her in-box had dinged again. "LOL," the other Diana had written. "I'm a corporate consultant based in NYC. It's nonstop glamour." With the rolling-eye emoji after that.

"Anything is more glamorous than my life," Daisy typed.

"I have a teenager who hates me, a husband who's never home, and an old dog with digestive issues." She hit "send" before she could rethink it. "Sorry, Lester," she murmured. Lester gave her a mournful look, loosed a sonorous fart, and rearranged himself against her leg, where he promptly went back to sleep . . . and, then, again, her in-box was pinging. This time Diana had sent three emojis, all of the scrunched-up, tears-coming-out-of-its-eyes laughing face. "I don't have any children, but I have teenage nieces. I truly believe that teenage girls are God's revenge on women for what they did to their mothers," she wrote.

"I know she doesn't really hate me. She's trying to be independent. It's what she's supposed to do," Daisy wrote back. After three different people had recommended it, she'd read a persuasive book that made the case about teenage girls and the work of separation, and she was trying hard to believe the words as she typed them.

"You're right," Diana replied. "But it still must be hard."

"She's probably going to be expelled from her school," Daisy typed. "My husband and I are leaving first thing in the morning to drive to New Hampshire to meet with the dean." Daisy, who'd been raised casually Jewish, had never been to a confessional, but she imagined the rite to feel something like this, sitting in the dark and telling all your sins to a stranger.

"Yikes," wrote Diana. "Is that why you're awake at two in the morning?"

"I have insomnia," Daisy wrote. "Me and every other middle-aged woman."

"Same here," wrote Diana. "It's the worst. And I'm sorry about your daughter." Daisy appreciated that the expression of sympathy wasn't paired with a request for information, a demand to know what Beatrice had done to get in trouble. "Do you feel like you're the one who's been called to the principal's office?" Diana wrote.

"Dean, not principal," Daisy typed, rolling her eyes, even as she felt grateful. For all his complaining, for all of his fury at Beatrice, Hal hadn't seemed to realize that Beatrice's expulsion had left Daisy feeling like she'd been the one found lacking. "And yes. I feel judged."

For a moment, there was nothing. Then another email appeared, "I bet you could use a treat. If you've got a free night and can meet me in New York, I'll buy you the best Bloody Mary of your life." And again, Daisy barely hesitated before she typed the word *Yes*.

Six hours later, Daisy saw Hal's jaw tighten as he pulled into a visitor's parking spot on the Emlen campus parking lot. He turned off the car's engine, unfolded his legs, stood up, and slammed the door harder than he had to. Daisy stared down at her lap for a moment, gathering herself, before opening her own door and stepping out into the early-spring chill. It was a gray, windy afternoon, with patches of snow visible under the leafless trees.

They crossed the quad, following a wide slate path up the hill to Shawcross Hall, a brick building that had been constructed, the tour guides liked to say, at the turn of the century—"the eighteenth century." Each of the stone steps leading to its front door had a shallow depression at the center, worn from centuries of students' feet. The panes of window glass were thick and wavery, and the room where they were told to wait for the dean, Dr. Baptiste, was dim and low-ceilinged. She and Hal perched on a pair of spindly-legged antique chairs, with Hal in his newest chalk-striped gray suit and Daisy in a black wool jersey dress, already sweating beneath her arms and at the small of her back. A radiator clanking in the corner filled the room with steamy air and the smell of wet wool. Daisy sighed and fanned her face with one of the admissions brochures arranged on the coffee table, until she saw Hal frowning. Carefully, she set the brochure back down.

The dean's door swung open. "Mr. Shoemaker? Mrs. Shoemaker?" Hal and Daisy got to their feet and went into an expansive office that must have been remodeled, or added on. Unlike the warren of small, dark rooms, this room was airy, with high ceilings. A bay window looked out over the quad; a skylight admitted the grainy afternoon light.

Dr. Baptiste, a handsome man in late middle age, with glowing light-brown skin and dark hair that had gone a striking, snowy white at the temples, sat behind his fortress of a desk. He'd been one of a handful of Black students to attend Emlen back in the 1970s, when, Beatrice had told her parents, he'd sported an epic Afro. He'd gone on to Harvard, gotten a PhD in education, and been at Emlen since the mid-1990s. During that time, Emlen had gone co-ed and had gone from being viewed as one of the less desirable of the old New England prep schools—a place to deposit a wayward son who'd been booted from Exeter or who'd flunked out of Choate—to, once again, one of the top prep schools in the country, not quite on par with Andover or Exeter but certainly moving in the right direction. Dr. Baptiste had restored much of the school's lost luster and rebuilt its endowment, which was currently in the hundred-million-dollar neighborhood. He'd overseen three capital campaigns; the construction of a new arts wing, with a state-of-the-art theater, and a natatorium; and the renovations of the campus cathedral. Daisy assumed that these accomplishments had overcome any reservations the more old-school (translation: racist) alums might have had about his role.

Beatrice was waiting for them, sitting in one of the wingback chairs, dressed in a black-and-green plaid kilt, a green sweater, and a primly high-necked white blouse with a pie-crust collar. In spite of the cold, her legs were bare, the skin chapped-looking and goose-pimpled. Her daughter's jaw had the same stubborn set that Hal's did, but she smiled, very slightly, when Daisy hugged her.

"Hi, Mom."

"We missed you," Daisy whispered. Beatrice smelled like unfamiliar hair conditioner and cold New Hampshire spring. Daisy struggled to look stern as she took a seat, but it was hard to keep from smiling. Her daughter! Even in her handful of months away, she'd changed; the bones of her face shifting, childhood's extra padding melting away to reveal the adult she was already on her way to becoming.

"Beatrice," Hal said curtly.

"Hi, Dad." Beatrice's voice was raspy and low.

"Shall we get started?" The dean wore a blue sports coat, a tie in the school colors with a gold tie tack, and, on his feet, dark-brown wingtips, in defiance of the snow. A gold watch gleamed on his wrist, along with gold cuff links, a wedding band, and a heavy gold Emlen class ring. "Would anyone like anything? Coffee? Tea?"

"No thank you," said Hal, and Daisy, who could have used a drink of water, said, "I'm fine." She adjusted herself, sitting up very straight, wondering what it was about this room, or the dean, or Emlen itself, that made her feel so small, like she was Alice in Wonderland, like every chair would leave her feet dangling inches from the floor and every adult was a foot taller than she was. Maybe it was the visits she'd made as a little girl, on Parents' Weekends and to watch her brothers graduate. Maybe when you first experience a place as a six-year-old, you become six again, every time you return.

The dean sat behind his desk, settling his elbows on the leather blotter. "I appreciate your willingness to come on such short notice."

"We're taking this very seriously," Hal said.

"I'm glad to hear that," said the dean. "It's a serious matter." He looked at Beatrice. "You understand that you've violated several of Emlen's Core Practices?" Daisy could hear the capital letters in "Core" and "Practices."

"I know." Beatrice raised her chin. "I also know that Colin broke a few of them, too."

"We're not discussing Mr. Mackenzie," said the dean.

"Why not?" Beatrice demanded. "I mean, is anyone going to talk about what he did? Like, ever?"

"Of course we are," the dean said smoothly. "But that's a matter for Mr. Mackenzie and his advisors and his family. Right now, we're here to talk about you."

" 'An Emlen student is to conduct herself with honor and integrity,' " Beatrice said. "That's all I was trying to do."

The dean sighed. "You understand, though, that there's such a thing as due process? That your expression of honor and integrity cannot impugn the character of another student?"

Beatrice shrugged.

"And that we can't just punish students on one another's say-so? That we have to take our time, gather the facts, do our due diligence? That we can't resort to vigilantism and vandalism?"

Beatrice crossed her arms against her chest, chin jutting, eyes narrowed, her brows—dark and emphatic like Hal's—drawn down. "Tricia followed the procedures. She told our RA, she told the dorm leader, she told her advisory leader, and she went to the counseling center. But nothing happened. Because nothing was ever going to happen. Because Colin matters more to you—to Emlen—than Tricia does."

The dean pulled off his glasses and massaged the indentions on either side of his nose. "You understand that the deliberations of the Honor Council have to remain confidential?"

Beatrice shrugged.

"Beatrice, answer the dean," Hal snapped. Spots of color had risen in the middle of each of his cheeks.

"I understand," Beatrice said in a robotic monotone. Daisy's mouth felt dry, and her heart was beating very fast.

"You understand that we'd extend the same courtesies to you, had you been the one accused?"

"Of raping someone?" Beatrice scoffed. "I'm sure that happens a lot." The dean started to talk again, but Beatrice spoke over him, her voice thin but steady. "Look, I've made my point. I know that what I did was against the rules, and the Code, and whatever, but I don't think I did anything wrong, and I definitely didn't do anything as bad as what Colin did. So kick me out, or suspend me or whatever, but don't make me sit here and think I'm going to agree when you say that it's fair." She practically spat the last word before leaning back, a mottled flush creeping up her neck.

"Beatrice," said the dean, "please wait outside."

Beatrice bent down, jerked her backpack off the floor, slung it over her shoulder, and stomped out the door. Dr. Baptiste sighed.

"Sir, if I could . . ." *Here comes Hal the lawyer*, Daisy thought, as her husband, smooth-voiced and perfectly calm, armed with many facts, explained that Beatrice understood that she'd done wrong, and that if it wasn't clear to her at that point, "her mother and I will help her understand that she's not responsible for determining the innocence or guilt of her classmates."

The dean listened. Or, at least, he gave the impression of listening. When Hal finished, he cleared his throat. "Emlen is a fine institution," he began. He opened the top drawer of his desk and removed a pipe and a leather pouch full of tobacco. When he opened it, the rich smell of tobacco filled the room. Daisy watched as he pinched leaves between his fingertips and let them trickle into the pipe's bowl. "A terrible habit, but I can't seem to give it up," he said. His tone was apologetic, but Daisy suspected he was enjoying the performance. She wondered how many students had sat where she was sitting, feeling like their lives were hanging in the balance as this ritual unfolded.

"Emlen is a fine institution," he repeated. "Which, of course, you know." Hal nodded quickly. Daisy could feel him beside her, thrumming like a guitar string stretched too tight.

"Can I—excuse me. If I may." Daisy felt her cheeks get hot as both men turned to face her. The dean's expression was neutral. Hal did not look happy. "It's probably none of my business, and if this is confidential, of course you don't have to tell me anything, but . . . well, what did happen? With Beatrice's roommate and that boy?"

The dean let more tobacco fall into the pipe, then used a metal tamper to press it down. He lifted the stem to his lips, drew on it, and, once satisfied, set it back on the blotter and began filling the bowl again.

"What have you heard?" he asked.

Daisy started to speak, but stopped when she felt Hal's hand on her forearm, squeezing with a pressure that said *Let me handle this*. "What Beatrice told us was that her roommate told her that a young man forced himself on her, over her objections. We told Beatrice to encourage her roommate to take the steps she mentioned—to tell her RA, and the dorm parent, and her advisor. We certainly would never tell her to take matters into her own hands." Hal gave the dean a man-to-man smile and said, "Teenage girls. They get emotional. As I'm sure you know."

"Okay, but what *happened*?" Daisy's voice was too loud, and both men swung their heads around to stare at her, like she'd suddenly sprouted wings. She rubbed her hands against her legs. "Did that boy . . . did he do what Beatrice told us?"

"I'm afraid that's confidential." The dean's voice was cool. "I can assure you that we take any allegations of this nature seriously. We take our responsibilities, in loco parentis, and the health and well-being of our students seriously. Nothing matters to us more."

"Of course," Daisy said, thinking that the dean had just used a lot of words that told her less than nothing. The dean picked up a heavy gold lighter, spun its wheel, and applied the flame to the pipe's bowl, moving it in circles as he puffed gently, wreathing his face in smoke and filling the room with the warm scent of burning tobacco.

"I've been here for almost twenty-five years, and in that time, I pride myself on being able to tell whether Emlen, with all it has to offer, is or is not the best place for a student. I think we can all agree that it's not a matter of the best school, but a matter of finding the best place, the right place, for each individual student. And in this case," he continued, his voice almost kind, "I'm afraid that it's become abundantly clear . . ."

Oh, no, thought Daisy, as the hinges of Hal's jaw bulged. ". . . that Emlen is not the best fit for Beatrice."

"Please," Daisy murmured, even though she wasn't sure what she was pleading for. She suspected that the dean was probably right. Emlen had been the right place for Danny and David, and it had unquestionably been the right place for Hal, who'd made lifelong friends here; who spoke of his years at Emlen as the best years of his life. But Emlen, Daisy thought, had never been the right place for her daughter.

Hal got to his feet, unbuttoning his jacket and smoothing his tie, his lips pressed so tightly together that they'd vanished in his face. Daisy rose with him, and settled her hand on his arm, feeling the coiled tension of his muscles. She squeezed, a gesture that she hoped would communicate the futility of yelling or threats; that would speak of her desire to leave with their dignity and their daughter, even if it wasn't Hal's preferred outcome. This was her role in their partnership: she was the guardrails that kept Hal from veering off the road; she was the civilized counterweight to his most brutish instincts.

"Thank you for your time," she said to the dean, and led her husband into the antechamber, to collect their daughter. She put her arm around Beatrice's shoulders, pulling her close, and, just for a moment, Beatrice allowed the contact. "Let's go home."

2

Beatrice

Class, let's welcome the newest member of the class, Beatrice Shoemaker."

Beatrice stood up, smoothed her pale-blue cardigan, and gave her new classmates the smile she'd been rehearsing—cheerful, but not goofy; friendly but not desperate. "Good morning, Beatrice," the kids droned. Bea waved, took her seat, and looked around. Her first period, A Block ("It sounds like jail," she'd overheard her father saying), was ninety minutes of American Literature. Followed by World History, followed by lunch. There were fourteen other kids in the class, a testament to Melville's "commitment to small, intimate classes where your child can shine." Beatrice recognized just one girl, Doff Cartwright, a former classmate from junior high. The other kids were strangers, and the school itself was a significant come-down from the Emlen Academy. Emlen had a campus, with a collection of gray granite and redbrick buildings crawling with ivy. It had three senators and a vice president among its alumni, not to mention novelists and journalists and researchers and nuclear physicists. Its motto, *serve hoc mundo*, meant "we serve the world," and the dean and the teachers were forever talking about the students' obligation to give back, to use their brains and skills and their talent to make the world a better place.

Beatrice had hated it. She'd hated the bright-eyed, well-behaved students who talked endlessly about their resumes and the colleges to which they'd apply. She hated the cold New England weather, the bland dining-hall food, the way the other kids, including her roommate Celia, treated her crafting as a waste of time. She hated, too, how she'd gone from being one of the smarter kids in her grade to average. Not even average, really. Below average. One of the girls in her dorm had won an international piano competition when she was twelve, and a boy on the next floor was the son of the Senate's minority whip. The level of ambition, the constant scrambling after achievements and prizes, the anxiety and sleeplessness that preceded every exam or paper's due date, the way the girls' bathrooms would reek during finals, when the girls who threw up because they were anxious joined the girls who threw up after they binged. All the kids bragged about how little sleep they'd gotten and how much coffee they'd consumed. To Beatrice, it all felt wearying and pointless. Especially because Beatrice didn't want to run for president or conduct an orchestra or discover a cure for cancer when she grew up. What she wanted to do was crafts. Knitting and needle-felting, mostly, but she also embroidered and crocheted, none of which were skills appreciated or encouraged at Emlen.

So now she was at this new school, which had been founded thirty years after Emlen and had barely any ivy at all. Melville had a good reputation locally, but it wasn't a nationally known school the way that Emlen was, and she knew, from the way his lips had tightened in his face and his hands had tightened on the steering wheel when he'd dropped her off, that her father was disappointed.

Oh, well, Beatrice thought, and tried to ignore the twinge of disappointing her dad. On her left, two boys were staring at her. As she watched, one of them whispered something to the other, and they both sniggered. Beatrice was especially proud of that day's look: an ankle-length prairie-style dress with many ruffles and a petticoat under its skirt and a loose-fitting cardigan with pearl buttons that she'd bought for six dollars at the Thrift for AIDS shop in Queen Village on top. Her hair had been cut in a chin-length bob and she'd dyed it a silvery lavender over the weekend. She wore knee socks and her favorite canvas Chuck Taylor basketball sneakers on her feet. She dressed to please herself, and to feel comfortable, and if these boys believed that her body was an object that existed for their pleasure, she'd be happy to tell them otherwise.

On her right, her old classmate Doff had pulled out her phone and had it half-hidden in her lap. Beatrice could see what she was looking up: PLAN B NEAR ME and PLAN B CHEAP and DOES PLAN B ON AMAZON WORK and IS PLAN B ON AMAZON REAL.

Oh, dear. Beatrice was a virgin. She'd never had sex, let alone a pregnancy scare. The year before, her mother—she still shuddered at the memory—had come into her bedroom one night. Beatrice had just gotten through straightening things up. Her favorite books (*Frankenstein* and *The Sandman* and *The Gashlycrumb Tinies*, the collected works of Emily Dickinson and Christina Rossetti) were in neat rows on her bookshelf. Her lavender-scented candle was burning, she'd made herself a cup of tea, and she was getting ready to sort through her sewing kit when her mom had knocked at her door. "Do you have a minute to talk?"

Before Beatrice could answer, her mother came and sat down on Beatrice's bed, in the gray fleece overalls she insisted on wearing around the house (Beatrice thought she would actually die of shame if her mom ever wore them out in public. Twice, she'd tried to sneak the overalls out of the dryer and into the trash, but, both times, her mom had rescued them. "Oh, sorry," Bea had said innocently. "I thought they were rags").

"I want to talk to you about sex before you go to boarding school," her mom had announced.

Cringe. "Okay."

"Now, I know you've taken biology, right?" her mom began, in a strangely upbeat tone, smiling like she was trying to impersonate someone she'd seen on daytime TV. "And sex ed in sixth grade? So you know all the names of the parts, and what goes where."

Oh my God, Beatrice thought. Her mom had flour on her midsection and crumbs on her bosom. She'd been making brioche, and she smelled like yeast and sugar. It was like a loaf of bread had invaded her room. A loaf of bread that wanted to talk about sex.

"And, you know, now that you've entered puberty . . ."

Beatrice prayed for a tornado, a tsunami, a meteor to crash through the earth's atmosphere and through her house's roof and to somehow make her mother stop talking. She prayed for a supermoon to cause the tides to surge and sweep her house away. A hurricane would do nicely. But no meteorological event was coming to save her . . . and, she realized, her mother was at least as uncomfortable as she was. Which meant that maybe she could have some fun.

"I wanted to talk to you about the emotional part of it." Her mother made a point of looking right into her eyes. "When girls have sex, their hearts get involved, too. Whether you want that to happen or not. I think that women are just built that way." Her mom had a faraway look on her face, like maybe she was thinking about someone she'd had sex with, once. *Ew.*

"How do you know I even want to have sex with guys? Or with anyone?" Beatrice had asked, just to make trouble. First her mom had looked shocked, then she'd hurriedly smoothed out her face, which only made it look like she was trying super-hard *not* to look shocked. Which was exactly what Beatrice knew would happen. Her mom loved to talk about how progressive and accepting she was, how happy she was that her brother lived in a world where he could marry the man he loved. But of course, Beatrice thought smugly, it would be different if it was her own daughter.

Her mom had cleared her throat, rubbing her hands up and down her fleece-covered legs. "Well, whoever you end up having sex with—if you have sex with anyone—that person can hurt you. I'm not going to tell you to wait for marriage, but I hope you'll wait until you're older, and strong enough to handle getting your heart broken."

"I'm strong," Beatrice said. "You don't have to worry about me." *Get out,* she was thinking. *Get out of my room and never come back.*

"But I do," said her mom, clasping her hands earnestly. "I do worry. That's my job." She squared her shoulders, like she was getting ready to plow a field or raise a barn. "Do you have any questions?"

"I do not."

"Anything you want to know?" Her mom made another attempt at a smile. "You can ask me anything."

How soon can this conversation be over was the only thing Beatrice wanted to know. "I'm fine. Really. No questions."

"Oh, and I wanted to talk to you about masturbation!"

Oh, no. Beatrice couldn't stop herself from making a dismayed squeak, which her mother either didn't hear or decided to ignore.

"You probably know this already, but masturbation is perfectly natural and normal, and it's nothing to be ashamed of. And if you do it, it doesn't mean you aren't a virgin, or anything like that. It's very important that you, um, know what makes you feel good before you're intimate with someone else. Sex is about pleasure . . ."

Please stop talking, Beatrice prayed.

". . . and you deserve pleasure," her mom was saying earnestly. "Every woman does. You should be enjoying yourself just as much as the boy. Or, um, the other person."

"Or people," said Beatrice, straight-faced.

"Or people! Whatever! I just don't want you to be in a relationship where sex is something you do for the other person. It can be the most wonderful thing in the world, and you should be exploring. By yourself, before you start with other people. Your body is a wonderland!" her mom had said, and she'd actually tried to wink. "And if you don't know how to have an orgasm on your own, you aren't going to be able to share that with your partners."

Maybe I'm dead already, thought Beatrice, with a kind of faint wonder. *Maybe I'm dead and this is hell: my mom quoting John Mayer songs and talking about orgasms.*

"I got you some books . . ." Her mom had handed her *A Girl's Guide to Her Body* and *The Care and Keeping of You.* "And if you have any questions, I'm here."

"No questions," Beatrice said, very firmly. "Thank you for this instructive interlude." Her mom opened her arms, and Beatrice couldn't back away quickly enough to avoid being hugged, and then finally, *finally*, her mom had departed, leaving only an indentation on the comforter to show that she'd been there. Beatrice had placed the books in the very bottom of her bottom dresser drawer, underneath the sweaters she never wore, and closed the drawer and told herself she'd never look in there, or even in that direction, again.

"Let's open our MacBooks to a new Google Doc, please," said Dr. Argan. "Beatrice, we usually start off on Thursdays with some free writing. Half an hour on the subject of your choice." The other kids had already started clickety-clacking away, but her face must have looked as blank as her brain felt, because he looked at her kindly, and said, "Tell me who you are. Tell me about your hobbies. Heck, tell me what you did on your summer vacation! Just something so that I can get to know you."

Great. Beatrice stared at the cursor, which pulsed evilly and refused to form words on its own. She buttoned and unbuttoned the top pearl button on her cardigan and smoothed her hair behind her ears. She thought about telling the story of sixth-grade art class, how the teacher, Ms. Perkins, had shown them how to use wire and papier-mâché to make a sculpture, and how, almost the instant she'd started bending the wire in the shape of their dog Lester's body, Beatrice had felt a magical click in her brain, the sense that this, not math or English or being a lawyer or giving cooking lessons, was what she was made for. Ms. Perkins was short, with curly hair and thin lips and pointy ears, one with seven piercings, including one through the tragus. By the end of the year, to her mom's amusement and her father's dismay, Beatrice had stopped wearing jeans and sneakers and began finding an aesthetic of her own, one that involved vintage Laura Ashley and Gunne Sax dresses, delicate gold rings, pearl necklaces and embroidered carpetbags and bouquets of tea roses and baby's breath.

Beatrice could write about art and fashion. But then she decided there was a different story she could tell.

"Last year a woman was murdered in the house next door to mine," she typed.

There. She was off to a banging beginning. Now for some details. "Every summer I go to Cape Cod with my parents. My father's father owns a house on the Outer Cape, right on the water. My dad's brother and his wife and their kids get it for three weeks, then my mom and dad and I get it for three weeks, and for the last part of the summer we're all together." When she was younger, that had been her favorite part of the summer. Uncle Jeremy was like an older, grayer, more profane version of her dad. He had a bit of a beer gut (maybe because, unlike her dad, he drank beer), and a skinny, anxious, slightly bucktoothed wife. Every year when they arrived, Beatrice's mom would hand Aunt Janie a large gin and tonic and lead her to a seat out on the deck, and Uncle Jeremy would coax her father out of his office. "C'mon, Hal. Live a little!" he'd say. Whenever her dad would try to claim that he couldn't go fishing or to the beach or out to lunch because he had work, Uncle Jeremy would say, "Don't be such an old woman!" in a funny, quavering voice . . . and it would work. Her dad would trade his button-down shirts for ancient T-shirts advertising old bands like R.E.M., and sometimes he'd even skip his daily five-mile run and go to the beach, or for bike rides with Beatrice and her cousins Oliver and Tallulah (both were nice enough, with their mother's unfortunate overbite). Once every summer, at the end of her dad's designated vacation week, they would charter a fishing boat for the day, and even Aunt Janie would come, after dosing herself with Dramamine and ginger candy. They'd take turns pulling in stripers and bluefish, and her mom would pack a picnic, which they'd eat while the boat was at anchor, rocking gently on the waves. There would be bonfires on the beach, and her grandfather would come for the big barbecue, where they'd invite all their friends and other visiting families, people her dad and his brother had grown up with. The party would go late into the night, with parents stashing the kids in her bedroom, with its two sets of bunk beds. Beatrice could remember being very young, waking up to find her room full of sleeping children, in the beds or curled up under blankets on the floor, hearing laughter, and music, and the splash of one of the dads cannonballing into the swimming pool.

"Cape Cod is my favorite place in the world," she typed, and thought about one of her favorite Emily Dickinson poems, the one about how she's never seen a moor, and never seen the sea, "yet now I know how the heather looks, and how a wave must be." It was a poem about faith, and not beach vacations, but the

line *how a wave must be* had always called the Cape to mind.
For years, her parents had sent her to nature camp and art camp
and, finally, the sailing camp in Provincetown that her dad had
attended. Beatrice had been prepared to hate it, but it turned
out that she loved to sail. Once she passed her skipper's test, she
begged her father to buy her a used Sunfish—"It can be a whole
year's worth of birthday and Christmas and Chanukah presents,"
she'd said. He'd agreed. Beatrice had gotten her boat the next
year. That summer, she'd spent long days on the water, all alone,
tacking back and forth around the bay.

"Last summer, my dad's family rented the house out for a
week," Beatrice typed. When Uncle Jeremy had called, her dad
had put him on speaker, so Beatrice overheard her uncle's voice,
tense and eager, as he'd said, "They'll pay us whatever we want.
They need a place to put their guests, and they're trying to rent
every house on the street."

"Not interested," her dad had said. "We've never let anyone
stay there who wasn't family, and we're not going to start now."

"You have all your Emlen buddies stay there," Uncle Jeremy
argued, and her dad had said, "That's different. I'm there with
them." Uncle Jeremy's voice had gotten almost shrill, as he'd said,
"It's twenty thousand dollars, Hal. Maybe that doesn't make any
difference to you. But it makes a difference to me."

That was when her dad had spotted her. He'd frowned,
walked across his office, and shut the door, but Beatrice guessed
that Uncle Jeremy had talked him into it. Instead of going to the
Cape for the last week of June, they'd gone to the Bahamas. Her
parents had forced her to ride a bike all over the island. They'd
eaten conch fritter and her mom had pointed out the pink sand
at least four times a day, saying, "Isn't it beautiful!" with a longing
sigh like she missed the beaches already, even though they were
right in front of her. On the last day of their vacation, they'd been
packing, getting ready to go to the airport, when Beatrice's phone

had started blowing up, with her friends texting her things like: OMG and DID YOU SEE and THAT'S YOUR HOUSE ON CNN! She'd checked the news, then hurried through the suite's living room and into her parents' bedroom, to find her mom sitting about six inches from the TV screen with her mouth hanging open and her dad on the phone with Uncle Jeremy, saying, "I knew this was a bad idea!"

"The woman who died was an Instagram influencer named Drue Cavanaugh. She'd come to the Cape to get married," Beatrice typed. "She was murdered on what would have been her wedding day." Beatrice hadn't known the dead woman, but she knew her grandparents, the Lathrops, an elderly couple who lived in an enormous house on the same dune as the Shoemakers. The Lathrops would call to complain if Lester ever chased a chipmunk into their yard, back in Lester's chipmunk-chasing days, and when Beatrice and her mom saw Mr. Lathrop at the post office, or Mrs. Lathrop at Jams, they'd just get a single stiff nod. "WASPs," her mom had said with a shrug when Beatrice had asked why they were so mean. When Beatrice was little, she'd thought that maybe the Lathrops were actual insects, hiding their wings and their stingers underneath Lilly Pulitzer dresses and Brooks Brothers shirts. Drue Cavanaugh had been their granddaughter.

Beatrice stared at the cursor for a moment, imagining what Mrs. Hardy, one of the only teachers she'd liked back at Emlen, would have asked. *Why are you telling us this story? How do you feel about it? What does it mean to you?*

"I thought about the murder all last year," she typed. "How I probably walked on the sand, exactly where the dead woman walked. How we'd been swimming at the same beaches, and probably eaten in the same restaurants."

The dead girl had been easy to find online. She'd looked so perfect, rich and beautiful and perfect, with honey-blonde hair and sun-kissed white skin and the kind of slim-hipped, big-busted body that it usually took a surgeon to achieve. She'd had a Harvard degree and a man who'd loved her, money, about a million followers on social media, and a huge, global brand. Only none of it had been real. The dead girl's death had exposed the truth of her life, the way she'd been two people, the real one and the one she'd portrayed on social media.

For the rest of the summer, Beatrice thought about Drue Cavanaugh. Maybe Drue had learned to swim at Gull Pond or waited in line to buy croissants at the boulangerie on Route 6 in Wellfleet; maybe she'd walked into the bay at low tide, with a bucket made of metal mesh banging against her hip, feeling for clams with her feet. Maybe she'd eaten fresh oysters at Moby Dick's or gone fishing for stripers with her father. It had made Beatrice feel strange in a way she couldn't describe; newly aware of the world, and the people around her. It had made her think about her own future: what she wanted, where she'd live, what kind of life she'd have, when her choices were her own. Right now, she could run her Etsy shop, she could pierce her ears and color her hair and wear long Laura Ashley dresses instead of Lululemon leggings, but when she'd timidly brought up the topic of applying to one of the city's magnet art schools, in the car on the way home, her dad had said, curtly, "You'll go to Emlen, and after that you'll get a liberal arts degree. Do whatever you want after that." He'd concluded with one of his favorite sayings: "He who pays the piper calls the tune," and her mom had closed her eyes like her head hurt.

Tomorrow isn't promised, Beatrice typed. She couldn't remember if she'd read that somewhere, or just seen it on a handmade sign at a store, next to the ones that said LIVE LAUGH LOVE and IT'S WINE O'CLOCK. She sighed and erased it, hearing Mrs. Hardy say *cliché!* She thought for a moment about how to express what she was trying to say, and the difference between being a thing and only seeming that way, and, when the bell rang, she finally wrote, "Cape Cod is one of the most beautiful places in the world. It's always been my favorite place, the place where I've made some of my happiest memories. But what I learned last summer is that it isn't a safe place. Maybe there are no truly safe places for girls and women. Drue Cavanaugh and I probably looked up at the same stars from the same spot on the beach and thought about our futures. Only now she'll never have one. And I am thinking even harder about mine."

3

Daisy

In 2019, the iconic signboard at Thirtieth Street Station, the one that had clickety-clacked through train numbers and gate assignments and destinations, had been replaced by a new, blandly digital one. Preservationists had written petitions, newspaper columnists and the Historical Society had complained, every passenger Daisy had ever met preferred the old version, but the outcry had not been enough to get the Amtrak executives to change their minds. Daisy missed the sign, even though the station retained its grandeur, with soaring ceilings and gold marble and the enormous statue of Winged Victory, her arms enfolding a man's body, in honor of Philadelphia's wartime dead.

On Sunday morning, Daisy arrived at the station an hour ahead of time, and it only took her two tries to liberate the ticket to New York City that she'd reserved from the machine. At a coffee shop near the waiting area, she bought herself a cup of coffee and, after some deliberation, a warm chocolate croissant.

She and Beatrice used to go to New York City every year, for Beatrice's birthday. They'd get their nails done ahead of time and purchase a new dress for Bea. They would take the train up, and see a Broadway show, and spend the night in a hotel, and have brunch at the Plaza. Daisy still had the Playbills in a box in her closet: *Waitress* and *Avenue Q*, *Wicked* and *Legally Blonde*. The last time she'd mentioned her birthday and the possibility of a trip, Beatrice had said, "I'm going to do something with my friends." She hadn't been rude, or dismissive, or sarcastic. In fact, she'd spoken so gently that Daisy suspected that Beatrice was worried about hurting her feelings. Which, of course, had injured her more than sarcasm would have.

Sighing, she thought of Hannah, and wondered what her friend would have said. *Don't take it personally*, she imagined, and pictured Hannah's pale, freckled skin, her reddish hair and eyes like dark chocolate drops, her sly smile.

Daisy had met Hannah when she was eight months pregnant and had ended up alone in a Bradley Method birth class. Hal had been scheduled to be there with her, but he'd been called away to Ohio for a case that had unexpectedly gone to trial, and Daisy had ended up sitting by herself, stiff and self-conscious in a Pennsylvania Hospital conference room, aware that she was younger than the rest of the women in the room by at least six or seven years. She could feel their eyes on her, and was fiddling with her engagement ring so they wouldn't think she was a single mom when Hannah hurried through the door, plopping down in the seat beside her just as the lecture began.

"Birth is a natural process," said the instructor. She was middle-aged, and wore a long strand of chunky amber beads over a long-sleeved black dress, black leggings, and black clogs. "It's a task your body was built to perform, and there's no reason for interventions like epidurals, or drugs to hurry labor along. Now, Dr. Bradley developed this method in the 1950s, when most women labored in what was called twilight sleep."

"Those were the days," murmured Hannah (they hadn't been introduced yet, but they'd all been given name tags). Daisy glanced sideways, as discreetly as she could. Hannah was petite, one of those pregnant women who looked like she'd stuffed a basketball under her shirt while staying skinny everywhere else (as opposed to Daisy, who just looked bigger everywhere).

"Dr. Bradley was raised on a farm, where he saw many animals giving birth. As a result of what he saw, he believed that women could give birth without drugs or distress."

"Moo," said Hannah softly. Daisy bit her lip. Hannah raised her hand.

"Yes?" said the instructor.

"I'm just curious. How did Dr. Bradley know that the animals weren't in pain?"

The instructor, smiling tightly, said, "I'm assuming he was able to tell whether or not a horse or a cow was suffering."

"But how? They can't scream, or moan, or curse, or anything like that. Maybe they were in absolute agony, and just, you know, suffering in silence. Maybe," Hannah continued, "if they could have asked for epidurals, they would have."

"I guess we'll just have to take Dr. Bradley's word for it," said the instructor. "And remember that more than eighty-five percent of the women who've completed the course have had natural, vaginal births."

Daisy didn't like the word "vaginal." She supposed, if she stuck with the course, she'd be hearing it frequently. Hannah tapped Daisy's shoulder. "Want to be partners?"

Daisy looked around. The instructor was removing a stack of pillows from a closet, and the other couples were grabbing pillows and arranging themselves on the floor.

"Which one of us gets to be the mother?"

"We can take turns. Or," Hannah whispered, "we can go get a burger." When she saw Daisy hesitating, she pointed at the stack of documents they'd been given, whispering, "Protein! It says we're supposed to be eating lots of protein!"

They'd slipped out the door and gone to Butcher and Singer on Walnut Street. "How'd you get interested in the Bradley Method?" Daisy asked as they walked.

"My sister gave birth to twins in her bathtub," Hannah said, lifting her narrow shoulders in a shrug. "I'm competitive. But I think in this case I'm going to let Rose win."

Daisy learned that Hannah was a preschool teacher, that her husband was a nurse at Pennsylvania Hospital, that they lived in Bella Vista, the neighborhood right near the Italian Market, and that they, too, were expecting a girl.

"What about you? Are you really going to do this Bradley stuff?" Hannah had asked Daisy.

"I'm investigating," Daisy said. "My husband's a fan of natural birth." She finished her glass of water. "My husband was also supposed to be here tonight, but he got stuck at work."

"And he's not the one actually having the baby," Hannah pointed out. "Shouldn't this be your call?"

Daisy toyed with her ring again. She lived in Hal's house, supported by Hal's money. She honestly didn't feel like much of anything was her call these days. "I guess." She tried for a smile. "Honestly, if they were still doing twilight sleep . . ."

"Ha!" Hannah's bark of laughter, startling from such a small woman, was so loud that Daisy saw heads at other tables turning. "I know, right! I mean, I understand it's supposed to be better for the baby if we don't get drugs. It makes sense. But we're people, too, right?"

"We are people, too," Daisy affirmed.

"So what's your story, morning glory?" Before Daisy could answer, the food arrived. Hannah's face lit up, and she lifted her burger with palpable gusto, her jaw seeming to unhinge as she took a gigantic bite. "Oh, God, that's good," she said after she'd swallowed. "I'm so hungry all the time. Are you hungry all the time? What have you been craving?"

"I was hungry all the time before I got pregnant," Daisy admitted. "And I'm eating a lot of grilled cheese."

"Grilled cheese!" Hannah said. "Ooh. I haven't had a grilled cheese sandwich in forever. I shall add it to my list." She'd pulled out a BlackBerry and typed it in. "So, back to you." She'd looked Daisy up and down. "Where do you live?"

"Gladwyne. And I'm twenty-two," said Daisy, even though Hannah hadn't asked.

"Wow. I remember my twenties. Vaguely." Hannah ate another bite of burger. "How long have you been married?"

"Almost two years," Daisy said. It was closer to a year and a half, but she wanted to make it clear that she'd married Hal because she wanted to, and not because she'd needed to.

"Mazel tov," said Hannah, and licked her fingers.

"How old are you?" asked Daisy.

"How old do you think I am?"

Daisy took her honest guess and revised it downward by two years. "Thirty?"

"Ha! I'm thirty-five. A crone!" Hannah patted her lips with her napkin and looked around for their waiter. "Do they have ice cream here?"

They ended up at Scoop DeVille, where they shared a banana split, and when Hannah said, "Do you want to meet up and go for a walk tomorrow?" Daisy hadn't even had to think about it.

"Yes," she'd said.

Daisy knew that she and Hannah were going to be friends. She'd hoped that Hal and Hannah's husband, Eric, would like each other; that they could be couples who did things together, but they'd never really meshed as a foursome. Hal said he liked both of the Magees, but Daisy could tell that he was irritated by Hannah's loudness, her brassy voice, the way she never wore makeup or heels and would ask anyone anything. Her house was comfortable in Daisy's opinion, "a mess" in Hal's (and Daisy had to admit that there was a certain amount of dog hair on, and in, things at the Magees). As for Eric, Daisy figured her husband would dismiss a male nurse as a man who hadn't been able to make it through medical school, a man who probably wasn't as smart or accomplished and who definitely wasn't as well-off as he was. "If you like them, that's what matters," he'd said after an uncomfortable dinner at the Shoemaker house, where Eric had done his best to act interested in bass fishing, and Hal had barely tried to act like he cared about European League soccer, which was Eric's passion. "They're your friends, not mine."

It turned out that the group that clicked didn't involve Hal at all, but Daisy and her brother and Danny's husband, Jesse. Jesse worked in an art gallery and taught dance, and Danny was a counselor at a high school in Trenton. Every month or two, they'd all meet for dinner, sometimes in the city, sometimes in Lambertville or New Hope, or at Daisy's house, where Daisy could cook. For years, Daisy had been trying to coax the Magees out to the suburbs. "Forget it, I'm not going to the dark side," Hannah would say. Still, every time Daisy saw a listing for a house she thought would work, she'd text the listing to Hannah, and Hannah would text back GET THEE BEHIND ME SATAN.

And then her friend had died. "Bad news, kiddo," Hannah had said on the phone one afternoon, her normally ebullient voice so muted that Daisy almost hadn't recognized it. "The docs found a lump." She'd named it—of course she had—but even after Larry the Lump had been excised, even after a round of radiation and three months of chemotherapy, there'd been more lumps. Son of Larry, and Return of Larry, and Larry Two: Electric Boogaloo. Then they'd found masses in her liver, and spots on her lungs, and Hannah had stopped making jokes.

"I don't think I'm going to beat this," she said. She'd lost her hair and thirty pounds by then, and was sitting in bed, her tiny frame swimming in a flannel nightgown, with thick fleece socks on her feet. "To the extent that it was ever a battle or a war, I'm pretty sure my side isn't winning."

"Yes, you are. Don't say that!" Daisy had taken her hand. "Zoe needs you. Eric needs you." She'd swallowed hard. "I need you."

"Oh, kiddo." Hannah had squeezed her hand, but her eyes were far away, and Daisy thought, *She's already only mostly here. Part of her is already gone.* She'd thought Hannah had fallen asleep, but then her friend had licked her lips and opened her eyes again.

"I need you to promise me something," Hannah had said.

"Of course," Daisy said. "Of course. Anything."

With a visible effort, Hannah rallied herself. She'd licked her dry lips again and said, "I've already given Eric permission to remarry," she said. She stared up into Daisy's eyes, her cold hands feeling claw-like as she pulled Daisy closer. "But you have to promise—and this is my sincere dying wish, so you have to swear to me—to keep him away from that whore Debbie Conover."

Daisy started laughing. Then she'd started crying. Sniffling, she'd squeezed her friend's hand. "I promise," Daisy said. "I promise."

Three days later, Hannah had died. A few months after that, Eric had put their row house on the market, and he and Zoe had moved to Wisconsin, to be closer to his parents. Daisy missed her friend with a pain that felt physical, a wound that refused to close. She had plenty of acquaintances, other moms she could call up for coffee or a barre class, but Hannah had been her only real friend.

In preparation for her meeting with Diana, Daisy had done her googling, but she hadn't learned much. Diana.S@earthlink was Diana Starling, the founder and principal of a business called DS Consultants. She had a website, but it was full of lingo that Daisy, as a non-businessperson, found completely incomprehensible. *We help our clients transform and evolve in our fast-moving modern age and embrace transformation and disruption as a continuous way of working.* She knew what each of those words meant, on its own. Combined, though, they might as well have been a language she'd never learned.

There was a picture of the other Diana on the website, a headshot of a middle-aged white woman with dark hair and a confident look about her. The "about our principals" page listed her degrees: undergraduate from Boston University, MBA from Wharton, and no information about when those degrees had been awarded. From what she knew about the working world, Daisy supposed it made sense. Young women were seen as ditzy and clueless and inconstant; flighty things who could quit at any moment to have a baby. Older women were barely seen at all. "Ms. Starling is based in New York City," read her bio. There were no details about where the other Diana had grown up, or any hobbies she had, or if she had a spouse or a family.

Daisy had continued her search on social media. The DS Consulting Twitter account specialized in bland retweets of *Wall Street Journal* and *Business Today* stories and *Contact us today to see what we can do for your business!* It also seemed to delete its tweets after six weeks, which didn't give her much of a history to peruse. Diana Starling was on Instagram, but her account was private, the picture it displayed a version of the headshot on the corporate website. Same with Facebook. The only information Daisy was able to glean came from the misdirected emails, which suggested a life of revelry and glamorous destinations; parties and dinners and girls' nights out, although the other Diana had been quick to assure her that this was not the case. *I promise you, these are work obligations disguised as parties.*

"Regional train one eighty-six making station stops in Trenton, Metro Park, Newark, and Penn Station, New York. All aboard!" called the conductor. Daisy brushed croissant crumbs off her top and got in line. When she boarded the train, she found two empty seats in the quiet car. An excellent sign. She sat, settling her purse in her lap and wondering if she would look hopelessly dowdy next to the other Diana. She'd blown out her hair, to the best of her abilities, and packed a black knit jersey tunic to wear over leggings and black boots, along with a necklace made of gumball-sized blue glass beads that the salesgirl at J.Crew told her was a statement piece. As a size fourteen, her options were limited, but even if they hadn't been, fashion had never been her thing, and she was too old to reinvent herself as a fashionista.

"All tickets, please!" called the conductor. Daisy handed over her ticket, which the conductor scanned with some kind of chirping electronic device that looked like a phaser from *Star Trek*. It gave Daisy a pang, remembering how the conductors used to use a hole punch, leaving the car littered with tiny circles of paper. She had half a dozen paperbacks with old Amtrak tickets as bookmarks, relics of the trips she'd made to the city with her husband and her daughter. That made her feel even worse, realizing that she was now one of those annoying women, prattling on about how much better things used to be.

I'm getting old, she thought, and settled back with a sigh. She had a book, Alice Hoffman's latest, and there was always her phone, with its games and social media apps and the entirety of the world's collected knowledge. She could sort through her photos, which she'd been meaning to do forever; she could email the school's decorating committee, which she had recently joined, to see if anyone had any great ideas for giving Melville's all-purpose room the feel of a glamorous destination (their theme was "A Night at the Opera." Hal's single, non-helpful suggestion had been hiring a fat lady to sing).

But she didn't want to read, or scroll through Facebook, and see all the other happy families, the other moms and dads and kids posing on their spring-break vacations. When she'd told

Hal about her plans, he'd given her a distracted nod, and barely seemed to be listening. He'd been in a mood ever since their return trip from Emlen, and she wasn't sure whether it had to do with his only child getting kicked out of the prep school he'd attended or if this was lingering sorrow over his classmate's death.

Daisy shifted in her seat as the train rounded a curve. The night before she'd asked, one more time, if Beatrice wanted to come with her. She'd found her daughter sitting in the corner, in one of her long, drab dresses, knitting by the light of a candle on her dresser. She looked, Daisy thought, like an eighteenth-century consumptive.

"You sure you don't want to come with me?" she'd asked.

"No, thanks," Beatrice replied, shaking her head. She was murmuring *knit one, purl two* under her breath, and Daisy could tell she was annoyed at the interruption. The electric kettle they'd ordered her at school was steaming on her dresser, next to a biscuit tin and a box of PG Tips teabags. A tiny swashbuckling mouse was posed on Beatrice's desk. It had a little silvery sword in its hand, clever black boots on its feet, and a black mask over its eyes.

"This is so realistic!" Daisy had marveled, picking it up for a closer look. "Is this real fur?"

"Well, yeah, it's real fur. It's a real mouse."

Daisy, who'd assumed she'd been handling something made of wool, had screamed, and dropped the thing. Well, maybe she'd actually (unintentionally!) thrown it a little. And then she'd had to wrestle it away from Lester, who'd tried to eat it.

"Hey, I made that!" Beatrice said indignantly.

"Sorry," Daisy said. Her voice sounded faint. "Are you . . . did it . . ."

"It's from a pet store."

"Was it . . ." She couldn't think of how to ask if the mouse was dead or alive when Beatrice obtained it. She wasn't sure she wanted to know the answer.

"Don't worry. I'm being very sanitary." Daisy looked down at her daughter's desk. Once, there'd been a stack of vintage Nancy Drew books there, a collection Daisy had painstakingly assembled a book or two at a time. There'd been a pair of lamps with pink polka-dotted shades and a jewelry box that had once been Daisy's, with a ballerina who spun to "The Blue Danube Waltz" when you lifted the lid. Now there were bags of cotton batting and cotton balls, loops of fine-gauge wire, scissors and pliers and scalpels, all lined up neatly in a row, along with a box of rubber gloves, and a small dish of tiny beaded eyes.

"So you're doing taxidermy?"

"Yep."

"No more needle-felting?"

"No, I'm doing that, too. I've actually got two commissions to do this week. A goldendoodle and a Great Dane."

"Well, I left you and Dad the Indian chicken you both like. You just need to—"

"Put it in a saucepan, heat it on a low flame for twenty minutes."

"Okay, well, have a good day at school."

"Bye," Beatrice said, without looking up from her knitting.

As the train picked up speed, Daisy turned her head toward the window. She saw her own reflection—brown hair, full cheeks, heart-shaped face, lines, faint but discernible, around her eyes—and watched the backyards of New Jersey flashing past. She was thinking about her father, who'd been on her mind.

Jack Rosen had been a businessman—or, as he put it, an entrepreneur, forever in search of the next big thing. For the first ten years of her parents' marriage, money had been scarce. Her father had invested in opportunities that hadn't panned out—a jewelry store franchise that had been doing fine until a Kay Jewelers opened up in a nearby mini-mall; a fur-storage facility that had gotten picketed every week by animal rights protestors; a fondue restaurant that had given Jack and his wife two good years, until people stopped eating fondue.

Then, in the 1970s, her dad had gotten lucky with Jazzercise studio franchises, and when the 1980s arrived, her father had presciently invested in movie-rental shops. The next twelve years had been good ones. They'd moved out of their duplex and into a rambling Victorian mansion in Montclair, New Jersey. He'd sent his sons, Daisy's brothers, to the Emlen Academy, the storied boarding school that had only admitted a handful of Jews until the 1960s.

Jack Rosen had loved his sons, a love that was tinged with something close to awe as they'd grown into the kind of young men he'd never been, sporty, preppy fellows who'd traveled the world, tagging along with wealthier friends to Nantucket and St. Barts and Banff. His sons skied and sailed; they played tennis and eventually knew how to order wine. David had played baseball at Emlen, and Danny, who was short and slightly built, like their dad, had coxswained the men's eight for the crew team. Daisy could sense that the sports and the slang, the way her brothers seemed to speak a coded language full of nicknames and casual references to people Jack had never met and places he'd never been, made her slight, asthmatic father proud, and also left him slightly bewildered. She'd been very young when her brothers had been at Emlen, but she could still remember, vividly, her father wearing an Emlen hoodie around the house during the winter months and an Emlen T-shirt in the summer. At graduation, he would dress in a tweed sports jacket, no matter how hot it was on that day, and a tie in Emlen's colors, and take pictures of everything—the ivy-covered dorms, the dining halls, benches on the quad, with their brass plaques, the crew shells, even the other families, whose dads wore dress shirts with the cuffs rolled up and madras shorts and boat shoes on warm afternoons. There'd be sweat pouring down her father's bald head and cheeks, and her mother, tottering beside him in high heels, would hiss, *Jack, that's enough* as he'd surreptitiously fire off his camera. Daisy always liked visiting Emlen—they set up a tent where other families could drop off their children, so there were other kids to play with, and good things to eat. It wasn't until she was older that she understood how complicated it must have been for her parents, the way they must have felt both proud and out of place.

Daisy adored her father. She'd been a late-in-life baby, arriving when her mom was thirty-eight and exhausted and, Daisy suspected, pretty much ready to retire as a mom, but her father had loved her unreservedly. *Me and my shadow*, her dad used to say. She'd tag along with him whenever she could, when they'd visit his businesses, or his mother, Daisy's grandmother, who lived in an apartment in Riverdale in the Bronx. Her father did much of the family's cooking, and all of the baking, and it was from him that Daisy learned to prepare hamantaschen and rugelach and sufganiyot. *Princess Diana*, he'd called her, and he'd say, "Nothing is too good for my little girl." Every Saturday they spent together would end with the two of them browsing at a bookstore—sometimes the Waldenbooks in the nearby mall, sometimes the Strand in New York City. Her father would let her buy a stack of books as high as her knee. Daisy had her own bedroom and her own bathroom, a closet full of Girbaud jeans and Benetton sweaters. Every summer she went to Camp Ramah in the Catskills, and for her bat mitzvah she'd had a casino-themed party, which had featured a roulette wheel, blackjack tables, a popcorn stand, a photo booth, and a crew of "party motivators" to coax the awkward preteens out onto the dance floor. For favors, there were customized pairs of socks, pink for the girls, blue for the boys, that had I DANCED MY SOCKS OFF AT DIANA'S BAT MITZVAH embroidered on the soles. Daisy had worn a pink dress with a tulle skirt and silver paillettes stitched into the bodice, and had gotten her hair permed. She'd never felt more pretty, or more grown up.

Eighteen months later, things had taken a turn. First, her dad had gotten his money out of the movie-rental franchises, convinced that the public's appetite for at-home movies was waning, and put everything into a local chain of rotisserie restaurants called Cluck It. Then people stopped wanting roast chicken. Or maybe they wanted it from Boston Market. Or maybe Cluck It wasn't as much of a draw as investors had hoped. Whatever the reason, three of the four restaurants had closed within a year, and the Rosen family had downsized. Instead of fancy vacations, at the beach or in the mountains, there were long weekends at the Jersey Shore, with Judy sulking for most of their stay, crying when she thought the kids couldn't hear her, and asking, "What do you mean, it's all gone? How could you not have saved anything? How could you have let this happen to us?" Her dad ended the lease on his Porsche early, her mom went from a Cadillac to a Toyota, and they'd put the Montclair house on the market—"It's too big for just the three of us," her father had said, and Judy had nodded woodenly, swiping at her red-rimmed eyes. On their last night there, Daisy's mother had been the one with the Pentax, taking pictures of the bay window in the living room, the walk-in pantry and the custom tiled floors in the kitchen, and the in-ground pool in the backyard, walking through the house like a ghost, with her fur coat draped over her nightgown's shoulders.

Daisy liked to think that if she'd been a bit older, or if her parents had been a little more forthcoming, she would have behaved better. But she'd been fourteen and clueless, and her last conversation with her father had revolved around her insistence that if she didn't get the pair of cherry-red patent-leather Doc Marten boots, the very ones she'd seen in a Smashing Pumpkins music video, her life would be over. "Sure, Princess," her dad had said, sounding a little distracted. Later, Daisy would remember the lines around his eyes, the weary slump of his shoulders, but at the time, her only thoughts had been for those red boots. "I'll be home for dinner, and I'll bring you those shoes," were the last words her father had spoken to her as he'd passed through the kitchen on his way out the door on Monday morning. Daisy would have given a lot—years off her life, the use of her right hand—to have told him that she loved him, instead of saying what she had said, which was, "They're not shoes, Daddy, they're boots, and if you get the wrong ones you'll just have to return them."

They'd heard the front door closing, the sound of her dad starting his car. Then, an instant later, they'd heard the crash. Her mother ran out of the house. Daisy had gone to the window and seen her father's car, its rear end crumpled against a car parked across the street, with her father slumped over the wheel. Her mom had screamed "Call 911!" and Daisy had raced across the kitchen for the cordless phone. Too late. Her father had been dead before the ambulance had arrived.

At the house in Montclair, Daisy's mother had a quarter-acre patch in the backyard where she grew vegetables and flowers. From spring through summer and into the early fall, that was where she spent most of her free time, tilling the soil, planting and weeding and watering, hand-pollinating eggplants with a tiny paintbrush, or sprinkling ground-up bone meal on her roses and zinnias, to keep the ants away. Daisy would help her to put up the vegetables she'd harvested, turning cucumbers into pickles and tomatoes into marinara sauce.

After Jack Rosen died, the house was sold—quickly, and, Daisy gleaned, for not as much money as Judy might have hoped. Daisy and her mom had moved out of Montclair and into the two-bedroom apartment in West Orange. There was no garden, no yard, no outdoor space at all, just a little strip of concrete balcony with a waist-high metal railing. Daisy's mom had filled every inch of it with pots and hanging baskets. She'd grown what she could, but it wasn't the same. Nothing had been the same. There wasn't money to send her back to summer camp, and when she'd started at her new high school, she hadn't let anyone get too close. She'd worked hard to earn good grades, knowing she'd need assistance for college, and once she'd made it to Rutgers, she'd worked two jobs all year long, while maintaining the GPA that her scholarship required. Then, the summer after her junior year, she'd met Hal, and then Beatrice had come along. And then there'd been Hannah, the one friend she'd made, and kept, until Hannah had died.

Maybe she'd gotten out of the habit of friendship, she thought, as the rhythm of the train's motion drew her down toward sleep. Maybe this stranger, the other Diana, would be a chance for her to try again.

4

~~~

Daisy

On their usual trips to New York City, the Shoemakers stayed at a hotel on Central Park South. One of Hal's old Emlen classmates was a national manager for the hotel chain that owned it. Usually they got upgraded, and there was always a basket of fruit and a bottle of wine, with a note welcoming them back, waiting in their room when they arrived. *Just one of the perks of being an Emlen man*, Hal would say, as if Daisy needed to be reminded of how the world's doors swung open for Emlen men, in ways that were completely legal but still didn't seem entirely fair. An Emlen man, Hal's guidance counselor, had written Hal's letter of recommendation to the Emlen man who ran the admissions department at Dartmouth, and Hal had gotten in. A different Emlen man had recommended Hal to the alumnus who was dean of Yale Law, and Hal had gotten in there, too. While he was at law school, an Emlen man had hired Hal as a summer associate at Lewis, Dommel, and Fenick in Philadelphia. Hal had gone to work there when he'd graduated.

Daisy had her own thoughts about Emlen, few of which she'd shared with Hal. She wasn't quite sure how she could begin. She could see all the privileges that Hal enjoyed, and why he would want his daughter to be able to access that aid. She could see, too, some of her own complicity, the way that she benefited from his status by proximity, and how, instead of protesting or pushing back or trying to make it right or share what she'd been handed, she mostly went along with it, quietly enjoying all those unearned benefits. Her single act of rebellion was slyly asking Hal how much he'd donated to Emlen and then writing a check for an equal amount from their joint account to the NAACP, a gesture that seemed to amuse her husband more than it angered him. "Really, Daisy?" he'd asked her, and when she'd said, "It's the least we can do," he'd said, "You didn't have to go behind my back," before giving her the kind of indulgent look that made her want to throw a pizza stone at his face and then kissing her on the forehead.

On this trip, Daisy had wanted to be independent. Or, more accurately, she had wanted to enjoy the illusion of independence. When Diana had proposed meeting at the King Cole Bar at the St. Regis, Daisy booked a room there, telling herself that, after all of the year's upheavals—Hannah's death, Beatrice's expulsion, the death of Hal's classmate and Hal's subsequent funk—she deserved a treat.

When the train arrived, Daisy escaped the underbelly of Penn Station as fast as she could and walked up the escalator, past the cab line and into the cool spring air. She walked along Broadway, marveling as she headed uptown at how different New York City was from Philadelphia, or, really, from any other big city in the world. Everyone hurried. They swung their arms briskly at their sides; they dodged and wove around their fellow pedestrians, and charged every crossing signal. To what end? Daisy always wondered. What could possibly be so urgent? And had she ever felt such urgency about anything in her whole life? Not since childbirth, she thought, and she smiled thinly, remembering how she'd wanted to go to the hospital as soon as she'd felt the pain of the first contraction, and Hal had made her wait until he'd finished eating his lunch, and made sure that they'd locked the door behind them.

"Good afternoon, Mrs. Shoemaker," said the woman behind the front desk at the St. Regis. She was beautiful, with an oval face, heavy-lidded dark eyes, golden skin, and dark hair pulled back at the nape of her elegant neck. Daisy half-listened to her speech about the butler available to take care of any needs that she might have, and how room service was offered twenty-four hours a day, trying to place the woman's accent and wondering if she had even considered calling Daisy "Miss" instead of "Ma'am."

"Enjoy your stay, Mrs. Shoemaker." Daisy accepted her key card and took the elevator to the eighth floor, where she found her room, elegant and pristine, with a pale-gray carpet and ivory-colored drapes and a luxurious king-sized bed. She eased off her shoes, lay on her back, spread her arms and her legs as widely as she could, set an alarm on her phone for an hour, and sank into a deep and satisfying sleep.

At six o'clock, the King Cole Bar was hushed and welcoming, filled with low chatter and soft music and candlelight. The famed Maxfield Parrish mural seemed to glow behind two bartenders who were serving a row of drinkers. In the corner, a piano player was doing a rendition of "Some Enchanted Evening." Couples made quiet conversation at the tables for two; at a table for four, a quartet of boisterous businessmen were laughing loudly over what sounded like the punch line of a dirty joke. As she looked around, Daisy could feel herself relaxing, and when she spotted a dark-haired woman using her phone's flashlight to examine a menu, she thought, *That's her. It has to be.*

As if she'd heard Daisy's thoughts, the other woman put

down her phone and got to her feet. She wore a gold bangle on her wrist that flashed in the candlelight as she waved.

"Daisy?" the woman asked. Smiling warmly, she extended her hand. "Diana Starling," she said. Her voice was low and pleasant, and Daisy thought she heard, very faintly, the hint of a Boston accent.

"Daisy Shoemaker." The other woman's grip was warm and firm, and her smile seemed genuine, as if Daisy's arrival was the best thing that had happened to her all day. She didn't look a thing like petite, freckled Hannah Magee. She was taller and darker, her features more severe, but Diana had to be about Hannah's age, and there was something about her that reminded Daisy irresistibly of her old friend.

"It's so nice to meet you," Daisy said.

"It's nice to meet you, too." Diana sat down, rolling her eyes. "I spent the last six hours with a guy who called me sweetie, and I'm not sure if it was because he'd forgotten my name, or because he'd never known it in the first place. I've been looking forward to this all day!"

Daisy smiled and sat, congratulating herself on her guess-work. Diana Starling was tall, like she'd imagined, with a poised, confident manner. She wore a black business suit, crisply tailored, with a cream-colored silk top with an artful bow tied at the neck, the kind of shirt Daisy would have never been able to pull off (her bosom made button-downs impossible, and the bow looked complicated). Significant diamonds flashed at Diana's ears. There were no rings on her fingers, but she was wearing perfume, something dark and emphatic, with notes of musk and tobacco. Diana's dark hair hung in loose waves against her shoulders. She had a broad forehead, two faint lines between her eyebrows and more at the corners of her eyes, high cheekbones, and a square chin. Daisy saw the eyelash extensions she'd imagined, blush and bronzer and lipstick that left a dark-red bow on her water glass's rim. It was more makeup than a typical Bryn Mawr mom might have worn for drinks, but it suited the other Diana. Daisy guessed that she was about fifty, but a well-maintained fifty, a groomed and fit and hydrated fifty. She looked healthy and attractive, and didn't seem like she was trying desperately to look young. Daisy imagined private Pilates classes and a lap pool; regular blowouts, facials and waxings and a personal shopper to find those suits and silk blouses. When the other Diana traveled, it was probably first-class, and when she stayed in a hotel, it was probably five stars. It made Daisy insignificant and ordinary, with a handful of wholly unremarkable achievements: she'd married a man, produced a single child, and started a very small business, and how hard was any of that?

A waiter approached and bent over them solicitously. "Ladies, welcome to the King Cole." He handed Daisy a menu, refilled Diana's water glass and gave Daisy one of her own, and set a silver dish of warmed, spiced cashews, and another one of chicharróns, in front of them.

"Mmm," said Diana, biting into a nut. "Delicious."

"Nuts are always better when you heat them up," said Daisy. "I tell that to all my clients. Five minutes in the toaster oven and they're a hundred times more impressive." She realized that she was showing off a bit. It felt good, though, to have someone look at her like she was the expert, like she had wisdom to impart. Normally, she only experienced that kind of regard from a distance when she was with Hal, watching as people pumped him for legal advice or asked if he knew any secrets for getting into Dartmouth.

"I want to hear everything. But first . . ." Diana opened the menu. "I'm getting a Bloody Mary. They say they invented them here, you know."

"Sounds perfect," said Daisy. She had planned on ordering

her usual glass of white wine, but a Bloody Mary sounded like exactly the thing.

"And is it okay if we get some snacks?" Diana made a funny, self-deprecating face again, and Daisy felt gladdened to know that Diana was an eater. "I had one of those working lunches, where they bring in platters of pastrami and corned beef sandwiches for the guys, and there's always that one salad in a plastic clamshell, and it's always the saddest salad in the world. And I have to eat it, because I'm a girl."

"Can't you eat the corned beef?" asked Daisy.

"The one time I attempted a sandwich at a business meeting, I ended up with mustard all over my blouse. A Shout wipe can only do so much."

That made Daisy feel a little bit better, even though she suspected that Diana was probably lying, or that if the event she'd described had happened, it had occurred only once, years ago, and Diana had related the anecdote for the sole purpose of putting Daisy at ease. Daisy felt grateful for the effort, even though she couldn't imagine this elegant, composed, confident woman with mustard on her blouse or dog crap on her shoes or walking into a PTA meeting with the back of her skirt tucked into her tights, which had happened to Daisy just three weeks ago.

They agreed to share the cheese plate and the calamari. When the drinks arrived, Diana lifted her tall glass of horseradish-flecked tomato juice and vodka. "To Dianas," she said.

"To new friends." Daisy clinked Diana's glass with her own, and gave her drink a stir with the celery stalk, before taking a sip, relishing the heat of the spices, the slower burn of the booze. "It's such a weird coincidence. And honestly, nobody's called me Diana in years. My husband renamed me."

The other woman tilted her head. *And you let him?* Daisy imagined her thinking, but what she said was, "Daisy's a lovely name."

Daisy thought her name was sweet more than lovely, and she wasn't sure how the notion of a man renaming an adult woman was resonating with her new friend. "So what are you doing for work, right now?" she asked Diana. "I know you're a consultant, but ..."

"I know, I know," Diana said, with a good-natured shake of her head. "A word that means nothing. In my case, businesses— mostly pharmaceutical firms these days—bring me in to spend a few months looking around, to find the deadwood and the soft spots. And then do the cutting." She shrugged, smoothing a glossy lock of hair. "I'm the angel of death, more or less. I bring the axe down, and I leave while the blood's still on the floor."

"That must be hard," Daisy ventured. She could picture it: this assured, competent woman inviting underlings into her office, saying, *Close the door and have a seat*, then telling them that they were no longer needed. "Do people ever—you know—react badly?"

Diana's lips turned up slightly. "Some of them cry. Some of them call me names. I've had a trash can thrown at me."

"You must be good at talking people through it."

Diana shrugged. "Actually, I've just got good reflexes." She mimed ducking out of the way of a projectile, making Daisy laugh.

The waiter arrived and set down the plates with a flourish, arranging them just so, handing around cheese knives and small plates. Diana spread warm goat cheese on a round of baguette, gold cuff flashing in the candlelight, and took a bite with evident enjoyment. Daisy got another whiff of Diana's perfume, and could see that her eyes were hazel. They seemed to glow, cat-like, in the candlelight. Or maybe that was just the effects of the Bloody Mary, which, somehow, was already half-empty.

"Yum," Diana said after her first bite of bread and cheese. Daisy nibbled a calamari ring, watching Diana eat. She wondered if, in another life, she herself could have been a businesswoman, in black suits, causing waiters to scurry and hustle to make her happy, and not the kind of woman who'd gotten married before she turned twenty-one, who'd dropped out of college and had spent her life cooking and keeping other people happy. With a sigh, she thought, *Probably not.*

"I want to hear more about what you do," Diana said. "How'd you get to be a chef?"

"Oh, I'm not a chef. I haven't had professional training. I'm just your basic home cook." *A home cook with pretensions*, as she'd once overheard Hal describe her, and when she'd told him how that made her feel, how diminished and belittled she'd felt, he'd looked puzzled before he'd said, *You're right, Daze. I should have said ambitions, and not pretensions.* She'd accepted his apology, but felt like the incident had given her a window into Hal's mind. She'd seen his true feelings, and they were not flattering.

"I always loved cooking. And my mom didn't." Daisy felt a pang, remembering her mother's gardens. "She liked growing food, but she really didn't like to cook it. And I have two brothers who are twelve and thirteen years older than I am. I think that, after feeding two teenage boys, my mom would've been happy if she'd never had to see the inside of the kitchen again. And then my father died when I was fourteen."

"Wow. I'm sorry," Diana murmured.

"Yeah. It knocked my mom for a loop. She wasn't really interested in cooking." *Or in anything, for a while*, Daisy thought. One of her dad's former business partners, one of the men who'd bought out her father's shares in the video rental stores, had helped her mother find a job, doing the books for a car dealership. Her poor mom, who'd once worn a diamond tennis bracelet and designer gowns, reduced to working nine to five, under harsh fluorescent lights, dealing with their former neighbors who'd come to get their BMWs and Jaguars serviced.

Daisy made herself look cheerful. "I used to bake with my dad, and my grandma. So it wasn't a big step to take over the meals, too." Her mother would give her grocery money at the beginning of the week, and Daisy would shop after school, stopping at the Key Food that was on her way home. At night, Judy would sit on the couch, drained from her day at work, and Daisy would bustle around behind her, walking the circuit from the refrigerator to the counter to the stove, trying to cook something— anything—that would coax her mother to the table. Chicken Francese, or lamb chops, or plump spinach gnocchi that she'd roll out by hand and drop into boiling salt water. When her brothers came home for the holidays, she'd spend days in the kitchen, preparing airy latkes and sweet and sour brisket; roast turkey with chestnut stuffing; elaborately iced layer cakes. She'd stay in the kitchen for hours, cooking dish after dish, hoping that all the food would somehow conceal their father's absence; hoping that the meals would take the taste of grief out of their mouths.

"After my father died, I think cooking saved me. It was the only thing that made me happy. Everything else felt so out of control. But if I followed a recipe, if I used the right amounts of the right ingredients and did everything I was supposed to do ..."

She tried to explain it—how repetitive motions of peeling and chopping felt like a meditation, the comfort of knowing that flour and yeast, oil and salt, combined in the correct proportions, would always yield a loaf of bread; the way that making a shopping list could refocus her mind, and how much she enjoyed the smells of fresh rosemary, of roasting chicken or baking cookies, the velvety feel of a ball of dough at the precise moment when it reached its proper elasticity and could be put into an oiled bowl, under a clean cloth, to rise in a warm spot in the kitchen, the same steps that her mother's mother's mother would have followed to make the same kind of bread. She liked to watch popovers rising to lofty heights in the oven's heat, blooming out of their tins. She liked the sound of a hearty soup or grain-thickened stew, simmering gently on a low flame, the look of a beautifully set table, with place cards and candles and fine china. All of it pleased her.

"Do you like to cook?" she asked Diana, who looked rueful as she shook her head. "Too much travel, and too many business dinners. I can make tuna-noodle casserole and heat frozen dinners. That's about it. What about your husband and your daughter?" Diana asked. "Do they like to cook? Or do they even bother when they've got a pro in the house?"

Flattered, Daisy said, "Hal can do the basics. Beatrice isn't really interested in learning." She felt her smile fade as she considered Beatrice's and Hal's indifference to her life's work. Her husband would eat pretty much anything, with the same degree of enthusiasm. "Tastes great, dear," he would tell her, whether she'd served him salmon *en papillote* or beef Wellington, with mushroom duxelle and puff pastry made from scratch, or a hoagie she'd picked up at Wawa. Meanwhile, Beatrice's favorite food these days was cucumber sandwiches with the crusts cut off. And even the most perfect, most lovingly prepared cucumber sandwich was still, at the end of the day, cucumbers, butter, and bread. Worse, she suspected that Beatrice thought that cooking, cleaning, homemaking, all of what used to be called the *domestic arts*, were women's work. A yoke that Daisy wore, of her own choosing, boundaries past which she did not stray; all of it part of a world that Beatrice and her generation had evolved beyond.

Diana seemed to sense her discomfort, and deftly changed the subject. "How did you start giving lessons?"

"Ah," said Daisy. She'd expected the question. Most of her clients would ask—*hey, how'd you get into doing this?*—so by now she had a story as polished as a silver serving piece. "My sophomore year of college, I had three roommates. We had this tiny little shoebox of an apartment. One night, I made chicken marsala for dinner. Chicken, rice, a green salad with vinaigrette. Basic stuff."

"It doesn't sound basic to me!" Diana said, and Daisy felt herself flush with pleasure. "How do you do it?"

"Well, you start with chicken breasts. And you have to pound them thin." She remembered how they didn't have a mallet, and how they'd wrapped a can of soup in tinfoil and used that instead, taking turns, thumping the cutlets to the beat of ABBA. *Pretend it's your ex!* Louisa had said.

"Then you dredge the cutlets in flour, sauté them in butter, and deglaze the pan—that just means you put in some broth or some wine, and scrape up the browned bits. And then you add mushrooms, a little cream, whatever herbs you like. There's really not much to it."

Diana shook her head, and Daisy repeated that it was easy, that anyone could do it. But she could still picture her roommates, hovering around the pan wide-eyed as Daisy touched a match to the liquor and sent flames jumping out of the pan; how they'd watched the sauce come together like it was a miracle. How it felt to have their attention and approval, when usually she felt herself overlooked, the least pretty of the roommates, the one boys' eyes skipped past. *This is better than anything I've had in a restaurant*, Louisa had said, and Marisol had said, *Daisy, you're a genius!*

"And vinaigrette? How do you make that happen?"

"Oil, vinegar, salt, pepper, and a whisk. It emulsifies."

Diana raised her hands. "Taking your word for it." From her expression, Daisy could tell that the word "emulsify" meant as much to Diana as the word "consultant" meant to her.

"It means the two liquids combine to become something different." In her mind, she was back in the apartment's tiny galley kitchen, remembering they'd sung along with "Waterloo," and done rock, paper, scissors to determine who'd have to find her fake ID and make a trip to the liquor store. That year, cooking had gone from being a lonely, solo activity to being communal, loud and a little slapdash in the crowded kitchen, and a lot more fun. Each girl would pour herself a glass of wine while they cooked. Marisol had taught them her grandmother's recipes for *pernil*, and *arroz con pollo*, and Louisa had made her mother's rosti, and Gretchen had mostly watched and washed the dishes because her parents had both worked, and most of their food had come from cans and boxes. It had felt so good, Daisy remembered, having people who appreciated what she made, after years of watching her mother pick at her cooking, indifferent and unappreciative, pushing whatever Daisy had prepared into her mouth like it was Soylent Green and not a gourmet meal.

"So, fast-forward a few weeks, and Gretchen's in a panic, because her boyfriend's bringing his parents down to meet her, and he wants her to make, quote, 'that chicken thing' for all of them." Daisy could still remember the terror on her roommate's face as she'd racewalked through the library to find Daisy. *He gave me a hundred bucks to buy groceries*, she'd whispered as other students had glared and tried to shush them, *and he swears he told me that his parents were coming to town, only I don't remember him saying anything about it, and I can't tell him I was lying, please, Diana, you have to help me. I'll do anything!*

"I took Gretchen to the grocery store and we bought everything we needed. Then we went home, and I showed her how to do it."

"She didn't want you to cook it yourself?" Diana asked. "You know, Cyrano the dinner?"

"Oh, she absolutely wanted that." Daisy remembered how Gretchen had begged. But Daisy hadn't wavered.

"I told her, 'Give a man a fish, he eats for one meal; teach a man to fish, and he'll never go hungry.' I made her do the whole thing." Daisy could still see it: Destiny's Child on the stereo, Gretchen, with her hair in hot rollers, scooping textbooks and magazines and discarded sweatshirts off the floor; Marisol following after her with the vacuum cleaner.

"Gretchen paid me to give her mother a lesson for Mother's Day, and her mom referred me to some of her friends, so I did it that way for a while. Word of mouth. And then one of my brother's friends hired me to help his dad." She could still remember Danny's voice on the phone, asking if she remembered him mentioning Hal Shoemaker, an Emlen classmate, the stroke of the men's eight. "I gave him your number. I hope it's okay." Hal had called, not ten minutes later. Daisy remembered how he'd sounded, his voice clipped and terse. *My mother died six months ago and I think my dad's going to starve or get scurvy.*

"And I married him. The guy who'd hired me, not his father," she explained.

"So, like, right out of college?" Diana looked startled.

"It was actually in the middle of my senior year," Daisy said, feeling the familiar twinge of embarrassment she got when confessing that her only diploma was from high school.

"Wow. You must have been a child bride."

Daisy swallowed hard, again hearing echoes of her friend. Hannah had teased her, calling her *kiddo* sometimes, or *teen mom.* "I was almost twenty-one. That's actually kind of average for lots of the country, but, yeah, it's young for around here."

Diana was looking at her with an expression that Daisy couldn't decipher. "You must have been sure of him."

"I guess I was." Daisy sipped the watery dregs of her drink. "Although sometimes I think that all I was sure about was marrying someone, and Hal was just the first one who asked." The words were out of her mouth before she'd thought about them, and, as soon as she heard them, she felt her cheeks get hot. This wasn't something she'd ever said out loud. Not even to Hannah.

"God, that sounds horrible. I mean, I wouldn't have married just anyone."

"Of course not," Diana said, even as Daisy wondered if it was true, if she'd have snatched up any guy with Hal's education and prospects. It wasn't something she enjoyed thinking about.

"I love my husband."

Diana nodded, and looked across the table, watchful and waiting.

"It was just . . ." Daisy's boots were squeezing her toes. She shifted in her seat, discreetly easing her right foot partially free. "It was pretty grim, after my dad died. I think if I hadn't gotten married, I would have felt obligated to live with my mother." Daisy suppressed a shudder, remembering, in spite of herself, the dark apartment that always seemed to smell like cabbage, even though she'd never cooked it; her mother's vacant expression as she sat on the couch; and how she'd felt like a wind-up car, frantically whizzing this way and that, trying to distract her mother, to jolly her out of her misery and get her back in the land of the living. The memory of falling asleep every night with the weight of her failure like a lead ball in her gut.

"So Hal was your escape hatch." Daisy must have looked startled, because Diana quickly said, "I don't mean that in a dismissive way. Given what was going on with your mother, it sounds like anyone would have wanted to escape."

"Hal's a wonderful guy," said Daisy. She had been in love with Hal; completely, head over heels in love. She could remember those feelings vividly. They'd been real. But there'd been more to it. She had wanted a soft place to land, and Hal, who'd already made partner at his law firm, who'd inherited a house and had money in the bank, had been just that landing place. She also had no doubt that her mother was glad to have Daisy's future settled, to have Daisy be someone else's responsibility. And Hal had wanted a comfortable nest; he'd wanted ballast, things that could tether him to his responsible, straight-arrow life. A house, a mortgage, a wife and a child; those things could keep him in place and serve as a barrier between his old life and his new one. As to exactly what that old life encompassed, Daisy still wasn't entirely sure. She'd never asked him much about it. She'd never wanted to, and told herself she didn't have to push or probe. Thinking about Hal's history was like walking into a dark room and touching the side of a monster. You didn't have to do more than sense its contours, its shape and its bulk, to understand that it was bad.

Diana was looking at her closely, with interest but no judgment on her face, as Daisy said slowly, "I think sometimes, if I'd been a better person, I would have stayed with my mom, and been there for her, and not complained. But I always knew I wanted to get married and have children, and a home of my own. I just ended up doing it sooner than I'd planned." When she'd told them the news, her roommates had performed something resembling an intervention, sitting her down on the couch, asking, one after another, *Are you sure? You don't think this is all really fast? You're sure that you know him?* Not *love* him, but *know* him. Marisol had asked her that, Daisy remembered, and she'd said, *Yes, of course I know him,* even as she'd thought, *How much does anyone know anyone else? And how can anyone be sure about anything?* What she'd known then was that Hal was, by far, the best-looking guy who'd ever shown any interest in her; he was handsome and accomplished. She knew no one better would ever come along, and she saw no reason to wait.

"What about your brothers?" Diana asked. "They were adults, right? Couldn't they have helped?"

Daisy felt herself squirming under the other woman's gaze. She forced herself to sit still. "David was married and living in Kentucky, and Danny was in New York City, but he was in graduate school, so he hardly ever made it home. I was the only one left.

And—well, I was the girl. It just felt like the household stuff naturally landed on my shoulders." With her forefinger, she wiped a bead of condensation off her glass. "The thing is, it wouldn't have even been for very long. Six months after I got married, my mom met Arnold Mishkin, the guy who lived in the penthouse in her apartment building. He was a retired doctor, so he had plenty of money. A romance for the ages," Daisy said, trying to smile and not think about how it had hurt to see her mom smiling again, and know that it was this new man, this stranger, who'd done what Daisy couldn't. "My brother Danny calls them the lovebirds." She drew herself up straight in her seat, which seemed to be trying to coax her into a slouch, and said, "What's the best city you've ever visited?"

They talked about Paris, where Diana had spent a whole summer when she was in her twenties, about chocolate croissants and macarons and the best patisseries. Diana mentioned stints in Los Angeles ("terrible traffic") and Phoenix ("incredible shopping") and Cleveland ("better than you'd think"). Her hands moved gracefully as she spoke, her voice rising and falling in a way that Daisy found extremely soothing . . . although, again, that might have been the vodka.

Diana talked about visits to Tokyo and Rome. Daisy listened, wistfully recalling her own grand plans. When Beatrice no longer needed bottles or sippie cups or an endless supply of chicken nuggets, Daisy had wanted to travel, and Hal had been perfectly amenable. The problem was that his idea of a perfect vacation was not Europe but, instead, a resort with a golf course that could be reached by a direct flight from Philadelphia International Airport, while Daisy wanted to eat hand-pulled noodles in Singapore and margherita pizza in Rome and warm *pain au chocolat* in Paris; she wanted to sit in a sushi bar in Tokyo and a trattoria in Tuscany; to eat paella in Madrid and green papaya salad in Thailand; shaved ice in Hawaii and French toast in Hong Kong;

she wanted to encourage, in Beatrice, a love of food, of taste, of all the good things in the world. And she'd ended up married to a man who'd once told her that his idea of hell was a nine-course tasting menu.

"Are you close to your brothers?" Diana was asking.

"Well, David's still in Kentucky. I only see him once or twice a year. But Danny's nearby. He and his husband live about an hour away from Philadelphia, and they're terrific." Daisy studied Diana's face for any signs of surprise or distaste at the mention of Danny having a husband, but all she saw was the way Diana's head was cocked as she listened closely. *Of course she's not a homophobe*, Daisy told herself. She's educated and sophisticated. She lives in New York City and she travels the world. If anything, a gay brother would probably give Daisy cachet instead of being counted against her.

"Jesse teaches dance, and works in an art gallery, and Danny's a counselor at a high school in Trenton." Daisy rummaged around with her toes, searching for her boot, which was now completely free of her foot and had escaped somewhere underneath the table. "And they live in Lambertville, which has this lovely downtown, with all kinds of shops and galleries." She couldn't stop herself from sighing.

"You prefer city living?" Diana asked.

"If it had just been me, I think I would have loved to live in a city. But Hal had strong feelings about raising kids in a place where they could ride their bikes and have backyards. And I got pregnant a year after we got married." Daisy sighed again, and Diana looked sympathetic.

"Was that hard?" she asked.

"Oh, it was about what I should have expected. Colic. Screaming all night long. Feeling like a failure, because I'd wanted to breast-feed for a year, and Beatrice wouldn't cooperate. Even when she was six weeks old, she wanted nothing to do with me."

Daisy tried to smile, to make it sound like a joke and not something that had wounded her deeply, something that pained her still. "My mom came for a week, right after Beatrice was born, but she wasn't a lot of help. And then . . ." Daisy looked down into her empty glass. "Well, after my mom went home, it hit me."

Diana looked at her expectantly, eyebrows raised.

"That I wasn't going to get to go anywhere," she explained. "That the years I probably should've spent living on my own, or seeing Europe on a Eurail Pass, or living with three girlfriends in New York, I was already married with a kid, and a husband who's not crazy about travel."

"Couldn't you travel on your own? Or with friends?"

"I could go with friends. I did, sometimes." She and Beatrice had made a few trips to the Poconos with Hannah and Zoe; they'd done overnight trips in New York. But they'd never gone very far, or stayed very long. "It's not that Hal wouldn't let me go. It's just that he needs me." If she hadn't had the better part of that Bloody Mary inside of her, she wouldn't have said it; and if she'd said it, she would have surely stopped there, but the combination of spices and horseradish and vodka and being in a room full of adults with a new friend who was listening with interest kept her talking.

"Needs you for what?" Diana was asking. If there was judgment in her tone, Daisy couldn't hear it. "To take care of your daughter?"

"Well, definitely that, at first." Daisy could still picture Hal, shirtless, with the baby in his arms, because the nurses at the hospital had encouraged skin-to-skin contact; Hal pacing back and forth along the upstairs hallway, insistently chanting, "Go to sleep, go to sleep, go to sleep," and with Beatrice's small pink body pressed against his chest for all of ten minutes, before handing the baby back to Daisy. He'd needed her to manage the baby, and their house, and, eventually, Beatrice's schooling and her schedule, needed her to remember his father's birthday and the anniversary of his mother's death, and set up doctor's and dentist's visits and buy groceries and gifts, to drop his suits at the dry cleaners and pick them up again. "Just everything. All of it. Our life. He needed me to run our life."

Daisy tried to smile, to shake off the memories of those bad years, the exhaustion born of sleepless nights and busy days, and how it felt when Hal would just hand off the baby, mid-meltdown, so he could go shower and shave. "You're lucky you never had to deal with any of this."

"Oh, sure," said Diana, rolling her eyes. "Because the world is just so delightful to women who don't get married or have kids. Nobody ever thinks there's anything wrong with me, and nobody ever asks if I've frozen my eggs, or when I'm going to meet Mr. Right." Diana raised her glass. "To the grass always being greener."

Daisy looked down and discovered a fresh drink in front of her. "To green grass," she said, and hoped she hadn't allowed the conversation to dwell too heavily on herself, and her own disappointments. "Did you fire anyone today?"

Diana touched a lock of her expensive-looking hair, and tucked it behind her ear. "I should have. There's this one manager. He deserves to be fired, but I think the most I can hope for is getting him reassigned to a place where he won't do as much damage." She shook her head. "White guys—especially white guys who are part of a family business—they fail upward, or they move sideways. And they always come out fine in the end."

"Ugh, right?" Daisy said. "My husband went to prep school. This place called Emlen, in New Hampshire. I swear to God, those guys . . ." She stifled a hiccup against the back of her hand. "They hire each other, or each other's businesses; they give each other's children internships and jobs. Like, one of my husband's classmates was down on his luck for a while—he'd had a couple of business ventures that hadn't worked out, and then he'd had a really horrible divorce. So first, he goes to one classmate's summer house in Maine for a few months, to lick his wounds. Then he moves to New York City, into an apartment in a building that another classmate owns, where he decided that what he really wants to be is an artist. So he goes back to school for an MFA in painting, while he's spending the year in the one guy's New York City apartment, and his summers at the other guy's place in Maine, and *then* . . ." Daisy paused for another sip. ". . . when he graduates, and has his student show, half the class shows up, and they buy every single painting."

Diana was staring at her, eyes wide. "That cannot possibly be true."

"Swear to God!" said Daisy. "We've got one of his watercolors hanging in our living room." She lowered her voice. "It's really awful," she said, and hiccupped again. She hadn't realized, until she started speaking, how irritating she found it. If she screwed up her job or her marriage, there wouldn't be an Old Girls' Network waiting to catch her and buoy her, with beach houses and New York City apartments and a whole new career when she was ready. "I don't know, maybe things are changing. Maybe they'll be better when my daughter's all grown up."

"She's really putting you through it," Diana murmured. Daisy had, of course, confided in her new friend about Beatrice's expulsion. She kept talking, her words coming faster and faster, like someone had pulled out a stopper and released a torrent of frustration.

"You know, I was so happy when I found out I was having a girl. I thought we'd go to high tea, and the ballet, and get manicures together and go shopping. And she put up with that, for a while. But Beatrice . . ." Daisy thought of her daughter, sitting tranquilly in her rocking chair, knitting needles clicking. "Well, she's just always been exactly who she is." Somehow, there was another drink in front of her. She hadn't remembered ordering it, but she lifted it and sipped from it gratefully. Diana was waiting, looking at her, but Daisy couldn't tell her that she and Hal had agreed that they'd have two children. They'd tried for years. Daisy had had two miscarriages, one the year after Beatrice's birth, just days after she'd found out she was pregnant, the other when Daisy was twenty-five, after she'd passed the twelve-week mark, which had been painful and messy and had left her sad for months. Then Hal had gotten a vasectomy. Daisy had argued against it. *We can keep trying*, she'd told him. My mom had me when she was thirty-eight! *When you're thirty-eight, I'll be over fifty*, Hal had said, his voice distant. *That's too old for diapers, and waking up in the middle of the night.*

"Sometimes I feel like a failure," Daisy said quietly.

"You're not a failure," Diana said. She reached across the table and took Daisy's hand, and her voice was so warm, and her expression so sincere, and maybe it was the drink, the room, the music; maybe it was being in the company of men in suits and ties and women in expensive shoes, or the smell of perfume and the flowers on the bar, but Daisy felt a sob catch in her throat. How long had it been since she'd had someone's complete attention this way, for this long? How long since she'd felt like she was with someone who could see her, and could see how hard she was trying? At least since Hannah's death, and that had been nine months ago.

"Thank you," she said, and thought of something Hannah had told her once, long ago, about how, for old married ladies like them, making a new friend was the closest they could get to falling in love.

5
~~~~~

Diana

Leave, Diana told herself, in a voice that rang through her head like a bell. *Get out of here.* Pay the bill, leave the table, get out of this ridiculous bar full of ridiculous rich people, where they have the nerve to charge twenty dollars for a drink. Don't ask her any more questions. Stop talking to her. Stop falling for her. It was a ridiculous thing to think, that she was falling for Daisy, that she was like some giddy, innocent teenager with her first crush, but there it was, the awful truth: she liked this woman. Daisy Shoemaker, with her earnest face and her carefully done hair and her I-got-dressed-up-for-the-big-city necklace, was very easy to like; she was nothing like the rich, brittle, Main Line trophy wife Diana had been expecting. She was sweet, and forthcoming, and, my God, she was so young! There was barely a wrinkle on her round, full-cheeked face, and her mouth seemed to relax naturally into a smile. She was friendly and funny and cute when she got tipsy, hiccupping and trying to describe the terrible watercolors she and Hal had purchased from his class-mate. Diana liked her, and it was almost impossible to think about causing her pain.

"So what about you?" Daisy was asking. From the way she was wriggling in her seat, either she needed the bathroom or she'd lost a shoe. "Where'd you grow up?" Diana gave her pieces of the truth: that she'd grown up near Boston, that she'd spent time on Cape Cod. Daisy's face had lit up at the mention of the Cape. *Us, too!* she'd said, pleased as punch. We go there, too!

Diana told Daisy that she'd never been married, but that she was in a long-term relationship. She couldn't say that she was single. It felt like betraying Michael, and she couldn't do that. She said that she had two sisters, three nieces and two nephews. She struggled to remind herself that this woman was not a new acquaintance, or a potential friend; she tried, as subtly as she could, to keep the drinks coming and keep the conversation focused on gleaning information about Daisy, and her life, her family. Her brother and her husband.

She learned Hal had quit drinking not long before he met Daisy, that he'd paid for their wedding, brought Daisy to Pennsylvania, and given her a credit card and carte blanche to decorate his house.

"He'd bought it before he'd met me, and it was furnished in Early American Empty—"

Daisy paused, and Diana couldn't keep herself from smiling.

"It was such a guy place! He only had furniture in three rooms. There were bookcases in the living room, and the world's most gigantic TV, and then a bed in the bedroom—no headboard, no chairs, no dresser, just a king-sized mattress and box spring—and two barstools in the kitchen. I think those actually came with the house."

"Wow," said Diana, shaking her head. She had a million more questions, a million things she needed to know, but Daisy had pulled out her phone and was frowning at the time.

"Oh my goodness, my show's going to start soon! I need to get going."

"I'll walk with you." Daisy reached for her credit card, but Diana had hers ready. "Oh, no," she said. "My treat."

Outside, Daisy rechecked the address of the theater where she'd be seeing *King Lear*. Diana braced herself for the glare of the sun, the crowds and the cacophony of taxi horns, but New York delivered one of those rare, perfect autumn twilights. The air was cool and faintly fall-scented; the sky was a rich, lustrous blue, and everyone seemed to have slowed down enough to appreciate the night's beauty.

"Oh, wow." Daisy gave a dreamy sigh, then looked sideways at Diana and smiled. "You probably think I'm a total country bumpkin."

"No," said Diana, because she could see what Daisy was seeing. "Magic hour. That's what photographers call it. That light at the very end of the day." Out of the candlelight's glow, Diana could see how young Daisy was. No crow's feet, no age spots. Her hair was still lustrous, her skin still smooth as a pour of cream. She walked with a jaunty bounce, and she looked around at everything—the sky, the buildings, the people—with undisguised appreciation, even wonder.

Diana, meanwhile, was feeling increasingly desperate, scanning the street for a likely-looking building, a place to escape. There was a skyscraper at the end of the block, a silvery needle that seemed to pierce the sky. "This is me," she said, quickening her pace. "My apartment's in the Village, but if I'm only here for a short stay and I'm working in Midtown, I Airbnb my apartment and let the company put me up," she said, lying glibly.

"Thank you for doing this," Daisy said.

"My pleasure," said Diana. She was going to offer her hand, but before she could do it, Daisy had drawn her into a hug. Diana smelled her shampoo. She felt her warmth and the strength of her arms. She stiffened as Daisy drew her close, then, without planning it, she found herself relaxing, and hugging Daisy back.

. . .

Diana waited in the lobby for ten minutes, until there was no chance that Daisy could still be anywhere nearby. She smiled at the doorman, who nodded in return, and stepped back outside, quietly blessing whoever had come up with a catchall term like "consultant," which could have been tailor-made for the purpose of pulling the wool over suburban housewives' eyes.

The night air was still cool, the sidewalks not too crowded, and she could feel the pavement thrum underneath her every time a train went by. She had a reservation on a ten o'clock flight from Kennedy to Boston, and a seat on the last Cape Air flight from Logan to Provincetown, but there was still plenty of time to get to the airport. Walking would give her time to think and, she hoped, to shake the discomfort that had grown with every moment of her time with Daisy Shoemaker. *Think about what you learned, not how you feel*, she told herself. When that didn't work, she tried to stop thinking at all.

In the airport bathroom, she locked herself in the handicapped stall and unzipped her tote. She'd been watching drag queens for years, observing as they transformed themselves, painting their faces and putting on custom-sewn hip pads and silicone breasts that looked, and felt, almost like the real thing, until they looked completely authentic, more beautiful than most biological women. The older ones would talk about the ballroom scene in New York City in the 1980s, where it hadn't all been about looking like a beauty queen, with sky-high wigs and mile-long lashes and six-inch platform heels. Back then, there were categories like Executive Boss Lady Realness or Butch Queen Realness, where the goal wasn't beauty or glamour but authenticity, of being believable, looking like a real female executive or a real straight male, inhabiting the character you were playing so completely that you could walk down Fifth Avenue at noon without drawing a single sideways glance; that you could pass in the real world.

In the bathroom, Diana removed her drag carefully. She peeled off the false lashes and wiped off the makeup; she slipped out of the suit she'd borrowed from Rent the Runway and folded it, and the blouse, carefully in a garment bag. She pulled on jeans and a plain jersey top and replaced her suede kitten-heel pumps with sneakers. She removed the earrings, zircons she'd borrowed from a work friend, and slipped them in her pocket. She brushed the spray out of her hair, which she'd had done at a blowout bar that morning. When she washed her hands, she avoided her face in the mirror. She felt, for reasons she couldn't name, as if she might not recognize the woman staring back at her.

When the plane touched down, at just after eleven o'clock, Diana pulled her leather carry-on over her shoulder and stepped down the three steps of the plane's staircase. The airport was the size of a small-town post office, and was almost empty at that hour. Outside, two cabs idled at the curb, the drivers standing beside their vehicles, scanning the terminal for passengers. A heavyset man with a thick beard and red hair threaded with silver was waiting, too, leaning against a pickup truck.

"You didn't have to come," Diana said.

"Didn't have to," he said agreeably, reaching for her bag. "I wanted to." He held the door as she got into the passenger's seat, and waited until she'd gotten her seat belt buckled before he started to drive.

"So how'd it go?" he asked, swinging the truck out onto the two-lane road that ran from Route 6 to the National Seashore.

Diana thought about how to answer. "Okay," she finally said. "I think it went okay."

He didn't press her, but she could feel his disapproval fill the space between them. Ignoring it, she bent over the phone, tapping out the message she'd send in the morning. *Really enjoyed meeting you. Hope we'll get to do it again soon. I'm getting my next posting on Monday. Will let you know where I land!*

They were silent as he turned up the driveway to the cottage. He pulled up beside the deck and turned the engine off. Diana rolled down the window and took a deep breath, imagining the smell of salt and the feel of the ocean replenishing her, scouring the grime of the city off her skin. "I liked her," she blurted, then pressed her lips shut. She hadn't planned on saying anything, and she definitely had not planned on saying that.

"The other Diana?"

"Daisy." Diana's lips felt numb. "She calls herself Daisy. Isn't that sweet?" Her voice caught on "sweet." She'd meant to sound sarcastic, but instead she'd sounded like she was going to cry. Because Daisy was sweet. She was sweet and young and innocent, and Diana was going to come smashing through her life like a wrecking ball. She was going to hurt her, whether she wanted to or not. The wheels she'd set in motion were turning; the train was racing down the tracks, and Diana couldn't stop it, not even if she'd tried.

Part
Two

~~~~~~~~~~~~~~~~

Our Lady of Safe Harbor

6

Diana

After that summer, Diana came back to a world that felt bleared and grease-streaked, gray and dingy, permanently corrupted. For three weeks she felt like she could barely breathe, or eat, or sleep, and when her period came, she fell on her knees on the bathroom's tiled floor, shaking with relief. Her bruises faded, and she didn't have any symptoms of diseases unless he'd given her one of the sneaky kinds.

"Honey, are you okay?" her mom asked, the first night at the dinner table. She'd made Sunday gravy, a sauce that simmered all day long, with chunks of pork shoulder and sausage from the market at Faneuil Hall. It was Diana's favorite dinner. Or, at least, it had been. That night, all she could do was poke at it and nod, knowing that the lump in her throat wouldn't allow her to speak.

After dinner, her sister Kara cornered her in the hall. "All right, what happened?" Kara asked in a low voice.

"What? Nothing."

"You're walking around with a face like . . ." Kara made a hideously mopey expression and knuckled fake tears off her cheeks. "So what happened?"

"Nothing," said Diana.

Kara's expression was not without sympathy. "Older guy? College guy? Married guy?" Her eyes widened. "It wasn't Dr. Levy's husband, was it?"

"No," Diana said. "He was fine. They both were."

"So what, then? It was a boy, wasn't it?"

Diana nodded. She knew she wouldn't be able to tell the truth. Not to her sister. Not to anyone. Let them think that some boy on Cape Cod had broken her heart. It was, at least, a version of the truth.

Kara sat on Diana's bed. "It sucks," she said. "I know. It's the worst feeling in the world. But school's going to start again, and there're plenty of fish in the sea." She grinned. "The best way to get over one guy is to get under a different one!"

Diana had tried to smile. Meanwhile, she thought, *I'll never have sex again.*

The school year passed in a lurching blur. Sometimes Diana would sit down at the start of class and blink to discover that forty-five minutes had passed and the bell was ringing and she had no memory of what the teacher had said or what material had been covered. Sometimes, the time dragged like cold mud, making the days and hours feel like an endless slog. Her nights were restless, her sleep interrupted by bad dreams. She'd skip two, three, four meals in a row, and then find herself at the refrigerator, gorging on whatever came to hand, once spooning the entire contents of a jar of blue cheese salad dressing into her mouth. Her middle softened. Her clothes stopped fitting. Her grades slipped. Everyone worried.

Tell me what's wrong. Her mother asked; her friends asked, her sisters asked. Her former soccer coach asked when he saw her in the hall, and her favorite English teacher from the year before cornered her in the cafeteria. She knew that her mom had called Dr. Levy to see if anything had happened, and she prayed she'd been a good enough actress during those last two days for Dr. Levy to say "no." "But she's worried about you," her mother reported. "So am I. We're all worried." Like that was a news flash; like she'd somehow missed the incessant chorus of *Tell us, tell us, tell us what happened. We can't help you if we don't know what's wrong.*

Nothing's wrong, Diana would say. I'm just tired.

Finally, her mother had taken her to her pediatrician, the man who'd given her Disney stickers and cherry lollipops after her shots. Diana had loved to bite them and feel the candy shatter on her tongue and cling to her teeth.

Dr. Emmerich shuffled through her chart and finally said, "Your mother's worried you're depressed."

"I'm not depressed," Diana said. "I'm fine."

He gave her a probing look. "Is it a boy?"

She shook her head, hair swinging around the soft, pale moon of her face.

"A girl?"

She shook her head again.

"Drinking? Drugs? Too much pressure at school? Anything you tell me is confidential. I won't tell your parents. That's a promise. But they're worried, and I am, too." He sighed, and put his hand on her arm, gently. "I don't like to see a girl's spark go out."

Somehow, after all the questions, all the people asking and begging and insisting that she tell them what was wrong, that was what made her start to cry. His hand on her arm; the kindness in his voice, the idea that her spark had gone out. The idea that she'd ever had a spark, and that it had been stolen from her.

"I'm fine," she said again, in her robot voice.

Dr. Emmerich sighed and wheeled his stool away from her, back toward the counter. "I'm going to give your parents the names of two psychologists. They're both women, and they're both excellent. Even if everything's okay, it can be good to have someone to talk to." He wheeled himself back and looked her in the eyes. "People care for you. They want to help. You just have to let them."

But she couldn't. She couldn't, because there was no helping her; no fixing her. She was a broken thing, thanks to her own stupidity, her own dumb, naive, trusting nature. And now, for as long as she lived, she'd be hearing those boys laughing at her. She'd remember what had happened; what they'd done. It would be the first thing she'd think of in the morning and the last thing she'd remember at night.

Tenth grade, eleventh grade, twelfth grade all went by, in the same unhappy gray miasma. Hours felt like they were endless; months passed by with Diana barely seeing the oak tree outside her bedroom window that had once been her preview of the seasons. Now she hardly noticed when the leaves were changing, or when leaves were gone, or when they'd come back, fresh and new and green again. She ate, late at night, until she couldn't feel anything, stuffing cookies on top of cold chicken on top of ice cream on top of bread. Sometimes she'd eat so much she'd vomit. More often, she'd just stumble to bed and lie there, half-asleep, her stomach aching as much as her heart did.

College, said her parents. So she went to the University of Massachusetts, where she lasted three semesters. It was the boys that were the problem. She'd be walking across the campus and catch sight of someone whose hair and height reminded her of Poe, or she'd be in the student center, eating lunch, and hear a laugh that sounded like one of the boys from the beach. Her roommates dragged her to parties, but the taste of beer made her gag. Her sisters came and collected her for a road trip to Florida, but the smell of sunscreen made her queasy. After three semesters' worth of Ds and Fs, her parents had let her come home.

It's a waste of money, she heard her father saying wearily to her mom. *If she doesn't want to be there, we shouldn't make her stay.* He'd gotten old in the years since her summer on the Cape. There was a gauntness to his features; hollows under his cheekbones, circles under his eyes. His skin hung loosely on his face, like he'd lost weight he couldn't afford to lose.

Diana tried temping, working nights in banks and law firms, entering data into computers, but the problems that had started after her return continued to plague her. She'd sit down with a stack of invoices, then blink, to find that an hour had passed without her having typed in a single number. After a few months, the firms were no longer able to place her, and her mother got her a job working the graveyard shift in the custodial services department at Boston University, cleaning offices and classrooms between ten p.m. and six in the morning. A van picked her up at the distant parking lot where she was allowed to leave her car; a supervisor gave her a mop and a bucket of cleaning supplies at the drop-off point; a different van picked her up in the morning. Her coworkers chattered, talking about their kids or their boyfriends or their husbands. They traded parts of the dinners they'd packed—half a meatball grinder for a Tupperware full of chicken with mole; baked ziti for spicy beef patties. Diana kept to herself, and, after a while, her coworkers left her alone. She didn't mind doing the dirty jobs—prying chewing gum off the undersides of desks, scrubbing toilet bowls, mopping the men's room floors. At least she could be alone, with her Walkman earphones plugged into her ears. She would mop, or spray down the mirrors and wipe them clean without ever looking at her own reflection, and, while she worked, she would think about whether she could kill herself and make it look like an accident. The world hurt; every man she saw was a man who could hurt her. Could she drive the car off the road on an icy night and hope the police would think she'd lost control? "Accidentally" step in front of the T?

She thought about the Dorothy Parker poem:

Razors pain you;
Rivers are damp;
Acids stain you;
And drugs cause cramp.
Guns aren't lawful;
Nooses give;
Gas smells awful;
You might as well live.

You might as well live, she told herself, and went plodding through her nights and sleeping her days away until, one morning in April, when her parents were both at work, there was a knock on the door. Diana tried to ignore it, but the knocking persisted, loud and ceaseless, like a cold spring rain. She pulled on sweatpants, went downstairs, and yanked the door open, preparing to hurl abuse at whatever inconsiderate delivery person or proselytizer had disturbed her. But it wasn't a Mormon, or the UPS guy. It was Dr. Levy, dressed in a belted trench coat and leather boots, with a worried look on her face, a look that quickly turned into shock.

"Diana?"

Diana looked down at herself. She wasn't fifteen anymore, and she knew she'd changed since that summer. Her face was a pale, bloated moon, and her hair was long and wild, witchy and untended. Dr. Levy looked different, too. Her hair was sleek. She wore red lipstick and gold earrings and an expensive-looking bag on her shoulder.

"Can I come in?" She held up a white cardboard box tied with twine. "I brought cannoli."

Wordlessly, Diana held the door open. She led her former employer to the kitchen, a small, cheerful space, with goldenrod-yellow walls and a red-and-yellow floral-patterned tablecloth on the table, and her mother's prize Le Creuset Dutch oven, enameled deep blue, sitting on the back burner of the stove. "Can I get you something to drink?" Diana asked. Her voice was a rusty croak; her tongue felt thick and balky. "Coffee? Tea?"

"Nothing for me, thanks."

Diana gathered a tea bag, a mug, a bottle of honey, plates for the pastries, forks and napkins, which let her keep her back to her visitor. She turned on the radio to fill the silence with the sound of classical music.

"How are you?" Dr. Levy asked as Diana turned on the gas beneath the kettle, wishing she'd had time to shower, or at least comb her hair.

"Fine," Diana said. Dr. Levy didn't ask anything else, so Diana didn't speak again, until she'd made the tea and there was nothing left to do but take a seat.

Diana sat and groped for the tools of polite conversation. "How are Sarah and Sam?"

Dr. Levy's expression brightened. "They're fine. In fourth grade, if you can believe it. They're growing up so fast! Sam's taking saxophone lessons. He can't really play notes yet, but he can make these noises . . ." Dr. Levy made a squeaky honk, and Diana startled herself by laughing. "And Sarah's in Girl Scouts. She's taking it very seriously. Trying to rack up as many badges as she can." Dr. Levy looked right at her. "But I came because I want to talk to you."

Diana looked down, straightened the salt and pepper shakers at the middle of the table.

"Your mother tells me you've been struggling."

"I'm fine," said Diana reflexively.

"She thinks," Dr. Levy continued, as if Diana hadn't spoken, "that something happened on the Cape. When you were staying with us."

"Nothing happened," said Diana, shaking her head.

"Are you doing all right, though?" Dr. Levy's voice was as

gentle as a hand on her forehead, as kind as Dr. Emmerich had been, years ago.

"I'm fine!" Diana's voice was too loud for the little room. And what right did Dr. Levy have to come swanning in with her leather boots and her fancy bag, asking about things that were none of her business? Diana lowered her voice. "Really. I'm okay. I'm figuring things out."

"I want to make you an offer." Dr. Levy clasped her hands and set them on the table. "I don't know what happened that last weekend you were with us, or if anything happened at all, but I suspect that something did. On my watch." She spoke each word clearly and deliberately. "You got hurt while I was supposed to be looking out for you, and I feel terrible about that. I can't undo it, but I'd like to try to help you now."

Diana felt her throat tighten and her eyes begin to sting.

"I told you that my parents used to bring me to Truro when I was a girl, right? That they had a little cottage?" When Diana nodded, Dr. Levy said, "The cottage is still there. My mother died, my dad's not well enough to be up there alone, and my sister's in California, so I've been renting it out for the summers. But it isn't rented for this year yet." She refolded her hands on the table. "I don't know, maybe the Cape is the last place you'd ever want to be. But if you do want a place to stay, to get away from the city, and be on your own, and clear your head, and figure things out, like you said, I'd be more than happy for you to stay there."

Diana blinked. Even in her misery, she could recognize that she was being offered something significant. She felt her heart lift, and realized that there was some part of her that remembered Cape Cod, and how it had felt before it had gone bad: the particular slant of the light in midmorning, the exact green of the marsh grass and the darkness of the water, the sun setting over the bay, in a swirl of flame and molten gold.

Dr. Levy was still talking. "It's not like the big house, but it's a sweet little place, right on top of the dune. I used to go there, when I was single, and then Lee and I went, when we were first married." A smile curved her lips. "It's just one room, with a sleeping loft, but there's a full kitchen, and a deck, and an outdoor shower, and—"

"Yes," Diana blurted. She felt a spark of something unfamiliar and faint, something she recognized as hope. Maybe there was a path forward; a place she could go and hide, and heal. She took a gulp of her tea, scalding her tongue, swallowed, and said, "Please. I'd like that very much. But could I go after the summer's over? I could pay you rent . . ."

Dr. Levy shook her head. "No, no, don't worry about that. Honestly, you'd be doing me a favor if you stayed. You could make sure the mice don't move in." She refolded her hands. "There's a woodstove. And there's oil heat. At least, there's an oil tank. Theoretically, it's a four-season house, but I've never been up there past Thanksgiving, so I'm not sure how warm you'll be, if it ever gets really cold . . ."

"I'll get a space heater." It felt strange to be making plans, strange to feel a smile on her face, and to feel a tiny pinprick of hope, after feeling hopeless for so long. "I . . . thank you. It sounds really great."

Dr. Levy said, "I'll put the keys in the mail, and send you directions. It's on an unmarked road, so it's kind of hard to find." She got to her feet. Diana stood up, too.

"Thank you. I . . ." She didn't have the words for what she wanted to tell her former employer, so she just said, "Thank you," again.

Dr. Levy nodded. "Take care of yourself." She paused in the doorway, giving Diana a long, level look, and then a smile. And then she was gone.

Diana walked back to the kitchen. Most days, she slept until the sun went down, right through dinner. She'd come downstairs at nine or so, eat something standing over the sink, and drive to work. That afternoon, she put Dr. Levy's cannoli in the refrigerator, then stood there, considering her options, before pulling out eggs and butter. There was bread in the breadbox, a just-ripe-enough red plum in the fruit bowl. She put butter in the pan, bread in the toaster, cracked the eggs, and took a bite of the plum. Ten minutes later, she sat down to one of the rare actual meals she'd eaten since that summer. She sprinkled salt over her eggs, twisted the pepper mill three times, and sliced through the first egg, watching the yolk spill its gold onto the plate, thinking, *Am I really going to do this? Am I going to go back, and live there, where it happened?* Part of her whispered that it was folly, crazy to even consider, the worst idea she'd ever had, but another part remembered the freshness of the air and the colors of the sunsets. Those boys were only summer people, she thought, and the beach was just a beach, not to blame for what had happened there. Besides, there were lots of beaches in Truro. She'd never have to visit that one again. Five months later, she packed up her clothes into trash bags and cardboard boxes from the liquor store, and climbed into the ancient Honda that had been Julia's, then Kara's, and was now hers, heading to the Cape.

7

~~~

Diana

The cottage stood at the end of Knowles Heights Road in North Truro, on the crest of a dune overlooking the bay. A screen of scrub pines, crabapple trees, and beach-plum bushes hid it from its neighbors, and it had expansive windows facing the sea. It wasn't grand. There were no airy rooms or walls of glass, no pool or hot tub or stainless-steel kitchen. It was just one room, a building like a child's drawing of a house, with a peaked roof, white walls, and black shutters, and a small deck out back. Inside, there were stained wood walls and bright rag rugs on the hardwood floors, and a couch in a white canvas slipcover. A short staircase past the kitchen led to the sleeping loft, tucked under the eaves, with room for a futon on a box spring, with a stack of books beside it. The roof formed a peak over the bed, and a pair of small windows let in the light.

Diana set a box of books down on a coffee table made from a glass-topped ship's helm. "Ahoy, matey," she murmured. Just ten steps took her from the front door, to the far windows, but when she got there, she saw that the views were almost the same as the ones from Dr. Levy's house. The ocean was spread out below her, as close as if she were standing on a ship's deck. There were seagulls skimming low over the waves, and in the distance, a sailboat with two masts, its white sails full-bellied in the wind.

Diana walked the length of the cabin, back and forth. She had the same feeling she got when she set down a heavy backpack or took off a too-tight bra—the same easing, the same sense that she could breathe freely, and move without restraint. She rolled her shoulders, still stiff from the drive, and imagined casting off all her years of numbness and sorrow, and turning into someone else. Maybe not the woman she'd once dreamed of being, the writer, the artist, the professor, but at least someone different than she'd been back home.

Diana continued exploring. There was a stereo with a CD player tucked into a nook in the kitchen. Simple white curtains hung over the eye-level windows. The woodstove Dr. Levy had mentioned stood in the corner, and the bathroom had a grand, antique claw-footed tub that barely fit in the tiny room and looked as out of place as a dowager at a tailgate party. Diana stared at it, bemused, then went back to the main room, where a narrow shelf ran around three walls of the house at eye level. She saw paperback books, bits of sea glass, and driftwood. A dried starfish was propped up next to a glass jar filled with shells. On a small rectangle of canvas, someone had painted a competent seascape.

Outside, on the deck, were a barbecue grill and picnic table. Around the corner, behind a screen of shrubs, there was an outdoor shower with a mural of a mermaid painted on the wooden wall of its enclosure.

Diana opened the windows to chase away the lingering, musty smell of closed-up house that she remembered from her stay with Dr. Levy. She put her clothes in the wooden dresser, hearing the creaks as she worked its water-swollen drawers open and shut. She put cans of tuna fish and bags of dried beans on the empty shelves in the kitchen, and put eggs and milk and half-and-half into the small refrigerator, noting, with approval, the coffee maker and the knives. That night, she fell asleep easily and didn't wake up until almost eight o'clock in the morning. It was the longest and the latest she'd slept in years. She lay in bed with the windows open, listening to the sound of the wind, the surf, the kids on the beach. It was the third weekend in September, the water still warm enough for swimming, families still squeezing out the last drops of summer with beach trips and picnics and ice-cream cones. She imagined she could even hear the foghorn blast of the Lewis Brothers ice-cream truck. *Maybe I'll stay*, she thought.

But she'd need a job.

On Monday morning, she got up early and walked on the beach, then took an outdoor shower, and combed her hair before pulling it back into a ponytail. She pulled on loose-fitting cargo pants and a bulky T-shirt, slipped her Birkenstocks on her feet, and drove to Provincetown. She parked all the way out at the West End, where the houses and shops and restaurants yielded to the National Seashore, and walked down Commercial Street, past the restaurants and nightclubs, the art galleries and performance spaces, the sex shops and the fudge shops and bed-and-breakfasts and the bike shops and the bookstores.

At the end of the street she turned around, retracing her two-mile route, stopping in at every business where she'd seen a HELP WANTED sign in the window. In some cases, the signs had been put up to ensure a ready supply of employees during the summer months, and left up by mistake. "Come back in June," the woman behind the counter at Angel Foods told her, and the man at Cabot's Candy gestured at the crowded aisles and said, "Busy as it is in here right now, that's how empty it's going to be on Monday." The Portuguese Bakery actually was hiring, but they needed an experienced line cook. The sex shop, with its assortment of leather harnesses to hold strap-on dildos in the window, was hiring, but Diana knew she couldn't work there.

At the Alden Gallery, the older woman with cat-eye glasses and pink hair had looked her up and down, then asked, "Do you know anything about art?"

"Um," Diana said. "I know it when I see it?"

The woman had smiled, not unkindly. "That's pornography, hon," she'd said.

Finally, Diana had worked her way down to the Abbey, an upscale restaurant with a small but lush courtyard that featured a tinkling fountain, a pair of wooden benches, flowering bushes and stands of tall grasses, and a statue resembling Rodin's *The Thinker* (one of the few things she did remember from the art history class she'd taken). She'd never eaten there, but she remembered Dr. Levy mentioning it as one of the places she and her husband visited for date night at least once every summer. She sat on the bench for a minute to rest her feet and peruse the menu. Tuna sushi tempura (eighteen dollars for an appetizer). Almond-crusted cod with a mandarin-citrus beurre blanc (twenty-eight dollars) and butter-poached lobster (market price). The list of cocktails and special martinis ran two pages, and when she walked up the curved stone steps and stepped into the dining room, the views of the bay were gorgeous.

"Help you?" asked the young man behind the host stand. He had pale blue eyes, and a willowy, long-limbed body. He wore white chinos and a blue linen shirt the same shade as his eyes. A red bandana was tied jauntily around his neck, setting off the translucence of his pale white skin. Beside him, Diana felt large, and drab, and clumsy.

"The sign in the window says you're hiring?"

"I'll get Reese." The boy turned on his heel and went gliding through the dining room. A moment later, he was back with one of the first nonwhite people Diana had seen on the Cape. This man had medium-brown skin, a bald head, and a bushy white beard, gold-rimmed glasses, and a friendly smile.

"Hello, my dear. I'm Reese Jenkins. I run this asylum." He offered her his hand, which was warm and so large it made her own hand disappear. "And yes, because I can feel you wondering, I do play Santa at the Police Athletic League party every year. In Provincetown, Santa's a black man." He beamed at her, and the beautiful, willowy boy and turned his eyes toward the heavens with an expression suggesting he'd heard the line many times before.

"Now!" said Reese. "What brings you here?" When he cocked his head, gold glasses twinkling, she was tempted to tell him what she wanted for Christmas, and then, when she opened her mouth, she realized that he'd already given her a gift. She could choose a different name, any name she'd ever wanted, and that's what he would call her. That girl who'd been hurt, who'd been left on the beach like trash, whose life had been derailed—she didn't have to be her anymore. Or, at least, she didn't have to answer to her name.

So Diana smiled and gave him her hand. "My name is Dee Scalzi." If she got the job, she'd have to give her real first name and Social Security number on the paperwork, but she could always say that Dee was a nickname.

Reese shook her hand. "Are you hungry?" he asked.

She was. She hadn't eaten breakfast, or stopped for a snack during her trek along Commercial Street. She was ravenous, and footsore, too, but she had just ten dollars in her pocket. The only thing she would have been able to purchase at the Abbey were the oysters, at two dollars apiece.

"Could I have a glass of water?"

"Don't be silly." Reese turned to the beautiful boy (up close, Diana could see that there was a pattern of tiny blue whales on the red-and-white belt he wore at the waist of his chinos). "Ryan, we'll be at table twelve." Diana followed Reese through the restaurant. He walked like a sailor, in a rolling, bow-legged stride, which added to her impression that they were on a ship, riding the waves of the sea. Diana could feel herself relaxing, ever so slightly, as he led her to a white tablecloth–draped table for two by the window and held her chair for her, waiting until she was settled before taking his own seat.

"Chef's just finishing the specials for the night, and, as the manager, it's my responsibility to taste them." She could see a flash of gold way back in his mouth when he smiled. "Nice work if you can get it. Have you ever been to the Abbey before?"

"No." She could see waiters and waitresses, in crisp white shirts, black pants, and black bow ties, bustling through the dining room. One woman was setting a single tea light candle in a hurricane glass on each table, another arranged a spray of white calla lilies in vases for the four-tops. At the host stand, Ryan was straightening stacks of menus and wine lists; at the bar, the bartender was decanting cherries from a jar into plastic dispensers. As Diana looked around, a waitress came by with a cruet of olive oil, bread plates, and a napkin-lined basket that held squares of golden-brown focaccia. Diana felt saliva flood her mouth.

"So what brings you to the Cape?" Reese asked, helping himself to a square.

Diana looked down at her hands, with their chewed nails, red and raw and chapped from the chemicals she'd used for her cleaning. They looked incongruous and ugly as they rested on the tablecloth. "I spent a summer here a few years ago, and then I had the opportunity to come back. I remembered how much I liked it, and I thought I could use a change of scenery."

"Hmm. Any waitressing experience?"

"No. But I'm a hard worker," she said. She wanted this, she realized. Wanted this job, wanted to work in this lovely place, wanted this man's company. "I've been working for Boston University."

"Doing what?"

She thought about lying, then decided he'd probably check her references. "In the custodial department." Wiping up puddles of puke from the walkways and splatters of urine from tiled floors; a world away from this hushed, good-smelling, candlelit room with its spacious windows open to the sea. Reese was looking at her closely, in a way that made her feel like he knew some of what she wasn't telling him.

"You know," he finally said, "this building was once a church. Our Lady of Good Voyage." He leaned back in his chair with the air of a man preparing to tell a much-loved story. "There're a lot of Portuguese families on the Cape. They came over from the Azores in the 1880s, and they settled here to fish. According to the stories, a fisherman was out on the ocean when his oars broke. Or his mast, depending on who's telling the story. Anyhow, something broke. He prayed to the Madonna, and the seas calmed, allowing him to return safely to port."

Diana looked around. Other than a small stained glass window toward the top of the peaked roof, and the beams of the ceiling, there wasn't much that spoke of a house of worship. Reese pointed toward an iron loop, bolted high in a beam on the ceiling. "See that? That's where the church bell hung. And it's hard to make it out from here, but the window depicts the Madonna, holding a boat in her left hand." He put a piece of focaccia on her plate and poured oil beside it. "Go on," he said. "Please."

The square of bread was light, almost airy in Diana's hand. The top crust was chewy; the bread beneath it was pillowy soft. She tore off a bit and swiped it through a slick of olive oil and sea salt, and ate it, trying not to gobble or moan out loud, as Reese watched her approvingly.

"Good?" he asked.

She swallowed. "It's amazing." She wiped her hands on her napkin.

"I should tell you, Dee, that you're here at the wrong time, if you're looking to make a lot of money." He nodded at the dining room, where there were maybe fifteen tables for two and another ten for parties of four. A single long table with seats for sixteen ran against the back wall. "When it's high season, we run a happy hour from three to five o'clock. We have two dinner seatings: one at six o'clock, one at eight thirty. We turn every table in here, every single night, and there's a waiting list, in case we have no-shows."

The kitchen doors swung open, and a waitress came to the table carrying two large, steaming white plates. She set the first one down in front of Reese and said, "Here we have filet of roasted halibut, caught this morning right here in Cape Cod Bay. It's pan-seared in a sauce of black garlic, blistered cherry tomatoes, and shishito peppers, both from Longnook Farms, served over a bed of coconut-lime rice with sautéed bok choy." She set the second dish down in front of Diana. "Here we have a confit of Maple Hill Farm duck leg and roasted duck breast in a balsamic-fig reduction, served over sweet-potato hash, with local roasted ramps. Please enjoy," she said, and gave a little bow.

"Thank you, Carly."

Carly nodded and turned to go. Reese picked up his knife and fork.

"We have sixteen waiters on staff in high season. That goes down to eight during the winter months. A lot of our people have regular winter jobs someplace else. Carly's a year-rounder, but Marcia and Lizzie—you'll meet them—they spend their winters at an inn in Key West."

Diana nodded. The heady smell of the food, the garlic and tomatoes, the sweetness of the fish, the richness of the duck, was making her feel dizzy. As she stared, her stomach made an embarrassingly loud noise. She grimaced, but Reese just smiled.

"That's an endorsement if I've ever heard one." He deftly portioned out half of the fish and rice as Carly set two smaller plates on the table. He put the fish on one, reaching for Diana's plate. "May I?" She handed it over, and watched as he repeated the maneuver with the duck.

"Go on," he said, setting the plate in front of her. "Let me know what you think."

Diana loosened a sliver of halibut with her fork and slipped it into her mouth. She closed her eyes, tasting the sweetness of the fish; the tart, juicy tomatoes; oil and butter and garlic and thyme.

"Good?" asked Reese. His eyes were dark brown behind his glasses, and there was a deep dimple in his left cheek.

She chewed and swallowed. "So good." He was still watching her, clearly expecting more. "I don't even like fish, usually. But this—it's so sweet! The tomatoes . . ."

"They're from a farm in Truro. They turn into jam when you reduce them. They're my favorite," he said, voice lowered, like he was telling her a secret, or like he didn't want to hurt the figs' or the bok choy's feelings. "We source as many of our ingredients locally as we can. Our milk and eggs, our butter, our honey— everything we can get from around here, we do." He had a few bites of fish, a sip of water, and patted his whiskers with his napkin.

"You know what they say about the people on the Cape?"

She could tell that wasn't a question she was meant to answer, so she shook her head, ate her duck, and waited.

"You've got your native Cape Codders. People who were born here. People whose families have been here for generations. They're the only ones allowed to call themselves locals."

He ate another bite of fish. "Then you've got your summer people. No explanation needed there. And then, last but not least, you've got what they call washashores. The misfits and the weirdos. Some of them are kids who ran away from home. Or got kicked out of their houses." She thought she caught his eyes move toward Ryan at his podium. "Some"—he gestured at himself—"are grown-ups who walked away from their jobs. The folks who wash up here and decide to stay." He smiled, flashing his gold fillings again.

"Are you from New York?" she asked, because she could hear New York in his voice.

Reese nodded. "I had a big, important job at a big, important bank in New York City. I came here one summer, on a two-week vacation. Brought a briefcase full of work with me, too. But I woke up every morning hearing the wind and the water. All day long, I'd just walk around and watch things. The sunset over the marshes. The wind in the grass. And at the end of the two weeks, I just couldn't bring myself to leave." There was regret in his voice, sadness on his face. Diana wondered if he'd had a wife, or a partner, with him on that vacation; if that person had gone back to New York and he'd stayed behind.

"So here I am. And I feel lucky. This is a special place." Diana wasn't sure if he was talking about the restaurant, or Province-town, or the Outer Cape, or Cape Cod in general, but found herself nodding all the same.

"Excuse me." Ryan had come gliding over to the table. As Diana watched, he bent down to murmur something to Reese about an invoice from their olive oil purveyor. Diana picked up her knife and cut a bite of the duck breast, filling her mouth with its melting richness, with the seedy, pulpy sweetness of the figs and the slashing acid of the vinegar, and sighed, letting her eyes slip shut. When she opened them, Reese was looking at her with approval.

"So?" When she didn't answer, he said, "The job's yours, if you want it."

"I want it," said Diana, and found that she was smiling.

"Good. Be here tomorrow at three," he said. "Get yourself some black pants and a white shirt." He winked, and said, "Your bow tie is on me."

8

Diana

It didn't take long for Diana's days to find a rhythm. Every morning, for as long as the weather allowed, she would put on a swimsuit and descend the six steep flights of stairs to the beach. She'd leave a towel hanging on the railing, and walk south for half an hour. Then she'd get in the water and swim back. Back on the deck, she would take a shower, trying to enjoy the hot water beating down on her scalp and her shoulders, watching the steam rise into the cool morning air, with a part of her always alert for the sound of an approaching car or footsteps. The neighboring cottages were all empty. She could go for days without seeing another car on her road. Just as Dr. Levy had predicted, the Cape had cleared out for the off-season.

She'd read, or run errands; straightening up the cottage, doing her laundry, or restocking her pantry and fridge. At three thirty, she'd put on one of three white shirts and a pair of black pants, put her bow tie in her pocket, and make the fifteen-minute drive into Provincetown.

At four thirty, Reese would gather the staff to go over the day's specials. "Push the cabernet; we over-ordered," he'd tell them as they sat around the refectory table in the back room, or "Chef wants to know how it goes with the pumpkin ravioli. If it's a hit, we'll keep it on the menu." Chef was a towering, silent man named Carl. Each night he'd prepare an order of each of the night's specials, a large enough portion so that each member of the waitstaff could have a bite or two and, thus, give informed descriptions to the diners. He'd also make a staff meal, a simple dish, like burgers and sweet-potato fries, sausage grinders served with onions and sweet peppers; chicken schnitzel and potato rosti. At five thirty, Diana would visit the restroom to brush her teeth and touch up her makeup. Her shift began at six o'clock and went until one o'clock in the morning, or until the last check had been dropped, whichever came first.

Reese gave her four shifts: dinner on Tuesdays through Thursdays, then a split shift on Sunday, where she'd work brunch from ten to two, then have a break before the dinner service began. Fridays and Saturdays were the most lucrative nights of the week, but, as the newest hire, she didn't get to work them. She didn't mind. The slow pace suited her, as did the clientele. Most of their off-season customers were locals who'd come to celebrate a special occasion, a birthday or an anniversary or a kid coming home from college. They were almost always friendly; patient with her mistakes, and the tips, while not astronomical, were enough for her to cover her expenses and even start a savings account.

She got to know the people who made up what Reese called "our happy Abbey family." There were the waiters and waitresses; the bussers, the chefs and line cooks and dishwashers. For her first few weeks, Reese had her shadowing Carly, a single mother who lived with her daughter in an apartment off Shank Painter Road and attended, each morning, the AA meetings at the Methodist Church. Diana wondered if it was hard for Carly, delivering drinks to tables, watching diners get tipsy and jolly and, sometimes, a few drinks past that, but she was too shy to ask. Carly was brisk and unsmiling and laconic on every topic except her daughter, Melody. "She's very talented," Carly would say, her plain, narrow face glowing as she pulled out her wallet to show pictures of her daughter seated at a grand piano, in a velvet dress and a hair bow that was bigger than her head. Every few months Carly would take her daughter to Providence or Boston to compete in a pageant. Carly's plan, Diana learned, was to move to Vermont when Melody got old enough to compete in the Miss America pageant. "I'm from Texas. She wouldn't have a prayer back home," Carly said. "But do you know how many girls in Vermont competed to win their state last year? Seven girls. Seven girls in the entire state." She'd laughed, shaking her head in disbelief. "My God, back home there'd be a hundred girls in every local competition. Up here, nobody even cares!"

Diana met Jonathan, Reese's partner, who managed a local theater that, in the summer, brought in Broadway stars to perform for a few nights apiece while he interviewed them and accompanied them on the piano. Jonathan was an accomplished pianist who could play just about anything from the Great American Songbook, and any Broadway show produced after 1976. On Thursday nights he hosted a singalong at the Crown & Anchor that went until last call, and most of the waitstaff would stop by for a drink and a few songs.

Ryan, the host, had been standoffish at first. If Diana failed to recite the specials exactly as they'd been written, he'd act like she'd forgotten the nuclear codes; if she hadn't kept the bar supplied with citrus and celery, he'd act like she'd neglected to deliver a heart to a kid awaiting a transplant. His standard form of address to her was "Bitch," but she couldn't take it personally, because he called everyone, male and female, the same thing. He also called Diana "Miss Thing" when he was merely irritated, "Missy Miss" when he was really upset, as in "Where do you think you're going, Missy Miss, you've got to help Mario with the napkins." Sometimes she'd hear him whispering with Frankie the bartender, or Lizzie, one of the waitresses, and she'd be sure he was talking about her. Probably wondering why Reese had hired someone so inept, she thought.

Then, one night a middle-aged couple had come for dinner. Ryan's face had been pale as he'd led them to the table, his shoulders stiff and his hip-swinging sashay tamped down to a regular walk. The man had worn a suit and tie; the woman had hairspray-stiffened hair and a gold cross glittering at her throat. They'd sat in virtual silence through their meal, and departed the Abbey wordlessly, looking straight ahead as they walked out the door. Diana was walking to her car at the end of her shift that night when she heard someone crying. She peeked around the Dumpster, and there was Ryan, half-hidden in the building's shadow, head bent and shoulders shaking. She'd tried to get herself out of sight, to leave him alone in what was clearly a private moment, but then he saw her.

"Are you okay?" she'd asked.

"It's my birthday," he said, and started to cry harder.

"What are you, twenty-five? That's not that old!"

He'd made a noise somewhere between a laugh and a sob. "I'm not crying because I'm getting older," he said, his voice dropping. "I'm crying because those people? The ones I seated at table seven? They're my mom and dad."

It was Reese who'd told her the rest of the story: how Mrs. Halliwell had come home from work unexpectedly to find fifteen-year-old Ryan wearing one of her dresses. How she and her husband had given him an ultimatum, to renounce his perversions, attend a special summer camp for boys with his particular problem, or leave their home.

"So he left?"

"He did. Couch-surfed and stayed with friends until he finished high school, and then moved out here. His parents still don't speak to him. I guess he's been excommunicated from whatever church they attend, and he's got two older brothers who act like he's dead. But they come for dinner, every year, on Ryan's birthday. They won't speak to him, but they leave five hundred dollars on the table when they go."

"God, that's awful." Diana couldn't imagine how it would feel if her own parents had behaved that way toward her.

"It's a sad old world," Reese agreed.

The next morning, Diana got to Provincetown an hour early. She bought Ryan a birthday card at Adams Pharmacy, which had creaky wooden floors and smelled like camphor and menthol cigarettes, and, after carefully perusing the offerings of several different boutiques, a pair of cashmere socks. "They're like hugs for your feet," she told him.

"Oh, thank you, baby," he'd said, and hugged her tight. After that, Ryan was her champion. The night she'd dropped a tray of glasses and the whole restaurant had applauded, he'd hurried to her side. "Show's over," he announced, with his hands on his hips, and he'd helped her sweep up the mess. He'd slip her grease-spotted paper bags full of day-old malasadas and croissants from the Portuguese Bakery, where his roommate worked, and seat the best tippers in her section.

As the weeks went by, Diana acquired a few regulars. A drag queen who performed under the name Heavy Flo (real name: Phil Amoroso) would make it a point to sit in her section and greet her with "How is my beautiful girl?" Dora Fitzsimmons, a taciturn woman with frizzy gray hair who ran a sailing camp in the West End, would come in every Tuesday at five o'clock precisely and order a burger, well-done, served with a pile of curly fries. Curly fries weren't on the Abbey's menu. "But they served them when this place was still D'Amico's," Reese explained. That had been almost twenty years previously, but the chef kept a bag of fries in the freezer, and would throw two handfuls into the deep fryer for Dora. Dora never said anything to Diana, other than "please" and "thank you," once she'd given her order. She'd greet the bartenders, and give Reese a nod, then read the *Provincetown Banner* while she ate her dinner. She'd leave without a word of farewell, but there would always be a ten-dollar bill under her water glass.

Almost everyone was nice. But when the staff gathered at the bar at the end of the night to divvy up the tips, when shots were poured and plans were made to go to the Crown & Anchor for Jonathan's singalong, or to meet at the Boatslip for drinks, Diana would say good night and return to her cottage, to read for an hour or two, then fall asleep.

On a sunny Monday morning in October, she drove down to the dog shelter in Dennis. "I'm just looking," she told the woman behind the desk, who gave a knowing nod. "Take y' time," she said. Diana walked along the row of cages, looking into pair after pair of beseeching eyes. There were dogs that jumped, dogs that licked, dogs that whined as they nudged at her hand with their wet noses. At the very end of the corridor, she found a scrawny, shivering dog with a patchy white coat who just huddled in the corner of her pen and looked at Diana, too scared to even approach.

Diana crouched down with a bit of Pupperoni in her hand, and extended the treat through the bars. She waited, patiently, as the dog regarded her. "It's okay," Diana said. "I won't hurt you." Finally, she set the treat on the floor and the dog, trembling all over, made her way to the front of the cage. She took the treat in her mouth and held it there, looking up at Diana.

"Go on," said Diana. "It's okay. It's for you." Instead of eating it, the dog carried the treat back to her bed, where she carefully nudged it under a wadded-up blanket and curled up on top of it with a sigh. Twenty minutes later, Diana had filled out the forms, paid the fees, purchased a leash and a collar and a ten-pound bag of kibble, and was driving back to Truro with Willa on a blanket on the passenger's seat.

Willa's skin was dark gray beneath her patchy white fur. Her ears were enormous and pointy, and her bushy eyebrows protruded like fans over brown eyes that looked weary and sad. Diana knew that Willa had been found on Skaket Beach at the end of summer. Had some family that had loved her for years taken her on one last vacation, then abandoned her? Had she been startled by the fireworks on the Fourth of July, and run away from some campsite or cabin or hotel room and gotten lost? Or had she run from a home where she was kicked and yelled at, taking off in search of a better life?

"Poor Willa," Diana murmured as she led the dog into the cottage. Willa took a tour, carefully sniffing at the baseboards, the legs of the director's chairs, the bottom of the couch, and the refrigerator. "Are you hungry?" Willa had wagged her stump of a tail, and looked up with her head cocked to the left. In the kitchen, Diana filled a bowl with kibble, and another with fresh water, and watched as Willa nudged at the bowl, looking up after every few sniffs like she was trying to make sure no one would snatch it away. She ate a few careful mouthfuls, then looked up, this time with her head cocked to the right.

"Go on," Diana said. "It's okay." She lifted the bag. "There's plenty more where that came from."

Willa ate more, but she didn't empty her dish. Diana kept her distance, watching out of the corner of her eye as Willa took a mouthful of kibbles, walked to the corner, let them spill out of her mouth, and nosed them under the couch. Diana retrieved them and, under Willa's reproachful gaze, put them back into her bowl. "You can eat them or leave them, but you can't hide them," she said, and Willa wagged her stump, as if she understood.

That first night, after she'd made sure the door was locked and turned out the lights, Diana climbed into the loft and got into bed. She could see Willa's silhouette below her, sitting on her haunches at the foot of the stairs. "Come on, girl, it's okay," she said, patting the bed, and Willa had gathered herself, trotting up the stairs and leaping onto the mattress, her tail rotating madly. She licked Diana's hand, sniffed her way around the perimeter of the bed, then turned herself around three times and curled up on her side, with her back against Diana's hip. Diana wrapped her arm around the dog's head, and Willa rested her muzzle on Diana's forearm. That was how they fell asleep.

Diana bought a dog bed, and one of the bike shops sold her a used three-speed bike with a roomy wicker basket on its handlebars. She'd take Willa for a walk every morning, and, every few days, for a bike ride to the post office to collect her mail. At two in the morning, with the whole world quiet except for the waves and the wind's low keening, Diana would come home from work and unlock the cottage door to find the light above the stove still burning and Willa curled up on the couch, tail wagging in welcome.

Diana's skin got tan; the sun put streaks of gold in her hair. The biking and the swimming worked her heart and her lungs and her muscles, the nights of sound sleep erased the worry from her eyes. Day by day, week by week, with every walk on the sand and each stroke through the water, with each workday completed, and each deposit to her savings account, she felt stronger. A little more herself; a little more at home.

By October, all the trees were bare, except for the scrubby pines. The water got too cold for swimming, and the beach looked desolate. The town had emptied out, just as Reese had predicted. In Provincetown, Diana had her choice of parking spaces, and started becoming familiar with the faces of some of her fellow washashores and year-rounders: the clerk at the grocery store, the librarians at the public library, the guy with the shaved head who worked behind the counter at Joe.

One morning, she was sleeping late, dressed in a sweatshirt and a pair of boxer shorts with Willa curled up beside her. Reese had celebrated his fiftieth birthday at the Abbey the night before, closing the restaurant to the public and throwing a party for all his friends, which seemed to include every resident of P-town. Diana had spotted the woman from the art gallery, with her pink hair and cat-eye glasses, the guy who ran the copy shop, the meter maid and the cops and the shellfish constable and even the guy who directed traffic, dressed as a pilgrim, on busy weekends. The Abbey had been crowded, with three bartenders hustling to keep everyone's glasses full. Chef had made paella, studded with linguica and chunks of lobster meat and fresh clams, and, after dinner was served, Reese had insisted that his staffers join the party. It had been a long night, which had culminated with Reese, after much coaxing from Jonathan, standing on top of a table and singing "Let's Get It On." He'd started a capella, but at some point one of the patrons had produced an accordion, of all things, and then a few of the drag queens, powerless to resist the spotlight, had climbed on the table to join in. At one point, Reese had fought his way through the crowd to Diana, taking hold of her head and planting a resounding kiss on her cheek. "Dee! My baby washashore! Are you having fun?"

She promised that she was.

"And you're happy!" Reese, who Diana suspected was thoroughly drunk, was giving her a probing look.

"I'm fine!" She lifted her glass of champagne as proof. "I promise."

"Okay, then." He patted her upper arm and sent her back into the throng. Instead of returning to the party, Diana had gone to the ladies' room. She'd washed her hands and looked at herself in the mirror for a long time, wondering what other people saw. A tallish young woman with golden-brown hair, a girl who wore

baggy clothes and a wary expression. A girl who'd forgotten how
to smile.

When she came out of the bathroom, Ryan was waiting. He
grabbed her hand. "Come dancing," he said, and dragged her
toward the center of the room, where people were doing some
kind of line dance to "Love Shack" by the B-52s. Diana had let
herself be pulled toward the center of the action, throwing her
hands in the air with three dozen other revelers whenever Fred
Schneider sang "The whole shack shimmies!"

She hadn't made it home until after two in the morning, and
had immediately fallen deeply asleep without bothering to set her
alarm, because it was Saturday, one of her days off. She had just
opened her eyes when the knocking began. "Caretaker!" a loud,
male voice shouted.

She jumped up, badly startled, calling, "Just a minute!" as
Willa yelped and scrambled underneath the bed. Diana snatched
up the previous evening's white shirt, wincing at the combined
odors of tequila, cigarette smoke, and clam juice, which must
have gotten splashed on her sleeves during service. The dresser,
with the rest of her clothes, was downstairs, on the opposite side
of the cottage, and she could see a bulky male shape looming
outside of the screen door.

"Just hang on!" A few weeks ago, there'd been a sale at one
of the fancy home goods stores on Commercial Street, the same
place she'd bought Ryan's birthday socks, and she'd treated herself
to a blanket of soft knit wool, purple with fringed tassels. She
snatched it up, wrapped it around her waist, and came down the
stairs to stand on the opposite side of the door.

"Can I help you?"

"I'm Michael Carmody. I'm the caretaker," said the man. He
was a tall, heavyset, bearded fellow, thick through the chest and
thighs, and he spoke with a broad Boston accent. She guessed
that he was maybe five or ten years older than she was. He wore

a barn jacket, jeans, and work boots and a Red Sox baseball cap. Beneath its brim, she could see a round face, full cheeks, pale, faintly freckled skin, and a thicket of reddish-brown beard.

"I don't need anything taken care of," she said.

The man looked puzzled at this assertion. "Dr. Levy and her husband hired me. I do for them every year. This place, and the other."

"You do what for them, exactly?" She was slightly reassured that he knew the owner's name. Then again, anyone could have looked that up.

"I caretake," said the man, as if that single word should have been enough. When she waited, clearly expecting something more, he gave her another puzzled look, his brow furrowing. "I close up the houses at the end of the summer, and make sure everything's shipshape for winter. I make repairs. I nail down boards and oil hinges. Check the weather stripping; put up the storm windows. I keep an eye on things through the winter. Making sure that the pipes don't freeze, plowing out the driveways if it snows. I fix what needs fixing, order replacements for things that need replacing. Making sure nothing gets stolen, and no mice take up residence, so everything's the way it should be when summer comes."

"Did Dr. Levy tell you that I'd be staying here for the winter?" Standing on the porch—no, she thought, *looming* on the porch— he was making her small cottage feel even smaller. She hadn't had any guests, and hadn't realized how the place would feel like a doll's house with another adult nearby.

The man pulled off his baseball cap, poked at his hair, which was a few shades lighter than his beard, and put the cap back on. "She mentioned that they had a tenant, but she didn't seem sure about your plans."

Which made sense. Diana had only called Dr. Levy three days ago to ask if she could stay on. Dr. Levy had told her that was fine, that she was welcome to stay through the spring if she liked, but the news didn't appear to have made its way to Michael Carmody, Caretaker.

"Well, I'm going to be here," Diana said. "I can take care of the place."

"So you'll put up the storm windows?"

Diana didn't know what a storm window was, or where the ones for the cottage might be, but she wasn't going to tell him that.

"Tell you what," said the guy. "Call Dr. Levy to make sure I'm supposed to be here. Once you tell me it's okay, I'll take down your screens and put up your storm windows." He paused. "I usually put down mouse traps, over the winter, but it looks like you two have got that covered."

Diana looked down to see that Willa had made her way down from the loft, nosed the screen door open and was butting insistently at the guy's knee with her forehead. He bent down and scratched behind her ears, then under her chin, murmuring, "Are you a good girl?" Looking up at Diana, he asked, "Okay to give her a treat?" When Diana nodded, he pulled something out of his pocket that caused Willa's entire body to convulse with delight. He offered it to her on an open palm. Willa gobbled it up, put her paws on his leg, and gave him her most beseeching look, with her head cocked to the right.

"I waitress at nights," Diana said through the screen door. "In P-town."

"Oh, yeah? Whereabouts?"

"So I'm gone Tuesdays, Wednesdays, and Thursdays from four in the afternoon on. If that works for you," she said. "I'll call Dr. Levy first, though."

"Sounds like a plan," he said agreeably. If he'd noticed that she hadn't told him her name, or where she'd worked, or even opened the door, he didn't mention it. He scratched Willa's ears. Willa head-butted his calf, then thumped down on her haunches, look-ing up at him with her tongue lolling and her eyes bright. The guy reached into his pocket again, looked a question at Diana, and, at her nod, tossed Willa something small and round and reddish-brown. Willa hopped up on her hind legs and caught it on the fly, a maneuver Diana had never seen her perform, of which she'd never suspected Willa was capable.

"Dehydrated hot dogs," he said.

"What?"

"You buy a pack of the cheapest hot dogs you can find, cut 'em into slices, then nuke the slices in the microwave for ten min-utes. My dad taught me to always carry them around. Even the meanest dog will leave you alone if you give him a few of these." He tossed up another treat. This time, Willa did a running leap to snatch it out of the air, and he smiled. His eyes crinkled at the corners. "What's her name?" he asked.

"Willa."

"Is Willa going to give me any trouble if I show up and you're not here?"

"Does she look like she'll give you any trouble?" asked Diana, indicating the dog, who was, at that moment, staring up at him ardently, with her tail wagging like a metronome. *Some guard dog*, Diana thought, as Willa rolled over and waved her legs in the air.

The guy smiled and petted Willa's belly, which almost dis-appeared under his enormous hand. "They say that there's dog people and cat people, and I'm a dog person. Grew up with a golden retriever named Monty. Are the fireworks bothering her?"

"Not much." Every Saturday night, kids down on the beach would set off sparklers or Roman candles. The first time it had happened, the noise had sent Willa scrambling behind the couch, but, after a few Saturdays, she seemed to have realized that the noise did not portend any harm.

"Are you a brave girl?" the guy asked Willa. "Monty, he'd hide under the porch, every time. Come out with mulch and burrs all over him, with this embarrassed look on his face."

Diana didn't want to be amused. But she couldn't stop herself from picturing it—a big, dopey-looking dog, who'd match this big, amiable guy, slinking out from underneath a porch, looking foolish.

The guy straightened. "Well, I won't take up any more of your time." He pulled a business card out of his pocket, extending it toward the door. "Anything else goes wrong—roof starts leaking, toilet won't flush—you call me."

The card, she saw, had the same logo as the truck. "Thanks."

"Okay, then. Nice to meet you. See you around." He ambled to his truck and climbed behind the wheel. It was a substantial truck, but even so, it seemed to sag a little beneath his bulk, and the top of his baseball cap brushed its ceiling. He gave her a friendly wave and drove away.

When Diana got home that night, she found that Michael Carmody had tucked another business card between her screen door and the doorjamb. He'd also left a waist-high pile of firewood stacked by the door, with a Baggie full of dehydrated hot dog on top of it.

"I hope you told him that your affections can't be bought," she told Willa, who looked up at her, her tail rotating frantically. Diana sighed and gave Willa one of Michael Carmody's treats.

9

Diana

O h, Michael! He's lovely," Dr. Levy told her when she called. "I should have told you he'd be stopping by." Diana left him a message, reiterating the afternoons she'd be working. The very next night, she'd returned from work to find her storm windows in place. A week after that, Diana went to the bar to fill a drink order and was not entirely surprised to find Michael Carmody sitting there, with the barstool practically invisible underneath his body. He wore jeans, a plaid shirt, and his Sox cap.

"Hey, I found you!" he said.

"Yes, you did," she said.

"Did Willa like her treats?"

"She did. Thanks."

"I love dogs," he said, his voice meditative. "Except for those nasty, yappy little purse dogs." Turning to Frankie, the bartender, he said, "Hey, do you remember Mrs. Lambert? She'd come in here sometimes, back in the day, looking for her husband, and she'd have one of them whatchamacallems, a teacup poodle, in that monogrammed tote bag she used to carry?" He turned to Diana and said, "I bet she would've monogrammed the dog, if she could have figured out how."

Diana made a noncommittal noise.

"When your shift's over, how about I buy you a drink?" he asked.

"No thank you," said Diana. If she'd been interested in dating anyone, Michael Carmody would have been a reasonable prospect, even if he resembled John Candy more than John F. Kennedy Junior. He was cheerful, with a nice smile, and he seemed kind. And he liked Willa, too.

He spread his hands wide in supplication. She noticed, without intending to notice, that his nails were clipped very short, and they were scrupulously clean. "You don't want to hear about my childhood?" When she smiled briefly, but didn't answer, he said, "Well then, I will finish up this excellent gin and tonic, and be on my way." He nodded at the bartender. "Thanks, Frankie."

"Any time, Mike." Frankie was a sinewy, middle-aged woman, deeply tanned, with an anchor tattooed on one of her forearms, and her dark hair in a mullet. The waiters and the bussers wore white shirts and black pants, but Frankie, like Ryan, was exempt from the dress code. She wore her own uniform: black jeans, a black chambray shirt, and motorcycle boots with heavy silver buckles.

Diana tried to ignore Michael Carmody, but she saw him greet two of the waitresses, kiss Ryan on the cheek, and give Reese a lengthy hug, complete with back-pounding, on his way out the door. When he was gone, Ryan drifted over to the bar and sat down with a sigh. "Isn't he cute? Total bear."

Frankie nodded her approval. "You're missing out, Dee."

"Which bear are we talking about? Michael Carmody? I love him," said Ellie Ford, who was one of the waitresses, a petite, freckled strawberry blonde who'd spent her whole life on the Cape and knew everything about everyone in P-town. "He dated my sister's best friend for two years in high school."

"You could do a lot worse than be wrapped up in that," Frankie said to Diana. "Michael Carmody's good people."

Diana shook her head. "I'm sure he is. It's just, I'm not looking for anything right now." When she'd taken the job, she'd made vague allusions to a broken heart, and how her move to the Cape was a chance to start over. She'd answered follow-up questions as briefly as she could without being rude and politely turned down Ryan's attempts to set her up with single friends of both genders. She was sure her colleagues were engaging in some collective *Baby Boom* fantasy, where she was the bitchy, big-city ice queen who needed some salt-of-the-earth loving, maybe even a baby or three, to make her a woman again. *Not happening*, she told herself. She'd never wanted children, not even before that summer, and she wasn't ready for any kind of romance. On her way back from the kitchen, her hands full of lemons and limes, she realized that she'd have no one to call if the roof leaked or the toilet stopped flushing. Dialing Michael Carmody's number would automatically be seen as a capitulation. *Oh, well*, she thought.

The following Monday morning, Diana put Willa into her bicycle basket and rode to the center of town, where a single convenience store, two real-estate offices, a seafood market, and the post office, each housed in a single-story wooden building, comprised Truro's downtown. In the empty field next to the post office, across the street from the town green, bands and local musicians gave free concerts in the summertime. The summer people packed picnics and came to listen, letting their kids run and dance in front of the bandstand while they drank wine out of plastic cups and ate fried chicken from the Blue Willow or pizza from the Flying Fish in Wellfleet.

On Monday mornings, the field hosted a farmers' market. That day, half a dozen farms had come, displaying their wares on folding tables. There were jars of honey and beeswax candles, pumpkins and squash and turnips and wreaths made of cedar and pine. Diana was browsing the offerings when Michael Carmody appeared beside her, holding an enormous, oddly shaped tomato in one of his hands.

"Eight dollars for this?" he asked the young woman minding the cashbox.

"It's delicious," she said. "Last ones of the season."

"But it looks like a tumor." He held the tomato out for Diana's inspection. The tomato was more oval than round, big enough to fill his palm, with odd bulges beneath its yellow-gold skin. "Would you pay eight dollars for this?" Before she could answer, he turned back to the girl. "You know what, I think I'd pay eight dollars so I wouldn't have to eat it."

"Your loss," she said. "That right there is an Early Girl. Sweetest tomato you'll ever taste."

"Really?" He studied it skeptically.

"You get some good sourdough bread, toast it up, slice your Early Girl. A little mayo, little salt, a few grinds of pepper. Best sandwich in the world."

Michael considered the tomato, then handed the girl a ten-dollar bill and said, "Keep the change." Turning back to Diana, he said, "Want to split it? I'll buy the bread if you supply the mayo."

She shook her head.

"It's just a sandwich!" he said. "In broad daylight!" When she walked to the fence, where she'd left her bike, he followed her, and when she turned around, he was right on her heel.

She lowered her voice. "What part of 'no' don't you understand?"

"Well," he said equably, "I would like to get to know you. But I will respect your wishes. If you want to be left alone, I'll leave you alone. I don't want to make a nuisance of myself." He made a show of turning away from Diana, toward the center of the field, where an older man, gantry-thin with a dandelion fluff of white hair, was playing "Turkey in the Straw" on the banjo, with an adoring circle of children at his feet.

Diana had to raise her voice to make herself heard over the music. "Why?"

"Why what?"

"Why do you want to get to know me?"

From underneath his baseball cap, Michael Carmody gave her a look that was equal parts incredulous, annoyed, and amused. "Are you fishing for compliments?"

She looked down at her feet and didn't answer.

"You honestly have no idea why a man would be interested in you."

"I know why a man would want to sleep with me," she said bluntly. She'd meant to shock him, and, from his face, she could see that she had.

"Look," he finally said. "You're pretty, which you know, because, if I remember right, your cottage has a mirror. And you seem interesting. And your dog already likes me, which is half the battle." He rubbed his hands together. "But if you're not interested, that's okay. I promise, I can take no for an answer."

He looked at her for a minute. When she didn't say anything, he nodded, and said, "Okay, then. See you around, Early Girl." He turned around, cradling his tomato in one big hand. Diana watched him. Her heart was beating fast, and she could taste iron on her tongue. She felt relieved, and angry, her insides fizzing with adrenaline and the memory of terror. But she also felt something else, something it took her most of the bike ride home to identify as regret.

Fall burned down into winter. The skies were gray in the daytime, dark by five o'clock; the trees brandished bare limbs against the sky. Four members of the waitstaff and two of the line cooks left for Key West, where they had jobs waiting. Ryan used what he'd made over the summer to go to Los Angeles for a month for auditions. Reese warned her, again, that the tips in the winter months wouldn't amount to much. "Are you going to be okay?" he asked.

Diana promised she'd be fine. If she'd had to pay rent, it might have been a stretch, but Dr. Levy told her she could have the cottage through the spring.

"It'll get better in the summer," he said. "You'll make, like, triple the money in high season." Diana nodded, even though she'd already decided that there was no way she could stay on the Cape through the summer. Not with all the memories it would bring up; not when everything she saw and heard and smelled would remind her of that summer.

All through the winter, she took Willa down to the beach every morning, to frolic with her pack of regulars, a corgi and a golden retriever, two chocolate labs, and a few other rescues. The big dogs would chase tennis balls into the water, while the small dogs watched from the shore and gave each other looks that seemed to ask *Why on earth would they do that?* Diana met their owners; her fellow washashores, women and men who'd had other lives in other towns and cities, who'd landed on the Cape and decided to stay. One woman was a sculptor, one man was a writer; a married couple were university professors who kept a pied-à-terre in New York City for the school year. All of them loved the Cape, and couldn't imagine living anywhere else, and they were happy to tell Diana where to go and what to do.

On Sundays, she'd bundle up and join Charlotte the sculptor and ride her bike to Provincetown for a restorative yoga class. When it was over, she'd treat herself to a latte at Joe, then pick up a few groceries and pedal back home. On Wednesdays, she would go to the Truro library, where she got to know both of the librarians: Margo, who was older, bubbly and enthusiastic, grabbing Diana's hand as she led her to the New Release table; and Tessa, who was younger, quiet and tall. Both of them would put books aside for Diana's visits. She'd check out a stack to get her through the week; always fiction, tilted heavily toward mysteries. She'd make a fire in the woodstove, brew a pot of tea, and read the afternoons away on her days off. Her favorites were cozies, where a tea-sipping spinster or a group of knitters solved the crime, without ever resorting to violence. Happy endings guaranteed.

One night in December, Michael Carmody came to the Abbey for dinner, accompanied by a pretty young woman who wore dangly gold earrings and a dress of peach-colored silk. Diana could have never worn that color, but the shade made the woman's pale, luminous white skin seem to glow. Reese winked at Diana as he seated them in her section. Diana shot him a dirty look, but before she could head over with menus and bread and glasses of water, Ellie had swooped in, smiling and chattering, greeting Michael with a hug. "I've got this," she called to Diana.

Diana told herself that it didn't matter. She returned Michael Carmody's friendly wave, and tried not to watch as he held the woman's chair out for her, or to listen as her laughter rang out across the dining room. When she walked by to deliver desserts to a four-top, an hour later, Michael and the woman were talking intently, their voices low, leaning so close to one another that their foreheads were practically touching, and he never even looked her way as he escorted his lady friend out the door. *Well*, she thought, *that's that.*

Jane, a fellow dog walker, told Diana where to get her shellfishing permit, and taught her how to use a clam rake. All through January and February, every few weeks, at low tide, Diana would walk Willa out onto a sandbar. Willa would run, chasing gulls, while Diana, in wool socks and rubber boots and a puffy down coat, raked the sand, listening for the telltale clinking sound of shells against the rake's tines, and filled the wire bucket with clams. One weekend Jane, who was short, with cropped gray hair and clear blue eyes, took her to Pamet Harbor and showed her how to pry oysters off the rocks with a knife. Back at home, Jane watched, supervising, as Diana struggled to pry the shells open, finally managing to free six mangled oysters from their homes. She poured herself a beer and sliced a lemon into wedges, arranged the oysters on a platter, and ate them, with lemon juice and cocktail sauce, while she and Willa and Jane and Jane's Bernese mountain dog, Thatcher, sat on the deck in the thin winter sunshine.

She went oystering all through the winter, dressing in layers, with canvas gardening gloves on her hands and a wool cap pulled down over her ears. She tossed the shells into a heap at the corner of the deck, thinking about her summer with Dr. Levy, the way that she would boil the shells until they were clean, then throw them onto the driveway. "Okay, kids, do your thing!" she'd call, and Sam and Sarah would race outside to stomp on the shells, jumping up and down, crushing them to bits.

By March, her heap was almost knee-high. Diana thought about dropping some off as an offering, as a combination thank-you and hello, but she knew she couldn't. Even seeing the house would be too much. She picked up a shell and held it in her hand, turning it over, admiring its shape and the shades of cream and gray on its inner curve, underneath where the oyster had lain. She looked at them until she had an idea. Then it was just a matter of gathering supplies.

She found paper napkins in the clearance bin at one of the fancy home goods stores in P-town. "With the summer people gone," said the proprietor, "there's not much call for cocktail supplies." Diana bought a pack of napkins with a pattern of blue anchors and seashells on the white background, and bought gold paint, white paint, and Mod Podge at the hardware store on Conwell Street.

Back at the cottage, she gave the shells a soak in vinegar, and dried them in the sun. When they were dry, she picked the largest shell and painted its insides white, and then, with a fine brush, painted a layer of gold around its rim. When the paint had dried, she brushed on a layer of Mod Podge, then carefully peeled the two-ply napkins apart and pressed the colorful side into the shell. She trimmed off the extra, lacquered the paper, and rubbed the edges with fine-grained sandpaper. "See that?" she asked Willa, extending her creation for the dog's perusal. "It's a dish for my necklaces and earrings."

Willa sniffed the shell dubiously, and gave Diana a hopeful look. Diana tossed her the last of Mike Carmody's dehydrated hot dog rounds, and then, after painting and decoupaging the rest of the shells, she lined them up in a row. They were brightly colored, their gold rims vivid. From a distance, they looked like flowers, pinks and creams, reds and golds, unfolding in the sun.

10

Diana

On the last day of March, Diana woke up one morning to find the cottage so cold that she could see her breath. She wrapped her down comforter around her and padded, barefoot, down the stairs and over to the thermostat, which said that it was fifty-two degrees. She bent to put her hand down against the vent and felt no warmth, and no matter how many times she turned the thermostat's switch off and then on again, the cottage refused to get any warmer.

She pulled on jeans, wool socks, and her warmest sweater, which was made of thick cranberry-colored wool and came down to her thighs, and quickly kindled a fire in the woodstove. Then she called Reese. "There's no heat in my cottage," she said.

"Did you turn the thermostat on and off?"

"Yep. Nothing happened."

"Is there oil in your tank?"

She grimaced, vaguely remembering something Michael Carmody had said about an oil tank, back in the fall. "Shoot."

Reese's voice was not unsympathetic. "You've got a caretaker, right?"

Diana sighed. "I do." She'd thrown out Michael Carmody's business card, but he was in the Yellow Pages, and the cheerful-sounding young woman who answered the phone said, "I'll send him right over."

"Thank you," said Diana. She put on her down coat, and she and Willa went to sit on the deck and await Michael Carmody's arrival.

Twenty minutes later, the caretaking truck came rumbling up the driveway and pulled to a stop beside her Honda. Michael gave her a salute and opened his door. The truck's springs seemed to sigh in relief as he climbed out. He wore jeans, work boots, a canvas barn coat, a red and black plaid shirt, and his usual Red Sox cap.

"Tank empty?" he asked.

"I'm not sure." That was easier than having to explain that she'd never even located the tank.

Michael set off on a walk around the cottage. Diana followed along, thinking that Frankie hadn't been wrong to call him a bear. He didn't walk as much as lumber, and it wasn't hard to picture him spending a few months gorging on salmon and blueberries, getting ready to hibernate. She was smiling at the thought of Michael using his large, nimble hands to snatch salmon out of a river when he turned around.

"What's funny?" he asked.

"Nothing."

Michael made a grumbling noise. A bearlike noise. Diana bit the inside of her cheek to keep from laughing. A moment later, he was kneeling next to a round black tank, half-hidden behind a lilac bush, low on the side of the cottage. When he gave it a rap with his knuckles, she could hear the echo. "Yup," he said. "You're dry." He pulled out his cell phone and punched in a number. "Hi, it's Michael Carmody. Let me talk to Little Don." When someone—presumably Little Don—picked up, he said, "Yeah, I'm up here at the Levy cottage on Knowles Heights Road. They got an account?" He paused, then nodded. "Yuh. We'll wait." He pocketed his phone, said, "Shouldn't be more than an hour," then reached in his pocket and tossed Willa a disc of dehydrated hot dog.

"How's my girlfriend?" he crooned, as Willa bounced around the patchy grass, looking half-insane with joy. "How's my number-one girl?" His beard had gotten bushier since Diana had seen him last.

"How much is this going to cost?" she asked, trying to keep her voice businesslike.

"Well, I'm not sure." He turned to examine one of her shutters, lifting it from the bottom, then wiggling it back and forth before pulling a screwdriver out of his pocket and tightening one of the screws. "What's your deal with Dr. Levy? Is she paying utilities, or are you?"

Diana pressed her lips together. "I'm not sure," she muttered.

Michael tightened the second screw, then made his way back to the front of the house, where Diana had set out her shells to dry in the sun. He crouched down to examine them. "Hey," he said. "Did you make these? They're pretty." He picked up a shell that she'd lined with a lobster print. "Are you selling them?"

"What? No, no, I just . . . I needed a project."

"Come summer, these babies would fly out of the farmers' market. The summer people always want souvenirs to take home. You could make some money."

She shook her head, thinking no one would pay for a shell with a bit of paper glued inside. "I won't be here this summer."

He tilted his head, a very Willa-like gesture. "Oh, no?"

"No." Dr. Levy had offered, which was more than generous of her. *If you're happy there, please stay*, she'd said, but Diana knew that she couldn't.

"Where are you headed?" Michael asked.

"Back to Boston. I'll stay with my parents for the summer."

She'd already made plans to resume her old job, deep-cleaning the classrooms and the dorms over the summer, readying them for the students' return.

"That's too bad." He sounded honestly regretful as he looked at her, not in a predatory, leering way, but with great concentration. Like he was trying to memorize her, and there'd be a test later.

"Why?"

"Well, you're going to miss the best part of the year." He looked out toward P-town. "I've lived here all my life, and I never get tired of summer." He still wore that wistful smile as he turned toward her. "Business will really pick up at the Abbey. They open up the deck, and it's the best seat in town to watch the sunset, and Carl makes this incredible tuna Bolognese. It sounds weird, but it's out of this world."

"So what did you have when you came in?" Diana hadn't meant to interrupt; she hadn't even intended to let him know that she'd noticed him at the Abbey. She certainly hadn't meant for her voice to sound as sharp as it had.

"Huh?" He looked puzzled.

"In December," she said. "You were on a date."

For a minute, Michael just stared at her. Then he started to laugh.

"What?" Diana asked.

He shook his head.

"What?" she said again.

Shaking his head, he said, "Kate's my sister." He grinned. "But if I'd known that showing up with another woman was what it took to get you to notice me, I would have done it sooner."

Diana could feel her face getting hot. "I wasn't . . . I didn't . . ."

He held up his hands. "It's okay. Really. Like I told you at the farmers' market, if you're not interested, then you're not interested." He rubbed his hands along his thighs. When he spoke again, his voice was low. "I just wish you weren't leaving."

"Why?" she asked.

He looked at her for a long moment before spreading his arms wide. "Because I like you, dummy!" he hollered, his voice echoing out over the water. Willa gave a short, exclamatory bark. Diana tried her hardest not to smile.

"You don't even know me," she said.

"I know some things," said Michael Carmody as he sat down, uninvited, on the edge of her deck, and patted the space beside him. Immediately, traitorous Willa hopped up beside him, tongue lolling. Michael scratched her ears and said, "I know that you like to read Agatha Christie and Ruth Rendell. I know you like nutmeg on your lattes, but you only get lattes on Sundays, after yoga, and that you just get plain coffee the rest of the time. I know you like to swim and shuck oysters. Oh, and I know you're a dog person." He gave Willa another scratch. Willa laid her muzzle on his thigh and stared at him adoringly. *Damn dog*, thought Diana.

"You're a stalker," Diana muttered.

He shook his head. "I just pay attention." He took off his baseball cap, smoothed his hair, and put his hat on again. "Also, I know the guy who owns the coffee place," he said modestly. "And the woman who teaches the yoga class."

"And all the librarians," Diana muttered.

"Well, yes, seeing as how one of them's my mom," Michael said.

Diana made a strangled sound, realizing that there was a reason that the friendlier of the two librarians, the one with the curly red hair, seemed so familiar. "What else do you know?"

Michael Carmody looked her full in the face. "I don't know for sure, but I've got an idea that someone hurt you. And I'm sorry." He stood up and reached for her hands, and Diana shocked herself by letting him take them. With his eyes on hers, he said, "But I'm not that guy."

She pulled her hands free, turning away. "You're all that guy," she said.

"No." Michael's voice was gentle but insistent, and somehow he was right in front of her, turning her toward him, with one hand holding her hand, the other touching her chin, guiding her face toward his. "No, we're not."

They were so close that she could see his eyes were a mixture of hazel and green; so close that she could smell him, and whatever combination of soap and shampoo and aftershave he used smelled good to her. He was cupping her face, very gently, not pushing her, not forcing it, letting her be the one to move closer, to tilt her head up and look in his eyes and, finally, to press her mouth against his.

It was a sweet, chaste kiss, the first real kiss of her life, and Diana felt every part of it—the warmth of his palm on her cheek, his thumb, moving gently along her cheekbone; his lips, warm and soft amid the prickly patch of his beard; the comforting bulk of his body, blocking the wind, sheltering her, as surely as a house. He drew her against him, his hand at the base of her neck. "Okay?" he whispered.

Her skin was tingling, her breath was coming fast. Instead of answering, she put her mouth against his again, tilting her head back, deepening the kiss. She felt a sigh shudder through him. His barn coat hung open, and when he pulled her against him and wrapped his coat around her, it felt like coming in out of the cold to stand by a fire. His plaid shirt brushed against her chest, and she could imagine how it would feel if she was naked, her breasts pressed against the soft flannel. She shivered, and slipped her hands underneath his coat, gliding them down along his back and back up to his shoulders, letting her cheek rest against his chest. She could hear his heart, could feel her head rise and fall with his breaths. His hand made gentle circles on her back as he held her against him, and she felt like a storm-tossed dory that had come through the wind and the waves and had found its way back to the shelter of the shore. *Our Lady of*

Safe Harbor, she thought . . . but when he bent to kiss her again, she pulled away.

"I have to go," she said. "I—I have things to do."

Michael looked almost comically crestfallen. If he was a dog, his ears and his tail would all be drooping. "Tell you what," he said. He bent down and scooped up a handful of shells. "I could ask Maudie—the one with the tomatoes—to sell these at the farmers' market. When you come back—if you come back—I'll give you whatever she makes."

"Well, Maudie should get some of the money, if she's doing the selling," said Diana. "And what about you? Do you want an agent's cut?"

"I'll take an IOU," he said. "You promise to go on a date with me this weekend."

Diana considered. "Deal," she said, and extended her hand. Gravely, Michael shook it, then he pulled her into another bear hug. Diana leaned into his warmth, feeling safer, more at home than she had in a long, long time.

11

Daisy

The morning after she'd met the other Diana, Daisy slept through the night and woke up after seven o'clock, well-rested for the first time in what felt like months. She always slept more soundly when she had a bed to herself. It was as if she was so attuned to Hal's moods and his movements that every time he rolled over or sighed in his sleep, part of her would wake up enough to notice.

She took a long shower in the hotel bathroom, enjoying the selection of bath products. Once she'd checked out, she wheeled her neat suitcase to Petrossian on Fifty-Ninth and Seventh Avenue, where she sat at one of the four tables in the café at the back of the shop. She had smoked salmon eggs Benedict for breakfast and bought a pound of lox to take home before heading to the Pick-a-Bagel across the street. Philadelphia's bagels were just as good as the ones in New York, but there was no telling Vernon Shoemaker that, and woe betide her if she ever came back from the city without his everything bagels. She bought a dozen for Danny and Jesse, another dozen for her father-in-law.

Vernon still lived in the apartment in a retirement community in Bryn Mawr where he'd resided back when Daisy had first met him. Hal had called her, desperate for help, and the following afternoon, Daisy cut her last literature class of the year and drove two and a half hours to Bryn Mawr. Her client had turned out to be a scowling gentleman with pale, watery eyes and the most ridiculously elaborate comb-over she'd ever seen.

"Mr. Shoemaker?" Daisy had said, hand extended. "I'm Diana Rosen." Back then, she'd still been Diana.

Instead of returning her greeting, he'd said, in a querulous tone, "I didn't ask for this."

"Your son hired me," Daisy said.

"Well, I didn't ask him to," Vernon pronounced. "I'm doing fine on my own."

"How about you show me your kitchen?" Daisy suggested. She'd had half a dozen students by then, and was used to being greeted with everything from cheerful enthusiasm to naked desperation, depending on the circumstances. Meanwhile, her new student just looked stubborn and aggrieved.

"Fine," he grumbled, and stepped aside to let her enter.

The condo smelled of furniture polish and, faintly, of unwashed male body, and its rooms were crammed with a Tetris puzzle of furniture, coffee tables and armchairs and love seats and couches and highboys occupying almost every inch of space. An enormous television set was the single new addition to what had clearly been the contents of a Main Line mansion.

The condo had wall-to-wall carpeting, raked with vacuum-cleaner tracks, but Daisy could discern two paths branching away from the recliner. She could picture Vernon Shoemaker sitting in his chair like a king on his throne, leaving only to go to the left, to the kitchen, or to the right, where she guessed there was a bathroom.

In the kitchen, the sink was full of dirty dishes, and the trash can was overflowing, spilling empty cans, packets of soy sauce and mustard, plastic silverware, and more takeout containers onto the sticky-looking floor. "The girl comes Wednesdays," Vernon said with a negligent wave. The dining-room table was piled high with newspapers, magazines, and stacks of what looked like children's clothing. Daisy saw dozens of pairs of pants, shirts, shoes, and sweaters. Vernon saw her looking.

"Gifts," he said. "For my grandchildren." He went to the table and showed her a pile of boys' T-shirts. "I buy 'em on Senior Day at JC Penney. I get the twenty percent coupons from the paper, and *then* I go to the clearance racks, and by the time I'm done . . ." He cackled and pushed the T-shirts toward her. "You see all these? Guess how much. Guess how much I paid?"

"Hmm. Thirty dollars?"

"Twelve dollars and thirty-six cents," Vernon crowed. "They're practically paying me to take the stuff off their hands!"

"That's impressive," Daisy had said, remembering how her own father liked to say that no people were as cheap as rich people.

"See, I get it in all the sizes," Vernon said. "Newborn, and toddler, and . . ." He paused, appearing stumped about what stage of a child's growth might come next. ". . . and what have you." He waved his hand at one stack. "There's birthdays." He pointed at another pile. "That's Christmas."

"How many grandchildren do you have?"

"Two. A boy and a girl. From my older boy." He frowned. "None from Hal yet. He's thirty-two years old and he's still not married." He looked at Daisy, who'd been studying his comb-over in helpless fascination. The man appeared to have exactly one lock of gray hair, which had to be long enough to hang down past his shoulders when it was wet. He'd somehow combed it forward and coaxed it sideways, looping it around, pleating it, origami-style, and managing to cover—more or less—the entirety of his scalp. It was like a geometry problem. Is it possible for Elderly Man X with Y amount of hair to cover Z amount of surface area?

"So?"

Clearly, she'd missed something. "I'm sorry, what did you say?"

Impatiently, Vernon said, "I asked if you think he's a queer. He signed me up for cooking classes. In my day, you know what they called this? Home ec. And you know who did it? Girls." He glared at her indignantly.

Daisy thought of her brother Danny, whom she suspected was gay, even though he'd never said a word to her; Danny, who was charming and funny and ever so slightly wistful. She returned to the kitchen, which beneath layers of trash, had granite counters and a granite breakfast bar, stainless-steel appliances and glass-fronted cabinets. The ample counter space and deep sink were cluttered with empty cartons and bags and more dirty dishes. Daisy went to the sink to wash her hands, hoping to lead by example. "I think the first thing we need to do is get this kitchen up to code."

She expected Vernon to argue with her, or tell her that cleaning, like cooking, was women's work. Instead, he said, "Police this area."

"Sorry?"

"That's what they would tell us. In the army. 'Police this area!' your lieutenant would say, and woe to you if that area was not spotless. You ever heard of the white glove test? Your commanding officer would come and put on a pair of white gloves and run his finger along a shelf or a doorframe or what have you. You'd be on KP duty if he found any dust." Vernon bent down to pull a box of trash bags out from underneath the sink. He was wearing nylon track pants and a plain white T-shirt that hung loosely over his narrow chest and stretched to cover the protuberant curve of his belly. "See, back then, sending a man to work in the kitchen was punishment." His lip curled. "Not a hobby."

Diana located a pair of rubber gloves and pulled them on. "If you bag up the trash, I'll work on the dishes." Most of the dishes in the sink were covered in layers of spaghetti sauce or lo mein noodles. The bowls contained the dried-up detritus of milk and cold cereal. That, plus takeout pizza, seemed to have comprised the bulk of Vernon Shoemaker's diet in the wake of his wife's death. Daisy couldn't see any evidence of fruits or vegetables— not an apple core or a banana peel, or a hint of anything that had ever been green.

She had turned the water on as hot as it would go, added detergent, found a sponge, and started scrubbing as she made a mental list of everything they'd need to do before she felt comfortable enough to start cooking. The floors would need to be swept and mopped, the stovetop and counters sprayed with something disinfecting and scrubbed clean, and the refrigerator . . . God, she didn't even want to think about the refrigerator.

"So you've been eating mostly prepared foods and takeout?"

"You ever go to Wegmans?" Vernon asked. She'd expected him to stand there and watch while she did the work, but, to his credit, he seemed to be doing a decent job of collecting and bagging up the trash. "They've got all kinds of ready-to-go stuff. For the working mothers, I guess." He paused to unfurl another trash bag. "In my day, a mother stayed home with her kids."

"Times have changed," Daisy offered.

"Not for the better," Vernon said darkly. "Okay, chief, what's next?"

She instructed him to find a broom and a dustpan, while she loaded the dishwasher and ran it on its "sterilize" setting. Vernon started sweeping while she looked for some kind of cleanser to spray on the counters.

"Sometimes, I eat out," Vernon said abruptly.

"Oh?"

"Yep. In Atlantic City, or at Foxwoods, I get coupons for the restaurants. I go to the diner." He swept for a few minutes, then said, "Margie—my wife—she'd always want to go to the fancy places. The noodle place and the tappers place and what have you."

"Tappers?"

"You know, the Spanish stuff. Little snacks."

"Oh. Tapas."

"Like I said. She'd wanted that, or the fancy Chinese place. I never understood paying twenty bucks for a plate of noodles with some kind of mystery meat, but it made her happy." He tied a garbage bag shut. "Lots of Asians at the casinos, you know."

"Mmm." Daisy wasn't touching that one. She wondered if Vernon Shoemaker knew that she was Jewish. "Did your wife gamble?"

"Margie? Oh, no." Vernon went silent. Daisy finished wiping the counter closest to the stove. She held her breath and pulled open the refrigerator door, revealing the hellscape she'd expected.

"Can I have a trash bag, please?"

Vernon handed her a bag, peering over her shoulder as she started to toss half-empty packages of lunch meat. "Hey! Hey, that's still good!"

Daisy showed him the package. "It expired three months ago."

Vernon scoffed. "That's a scam. All those expiration dates. It's just companies wanting to get you to buy more food. Someone sent me an article about it."

Daisy unwrapped a block of cheese, revealing a layer of green mold. She showed it to Vernon, who shrugged. "I bet you could just scrape that off."

"You could," she said, and dropped the cheese into the trash. "You won't."

"Fine, fine," Vernon grumbled, as Daisy threw out Chinese-food containers and a desiccated lemon and poured a pint of curdled half-and-half down the drain.

"So what did your wife do in the casinos, if she didn't gamble?"

"Oh, she'd shop. Watch people."

"Did she like to cook?"

The question seemed to leave Vernon nonplussed. He moved the broom back and forth over a patch of floor he'd already swept, looking puzzled. "I don't know," he finally said. "She did it—you know, your steaks and your chops and what have you. Meatloaf. She made a fine meatloaf." He paused, still sweeping. "I don't know if she liked it. She didn't complain."

"Well, I love to cook," said Daisy. "I think it's fun. And can be an expression of creativity. Like art."

"Art," Vernon said, his upper lip curling. "Art that ends up in the crapper the next morning. Pardon my French."

"Preparing a meal," Daisy continued doggedly, "is a way of showing people that you love them. You're showing them you care. You're offering them sustenance."

"Money is sustenance. Food is just food," Vernon said.

"And, for a single person, cooking a nice meal, setting the table, and taking time to eat can be a way of taking care of yourself."

Vernon scowled. "I don't need taking care of." The way his lips twisted made Daisy wonder if his sons had proposed some kind of long-term-care arrangement after his wife had died.

"Hal and Jeremy, they wanted to put me in one of those places," Vernon said. *Bingo*, thought Daisy. " 'Assisted living,' they call it. You start out in a house or an apartment, and six months later you're in an old folks' home. Well, I don't need any assistance. I can look after myself." He gave her a baleful look. "That's why I said it was okay for you to come. I don't want Hal thinking I can't feed myself." Another glare. "I've been getting along fine."

Daisy thought of the rotted Chinese food and the chunky milk and kept her mouth shut.

"What's wrong with takeout?" Vernon demanded.

"It's not the healthiest option."

He pursed his lips, like he was tasting something unpleasant. "At my age, I should worry about health?"

"And," said Daisy, "it's not the most economical. I've read," she said, lying glibly, "that a single person who eats out three or four nights a week can save up to five hundred dollars a month by cooking those meals at home."

That caught Vernon's attention, just the way she'd hoped it would. "Really?"

She put her hand on her heart. "Swear to God."

He sucked his dentures, then sighed. "All right," he said. "Lead on, Macduff. At least it'll get Hal off my back."

Together, they scrubbed the kitchen spotless. She showed him how to operate his coffee maker, and how to set its timer so it would brew coffee for him every morning, and taught him how to make his favorite breakfast of eggs over easy and bacon and his favorite lunch, which was a patty melt, and his favorite dinner, which was steak. She seared his rib eye in a cast-iron pan, and instructed him as he scraped up the browned bits from the bottom of the pan, then added butter and flour and red wine and cranked up the heat to a boil. "Once it's reduced, you can add some fresh herbs and some more butter and you've got a sauce."

"Huh." Vernon didn't exactly look impressed, but he didn't look unimpressed, either. Daisy pulled the potato she'd baked out of the oven, gave a handful of sugar snap peas a quick blanch in boiling salted water, and mounded them on the plate, next to his steak and potato. "See? Doesn't that look nice? You've got to give a plate a little color."

"No," said Vernon, picking up his knife and fork, "you don't."

At the end of the lesson, Daisy gave him the printouts of menus and recipes that she'd brought with her, and the address of a website where he could buy a cast-iron pan. When the lesson was over, he'd said, gruffly, "You're a fine young lady," and pressed a hundred-dollar bill into her hand. Then he'd eyed her carefully, as if she were a horse he was about to bid on at auction. She was ready for him to ask to see her teeth, wondering if he'd proposition her.

"Are you married?" Vernon asked.

Oh, here we go, Daisy thought. Vernon smirked at her.

"Not me. My son. Hal's an attorney." Vernon was already heading to his desk, in search of pen and paper. "I bet he'd love to meet a girl who can cook." He'd handed Daisy a heavy piece of stationery, embossed with his initials, and a phone number written below. "Call him, don't call him. It's up to you."

Daisy hadn't decided whether she'd call or not. It had ended up not mattering either way because that night, Hal had called to thank her. "My dad spoke very highly of you."

"I'm glad to hear it," Daisy said. "I wasn't sure how much he was enjoying it. He was kind of hard to read."

"Hard to read," Hal had repeated, and laughed a little. "That's nicely put. I'm sure he was awful. And I would like to take you to dinner to thank you for putting up with him." Hal's voice was deep, warmer than when he'd first called. "My dad couldn't say enough about how great you were."

"I think he just liked being spoiled a little. Or maybe he misses having a woman around." As soon as she'd spoken, Daisy wondered if it had sounded like a criticism, but she was curious to know what kind of woman Vernon's wife had been; what kind of woman had endured decades of marriage to Vernon Shoemaker and his incredible comb-over.

"All I can tell you is that he was about the happiest I've heard him when he called me."

Hal had come to New Jersey to take her to dinner a few weeks later, when the school year was over, then to a play the following weekend, and to his house the weekend after that, where they'd slept together for the first time. By then, Daisy was madly in love with him, and her mom was madly in love with the idea of having Hal as a son-in-law. Six months later, they'd gotten married . . . and that, Daisy thought, had been that.

From the Trenton train station, it was just twenty minutes by Lyft to the house her brother and his husband shared. Daisy knocked on the door, calling, "I come bearing gifts," and waited until her brother came to take the bagels and usher her inside.

The brick single-story ranch home Danny and Jesse had purchased ten years previously didn't look special from the outside, but inside, thanks to Jesse's eye, and all of the art and keepsakes the couple had collected over the years, the house was as beautiful, and as welcoming, as any home Daisy had ever visited. Gorgeously patterned rugs, in shades of gold and indigo and deep, glowing scarlet, overlapped each other on the floor, in a way that would have looked chaotic if she'd attempted it. Charming assemblages of paintings and tapestries and mirrors and framed photographs covered the walls, and the mantel was decorated with arrangements of dried flowers, Chinese ginger jars and seashells, and a single vintage postcard of Coney Island on a wooden easel. Small paintings of birds on gold-gilt backgrounds hung along one grass cloth–covered wall; the bookshelves that lined the hallway were filled with books, and antique bookends shaped like terriers, and photographs of Jesse and Danny on their travels. Fresh flowers stood on the table in the entryway, along with a bowl full of chestnuts and an antique nutcracker. The air smelled like cinnamon and nutmeg and smoke from the fire that crackled in the fireplace. Daisy could hear classical piano music—Bach, she thought— and could hear Jesse's voice, low and calm, from the kitchen.

"Okay, now we're going to pat it until it looks like a circle. You want to try?"

"Hi, Di," said her brother, and gave her a hug. There was flour on his sweater, and an apron tied around his middle. She hugged him back, smiling. Danny's house was one of her favorite places. When Beatrice had been a toddler, Daisy had worried about bringing her to visit, afraid that she'd break something fragile, or pull the threads of one of the woven tapestries or plant hangers on the walls, but Jesse had put her at ease. "I think children need to learn to live with beautiful things. Besides, there's nothing in this place as precious as you and that sweet baby," he'd told her, and Daisy, her emotions already amplified by her hormones, had turned away so he wouldn't see her crying. In Gladwyne, Hal had made her put anything that Beatrice could possibly get at into a childproofed cabinet or up on a high shelf.

The house was mostly on one story, with three bedrooms. Danny and Jesse shared the largest one. The two others were kept child ready, one with a crib and a changing table and a toddler bed, the other with a set of bunk beds and two twin beds that could be pushed together to accommodate adult couples. Over the years, Danny and Jesse had converted the unfinished attic to a playroom, with a dollhouse and a toddler-sized train. While Danny and Jesse had no children of their own, they provided respite care for foster families, sometimes for an afternoon, sometimes for as long as a few weeks, and they didn't always know when, or for how long, they'd have a child, or children, to care for.

"Daisy, come meet Tasha," Danny said. Daisy followed her brother to the kitchen, where Jesse was peeling apples and a girl with brown curls was standing on a stepstool in front of the counter, carefully patting a disc of plastic-wrapped dough with her palms.

"Hi, Tasha," said Daisy. The girl looked up at her gravely, murmured, " 'lo," and went back to her task. Jesse was already filling the kettle at the sink. "Coffee? Tea?"

"Whatever you guys are having." Danny and Daisy had the same brown hair and hazel eyes, but Daisy had her mother's heart-shaped face, while Danny favored their father. He was short, with his father's delicate features, although he'd gotten rounder since his days as the coxswain. He wore steel-rimmed glasses and was almost entirely bald, with the neatly trimmed goatee he'd grown, as if to compensate, more gray than chestnut brown. Jesse was taller, lithe and graceful, with a dancer's muscled legs and back. His brown skin had golden undertones; his hair was still dark and glossy. He and Danny had met in New York City, where Danny was getting his degree in social work and Jesse was teaching ballet and modern dance in studios around the city, including the Alvin Ailey Theater, where he'd trained, and in whose troupe he'd performed for ten years.

"How long is Tasha here for?" Daisy asked, as Jesse poured scalding water into a marigold-colored ceramic teapot, then shook loose tea leaves inside, and poured more water on top.

"Just until tomorrow night. Her foster parents are at a wedding out of town."

"I wanted to be the flower girl," Tasha announced with a woebegone expression, as Jesse found a lacquered tray, with pressed flowers decoupaged around its edges, and set three mugs, mismatched but somehow harmonious, on top. He added a sugar bowl, a pitcher of cream, linen napkins, and a plate of shortbread cookies. Daisy watched enviously, knowing that, given a half hour to fuss and rearrange, she wouldn't have been able to make the snack look half as good.

"I hope you'll get to be one, someday. My daughter was a flower girl once." Daisy cast her mind back over the years, to a time when Beatrice had still been sweet and accommodating. "I remember we read a book, about a mouse who was a flower girl."

Tasha's eyes got wide. "*Lilly's Big Day!*"

"That's the one."

"Let's get Mr. Pie in the oven, and then we can read it, if you like," said Jesse.

Tasha giggled. "How do you know it's Mr. Pie? Maybe it's Miss Pie!"

"Maybe you're right."

They had their tea and cookies in the living room, by the fire, which crackled behind an antique wrought-iron screen that depicted a forest scene, deer and trees and a bear, lurking from the corner. Tasha selected two picture books from the basket full of them next to the fire, and, once each had been read twice, announced that she was going back to the playroom. "I'm building the tallest LEGO tower in the world," she told Daisy.

Once she was gone, Danny asked, "Have you heard from Judy?"

Daisy smiled at the thought of the Judy Rosen birthday drama, which inevitably commenced at least three months before the blessed event. "She texted me a list of birthday menus two days ago, then a different list yesterday, and then, an hour after that, told me to stick with the first list." Narrowing her eyes, Daisy said, "Which one of you taught her how to text?"

Danny pressed his lips together, while Jesse got busy reloading the tray with their dishes. "Okay, I might have taught her how to text," Danny said. "But Jesse showed her the emojis."

"Not the eggplant," Jesse said. "That one she found all on her own."

"So, how was your trip? How was the show?" Danny asked.

Daisy told them about the show, and about the new friend she'd made, the other Diana. "Good for you," Jesse said. "I know how much you miss Hannah."

"It would be nice to have a friend in town," said Daisy, who'd long since given up on finding a soulmate among the Main Line mommies. Maybe it was the age difference, or how most of them had put aside careers before they had babies—and certainly her husband's pickiness didn't help—but, since Hannah, she hadn't come close to making a real connection.

"A friend in New York isn't bad," Danny said. He smiled as Jesse refilled his mug, but Daisy could see circles under his eyes. His lips were chapped; his beard had new strands of gray. More worrisome was the way his hands trembled as he carried the tray back to the kitchen. She waited, hoping for a moment where she could get Jesse alone, while they chatted about work and Beatrice's return and the trip Jesse and Danny were hoping to take that summer. Finally, in desperation, Daisy said, "Jesse, can you come wait for the Lyft with me? I need to talk to you about something." She winked at her brother, hoping he'd think the conversation was about *his* birthday, and led Jesse outside. As soon as they were in the driveway, she said, "Is Danny okay?"

Jesse sighed. "So you noticed."

"What's going on?"

"I wish I knew. I've been trying to get him to tell me." Jesse pressed his full lips together, raking his hands through his curls. "Ever since February, he's been working nonstop. He stays late after school, every day, and when he's not there, he's at the Boys and Girls Club, and when he's not there he's at the soup kitchen. And I'm all for good deeds, but . . ." He tugged at his hair again, looking at the sky. "It's like he's trying to atone for something. And I have no idea what. And he won't say."

Daisy hoped her shock didn't show on her face. "Do you think that he . . ." She let her voice trail off.

"Cheated?" Jesse gave an inelegant snort. "I can't think when he'd have had the time. No." He put his hand on her shoulder and looked past her, off into the distance. "And when I ask him, he says everything's fine, and I'm worried about nothing. Which is making me feel kind of crazy."

"You're not crazy. I see it, too."

"Maybe you can ask him," Jesse said. "Maybe you'll have better luck."

Daisy wasn't sure about that, but she promised she would try.

12

Daisy

By four o'clock, Daisy was home, greeting Lester, who was wagging his tail and frolicking around her legs with an energy suggesting he'd despaired of her ever returning (and also suggesting that Beatrice, who'd sworn she would walk him, had, instead, only let him out the back door). She was gathering ingredients for dinner when Beatrice came home from school, arrayed in a frilly, puff-sleeved pink blouse, high-waisted jeans, Doc Marten boots, and her typical scowl. Her daughter's blue-tinged hair hung in ringlets, and she'd accessorized with a pair of black velvet gloves and a small hat with a bit of black netting that hung over her eye. It was, Daisy had to admit, quite chic . . . but she knew if she said one kind word, all of it would end up in the back of Beatrice's closet. After the age of fourteen, Beatrice treated Daisy's approval like the worst kind of insult. Meanwhile, Daisy remembered being so desperate for even the tiniest sign of approval from her own mom that she'd taught herself to make puff pastry dough from scratch, the better to prepare homemade spanakopita, which her mom had once enjoyed.

"Hi, sweetheart. How was your day?"

Beatrice shrugged, and muttered, "I must lie down where all the ladders start. In the foul rag and bone shop of the heart."

Daisy stared for a moment. "So . . . bad?"

Beatrice made a rude noise in the back of her throat. "Predictable." She dropped her book bag—not the sturdy JanSport backpack they'd bought her to take to Emlen, but a petit pointe satchel, embroidered with a pattern of forget-me-nots—by the front door, pulled a loaf of brioche out of the refrigerator, and ripped off a chunk.

"Could you use a knife to slice that, please?"

Beatrice made a face, stomped across the kitchen, selected a serrated knife from the block, and, with exaggerated slowness, trimmed the ragged ends off the loaf.

"Did you learn anything interesting?"

Beatrice shrugged.

"What do you think of your new classmates so far?"

"They're rich prepwads. So, basically, just like my old classmates. My life is like an ouroborus. A snake that eats its own tail, forever." Beatrice looked especially moody as she smoothed peanut butter and honey on an inch-thick slab of brioche.

Daisy swallowed the lecture she wanted to deliver about how lucky Beatrice was to attend such a well-regarded school, to have a beautiful home and plenty to eat, to know that college would be paid for and that, once she finished, she would never have to worry about not being able to pay the rent. Beatrice, having lived with those certainties every day of her life, would never understand. Talking to Beatrice about privilege was like trying to explain water to a fish.

"What clubs do you think you'll go out for?" At Emlen, Beatrice had joined the school newspaper and the creative writing club, information that Daisy had gleaned from careful perusal of the school's online newspaper and its Facebook page, because Beatrice would never actually tell her something about her life.

Beatrice gave her another shrug. Daisy turned her gaze away from her daughter and out at the kitchen, remembering the first time she'd seen their house. On their third date, Daisy had taken the train to Philadelphia. Hal had met her at 30th Street Station and driven her out to Gladwyne, along streets of rolling green lawns and houses that looked more like estates. He'd pulled up the driveway of a stately Colonial, with a white exterior and black shutters, a sloping lawn that looked the size of a soccer field, and a bright-red front door.

"This is me," he'd said. Certainly in size the house matched the one Daisy had lived in, before her father's death. But that house, with its wraparound porch and the eyebrow windows that accented the third floor, seemed, somehow, to have a friendly, welcoming character, the fun uncle who'd let you have a sip of his beer at Thanksgiving and slip you twenty dollars on your way out the door. This house felt more like a forbidding grandmother, one who'd frown at your outfit and tell you that you didn't need that second helping of stuffing.

Hal led her through an empty foyer, past an empty living room, and into an almost-empty kitchen, where he paused to put the two bottles of seltzer he'd purchased into an almost-empty refrigerator (Daisy glimpsed condiments, lemons, and half of a hoagie in a clear plastic clamshell).

Daisy turned in a slow circle that gave her views of the almost-empty living room and dining room. "Were you robbed?"

Hal looked puzzled. Then he smiled. "This is the house I grew up in. When my father moved, he took all the furniture with him. You may recall," Hal said dryly, "that his place felt cramped?"

Daisy nodded, remembering.

"I just haven't had time to shop for anything new."

"I understand." Daisy was studying a framed black-and-white portrait hanging on the wallpapered wall of the entryway. A man in an army dress uniform stood stiffly, his arm around the waist of a woman in a white dress.

"Your parents?" Vernon was handsome without his comb-over. The woman had long, dark hair and an easy smile. Instead of a veil, she wore a wreath of flowers in her hair. Daisy remembered what Vernon had said about his wife—that she'd liked people-watching, that she hadn't liked to gamble, that he didn't know how she'd felt about cooking. "What was your mom like?"

Hal shrugged. "She and my father had high expectations for me and my brother. I'm grateful now, of course, but when I was younger . . ."

Daisy studied the picture again. She was thinking of her own father's delight in his sons' accomplishments, how he'd brag to everyone about their grades, or David's skill at baseball, or how Danny had been picked as the coxswain of the senior boys' eight ("he's the one who steers the boat," Jack had explained to his own mother, who'd looked perplexed, perhaps at the notion of steering being an athletic endeavor). Had Vernon and Margie been proud of their sons? Or had they been the kind of parents for whom anything less than perfection was a disappointment?

Hal put his hand on the small of her back and ushered her through the French doors, out into an expansive backyard that held an inground pool, a Weber grill on a flagstone patio, and a single lawn chair.

"When did you move in?" Daisy had asked.

"About a year ago," he said, as he'd fiddled with the grill's knobs. "I'd been living in Center City, but most of the partners live in the suburbs. Easier to get to the golf courses."

"Got it," Daisy murmured.

"I figured I'd be buying a house here eventually, so when my dad was moving out, it just made sense to take over this one."

Daisy nodded again. It made sense, and even if part of her wondered why Hal hadn't wanted his own place, she also thought that if someone had offered her the house she'd grown up in, she'd have taken it in an instant.

Back inside, she was relieved to discover that the kitchen was clean enough to perform surgery. There was no trash piled up in the trash can, no dirty dishes on the counters or in the sink. This, it emerged, was the happy result of Hal having hardly any dishes at all. When she'd opened the freezer she'd seen stacks of frozen Hungry Man dinners, and, in the cabinet closest to the sink, there'd been rows and rows of canned Campbell's Chunky soup. There were two bowls, three plates, and two juice glasses in one cabinet; the drainer next to the sink held a single pot.

Hal had come into the kitchen just as she'd closed the drawer on his paltry supply of silverware.

"Do you just eat the soup out of the pot?" she'd asked.

"It's efficient," he'd said, holding her so that his chest pressed against her back. Daisy appreciated his assurance, the way there wasn't any awkward fumbling or hesitation. "Also, better for the environment."

"Oh, so you're an environmentalist."

"I'm a thoughtful guy," he'd said, nuzzling her temples, making her shiver. Then, almost as if he'd been waiting for a sign, he'd turned her around and pulled her against him, so they were thigh to thigh and chest to chest. "I'm just doing things out of order," he'd said. "Most guys find the right woman, then the right house. I got the house first. And now," he said, kissing her temple, then her neck, "I need you to make my house a home."

"Oh my God," Daisy had groaned. "That's a terrible line!" But she could already feel the voices of her roommates receding, the warnings they'd given her—*what does a guy that old want with someone our age?*—subsiding. Hal was mature enough to know what he wanted and confident enough to get it. When he pulled her close, murmuring, "I just want to be a good man. A good husband and father," she decided that she was lucky that he'd decided he wanted her.

She'd registered for all the kitchen basics that Hal had never acquired, and he'd told her to buy whatever she thought the house needed, from carpets and couches to dishes and glassware, outdoor furniture for the backyard, art for the walls, and everything she wanted for the kitchen. She'd made missteps at first—she still cringed when she thought of the first party she'd held, for a few of the firm's other lawyers and their spouses. Hal had said, "It'll just be casual. Just buy stuff to throw on the grill," but Daisy had prepared for weeks. She'd gotten the butcher to grind a mixture of filet mignon and chuck steak for the burgers, and had blended in mushrooms and blue cheese; she'd ordered hot dogs from Chicago, which came delivered in a cooler of dry ice. She'd made her own barbecue sauce, plus dozens of elaborate canapés, slivers of smoked salmon on cucumbers and a refined version of onion dip, where she spent an hour caramelizing onions. The day of the event, she'd gotten her nails done, and donned a brand-new Lilly Pulitzer sundress and Tory Burch flip-flops in a complementary shade of hot pink.

The party had not been a success. The guests had nibbled at the appetizers, praising the food to the heavens—"You're so creative!" "You have to give me the recipe for this!"—but the only thing they'd eaten with any enthusiasm were the hot dogs. Her smoked salmon was ignored; her fancy dip, barely sampled; and the burgers had come back untouched. "Because not everyone likes blue cheese!" Hal said. He wasn't yelling, but his voice was clipped in a way that suggested he wanted to yell. "I told you, Daisy. I told you, just get regular burgers, and regular hot dogs, and make regular onion dip from the Lipton soup mix, like everyone else does . . ."

"I don't want to be like everyone else!" Daisy hated her war-bling voice; hated that she was practically crying. Her party had been a failure, and she suspected that all the couples were talking about it on their way home—how desperately hard she'd tried, how pathetically eager to please she'd been. "This is what I do, Hal. I cook. I'm not a lawyer, or a psychologist, or an art therapist, I don't do global outreach for Penn. I don't even have a college degree!" The other women had been polite about it; nobody had gone out of their way to make her feel bad. Daisy had been per-fectly capable of doing that all on her own.

"It's fine," Hal had said, his voice remote. "You'll learn."

She had. "They're stupid white people," Hannah would tell her, usually through a mouthful of whatever dish Daisy was cooking.

"You're a white person," Daisy would tell her, and Hannah would say, "But, hopefully, not a stupid one." Hannah, like Hal, had grown up in a household where salt and pepper were the only seasonings, but she loved all kinds of food, the spicier, the better. "Fuck 'em if they can't appreciate you."

Daisy looked around her kitchen, at Beatrice, gobbling pea-nut butter, and the sunlight, streaming through the window over the sink. She'd gotten the kitchen of her dreams: a six-burner stove, imported from England, with navy-blue trim and gold-toned hardware. A deep, expansive farmhouse sink; new cherry-wood cabinets, a new backsplash, tiled in shades of cream and gold and celery green. She'd ripped up the old granite counters and replaced them with limestone, with an inset made of butcher block, for chopping, and another made of marble, which stayed cool when she was rolling out pastry. In one corner was a dining nook, with built-in benches on two sides, and in the middle of the room was Daisy's very favorite thing: an enormous fieldstone fireplace that opened to the kitchen on one side and the den on the other.

Hal had been away a lot the year of renovations, overseeing a trial in Virginia and another in Florida. Daisy sometimes suspected that the kitchen was a kind of apology–cum–consolation prize, a way for Hal to say sorry for his absence, and how she'd been the only one at school concerts and parent-teacher conferences and at Bea's soccer games, where the girls would run up and down the field in a cluster, kicking each other more often than the ball and hardly ever scoring. Sometimes, she suspected that maybe there was something else Hal was apologizing for— something that might have happened when he'd been out of town. But she'd never asked, and he'd never volunteered. *On such silences are marriages built*, she'd told herself at the time. Certainly she'd never seen her own mother evince any interest in her dad's business trips. And the kitchen was undeniably gorgeous. She kept her eyes on the skylight and tried not to sigh as Beatrice clomped over to the freezer and started rummaging around.

"Have you seen my mice?" she asked.

Daisy was certain she'd misheard. "What?"

"My mice," Beatrice said impatiently. "They were right here, on the top shelf, behind the pie crust."

Daisy looked at her daughter, who stared back at her calmly, as if she'd asked her mom for a glass of milk or a ride to the mall. "Beatrice," Daisy said, her voice faint. "Please tell me you haven't been keeping dead mice in the freezer."

"Why not?" Beatrice asked, shrugging. "They're, like, double-bagged. They're not touching anything."

"I don't care!" Daisy said. Or, rather, screamed. "I don't want dead rodents in my freezer, near food that you and I and your father are eating! Food that I'm feeding other people, who are paying me to learn how to cook! Jesus, Beatrice, what if someone got sick?"

"How are dead mice any different than dead chickens? Or

dead lambs, or dead cow?" Beatrice yelled back. "You're a hypocrite."

"Well, I'm also the adult. This is my house."

"Like you paid for it," Beatrice sneered. "Like either one of you did."

Daisy made herself ignore the jab, choosing instead to be grateful that Beatrice said it to her. God knows how Hal would have reacted to the idea that there was something in his life he hadn't earned—and, even if he had given his brother money amounting to what Jeremy might have realized from the sale, paying for half of this house had been significantly easier than paying for all of it. "When I tell you that you cannot keep your mice in my freezer, I expect you to have the courtesy to respect my wishes."

"So where am I supposed to keep them?" Beatrice asked, eyebrows lifted. "Do you want me to buy a completely separate freezer for a few mice?"

"Well, ideally," Daisy snapped, "I would like for you to have a hobby that doesn't involve dead rodents. But seeing as how you're not going to do something normal, like join the school paper or the choir, I would like for you to find somewhere other than my freezer for your mice."

Beatrice's lower lip trembled, her eyes welled with tears. "Well, jeez. I'm sorry that I'm not the *normal* daughter you wanted," she said.

Instantly, Daisy went from feeling furious to feeling sad, and deeply ashamed for making her daughter doubt herself, for making her cry. Beatrice turned and stormed out of the kitchen. "Wait," Daisy called. "Wait, Bea, you know that's not what I meant!"

"Yes, it is," said Beatrice. "I'm not the kind of daughter you ever wanted."

Daisy swallowed down the bitter taste of guilt, because hadn't she said something very close to that, in New York, when she'd been with Diana? "Trixie . . ."

"Don't call me that!" Beatrice shouted. Before Daisy could apologize, she said, "I'm sorry I'm such a disappointment," and ran up the stairs to her room.

Daisy's shoulders slumped, and the pleasant anticipation she'd been feeling in advance of preparing dinner disappeared. She plodded to the freezer, emptying the shelves one after another, removing pie crusts, the containers of chili and lentil soup and chicken and dumplings that she'd made and frozen, the pints of ice cream and the bags of frozen peas and corn and cranberries and the chicken fingers she'd kept as a kind of break-glass-in-case-of-emergency dinner for her daughter. Wedged into a corner of the top shelf, she found a plastic Ziploc bag containing six tiny gray frost-stiffened mouse corpses. She considered them a minute, her breath condensing on the icy plastic. How had Beatrice turned into a girl who played with dead mice and despised her mother? What had Daisy done to cause this, and how would the world treat Beatrice when she was an adult?

Slowly, Daisy put the mice back and surveyed Beatrice's leavings: the uncapped jar of peanut butter, the unwrapped loaf of bread, the open jar of honey, the sticky knife and the crumbs all over the counter. She refilled the freezer, cleaned up the mess, and finally got started on dinner. Cooking always soothed her, and she thought that it would help. She seasoned the pork roast that she'd thawed before her trip. She peeled russet potatoes, sliced them thin, and fanned them out around a buttered baking dish, layering in pats of cold butter and sprigs of thyme, sprinkling Parmesan cheese on top. The pork and potatoes were both in the oven, the table was set, and she was whisking vinaigrette when Hal came home.

"Birdie!" Hal usually sounded cheerful at the end of the

workday, although Daisy was never sure whether it was because she'd turned their home into such a cozy and welcoming respite, or if it was just that the law firm was so awful. "How was your trip?"

"It was fine." She thought her tone and slumped shoulders would give him a hint that something was wrong, but Hal just set his briefcase down and started flipping through the mail.

"How was the funeral?"

Hal's lips pressed tightly together. "Sad," he said. His tone did not invite additional questions. Hal opened his arms to deliver a perfunctory hug, but she pushed herself against him, resting her head on his chest, feeling his shirt under her cheek. He was down to his last three white ones. She reminded herself to stop by the dry cleaner's in the morning.

Hal gave her arms a quick squeeze, and took a sniff. "Dinner smells great."

"Hal, do you think . . ." She waited until he was looking at her, then she said, all in a rush, "Do you think Bea needs a psychologist?"

"What now?" Hal asked. It was the right question, but he asked it in that clipped, I-don't-really-want-to-hear-about-it tone.

Daisy shook her head, imagining what would happen if she told Hal about the mice in the freezer. "Just the usual awfulness."

He looked down at her, and, when he spoke, his voice was indulgent. "She's a teenager. You know what I say—kids get a pass on stuff they do before they turn twenty-one." Which was, Daisy thought, a version of his *boys will be boys* speech. He stepped away from her, loosening his tie, turning to the refrigerator and pulling out a can of seltzer.

"That's what Diana said."

"Who?"

Daisy opened the freezer, handed him a chilled mug, and went back to the counter and the salad dressing. Sometimes, she thought he saw her as just another fixture in the kitchen, another useful appliance, like the toaster oven that reheated his pizza or the blender that whipped up his smoothies. "Diana. The woman I met in New York last night. The one with my email address?"

"Oh, right, right. How was she?"

"She was nice," said Daisy. She didn't want to talk too much; didn't want to jinx what she hoped might blossom into a real friendship.

"Good for you." Hal hung his suit jacket on the back of his chair at the kitchen table and picked up the *Wall Street Journal*. Daisy pulled a block of tofu from the refrigerator and set it beneath a can of beans to drain, in case tonight was one of the nights Beatrice decided that she was a vegetarian and got offended if no one remembered. She whisked soy sauce and rice wine vinegar and maple syrup together, to make a sauce for the tofu, and had just added sesame oil to her cast-iron pan when her phone buzzed. It was an email from Diana. "INCOMING," read the subject line. Daisy clicked it open and read, "Guess who's coming to Philadelphia!!! I've got a contract with Quaker Pharmaceuticals. Moving to Philly for the next three months! Any chance you can give me cooking lessons?" She'd added a smiling emoji, and one for a loaf of bread.

Daisy felt her cheeks stretch in a smile. Instead of writing back, she hit the CALL NUMBER button. A moment later, Diana's voice was in her ear.

"Can you believe it? What a crazy coincidence!"

"I'm so glad," Daisy said. And it was true. She might have a difficult daughter, but now, at least, she had a potential ally. "Where are you staying?"

"Um . . . hang on. Rittenhouse Square? Does that mean any-thing to you? The company's got an apartment there."

"Yes. It's a great neighborhood. Lots of good restaurants."

"Which brings me to my next question. I wanted to ask . . ." Diana sounded almost shy. "After we met, I got to thinking. And it's kind of ridiculous that I'm almost fifty years old and I can't even make grilled cheese. I don't know how busy you are . . ."

"I'll make time," Daisy promised. "When do you get here?"

"Next week."

"So soon?"

"Yeah, they keep me moving. No rest for the wicked. I'm like a shark. I've got to swim or die."

"Well, just tell me when you want me."

"I'll text you as soon as I'm settled."

Daisy felt light as a balloon as she moved through the kitchen. The potatoes came out perfectly, crisped and golden on top, soft and buttery-tender in the middle. When Beatrice came down the stairs, dressed in sweatpants and a T-shirt illustrated with a raccoon and the legend TRASH PANDA, Daisy made herself smile pleasantly.

"I made you tofu."

"Why?" Beatrice glared at the caramelized squares as if they had insulted her.

"Never mind," Daisy murmured, imagining she could hear her husband's thoughts: *Why do you keep making her tofu if it's just going to end up in the trash?* She served her husband and her daughter pork roast, and used the spatula to put the tofu on her plate. Bea ignored the salad, and Hal took all the crispiest bits of the potatoes. When dinner was over, Hal said, "Delicious, dear," and drifted away to his office. Beatrice, meanwhile, just vanished, as if she'd been raptured, leaving Daisy to clear the table, wipe down the counters, put away the leftovers, do the dishes, and sweep the kitchen floor. She found herself whistling while she did it, scraping table scraps into the trash can and sweeping the floor, wondering if Hannah Magee was somewhere, looking down on her; if Hannah knew that she'd made a new friend.

13

Beatrice

C block was just getting out when a guy suddenly appeared at Beatrice's side as she walked out into the hallway.

"Hey!" he said, with a smile that showed his teeth. "You're new!"

"I am." If Beatrice wasn't mistaken, he was one of the guys who'd been snickering at her clothes the week before.

"I'm Cade Langley."

"Ugh, why?" she said, before she could stop herself, if she'd cared to try.

At first, Cade looked confused. Then he laughed. He was wearing pressed khakis, a blue sweater, boat shoes, and that big, toothy smile, and he had the kind of skin that seemed permanently flushed, in an outdoorsy, windburned way. Beatrice herself was wearing a black lace skirt, a black jersey top, and a black lace-up faux leather bustier that she'd pulled on after her mom had dropped her off, and she thought she could feel the boy looking her over, checking her out.

"Can I help you with something?" she asked as they made the turn into the cafeteria. She could see Doff, waving from a table in the corner. For the past week, Beatrice had been sitting with Doff and her friends. There was Mina, president of the Speculative Fiction Club, in a truly spectacular pair of rainbow leg warmers. Beside her, Austen, who ran the school's gay/straight alliance, wore a jacket covered from lapel to hem with pins that bore slogans or advertised affiliations or, in one case, said WORLD'S BEST MOM. *The misfit toys*, they called themselves, and Beatrice had fit right in, had known she was at home the first lunch period she'd spent with them.

Cade appeared taken aback by Beatrice's directness. He was probably used to girls falling all over themselves if he even looked their way, she thought. "I wanted to see if you wanted to sit with us at lunch." He nodded toward a table filled with boys dressed just like him, and girls in jeans and fancy boots and cashmere sweaters. Probably the stuff Beatrice's mother wished that she'd wear.

Beatrice looked over at Doff, who was staring, with her mouth slightly open. When Beatrice widened her eyes, hoping her expression communicated the question, Doff gave her a big thumbs-up and a nod so enthusiastic Beatrice worried about her vertebrae.

Shrugging, Beatrice pulled out a chair at Cade's table, where she was introduced to Donovan, Ian, Ezra, and Finn, and Lila, Lily, and Julia. Ezra was Black, and Julia was Korean, but if you only looked at clothing and attitudes, the kids at the table could have been siblings, all of them from the same rich family, the girls with the same hairstyle and makeup, the boys with the same clothes. This was the school's top social tier, the kids who terrorized the underclassmen and could ruin their classmates with a single word on Snapchat or a lone Finstagram post.

Beatrice felt uneasy as Cade, with a flourish, pulled out a chair at the round table, then took the seat beside her. Beatrice opened her zippered lunch case and removed the elements of her meal: sliced peppers and carrots, water crackers, and a small container of hummus. She didn't think much of her mom these days; she thought that she was timid and uninteresting, but still, Beatrice had to admit that her mom could tear it up in the kitchen.

The other kids eyed her lunch with interest, especially when she pulled out a wedge of banana bread. The boys were all eating pizza, the girls picked at salads, and Cade, who'd bought a cheeseburger from the hot food line.

Beatrice ate quietly, listening as Lila, or possibly Lily, described a party she'd attended the previous weekend. "It was MacKenna Kelso's house, and she said only seniors were invited, except some idiot freshpeople must've snuck in through the garage."

"No bueno," said Ezra, uncapping an energy drink.

"So one of them, this girl named Sharzad, like, climbed on the Ping-Pong table," Lila/Lily continued, "and it collapsed underneath her. So Sharzad goes, like, crashing to the ground, and then MacKenna sees them, and she's like, 'What are you assholes doing here?' So they start running, and half the boys go racing after them. It was epic." Lila/Lily smirked, ate a forkful of salad, and turned to Beatrice.

"You went to boarding school, right?" She waited for Beatrice's nod, then looked Beatrice's outfit over with a slow up and down. "Did they have a dress code there?"

"You just had to dress neatly. No crop tops, no shirts with political slogans. Other than that, you could wear what you wanted."

"Lucky," the other girl said with a sigh. "God, I'd give anything if I didn't have to live with my parents." She leaned closer to Beatrice, her blue eyes wide. "Could you like, do anything? Stay up all night? Have parties?"

"Um, we had dorm supervisors. So no, not really. I mean, kids did sneak out sometimes . . ."

Lily/Lila sighed, as if Beatrice was describing paradise, and not forays to drink warm vodka in the laundry room, or outside, if it was warm enough (between October and March in New Hampshire, she'd learned, it was hardly ever warm enough). "You could get expelled if you got caught."

Julia cut her eyes at Cade, who gave her a blank look before turning to Beatrice with his toothy Kennedy smile.

"So why'd you leave?"

"I got kicked out," Beatrice said, after she'd chewed and swallowed her cracker. That got the table's attention. All the girls were looking at her. Cade pulled back his chair for a better view. Even Ezra had put down his energy drink.

"Really?" asked Finn.

"What'd you do?" asked the girl who was either Lila or Lily.

Beatrice swiped her tongue over her front teeth to remove any traces of food. She could lie, and say that her expulsion had something to do with drinking or drugs or boys, and probably impress these kids. But she didn't think that these were kids she wanted to impress, so she said, "Part of it was that I was running an Etsy shop. I do a lot of crafting—crochet and needle-felting, mostly—and I was spending more time doing that and not"—she hooked her fingers into air quotes—" 'focusing on my academics.'"

"How much money were you making, doing that?"

"Oh, like four or five hundred dollars a month. It depended on how much work I took on." She pulled out her phone to show a few of the dogs she'd sculpted. "That's so cool!" said Lily or Lila, and Finn asked, "You get a hundred dollars for each one you make?"

"Sometimes more."

Finn looked impressed. Then Julia tossed her hair and said, "You guys remember Kenzie Dawes? Well, she makes bank on Instagram. She gets, like, older guys to tell her things to say to them, and then she says it. She doesn't, like, take her clothes off or anything. She just whispers stuff. 'You're my daddy,' or whatever, and they Venmo her, like, fifty bucks."

The other girls murmured approval at Kenzie's ingenuity. Beatrice felt herself scowling. She took a bite of carrot, chewed, swallowed, and said, "Another reason I got expelled was that two of my friends and I painted the word 'rapist' on a boy's door."

The table went very quiet. Julia's face was flushed, and the girl who was either Lily or Lila was glaring at her. "Why?" asked Finn.

Beatrice stared at him. "Because," she said, speaking slowly, "he raped one of my friends. And the school didn't do anything about it."

Julia nudged Cade, giving Cade a meaningful look, one that Beatrice couldn't read. But Cade's toothy smile was firmly in place when he turned to Beatrice.

"So you're an activist."

Beatrice patted her lips with a paper napkin. Looking right at Cade, and only at Cade, she said, "I think it's important to do the right thing." If this boy was really, actually interested in her, it was better that he knew who she was and what she believed in, right up front.

Cade looked impressed. But the girls, and most of the guys, all seemed to be varying degrees of shocked. Ezra and Finn both looked angry. Lily and Lila were whispering to each other, and Julia was glaring at Beatrice with unmitigated hostility.

"What?" Beatrice finally asked.

"I have a brother," said Julia, as if that was all the explanation required.

Beatrice shrugged. "Well, as long as he doesn't rape anyone, I won't spray-paint anything on his door."

"What if some girl just says that he did?" Julia asked. She turned to the other boys in appeal. "That's all it takes, these days, right? Some girl makes an accusation, and then the boy's guilty until proven innocent."

Beatrice made herself take a breath before she spoke. She kept her voice mild. "I don't think it's something girls lie about."

Cade clapped his hands. The color in his cheeks seemed, to Beatrice, even more pronounced than it had been at the start of the lunch period. She wondered what he was thinking, if he was flustered, or embarrassed. She wondered, again, what she was doing there, when he said, "Hey, how about we change the subject?" He turned toward Beatrice, and ran his hand through his dark hair. "A bunch of us are going to the movies Friday night. Want to come?"

"I don't get it," Beatrice told Doff after school as they sat on the steps in front of the school. Doff's fine blonde hair was drawn up into a ponytail, and she was using her tongue to push her mouth guard in and out of her mouth.

"You're the new girl," Doff said, as if this was totally obvious. "Most of the kids here have known each other since kindergarten. When Lily got here freshman year, it was like a movie star showed up."

Beatrice shook her head. "There's no way he actually likes me." Still, there was that prickle of excitement, a buzzing sensation at her knees and the small of her back. The smooth, handsome rich boy falling for the artsy girl from the wrong side of the tracks—or, in her case, the girl who just looked like she was from the wrong side of the tracks—that was the kind of thing that happened in old movies, the kind her mother watched. From her limited experience, it never happened in real life. Things that happened in real life were like what had been done to her friend Tricia, back at Emlen. She could still remember Colin Mackenzie sitting down next to them, at Chapel, putting his arm around Tricia and having the nerve to look confused when she shoved him away. She'd known then that nothing would happen to Colin. He'd just say he'd gotten mixed messages, or that he'd been confused, and he'd get to stay, and Tricia, who was on scholarship, would get sent home.

"Invite him to poetry club," Doff said with a smirk. "See if he asks you to take a look at his Emily Dickinson."

Beatrice snorted. "How long did it take you to think that up?"

"Most of lunch, and the rest of G block," Doff said, shrugging modestly. "I started with 'read his Charles Dickens,' but Charles Dickens is a novelist."

"What about his Philip K. Dick?"

"Who's that?" asked Doff.

"He wrote the book that got turned into *Blade Runner*."

"Ah." Doff pulled on her shin guards. "Do you like him?"

"Who, Philip K. Dick?"

"No, dummy. Cade!"

Beatrice considered. Cade looked like the worst kind of boy who ended up at places like Emlen, or Melville: preppy and privileged, entitled and swaggering. Once, at one of her mom's annual clam bakes on Cape Cod, she'd overheard her uncle Danny telling Uncle Jesse about someone he'd known at Emlen, someone he and his husband had run into at the Provincetown airport: *He's always been one of those born-on-third-base-and-thinks-he-hit-a-triple types.* That saying fit most of the boys she'd met there to a T. They thought they'd gotten where they were: at Emlen, on their way to Williams or Princeton or Yale, with nice clothes and straight teeth, because of how hard they'd worked, and not primarily because, as Tricia used to say, they were lifetime members of the Lucky Sperm Club.

Cade was yet another member of that club. But still, there'd been a moment when Cade, with his flushed cheeks, had looked at her, and his cheesy smile had fallen away, and she'd thought that maybe there was something there, something that wasn't detestable, a boy she could actually like. There was also the social capital an association with a boy like that could guarantee. If she had a popular jock boyfriend, it wouldn't matter what she wore, or if she said weird, abrupt things, or had absolutely no desire to get into a top-tier college. She would belong at Melville, her position secure. Her mother would approve. Not that she cared, one way or the other, only it might be nice to see something besides the frown that seemed to have established permanent residence on her mother's face since she'd come home.

"I don't know if I like him," Beatrice said to her friend. "Does it matter?"

"Not really," said Doff. "If he likes you, though. That matters. Gotta go," she said, and jogged off toward the Lower Field.

14

Daisy

If Diana Starling had only looked mostly like what Daisy had imagined, her apartment in Rittenhouse Square was exactly what Daisy had pictured: bright and airy and modern, on the top floor in an expensive new building, with enormous glass windows facing north and east, to give her views of manicured lawns and flower beds and the fountains of Rittenhouse Square Park, and beyond it, the grid of the city, narrow streets lined with brick row houses, and, finally, the Delaware River.

Diana hugged her at the door. Daisy felt the warmth of the other, taller woman's arms, and smelled her musky-sweet perfume. "Come on in!" Diana took her arm, smiling. "I'll give you the tour." Diana was dressed casually, in dark-rinse jeans and a crisp white button-down shirt, with her hair hanging in shiny waves and her short, oval nails polished pink. A fine gold necklace with a diamond pendant hung at her neck, matching the diamond stud earrings she'd worn the night they'd met. Her magenta suede flats with gold buckles were the most colorful thing in the place, which was done in cream and beige, with the occasional daring foray into peach and pale gold.

Daisy held her breath as she turned the corner, but it turned out she didn't have to worry. The kitchen was all stainless steel and black granite, with glass-fronted cabinets, and a wine refrigerator. There was a good set of German knives on the counter, a new Cuisinart, and, thank goodness, a stand mixer, which meant Daisy wouldn't have to haul hers along when they started making breads and pastries.

"It's beautiful," said Daisy.

"Well, it's better than what I'd expected. I've been in places where there's, like, a microwave and a bar sink." At Daisy's expression, Diana shrugged. "Mostly men do this kind of work, and they're either eating out, with the clients, or ordering in. Which . . ." She held up her hands with a self-deprecating smile. ". . . not gonna lie, is what I normally do."

"You don't need to learn to cook," Daisy said. She nodded at the window. "I mean, you're right across the street from Parc, and they make the best roast chicken in the world, and they also have this amazing walnut-cranberry bread. If I lived here, I'd probably eat there all the time."

"Oh, no!" Diana put her hand on Daisy's forearm, looking right into her eyes. "I one hundred percent want to do this. I've been thinking about what you said. About how cooking's like a meditation." She gave a small, wry smile. "Well. I could use some Zen these days. This job is going to be a bear. The firm's stuck in R and D with this new breast-cancer drug. They're going round and round with the FDA, and meanwhile, the marketing people don't have anything to do."

"Well, as long as you're sure . . ." Daisy handed Diana an apron and set her bags on the counter. "I thought we'd start with an easy dinner. Roast chicken, risotto, green vegetable. You can cut it in half, if it's just for you; you can double or triple it to feed a crowd. It looks impressive, and it's super flexible."

"And easy?" asked Diana, who sounded a little nervous as she regarded the uncooked chicken. "Like, foolproof?"

"Easy," Daisy said. "I promise." She could tell that Diana would be her favorite kind of client: willing, motivated, eager to learn. She had already tied on her apron and started tapping notes into her phone as Daisy laid out the ingredients: a whole kosher chicken; a bottle of olive oil, a pound of butter, a lemon. Onions, garlic, shallots, shiitake mushrooms, Parmesan cheese, and a container of arborio rice; fresh rosemary and thyme, a bag of carrots, a half-pound of asparagus, and a half-pound of sugar snap peas. That was for dinner. For pantry staples, she'd gotten flour, white and brown sugar, kosher salt and Maldon salt, pepper, chili, and paprika; for the refrigerator: milk, eggs, and half-and-half, and, for a housewarming gift, a copy of Ruth Reichl's *My Kitchen Year* and two quarts of her own homemade chicken stock.

"You're going to do great," Daisy said as she washed her hands. "Anyone who wants to learn how to do this is a person I'm happy to teach."

"Do you ever end up with people who don't want to learn?" Diana asked.

"Only all the time. There are the college kids whose parents gift them my services. They don't always see the point of cooking when they can order any food ever invented on their phones and get it in twenty minutes, and they're more than happy to share that opinion." She could still remember her last such assignment, a girl who'd brandished her phone in Daisy's face, saying, *Like, hello? Grubhub? DoorDash? Uber Eats? Why do I even need to learn this?* "College kids are bad. Widowers who've never cooked and are angry that their wives had the nerve to die on them are bad." Daisy told Diana the story of the older gentleman who'd quit on her, mid-lesson, shouting, "She was supposed to be here to take care of me! That was our deal!" before leaning over the counter to clutch the food processor as he'd cried.

Diana shook her head. "I can't even imagine what my mom would've done to my dad if he'd ever said something like that."

"Hah. Maybe someday you'll meet my father-in-law. He acts like it's a woman's job to handle anything related to the kitchen, up to and including getting him a glass of water." Even after their cooking lessons, even after she'd become his daughter-in-law, Vernon Shoemaker would summon Daisy to the kitchen from the den or the bedroom and wave his empty coffee cup, not even bothering to verbalize the request, let alone slap a "please" on the end of it. "I'm sure Hal can help you," Daisy had learned to say.

"What about your husband?" Diana asked. "Does he think it's your job to get his coffee?"

Daisy closed her lips on her first answer, a reflexive, "Absolutely not." Hal would never say that it was her job to take care of him—at least, not out loud—but she couldn't ignore the way that their lives broke down along gendered lines, with Hal as the provider and Daisy in charge of child and home. He went out to conquer the world while she made a nest for him to land in, and she liked it that way. At least, most of the time. "Hal isn't much of a cook," she said, answering carefully. "But he's good on clean-up." *When he doesn't disappear.* "Let's see what you've got for pots and pans."

In addition to the knives and the mixer, there was a deep roasting pan with a removable rack; pots from extra-large to extra-small, cutting boards and graters, a garlic press and a lemon reamer and even a cast-iron pan—unseasoned, but better than nothing. Daisy set out what they'd need for the chicken: a stick of butter and the herbs, lemons and garlic, onions and carrots.

"This is a no-fail, can't-miss recipe. Unless you forget it's in the oven, it's almost impossible to ruin."

"There's a first time for everything," Diana muttered, but she rolled up her sleeves and followed Daisy's instructions. Daisy had her preheat the oven, remove the chicken from its plastic, rinse it, and pat it dry. "Dry skin is crispy skin," Daisy said, encouraging Diana to blot the chicken skin until there was no moisture remaining. "Some recipes have you leave the chicken in the refrigerator, uncovered, for the moisture to evaporate from the skin. Some chefs even use a blow-dryer on the skin."

Diana looked at her skeptically. "You're kidding, right?"

"Hand to God," said Daisy. "It probably looks ridiculous, but I'm sure it works."

Daisy showed Diana how to rock the flat side of her knife against a garlic clove to loosen its skin. She had her season the bird with lots of kosher salt and fresh-ground pepper, and mix chopped herbs and garlic into the softened butter, then loosen the chicken's skin and work the butter underneath. Some people got squeamish at touching gizzards or raw meat, and Daisy was relieved when her student managed it unflinchingly, poking carefully, almost apologetically underneath the chicken's skin. "You're a natural," Daisy said, and Diana scoffed, looking pleased.

Diana asked Daisy how far away she lived, and about nearby grocery stores, and told her that she'd already found two bookstores and the La Colombe coffee shop on Nineteenth Street.

"How's your daughter?" she asked, after Daisy had her stuff a lemon and some onions into the bird's cavity, and showed her how to truss the bird's legs with twine.

"Oh, Lord," Daisy sighed. She gave Diana the brief version of the mice-in-the-freezer fight. "It's not that I was actually worried the mice were going to contaminate our food. It's more of the principle of the thing."

Diana nodded. "She invaded your space."

"With dead rodents!"

"I get it," said Diana. She was smiling, which made her look younger. "I had a boyfriend once who was a fisherman. He'd leave his worms in my fridge, in a mayonnaise jar with holes punched in the top. I remember once when I went to get the orange juice they were all there, wriggling around. That was traumatizing."

Daisy was wiping off the mushrooms, gathering Parmesan cheese and white wine. "Was this a serious boyfriend?"

Diana frowned. "He was," she said, but she didn't seem inclined to offer details. "You told me your husband went to boarding school with your brother. Did you meet him then? When you were a little girl?"

"Hal says he remembers meeting me when I was six. I don't remember this at all." Daisy couldn't recall many specifics of the occasions when her brothers had brought friends home from boarding school or college. It was more of a remembered sense of how busy the house got, her mother's mood of mingled excitement and exasperation. She could picture Judy bustling around with tablecloths and armloads of sheets for the guest-room beds; and how their cleaning lady would come for an extra day that week to help get ready. She could recall the roar of the vacuum cleaner while she and her dad worked in the kitchen, the smells of roasting turkey and pumpkin pie; the feel of powdered sugar on her fingertips as she snuck the almond cookies her *bubbe* would bring. In her memory, the boys themselves were an undifferentiated mass of loud voices, tall bodies, winter coats and hats and boat-sized sneakers left unlaced by the door. When she and Hal had started dating, she'd asked her brother. Danny had just shrugged, saying, "Must've been senior year. I brought—let's see—Hal and Tim Pelletier and Roger McEwan." He'd looked abashed as he'd said, "I had a crush on Roger." She'd wanted to push for more details—about the Thanksgiving visit, about what Hal had been like back then—but Danny's face was shuttered . . . and the next morning, Jesse had called.

"Hey, Daisy, I want to ask you for a favor."

"Sure," she'd said.

Jesse sighed, and said, "Your brother really doesn't like talking about Emlen. The Happy Land, or Happy Place, or whatever they call it in the school song—it wasn't very happy for him, you know?"

"I can imagine," Daisy said.

"No," Jesse had said, his voice not unkind, but very firm, "I don't think you can. Being in the closet back then, knowing your classmates would beat the shit out of you, or worse, if they found out . . ."

Daisy had apologized. She'd reassured Jesse, that, of course, she wouldn't pester Danny for any more Emlen reminiscence, or stories about Hal. Which meant she'd had to take Hal's word for it when he said that she might not have remembered him from that Thanksgiving visit, but that he remembered her: a round-faced girl in a flannel nightgown who'd stared at him and said, "You're tall."

Diana seemed charmed by that story. At least, she seemed interested. Head tilted, she said, "So he remembered you, for all those years."

"Ew, I hope not!" Daisy said, laughing. "No, I don't think he ever thought of me again until sixteen years later when his mom had died and his widowed father was living on pizza and lo mein. But, once we started dating, we both knew pretty quickly."

"So was Hal a close friend of your brother's?"

Daisy considered while she washed the cutting board and the knives. "There were only forty-two boys in Danny and Hal's class at Emlen. I think that all the boys ended up knowing each other to some degree. Danny and Hal were roommates for their last two years, and Hal was the stroke of the boys' eight—the rower who sits facing the coxswain. Which was Danny. So they definitely spent a lot of time together, but I really couldn't say how close they were. I don't think Emlen was a very happy experience for Danny. David loved it, but Danny . . ." Daisy pressed her lips together, aware of the other woman's gaze. "I don't think that prep school in the 1980s was a picnic."

"Was he out then?" Diana asked calmly. "Did Hal know?"

"Oh, Lord no. Danny didn't tell any of us until after college, after my father died. And even then . . ." Her voice trailed off.

Danny had made his announcement in the mid-1990s, right after David's wedding. David and Elyse had just gotten into the limousine, which would take them to the hotel, when Judy, a little tipsy and resplendent in her mother-of-the-groom beige gown, had turned to him. "Why didn't you bring a date?" she asked.

Arnold Mishkin put his hand on her arm. "Judy, leave it," he had said, his tone uncharacteristically sharp, but then Danny had spoken up.

"I am seeing someone," he said. His voice was calm, but his hands had been clasped in front of him, so tightly that Daisy could see the tendons in his wrists. "His name is Jesse. We've been dating for almost a year."

Daisy remembered her mother gasping, the sound very loud in the hotel lobby. Then Judy had managed a single, defeated nod, as if this was just one more disappointment in a long, long line of them.

"Even then, he wasn't an out-and-proud kind of guy," Daisy said. "He doesn't lie about it, but I don't think he advertises, either. If that makes any sense."

"Did he ever date girls?"

"Just casually," said Daisy. "I'm not sure he ever even kissed a girl. And his husband is wonderful. They've been together more than twenty years. They do so much good in the world. I think they want to make sure that the world isn't as awful for other gay kids as it was for them."

"That's great," Diana said. Her tone seemed slightly cool. Or maybe she just didn't want to sound too rah-rah enthusiastic, too *hashtag-love-wins*, as Beatrice might put it.

"Did you like high school?" Daisy asked, and Diana pursed her lips.

"Not the easiest time for me," she said. "No special reason. Just typical teenage-girl misery." She gave Daisy an assessing look. "Are you one of those people who thought it was the best time of her life?"

"Oh, God, no," Daisy blurted. She gave Diana the outlines of her predicament—new school, reduced circumstances—as she showed her how to heat the stock, then bring it to a simmer; how to zest a lemon and peel and chop garlic and shallots, how to brown the grains of rice in olive oil and cook them slowly with a splash of wine plus the aromatics, the mushrooms, and the chicken stock.

"Next lesson, I'll show you how to make your own stock," Daisy said. "It's better than what they sell in stores, and less expensive, and I promise, very simple to make."

"If you say so," said Diana, sounding dubious.

"I promise." When Daisy pulled it out of the oven, the chicken was beautifully browned. Clear juices ran when she pricked the thigh, and it looked so good that they both sighed when she set it on the cutting board.

"We did it!" Diana exulted. She pulled out her phone to take pictures, then picked up the bottle of wine, and looked a question at Daisy. "We only needed one cup for the rice, right?" Examining the bottle, she asked, "Is this wine just for cooking, or is it okay to drink?"

"Oh, that's actually important," said Daisy. "Don't ever buy cooking wine at the supermarket. Never, ever cook with a wine you wouldn't drink." She filled two glasses. Diana raised hers in a toast.

"To new cities and new friends," she said. They clinked, and drank, and talked about the restaurants Diana had to try, the best places to buy dresses and shoes and books and jewelry, where to go to hear live music. It was fascinating, Daisy thought, to imagine this as the life she could have led, if, back when she was twenty, she'd said, *Are you crazy?* to Hal instead of *I do.* Maybe then she could have been the glamorous single lady, on her own in a big city, in a high-rise apartment decorated in gold and peach with a closet full of beautiful clothes. Maybe she'd have gotten not just her bachelor's degree, but an MBA, too; maybe she'd be running a national chain of cooking studios. Briefly, she let herself picture a life of first dates instead of PTA meetings; dinners alone, with a book and a glass of wine, instead of with her husband and a sullen teenager, and no one to please but herself.

"You'll have to come over for dinner. Are you free Friday?"

"I'd love that," said Diana.

"And if you're here in May, you'll have to come to this party I throw," said Daisy. "My mom and Hal both have May birthdays, so I cook their favorites. You'll be able to meet Danny and Jesse, and see Beatrice and Hal in the flesh."

"There's no way of knowing exactly how long this will take—it's an art, not a science—but I'll keep you posted," Diana said. "And how about after that?" she asked Daisy. "What happens in Philadelphia in the summer?"

Daisy made a face. "Unfortunately, I think in Center City it's about a hundred degrees, and it smells like hot garbage."

"Oh, but you're on the Cape, right?" Diana said, and gave Daisy a look she couldn't read, tilting her head as she smoothed her hair behind her ears. "I almost forgot."

~~~~~

15

Diana

After Daisy gathered up her knives and cutting boards and departed, Diana locked the door and used the peephole to chart the other woman's progress down the hall. When she was positive that Daisy was gone, she opened all the windows and lit a few candles guaranteed to eliminate unpleasant odors. She slipped off her silk blouse and pulled on the T-shirt she'd packed in her purse. Then she got to work.

She'd allocated twenty minutes on regular cleanup, reasoning that if Daisy came back up to retrieve a lost lipstick or spatula, she'd find Diana involved in normal-looking tasks: washing dishes and sweeping the floor, the things she'd be doing if she actually lived in this place. Which, of course, she didn't.

She wiped down the counters, getting every last drip off the stovetop and the oven's interior, and the refrigerator's handles and shelves. She put the dirty dishes in the dishwasher. While it ran, she scrubbed every pot and pan and utensil that they'd used, drying them by hand and replacing them in their drawers and cupboards.

With those jobs completed, she felt safe enough to really get to work. She pulled a duffel bag out of the closet, and scooped the clothes out of the dresser and off the hangers, cramming them all inside. She'd brought the handful of designer garments she owned with her, borrowed more from her friends at the Abbey, and used a coupon to join Rent the Runway, which had supplied the rest of the high-end designer gear. Diana reasoned that even if Daisy spotted the Rent the Runway tags sewn into the clothes, she wouldn't think it was strange. Plenty of high-earning businesswomen used the service, instead of just buying clothes outright. Diana had read a piece in the *Wall Street Journal* about it when she'd been preparing for this role.

The toiletries in the bathroom went into a zippered case, and the case went into the duffel. The empty wine bottle went down the garbage chute, along with the rest of the trash. The chicken stock went into a tote bag. The cookbook Daisy had given her went into her purse.

Two hours later, the apartment was as spotless as it had been when she'd taken the keys that afternoon. The superintendent had been squirrely—"if anyone comes by and wants to see the model unit, I'm screwed"—so she'd pressed an extra twenty dollars into his hand and sworn to him that she'd leave the place immaculate, and no one would ever know that she'd even been there, and that if someone did come, she'd make up a story about a magazine photo shoot.

Before she left, she triple-checked everything—the cupboards, the refrigerator, the bedroom, and the closet, looking to see that she had every single thing she'd brought in. When she was satisfied, she closed the windows, blew out the candles, slipped them in her bag, and slung the duffel over her shoulder, with the cooler dangling from her left hand. She locked the door behind her and dropped the keys off with the super at the front desk. "Same time next week," she said.

Her Airbnb was less than a mile away. It, too, technically, was in Rittenhouse Square, but it was far less grand than the penthouse she'd borrowed. The layout reminded her of her cottage, as it had been when she'd first lived there: a single large room, with a half-sized kitchen on one end and windows on the other. As soon as she was inside, she locked the door behind her and sat on her couch, staring at the wall.

She thought about the kind of harm a person could inflict intentionally—through murder or robbery or rape—and about the kind that happened by accident, to people who weren't the targets at all, but just happened to be proximate, or in the way. Undeserving, innocent people who suffered for the crimes of others. She thought about women and children whose only crime was wandering into the blast zone, or being the son or daughter of the wrong man. The son, or the daughter, or the wife.

The lady or the tiger, she thought. *Truth or dare. Your money or your life.* No matter what she decided, she suspected that the other Diana's life, and the life of her daughter, would never be the same.

Part
Three

~~~~~~~~~~~~~~~

Little Bird

16

Diana

Michael left flowers in a mason jar on her porch, daisies and black-eyed Susans that breathed their fragrance through the room after Diana set them on the kitchen table. She repeated the steps she'd taken the year before, opening the windows, setting down her bags; putting her groceries away in the kitchen, checking for new additions in the rows of water-bloated paperbacks, making sure the starfish was still propped up in the bookcase over her bed.

Michael had made improvements during her absence. She saw that there was a new flower bed on the south-facing side of the cottage, and the shutters had been painted in her absence. There were new shelves in the kitchen pantry, a new, brightly colored rug on the floor, and a new drying rack next to the sink. The ladder to the sleeping loft had been replaced with a tidy staircase, and a miniature, dog-sized step had been built beside the bed. Diana thought about Michael Carmody, sawing and hammering, making these improvements for her, and felt her heart do a lazy flip.

When every shirt and pair of pants had been put away, when all the groceries had been set into the cupboards or the refrigerator, when Willa had been walked on the beach and had curled up in her favorite sunny spot on the deck, when there were no more chores to complete and nothing else with which she could procrastinate, Diana sat on the couch and picked up the cordless phone.

"Carmody Caretaking," Michael answered.

"It's me. Diana. Thank you for the flowers. And—and everything else."

"You're welcome. How was your summer?"

She smiled at the familiar accent that flattened "summer" into "summah." "It was fine. Very peaceful."

"Well, I've got a whole lot of cash for you."

For a moment, she didn't know what he was talking about. Then she remembered. "The shells?"

"Yeah. They sold out in three weeks. I know you told me five dollars apiece, but Maudie said she thought they'd sell better if she priced them at ten."

Diana was confused. "Wait. They'd sell better if they cost more?"

"Summer people," said Michael, as if those two words constituted an entire explanation. "You tell them something's valuable, and they believe you. I think Maudie made a sign that said they were handmade by a local artist."

"I'm not an artist!" Diana said, feeling her stomach lurch at the thought that she was misrepresenting herself.

"Sure you are." Michael's voice was easy. "She told 'em it was their chance to bring home a little piece of the Cape made by a local artist, and they couldn't hand over their money fast enough. Hey. I'm glad you're back. Tell you what. I've still got a few more houses to do, but I could pick up some stuff and swing by at six or so? I'll make us dinner."

"Okay," she said, her voice faint. She'd decided, over the last months and weeks, when she pushed her mop or wiped down mirrors and windows, what she would have to do. If there was any chance of whatever it was between them not dying, withering away before it had a chance to bloom, she needed to tell Michael her story. "I'll see you soon."

At five forty-five, Michael Carmody's truck came rumbling up the driveway. Willa planted her hind legs on the couch and her front paws on the windowsill and yipped in welcome, tail wagging. When Michael climbed out of his truck she nosed the screen door open and raced outside to meet him. Diana followed along.

"Hey there, rascal," he said, flipping Willa a treat. He smiled at Diana, approaching her carefully, seeming to sense that she didn't want to be hugged or kissed yet; that she needed to get used to being in the same room with him again.

He'd brought a six-pack of beer, two dozen oysters, four ears of corn, and a lusciously ripe tomato from Longnook Meadows Farm. "Want to slice this?" he asked. Diana had goat cheese in the refrigerator and olive oil and balsamic vinegar in the pantry. At the Abbey, the chef whipped the goat cheese until it was an airy foam, swirled it artfully around the edges of the plate, and fanned the tomato slices on top, drizzling balsamic vinegar and sprinkling roasted hazelnuts as a finishing touch. Diana didn't have hazelnuts, or the tools to whip the cheese, so she crumbled it on top of the tomatoes, and thought it wasn't half-bad.

They ate outside on the picnic table, which, she noticed, no longer creaked when she sat. Michael shucked the oysters and sipped a single beer. Diana polished off two, gulping them down fast, like they were medicine, and picked at her food until Michael put three oysters on her plate, doused in lemon juice, the way she liked them. "Eat," he said gently. "You've got to eat."

When the meal was done, and the shells piled up at the corner of the deck, Michael carried their plates inside, and came out of the cottage to sit beside her on the bench, and said, "How are you doing?"

"Fine!"

"No, really," he said, and put his hand between her shoulder blades. "You can tell me. How are you doing, really?"

Diana stood up and walked to the edge of the deck and looked out over the water, letting the wind blow back her hair. *A million-dollar view*, Michael had once told her the year before. Even if you don't have a million-dollar house to go with it.

She heard the creak of the deck's boards and felt his warm presence, as he came to stand beside her. Without looking at him, she spoke into the wind coming off the bay. "I love it here," she said. "I wish I could stay, year-round."

"What's stopping you?" he asked.

She turned away, shaking her head, and didn't answer. He put his hands on her shoulders. It was, she realized, as good of an opening as she'd ever have. She breathed in a long, careful breath, and said, "I need to tell you a story." With her eyes closed she could see it, all of it: the fifteen-year-old girl who thought she'd been in love, racing, barefoot, over the sand in her white sundress, running down the beach, to the bonfire, and the booze, and the boys.

"I was a mother's helper. A thousand summers ago. I worked for Dr. Levy. I met some boys, on the beach. At the end of the summer, right before Labor Day, they invited me to a party. A bonfire, on the beach."

As she approaches the fire, Diana slows her pace to a stroll and tries to catch her breath. She doesn't want to appear too eager or desperate, but it is hard not to run, to skip, to dance toward him; hard to hold herself back. Her mind is brimming with all kinds of wonderful thoughts: maybe tonight, Poe would kiss her. Maybe he'd ask her to be his girl-friend and visit him at college, and he'd come see her in Boston and meet her parents and her sisters. Maybe—her fondest wish, the best of them all—he would say that he loved her.

He's standing at the fire with his back to her, in khaki shorts and a hooded sweatshirt. When she taps his shoulder, he turns, smiling. He looks her over, from the slender straps of her dress all the way to her bare feet, and, impulsively, she twirls around for him, her skirt flaring like a blossom. "Hey, beautiful," he says. "Wait right there." A minute later, he's back, pressing a cup into her hand.

When she takes her first sip, the alcohol burns her throat and makes her eyes water. She gasps, spluttering, and almost spits it out. Her face glows hot as an ember when she hears a few of the guys laughing, and she thinks he's going to laugh at her, too, but all he says is, "Let me get you some punch." She watches him as he walks away, then studies the crowd, looking for familiar faces. Her friends have all gone home by now. Alicia's back in New York City and Maeve is back in Dublin and Marie-Francoise is in Breton. Kelly was the second-to-last of them to go. At Gull Pond that morning, she'd kissed Diana on each cheek, given her a postcard with her address on it, and said, "Keep in touch!"

There are girls at this party, older-looking girls. Diana sees one in cutoff shorts, holding a guitar, and another in an Emlen sweatshirt that must belong to one of the boys. Because, mostly, it's Emlen guys here, in T-shirts or sweatshirts that advertise their school, in jeans or cargo shorts or the pinkish-salmon shorts she's learned are called Nantucket Reds. When the wind changes directions, she can hear pieces of conversation: They went to Cape Cod and Early decision at Princeton, and, once, the word "townie," followed by a burst of unpleasant-sounding laughter. Her head swivels—was that meant for her?—but before she can figure out who was talking, or who they were talking about, Poe is back with another cup.

"Try this."

The drink is sweet, almost cloying, and it tastes like apricots and peaches, but it warms her pleasantly instead of burning on the way down. She sips, then gulps, because she's thirsty after her run and a day in the sunshine, and, suddenly, the cup is empty and Poe is off to get *her a refill, leaving her sitting on one of the driftwood logs that's been pulled up around the campfire, with the world gone slightly spinny and soft at its edges.*

"Hey, take it easy." She looks to see that there's a girl in the cutoffs, sitting beside her. The girl has a deep tan and about six bracelets on her arm, woven friendship bracelets and bangles that chime when she gestures. "That stuff sneaks up on you if you're not careful. Trust me, I know from personal experience." The girl's hair is long and brown, tangled by the wind, and she's got a narrow, clever face. There's a silver ring on her thumb.

"Thanks," says Diana, realizing that her bladder is suddenly, uncomfortably full. "Is there, um . . ."

"A bathroom?" The cutoffs girl makes a face. "Ha. I wish. The guys just go piss in the dunes. That'd be my advice."

Diana waits until Poe comes back. She sits by him and drinks with him and asks him questions, listening as he tells her about the previous night's adventures, which seem to have involved him and six of the guys he's staying with getting kicked out of a bar (or maybe it's a club?) called the Bomb Shelter. When she can't wait any longer, she says, "Excuse me," and stands up.

Tipsy. She's never appreciated the word before, but, now on her feet, she feels she might immediately fall over. The world is tilted, wobbling on its axis. She'd have fallen right over, if it weren't for his hand on her elbow.

"You okay?"

She isn't sure, but she nods, smiling brightly.

"I'll be right back." By then she's spotted a narrow path that threads through the saw grass. She follows it until she finds a sandy spot that seems secluded. She pulls up her dress and does her business. When she stands up, the world spins again. Maybe I'd better sit down, *she thinks, and finds a patch of sand, smooth as a fresh sheet, tucked into the curve of a dune. The night air is soft against her face, the sand is cool underneath her, and the stars are brilliant overhead, so close it*

looks like she could touch them. She lies back and wishes for Poe to come and find her, like she's Sleeping Beauty and he's the prince who will wake her with a kiss. She lets her eyes slip shut. When she opens them again, there's a boy on top of her.

"There were three of them," she told Michael, as she stood on the deck, looking out at the ocean, seven years after that terrible night. Her voice was dull, her shoulders hunched, as she watched the waves roll in and out; not stopping, not seeing, not caring. "One was on top of me. One was watching. And one of them . . ." She swallowed hard. "He was holding me down. And laughing." It was the laughter she heard in her nightmares, the boy's shrill cackle as he held her wrists and the way he'd chanted "Sloppy seconds!" He'd had a face as round as a pie plate, a snub of a nose, big round eyes, prissy, pursed lips, and brown hair combed back smoothly from his high, waxy-white forehead. There was something doll-like about him, like he'd been carved out of wood, then painted, and was waiting for someone to turn him into a real boy.

She could see him, looming above her: his smooth hair disheveled, his rosebud mouth drawn into a sneer, how, every minute or two he'd use his left hand to hold her wrists and his right hand to stroke himself roughly through his shorts. She could smell the sour cloud of beer that hung around his face. Worst of all, she could picture the face of the boy watching from the tall grass, his mouth hanging open and eyes wide and shocked. She'd waited for him to come save her, but he never did.

Michael pulled her gently against him, and she let herself lean into the warm bulk of his body. "Oh, sweetheart," he said, his voice a pained rasp, like it was his heart that was breaking. "I'm so sorry. I'm so sorry that happened to you."

She nodded, and breathed, and made herself tell him the rest.

"It hurt. It hurt a lot. I was a virgin." She remembered the pain when the boy tried to jam himself inside, how he'd spat on his hand, then smeared saliva between her legs, how she'd felt like she was being torn right in two. She remembered the dry, hissing noise her hair made against the sand as she tossed her head and bucked her hips, trying to free herself. She remembered the smell of the fire and the ocean; the sight of the sky, the moon obscured by a raft of clouds, cold and indifferent, a million miles away.

"When the first boy finished, he got off me, and then, before the second boy could get on, I hit him." She made a fist, to demonstrate, remembering how her hands had tingled after the boy released them, the meaty smack of her knuckles on his cheek, how the shock had traveled right up her arm and how the boy had yelped. Then she'd been moving, shoving her way past the watcher, stumbling through the saw grass as it sliced at her calves, the laughing boy so close behind her that she could feel his breath on her neck. She heard someone say, "That's enough. Leave her alone," but she didn't look back, she kept going, running until her thighs burned and she had a stitch in her side, turning her head every few steps to look behind her for pursuers, holding her ruined dress around her; her panties gone, abandoned back on the sand. She remembered realizing, as she'd dragged her poor, bleeding, hurting body up the Levys' beach stairs, that nothing had gone according to plan. She'd be going back to Boston in two days' time, and she still hadn't been kissed.

Michael put his arms around her and held her, and Diana felt herself rocking like a ship riding at anchor as his body kept her in place. When she finally raised her eyes, she looked for disgust in his expression, but she could see nothing but sorrow. Her throat ached and her eyes felt gritty.

"Wait here," he said. He got up and went inside, and got her a glass of water, and watched over her as she sipped.

"So," she said, and cleared her throat. "That's what happened.

That's why I can't be here in the summertime. That's why I dropped out of college. That's why . . ." Her voice trailed off. She knew she could never put words to how that night had changed her, re-shaping her sense of the world and of herself, turning her from an aspiring artist and writer to a custodian and a waitress. Nor did she want to hurt him by implying that there was something dishonorable or wrong about a working-class life. She couldn't say any of it, any more than she could get back everything she'd lost that night, that summer.

"It's just that I feel so stupid!" she said, in a loud, ragged voice.

"You weren't stupid. Don't say that! It's not your fault. You didn't do anything wrong."

"But I did. I trusted him. Poe. I thought he . . ." Her voice caught and broke, and when she spoke again, all she could man-age was a whisper. "I thought he liked me," she said.

She drained the water in breathless gulps. Then she sat, with Willa at her feet, and she waited for the world to crack open and swallow her whole, the way she'd always feared it would, if she said those words out loud: *I was raped*.

"Did you tell anyone?" he asked. "Dr. Levy? Or the police?"

She shook her head. "I couldn't. I felt so . . ." She raised her hands and let them flutter back down to her sides. "Not until now. You're the first."

"Listen to me." Michael put his hand on her chin. He tilted her face up so she had to look at him. "You didn't do anything wrong. Nothing that happened is your fault. It's their fault. Those guys. Their fault."

Diana nodded, sniffling. "I know," she said. "I know you're right. I'm trying to believe it."

"Well, for now just know that I believe it. One hundred per-cent." When he opened his arms, she shuffled close and leaned against his chest, crying so hard she was sure that his shirt had to be soaked. With her eyes closed, enfolded in a warm, Michaelscented darkness, she felt as close to safe as she had since that summer. Michael held her, and rocked her, and let her cry, and when she stopped he gave her more water, then went inside and fetched two more beers and sat beside her. They drank as the sun went down over the bay, drawing bands of gold and orange and indigo across the sky.

"So here's a question," he finally said. "What do you want to happen next?"

Startled, she turned to look at him. "What?"

"It's your life. You get to decide. How do you want it to be? Like, do you want to go back to college? Do you like being a waitress? Do you like living here?" He paused, then asked, his voice lower, "Do you like being with me?"

"I . . ." She swallowed hard.

"No pressure," said Michael. "But I like you. Like, a lot."

"I'm not sure . . ." He waited, while she sorted out what to say. "I'm not sure that I can be with anyone, is the thing."

She felt his body shift as he sighed, and saw his shoulders slump. "Yeah," he said quietly. "I understand."

"But . . ." She paused, and breathed, and then, in a rush, said, "If you can be patient with me, I think I want to try."

His smile was like the sun coming out after days of rain; like pulling on the softest sweater on a cold day.

"Can we take it slow?" she whispered.

"As slow as you need," said Michael Carmody. He reached for her hand. "I'm a patient kind of guy."

17

Diana

For the weeks and months of that year, through the fall and the winter and into the spring, Michael Carmody courted her, slowly, with great diligence and care. While the weather stayed warm, they did summer-people things. Michael took her to the Wellfleet drive-in, where they sat in the back of his pickup truck and watched a double feature of *Back to the Future* and *Jaws* with a giant bucket of popcorn propped between them. They played miniature golf with Michael's sister, Kate, and her husband, Devin, and spent afternoons visiting antiques markets and art galleries. On the first cool night he made her dinner, linguine with clam sauce, which, he claimed, was the only thing he could cook, and he took her fishing, cheering her on as she reeled in an eighteen-pound bass. In the cottage, he oiled hinges and replaced the showerhead in the bathroom and added a towel bar to the door. In the mornings on her days off, Michael would come over with coffee and scones from the Flying Fish. Together, they'd walk Willa, and Diana would get in the truck with him and help him make his rounds, keeping him company while he patched screen doors or nailed up drooping gutters or changed the chemicals in hot tubs ("can't tell you how many pairs of underpants I've fished out of this one," he told her, when they'd visited a mansion in Provincetown, high on a hill in the West End).

He invited her to spend Thanksgiving with his family, but Diana wasn't ready for that yet, so on Thanksgiving Day, he went to his parents' place in Eastham, and she went home to eat turkey with her mom and dad and sisters in Boston. Then, on Saturday night at the cottage, she and Michael prepared a two-person feast of a turkey breast, stuffing, sweet potatoes, and cranberry sauce made from the berries they'd picked together in the bog.

At Christmastime, she met his father, a larger, gruffer, gray-haired version of Michael, and was formally introduced to his mom the librarian, who was petite and round, with the curly reddish hair Michael had inherited. Mrs. Carmody—"call me Margo"—cupped Diana's face in both of her hands and said, "Finally—finally! He brings home a reader! You don't know how long I've been waiting!" before giving Diana a resounding kiss on the cheek and plopping down on the couch, looking smug. "My work here is done," she announced, and made a pantomime of dusting off her hands, as Kate and Devin gave Diana meaningful smiles, and Michael shoved his hands in his pockets, murmuring, "That's enough, Ma," looking endearingly abashed. Diana met Michael's friends—Victor, who ran a charter fishing company; and Eric, who owned a nursery; and Carolee, who taught at the yoga studio where Diana took her classes. She would have introduced him to Reese and Frankie and Carly and Ryan, her colleagues at the Abbey, except Michael knew them all already.

Some nights at work, toward the end of her shift, Michael would come and sit at the bar, waiting to bring her home. Sometimes she'd come home from work and find a gift on her doorstep—a palette of watercolors, a pair of earrings, a bouncy rubber Kong for Willa to chase on the beach, a perfectly shaped oyster shell for her to decorate.

The months went by, and all he ever did was hold her hand and kiss her. She knew he wanted more than that—she could see his face getting flushed and hear his heart beating faster; could feel the hard length of him, pressing against her, when she sat on his lap as they kissed on the couch—but he never pushed, never demanded, never asked her for more.

At the end of January, there was a blizzard. Snow covered the beaches, and black ice slicked the roads. Reese closed the Abbey for a few days. "Stay home. Stay safe," he said. "We're not going to get anyone in here anyhow." Diana hunkered down in the cottage, where she painted seashells and read, curled up with Willa in the sleeping loft. She thought Michael would want to be with her, but he picked up work plowing people's driveways and helping the town workers sand and salt the roads. He'd come home after dark, shedding layers of coats and sweaters by the door, and Diana would make him hot chocolate and build up the fire in the woodstove.

For his birthday, Diana took him out to dinner at an Israeli restaurant in Orleans. For her birthday, the first day of March, Michael told her to close her eyes. He walked her to the driveway, and, on the back of his truck, she saw two kayaks, one bright yellow, the other neon green. "His and hers," he said, and cleared his throat. "I thought we could go together." Left unspoken was *If you're still around when it warms up.*

March went by, then April, and she and Michael were out on the deck again, edging around the topic of the upcoming summer. Diana was trying to explain that she couldn't stay; that everything she saw or heard or smelled would remind her of what had happened.

"Do you think . . ." Michael began. He pulled off his baseball cap, then put it back on. "I just wonder. If there was some kind of punishment for the boys who did it to you . . . ?" His voice trailed off.

"There can't be," she said. "I didn't tell anyone after it happened. There's no police report. No pictures. No stained dress. No physical evidence. It would just be my word against whatever they say." Diana could already guess what that would be: *She wanted it. She was asking for it. She was drunk.* "So even if I figure out that guy's real name . . ." Her voice was querulous and high. "I don't know. I don't know what I want. I don't even know what's possible. I mean, do I find the guy and have someone rape him, so he knows how it feels?"

She'd thought Michael would be shocked by that, but his voice was its familiar calm rumble. "I guess that would be one way to go about it," he said. "And is it just one guy you'd want punished? Aren't all of them kind of to blame?"

Diana walked to the edge of her yard, across the patchy, sandy grass. She leaned out over the railing, looking down at the ruffled whitecaps, then up at the apricot sky, and waited until Michael had come to stand beside her. "I could blackmail the guys, if I find them. Tell them that I'd go public unless they paid me."

"Do you want money?"

"Doesn't everyone?" she snapped.

He raised his hands. "Hey, hey, I'm not trying to fight with you. I'm just asking."

She sniffled, wiping savagely at her eyes. "I don't know," she began, and then stopped talking.

"Don't know what?"

"I don't know what's fair. These guys . . . what they took . . . I mean, how do I ever get that back?" She made herself breathe, made herself loosen her grip on the railing. "I feel like they stole my life. Like they took the person I was supposed to be, the person I was on my way to being, and they killed her, and now I'll never get her back."

"But you're still here," he said gently. "You're not dead. Whatever they did do, they didn't do that."

"You don't understand." That old, familiar despair was back, welling up inside of her, pushing out every good feeling, every happy memory that she'd made. "I've got two sisters. They both went to college. One of them's a lawyer; the other one's a nurse. They're both married. Julia's got kids."

"Okay," he said. "So you've made other choices."

Other choices. She gave an ugly laugh, remembering one of her father's more pungent sayings: *You can't polish a turd.* "I'm a waitress," she said. "I dropped out of UMass after three semesters. I live in a one-room cottage, rent-free, because someone felt sorry for me. I'm basically a squatter. And when I'm not squatting here, I'm living with my parents and working as a janitor."

His voice was mild, but she could hear the rebuke in his tone. "There's nothing wrong with honest work."

Diana felt her face get hot. "I know," she said. "I know that. I do. It's just . . . I was good at school. I got good grades; I won a scholarship. My parents, my teachers . . . everyone expected more from me." She sighed. "I expected more from me. For me. But the girl who wanted that big life—I'm not her. Not anymore." *And I'm afraid*, she thought, but couldn't say. *I'm still so afraid.*

He settled his hand against her neck and rubbed gently. She pressed her face into his neck and leaned back into his touch, the warmth of his hand, the softness of his skin underneath the prickle of his beard. "I just want to stay here, in my house, with my dog, and work my job, and come home at night, and go to sleep to the sound of the ocean," she said into his chest. "And not hurt anyone."

"That doesn't sound bad to me at all." He was holding her close, and before she could lose her nerve she turned, stood on her tiptoes, took his face in her hands, and kissed him on the lips. He tasted like beer and lemons, and his mustache tickled her lips.

"Fuzzy," she murmured. She wanted to do something, to re-place the darkness inside of her with something light, and she knew what that thing might be. It was time. She took his hand and led him inside, onto the couch, and when he sat down, instead of sitting beside him, she arranged herself on top of him, her legs straddling his thighs.

"Mmm," he said, and touched her hair, then her face. He let his hands fall open on the couch as he leaned forward, nuzzling her neck. She shivered as the hairs brushed her skin, then leaned forward and pressed nibbling kisses on his cheek, then his beard, before finally shifting her lips to the soft, yielding warmth of his mouth.

His breath hitched as she leaned against him, pressing her breasts against his soft flannel shirt. He returned her kisses enthusiastically, his tongue a startling, delicious softness in the bristly tangle of his beard. But he didn't move his hands any lower than her waist, always letting her be the one to push herself against him, to deepen a kiss, to take the lead in whatever they were doing.

Michael's voice was a low rumble against her chest. "Are you okay?"

"Um, I think so."

He lifted one hand to stroke her cheek, then her hair. "I don't want to do anything you don't want. So you're going to have to tell me." He leaned close, whispering in her ear, making her shiver all over. "Tell me everything you want to happen. Everything you want me to do."

She kissed him again, feeling shame surge through her; panic trying to grip her. With an effort, she was able to put herself back in the present, in her body, in that moment. She concentrated on the sensations: the warm weight of his hand on her head, the slow brush of his thumb against her cheek, the persistent ache between her legs. Reaching up, she touched his hair, which was surprisingly soft. She combed through it with her fingers, scraping her nails gently against his scalp.

"Mmm," he rumbled.

She put the heels of her hands against his shoulders and looked down at him, gazing up at her. Leaning forward, she slid her palm down the side of his face, from the warmth of his skin to the prickles of his beard to the soft skin of his neck. She hesitated, then continued on, brushing her palm against his shirt, feeling the hard bud of his nipple. She gave it a tweak, heard him inhale, saw his eyes flutter shut. Still, he kept his hands motionless at her waist.

She began kissing his neck, warm, openmouthed caresses. When she nibbled at a spot just beneath his ear, he gasped, and stiffened, and his voice sounded strangled as he said, "Oh, wow, that's good."

She nibbled at him some more, tasting his salty skin, feeling the curve of his head against her palm. She sat up straight just long enough to pull off her sweatshirt and T-shirt. Michael leaned back and watched her, eyes wide. She smiled, and took one of his big hands, and brought it to her breast, and the plain beige bra she was wearing. He held his hand in place, then began sweeping his thumb in arcs against the skin of her chest. "Okay?" he whispered.

Instead of answering, Diana reached down and brushed her fingers over the solid mound behind his zipper, smiling at the strangled sound he made.

"You're going to kill me," he said, but he didn't sound unhappy about it.

She leaned forward, letting her hair brush his cheeks. "I want it," she whispered. "I want you."

He groaned, then stood up with Diana in his arms and carried her up to her bed. He laid her down as gently as if she was made of spun glass, as if she was some rare treasure. With great care, he undressed her, unlacing her shoes and easing each one off, pulling off her socks, unbuttoning her jeans and drawing them down over her legs. He looked at her for a long, airless moment, like she was the most precious thing he'd ever seen, and she had to close her eyes against the tenderness of his gaze, before it scorched her.

He leaned forward, mouth close to her ear. "I want to make this good for you," he rumbled.

"Mmm," she sighed.

"Anything you don't want, you tell me," he said. "If you want to stop, we'll stop."

She nodded. It made her heart ache to hear such consideration, and to know he was treating her with such care because of what had happened. *I'm damaged goods*, she thought.

"You're perfect," he said, as if he'd heard what she was thinking. Then he bent to her, kissing her ankle, her calf, the back of her knee. She could feel the softness of his hair, the prickles of his beard, the warmth of his lips and his tongue as he moved up, up, up. "Oh," she sighed, and she felt him kissing, then sucking gently, his beard tickling her thigh.

"Do you like that?" he whispered. She thought that the way she was squirming on the bed, her hips rising and falling with an unconscious, insistent rhythm, would have given him an answer, but clearly he needed to hear it. She'd almost worked out what to say when she felt his fingers pressing into the soft flesh behind her knee. When she felt his lips there, she arced right off the bed.

"Ooh!"

She heard his chuckle, felt his hands on her hips as he urged her onto her belly. Then he repeated the process on her other leg, kissing his way from instep to ankle to calf to, this time, the back of her knee. When she felt his tongue there, she made a noise so loud it would have been embarrassing, if there'd been any part of her that still had the capacity for shame. For once, she'd stopped thinking, her mind abandoning itself to sensation as Michael gripped her thighs, holding them firmly, but not with enough force to keep her in place if she wanted to move. She rolled her hips in the air, desperate for friction, frantic for him to touch her.

"Oh," she whispered, "oh, please, please, please . . ."

He brushed his thumb right between her legs. She squeaked, and did it even louder when he repeated the gesture with two fingertips.

"You're so wet," he muttered, and hooked his thumbs into the sides of her panties. "Okay?"

"Mmm," she hummed.

He drew them down slowly, slipping them over her feet, and his warm hands were gently urging her thighs apart. She had a brief moment to wonder how she looked, how she smelled, an instant to think *I should have shaved my bikini line*, before he dragged the tip of his index finger along the wet seam between her legs, so delicately he was barely touching her. His fingertip landed on her clitoris and flicked it gently, and she forgot how to think. He brought his face between her legs, and just breathed on her, gently, so gently that she could barely tell he was there. She lifted her hips, trying to spread her legs even wider, moaning, "Please, please, please."

He put his tongue against her, working his finger in and out as he licked, then sucked, then just pressed his tongue flat against her and letting her rub herself against it, like a cat arching its back into a waiting hand, and it was too much, and yet, still not enough. Her breath was coming in pants, and she was gripping the back of his head, holding him against her, feeling his beard, his lips, his teeth, his tongue, until her hips arced off the bed and she forgot everything she'd been thinking and everything she'd meant to say, all of it swept away in a torrent of pleasure.

"That has never happened to me," she whispered a few minutes later. She was smiling, and Michael was lying right against her. She had her arm underneath his neck. His head was on her shoulder, and she could feel his erection pressing against her thigh.

"With a guy?"

"It's never happened with a guy. And it hasn't happened at all since that summer."

"You don't, ah . . ."

"Masturbate? I've tried. But nothing works. This was the first time."

Tears were slipping out of her closed eyes, running down her cheeks, but, at Michael's look of alarm, she said, "They're happy tears. I'm okay. I promise."

He rubbed his thumb against her cheek and then, so gently that at first she could barely feel it, he kissed her tears away, which made her cry harder. Sniffling, she asked, "Where'd you learn to do that?"

He was, she realized, still completely dressed, in jeans and a flannel shirt, everything except his boots, which he'd left by the door. She stroked her hand along his back, then reached for the buttons on his shirt. He took her hand and held it still.

"We don't have to."

"What if I want to?"

He looked at her gravely. "Only if you want," he said.

"I do. I promise." He let her roll him onto his back, let her straddle him and unbutton his shirt, unbuckle his belt, unzip his pants. He helped her, sitting up when she told him to, lifting his hips so she could get his pants off. Then, finally, for the first time in her life, she was in bed, naked, with a naked man.

Michael was looking rueful. "I, ah, did the Atkins thing over the winter." He patted his substantial belly. "I don't know how I was supposed to lose weight eating bacon and eggs."

"I don't want you to lose weight," she said. She couldn't explain how much she liked his size, like he was solid and substantial enough to shelter her and keep her safe.

Michael was big all over, and hairy, his chest and belly and legs covered in reddish-gold curls. The curls were densest on his chest, and at his groin, a tangly nest from which his penis rose, red and curved and wet at the tip. She took it in her hand and gave it an experimental squeeze. He sucked in a breath, and his nipples puckered to hard points.

"Oh, boy." His eyelids fluttered shut. She kissed each one, then his cheeks, then his lips, kissing him gently at first before his mouth opened to hers and he put his arms around her shoulders, pulling her close. She breathed him in, smelling herself, and beer and balsamic vinegar and the scent that was his alone. Before she could lose her nerve, she straddled him, gripping his penis and rubbing herself against it, sliding back and forth until she was sure that it was wet, before gripping it, placing its tip at her entrance, and sliding slowly down until he was completely inside her.

They both groaned. Michael sounded ecstatic. Diana just felt full, unpleasantly full at first. She raised herself up, easing off him to lessen the pressure before she slid down again, letting him fill her. That time it felt good. No. Better than good. When she did it again, it felt amazing. Incredible. She raised herself up again, but he stopped her, gripping her hips.

"Wait," he rasped. "Condom."

"Oh, shit!" She clambered off him, so fast that there was an embarrassing wet popping noise. Michael reached over her, groping for his pants, removing his wallet from a pocket, opening the packet with his teeth. They rolled the condom over his erection together, his hand warm on hers. He lay back again, but she shook her head, and pressed her naked body against his.

"Come on," she whispered.

"Are you sure?"

She reached down, gripping his sheathed penis, and pressed her lips against his ear. "I need you to do this right now."

He groaned, so loudly that she imagined she could feel the cottage vibrating. She had an instant of doubt, a brief few seconds of fear. Then she reminded herself that this was Michael, Michael who knew her, Michael who'd helped her, Michael who maybe even loved her. She tilted her head and, as he kissed her, he put her hand on him and held still, waiting for her to guide him inside. She moved, tentatively at first, then faster, leaning forward so her hair fell down around him, enclosing their two faces, making a secret world.

"You know I love you," he said when it was over.

She'd been half-asleep, dozing against the warmth of his body, thinking it was like having a slow oven in her bed. When he said it, her entire body jolted, like she was a glass in the cupboard, rattled by some unexpected force. "What?"

"I love you. I've been in love with you a long time. Maybe even since the first time I came over, when you were so mean to me." He nudged her fondly. "Remember that?"

Diana cleared her throat. It felt like her tongue and her lips and her teeth were all new pieces of equipment, recently installed. "I was mean to you a lot of times."

"You sure were, baby," said Michael, and gave her shoulder a friendly pat. Diana laughed. The bed felt like a boat, small but sturdy, bearing the two of them in the sea of the dark, and she could picture his good-natured smile.

"Why?" she asked.

"Why what?"

"Why do you . . ." She could barely bring herself to say it. "Why do you love me?"

"Oh, honey." He turned on his side and took her in both of his arms, holding her against him. His hand was in her hair, and he was whispering her name. "Because you're my Diana. My beautiful Diana."

"And it's okay if I'm . . ." She swallowed in the darkness. "It's okay if I'm not . . . completely okay?"

He propped himself on his elbows so he could look down, right into her eyes. "You're perfect to me," he said.

For the next three days and nights, they barely left Diana's bed. On Tuesday night, when Diana went to work, Reese looked her over, then smiled. "I guess I don't have to ask if you had a pleasant weekend."

"What?"

He swatted her bottom with a bar towel. "Don't 'what' me, young lady. I know that look. That look is a look of pure sat-is-fac-tion." He nodded, pleased with himself, as Diana rolled her eyes. "Seriously, though, dear heart. You look happy. Healthy. Not quite so much the drowned rat I had the good fortune to meet last year." He put his hands on her shoulders, and looked her in the eyes.

"I'm happy for you, darlin'," he said, and walked off, humming a tune it took her a few seconds to recognize as "Sexual Healing." Diana shook her head, smiling, thinking that she was happy, too.

One night in the springtime, as they lay in the candlelit loft, listening to a thunderstorm roll in over the bay, Michael finally asked the question that had been looming between them since the first time they'd gone to bed. "Will you go back to Boston again this summer?"

"I don't know." She didn't want to go, but she still couldn't stand the thought of seeing one of those boys near the place that had started to feel like home.

Michael stroked her hair as the cottage shook with peals of thunder, and rain rattled against the windowpanes. When he spoke, her head was on his chest, and his voice was a warm rumble in her ear.

"You could stay."

She shook her head. "I can't."

"You really think those boys would come back?"

Diana didn't know what to say. Or, rather, she didn't know how to answer him in a way that wouldn't make her sound crazy. Years had passed since that night on the beach, but the truth was, part of her did think that the boys could come back, and she did think that they would find her, and they'd come for her again.

Michael's hand was warm and gentle. "Maybe you need a disguise."

Her voice was thick, and her mind stuck in the memories of the bonfire, the feel of that boy on top of her, the sound of her hair, swishing on the sand as she'd fought. She cleared her throat. "What?"

"Like a disguise. A secret identity. What if you had another name? You know, like how Superman is Clark Kent? And Batman's Bruce Wayne?"

At first, she didn't realize what he was saying. "Like what?"

"Well, I've always liked Carmody."

He rolled away to reach underneath the pillow, and when he turned toward her again he had a black velvet box in his hand.

"Diana Scalzi . . ."

She started to cry.

"Would you do me the great, great honor . . ."

She shook her head. "You don't want me," she sobbed, crying so hard she could barely speak. "I'm a mess."

"Hey," said Michael. "Look at me."

She looked.

"I love you," he said. "I love you, and I just want to be with you. No matter what." He was still holding the box, his face hopeful, his hand trembling, and she wanted nothing more than to open it, to slip the ring on her finger, to tell him yes and see him smile. But she couldn't do it.

"I need to tell you something."

"Okay," he said, and looked at her, a little anxiously. "Just as long as it isn't no."

She looked away, and then she forced herself to say it. "What if I don't want to have children?" When Diana had dreamed about her life, both before and after the rape, she'd considered many different versions of the future. Some of them involved traveling, or going back to school; some involved art, or writing, or teaching, but none of them had ever involved motherhood. She liked children—her nieces and her nephew, the kids she'd babysat when she was younger, Sam and Sarah Levy, from way back when—but she'd always been happy, at the end of a day or a night or a weekend, to give them back to their parents. Then the rape had piled another set of fears onto that initial reluctance. She was afraid of the appointments, of how it would feel to have her legs in stirrups and her body so exposed. If she had a girl, she'd be worried that something would happen to her daughter like what had happened to her, and she thought she wouldn't have any idea about how to raise a boy.

She explained herself as best she could, a recitation that left Michael looking troubled. "Is it nonnegotiable?" he asked.

"I don't think anything is nonnegotiable," Diana replied. "But . . . well, is it very important to you?"

He bowed his head. "I need to think," he said. She touched his shoulder, his dear face, the skin of his cheek so soft against his beard. "I love you very much," she said, and prayed that it would be enough. He blew out the candle and drew her down to the bed.

"Let's get some sleep," he said. Diana closed her eyes, but for hours she lay awake with her heart quaking in her throat. She imagined she could feel her entire body trembling with the thought of losing him, and she didn't know what she could say, or promise, to get him to stay.

The next morning, Michael went for a walk by himself, on

the beach. Diana cleaned every inch of the cottage, emptying out the refrigerator and scrubbing the shelves, pulling every book and shell and postcard off the shelf to dust them. She tried not to look at the time, or to entertain fantasies that she'd never see Michael Carmody again.

A few hours later, Michael came back. His face was very serious as he took her by the hands. "I always thought that the reason you got married was to have a family," he said. "I always thought I'd have kids, and be a good father to them, like my father was to me."

She nodded and felt like she'd swallowed a stone, like she'd just stepped off a ledge and was falling into the darkness.

"But I want you to be my family," he said. "I want us to be a family together. I want that more than anything."

She gave a hiccup-y half-laugh, half-sob. "You're sure?"

"I'm sure about you. But you have to be sure about this."

Diana squeezed her eyes shut and forced the words out of her mouth. "What if I don't deserve to be happy?" she whispered.

His inhalation was loud enough for her to hear it; the noise that meant that he was angry and trying to keep his temper in check. *Now is when he'll realize I'm crazy*, she thought. Now is when he'll leave.

Michael paused, then said, in a slow and deliberate voice, "Do you think you deserved what happened to you that summer?"

Diana shook her head. When she thought about the girl she'd been, young and trusting, running, fleet-footed, down the beach in her white dress, it felt like she was thinking of a stranger. But she knew that girl hadn't deserved what had happened to her. No girl did.

"Do you?" Michael's voice was still low and calm, but she could hear anger underneath it.

She shook her head. "No."

"Then why wouldn't you deserve to be happy?" When she

didn't answer, he bent down to gently brush his lips against hers. "Everyone deserves to be happy," he said. "Maybe you, most of all." Diana wrapped her arms around him, pulling him close, hearing him breathe.

"I love you so much. Please say yes," he whispered.

She watched him slide the ring on her finger. "Yes," she said.

18

Diana

They were married on the deck behind the Abbey, in the glow of a perfect September sunset with their friends and family all around them. Diana wore a white dress. Michael wore a blue suit. Willa wore a garland of white orchids and roses around her neck that she alternately sniffed at and attempted to eat. A Unitarian Universalist minister conducted the service, with Reese as an unofficial co-officiant, resplendent in a morning coat and a top hat.

Everyone was there: Diana's parents and her sisters and their husbands and kids; Michael's parents and his sister and her husband and their kids. Dr. Levy and Mr. Weinberg came. Maeve sent best wishes from Dublin, and Marie-Francoise from London, where she'd moved, and Kelly and Alicia were there, watching, as Diana walked down the aisle, a candlelit path in the sand.

Dora Fitzsimmons, silent as ever, wore a black pantsuit and black New Balance sneakers, and gave the couple a check for five hundred dollars and a pound of Cabot's fudge. Ryan, freshly returned from Los Angeles, gave them a birdhouse that he'd had commissioned, a version of their cottage in miniature, with a perch for a pair of lovebirds out front. Heavy Flo donated her services as a singer and DJ. She sang "Someone to Watch Over Me," and a rainbow appeared in the sky over the water as Michael waltzed Diana around the deck. Then she played "It's Raining Men," and everyone crammed onto the dance floor, laughing and singing along. It was, everyone agreed, the party of the summer.

At Michael's urging, Diana told her parents the truth that they'd long ago guessed at: she'd been assaulted that summer, and, while it had knocked her off the path she'd planned, she'd found a different one. "And you're happy?" her mother asked. "Because you look happy," she said, before Diana could answer. "I just wish . . ." she said, her voice getting thick.

"What, Mom?"

"I just wish you'd told us back then! I wish you'd let us help."

Diana wrapped her arms around her mother's shoulders, pulling her close. "I know. I wish a lot of things were different. But I promise, it all worked out okay." Her mother nodded, and wiped her eyes before pushing Diana toward the dance floor, where her father was waiting, looking healthy and strong, his shoulders straight and his skin less sallow. "Go dance with your dad, honey. He's been waiting for this a long time."

Diana had the money she'd saved up from years of living rent-free. Michael had a small inheritance from his grandfather. But even after they'd pooled their savings, it only amounted to ten percent of what they estimated the cottage would sell for on the open market.

"It can't hurt to ask," Michael told her, so a few weeks before their wedding, Diana approached Dr. Levy.

"I don't even know if you ever wanted to sell the place," she began.

"Actually, I've been giving it quite a bit of thought lately,"

Dr. Levy replied. "I think—wait, hang on." Diana waited. A few seconds later, Dr. Levy, sounding sheepish, said, "I had to close my office door before anyone hears me saying anything this woo-woo. But here's the truth: I think that people and things, and, maybe, sometimes houses, come into our lives for a reason. That cottage mattered a lot to my parents, and it was important to me when I was a young woman. Now, though, I think that you're the one who's meant to be its caretaker. Well, you and Michael."

Dr. Levy accepted their offer. Michael gave up the lease on his apartment in Wellfleet and moved in with his clothes, his collection of spy novels, and his television set. Diana worried that the cottage would feel cramped and claustrophobic, as the novelty of cohabitation wore off, but as soon as the weather was warm Michael started work on an addition, a living room with a second loft bedroom above it. In the warm months, they would use the deck, with its firepit and picnic table and the outdoor shower; in the winter, when it got dark early, they were happy to build a fire and huddle indoors, on the couch or in bed, tucked up underneath the eaves with Willa snoozing at their feet.

Michael replaced the creaky, drafty windows with double-hung, weatherproof ones that glided up and down at the touch of a finger and fit snugly in their frames. The next year, Michael dug up a patch of sandy earth and had a friend at a landscaping company haul in a truckload of soil, to make Diana a garden. That summer, they had a garden, and grew tomatoes and peppers and eggplants and corn.

Diana learned to bake, and Michael took up birding. They both became expert kayakers and proficient surf casters, standing on the beach in their waders, watching the horizon for signs. When they spotted clouds of birds massing, and the water roiling beneath them, they'd cast their lines and, more often than not, pull in a fish or two.

Michael bought a smoker, which he set on the corner of the deck and would use to smoke sea bass and make bluefish pâté. Diana began selling her embellished oyster shells to shops in Eastham and Orleans, and, just as Michael had predicted, when she raised the price, her sales first doubled, then tripled. For her birthday, Michael signed her up for watercolor lessons at the Castle Hill Center for the Arts, and Diana added painting to her hobbies. That summer, she displayed a few paintings at the farmers' market, next to her shells, and watched, surprised, as the summer people bought them. The year after that, she was showing her watercolors at local art fairs, and as the new century began, a gallery in Provincetown took her on. *Diana Carmody is a self-taught artist whose work explores the contradictions in nature and in the landscapes of the Outer Cape, where she makes her home. In still lifes and seascapes, Carmody forces the viewer to consider the spaces between the tranquility of sea and sky, the beauty of dunes and marsh grass, and the potent violence of wind and rain, thunder and lightning,* the gallery's brochure about her said. *In her work, nature is restless, motion is constant, the threat of danger implicit in the churn of the waves or a darkening sky or an animal lurking at the border. Her work invites the viewer to consider her own expectations about safety and beauty.* ("I don't know what it means, exactly," Diana confided to Michael, who'd replied, "It means they can charge five thousand dollars.")

Eventually, Diana found a therapist, one of Reese's friends, a woman named Hazel with short white hair and a thoughtful, quiet manner, who specialized in treating survivors of sexual assault. She taught Diana techniques for staying grounded, how to distinguish between her "emotion mind" and her "wise mind." In her soothing, melodic voice, Hazel would point out when Diana was catastrophizing or personalizing, and urge her to reframe her thoughts, to look for benign interpretations, and consider the facts in evidence when Diana talked about feeling empty or worthless or inconsequential, or on the days when she woke up so full of rage it was all she could do not to scream at everyone she saw.

Michael's sister, Kate, and her husband, Devin, eventually had three children, two boys and a girl. Diana's sister Julia's daughters were in elementary school, and Kara's son and daughter were seven and eight years old when Kate and her husband had their third (and, Kate swore, their final) baby. Diana watched her sister nurse the latest addition, a girl they'd named Addison. She watched Michael take the baby, his arms engulfing the blanket-wrapped bundle until it all but disappeared, his smile crinkling his cheeks and turning his eyes into slits, and waited to see if it would hurt. She probed her feelings the way she'd sometimes poke at a bruise, testing to see how it felt. The babies, she found, didn't break her heart the way she worried they would, and toddlers were exhausting. It was not until years later that she had cause to question her choices.

"I love it here," her fourteen-year-old niece Sunny said, her voice dreamy, when she and her sister came to stay for a long weekend while Diana's sister Julia and her husband celebrated their twentieth anniversary. "Aunt Diana, will you show us how to do the oyster shells?" Sunny asked, as Sasha, her twelve-year-old sister, stood slightly behind her, awaiting Diana's answer. Sunny and Sasha both had dark hair and dark eyes, but Sasha was a petite girl who moved in lightning-quick darts, like a lizard, while Sunny was taller, good-natured and tranquil, with hair that fell in ringlets and her mother's curvy build.

Diana showed them how to paint shells, and rode with them on rented bikes into Provincetown and all around the dunes. She took them to the cranberry bogs, and for walks along the jetty, and kayaking through the marsh. At night, Michael set up a tent in the yard, arranging camping lanterns in a circle around it. With a fire burning in the firepit, and the hot tub bubbling away, Diana thought it felt enchanted, even magical. The girls hadn't wanted to leave, had demanded that Diana and her sister settle on a date for their return before they'd get in Julia's car.

"You can send them here anytime," Diana said. "They're always welcome."

"I'll take you up on that. They look like they had a great time." She beckoned Diana toward the railing that overlooked the water, away from the car, and the girls. When Diana was at her side, she said, "I'm glad Sunny had a good time. She's been needing a break."

Diana felt a weight settle against her chest. "What's going on?"

"Oh, you know." Julia tried to sound nonchalant, but her face was bleak. "She was one of the first girls in her class to, you know, develop. I think some of the boys have been teasing her pretty bad."

And there it was, the rage that lived just under her skin, ready to come boiling up at an instant. Diana forced herself to breathe, to feel the ground beneath her feet and the wood of the fence under her fingertips, to relax her hands, which wanted to form fists. "It's just teasing? Nothing's happened?"

"No," said Julia, with an uncomfortable smile. "Nothing's happened. But I'm glad she's got this place. I'm glad she has you."

That night, Diana put away the tent and the lanterns, and straightened the clutter of shells and paintbrushes the girls had left on the deck. She called Willa, whose walk, in her later years, had become the stiff and oddly dignified gait of a queen. Slowly, they descended the beach stairs and walked along the sand. *I should have had daughters*, Diana thought, feeling her eyes sting with unshed tears. *I would have been a good mother. Those boys stole that from me.*

That night, in bed, when Michael reached for her, she rolled away, facing the wall. In a low voice, he said, "Want to talk?"

"Oh," she said, and cleared her throat, "just thinking about old times. I'll feel better in the morning." But it was a few mornings, and an emergency session with Hazel before she felt like herself again, like a human adult woman with friends and work and hobbies, a rich, fulfilling life, and a husband who loved her, and not like a broken thing that could never be made right. That winter, and into the spring, she went for lots of walks by herself, ranging for miles along the sand or the paths through the marshes and forests, trying to feel less empty, more at home in her skin and her life.

Fourteen years after Diana got her at the shelter, Willa died in her sleep, curled, as always, at the foot of their bed. Michael scooped up her body, wrapped in a blanket. He carried her out to the truck, then came back, and held Diana, in silence, for a long time.

Diana took it hard. It felt like another painful reminder that, however happy she felt, however safe and protected, there was always misery, crouching in the nearby shadows, waiting around the corner, and nothing could keep it away.

Michael didn't push her. When Diana finally felt ready, they went back to the shelter in Dennis and found a medium-sized mutt, a cheerful fellow with bushy brown fur and eyes like bright black buttons. He seemed to be the result of the union between a corgi and some kind of terrier, and, like Willa, he'd been abandoned, tied up underneath a bridge, starving, with his fur full of mats and burrs and every kind of bug. Diana and Michael brought him home. They brushed the remaining dirt and twigs and burrs out of his coat, and fed him kibble soaked in chicken broth, and tossed a tennis ball for him to fetch. Eventually, his favorite thing became sitting in the prow of a kayak with his back paws on the base of the boat and his front paws on its top, gazing out across the water as Diana paddled.

In 2010, more than twenty years after he'd fed her dinner

and given her a job, Reese called Diana into his office, a small, cramped space at the back of the restaurant that smelled of spices and industrial-strength cleaner. "Jonathan and I are retiring," he said.

"You're leaving?" she'd said, feeling her face and hands get cold. "You can't leave!"

He'd shaken his head. "We're not going anywhere." He waved his hands dramatically toward the sunset, and the drag queens on the street, visible through the window. "How could we leave all this behind? No. We'll be right here, except for a few months in the wintertime, when we'll decamp for warmer climes."

"So you're selling?" *New management,* she thought. A new menu and a new chef. Maybe the new management wouldn't even want to keep her. Maybe he, or she, would want eager young things, with their strong backs and their open minds, ready to adapt to new ways of doing things.

"That was what I wanted to discuss." He'd smiled at her and smoothed the white curls of his beard. "How would you feel about being the Abbey's new proprietress?"

She'd gasped, and said, "I don't have—I mean, I don't think—"

"Jonathan and I discussed it. We have what I consider to be a very reasonable mortgage. If the bank agrees, we'll let you take it over." Diana was silent, shocked into speechlessness, as Reese said, "You can even change the name, if you want. Call it Our Lady of Good Harbor again. Take it back to its roots."

She wiped away the tears that were spilling down her cheeks. "I don't know what to say. You're too good to me. I don't deserve this."

He'd shrugged, still smiling. His beard was completely white by then, but his skin was still the same smooth golden-brown, with his gold glasses twinkling against it. "Stop your sobbing." He'd reached for the box of Kleenex on his desk, the one he kept there for servers who'd come in crying about bad breakups or families who didn't want them, and handed it to Diana. "Go home, talk it over with that man of yours, and give me an answer in the morning."

She promised she would, knowing, of course, that the answer would be yes. And so, after all her years waitressing, Diana found herself the owner of a restaurant.

Sometimes, over the years, Diana would wake up, her night-gown soaked in sweat, her heart galloping, the cloying taste of peaches in her mouth and, in her ears, the sound of her hair swishing against the sand. Sometimes she'd turn away from Michael when they were in bed together. Sometimes, when they were making love, some sound or gesture would take her outside of herself. She'd find herself floating in the air, looking down, like she was watching a stranger moving on the bed. Sometimes, the sorrow of the road not taken would overwhelm her. Her sisters would visit with their children, or she'd talk with her nieces on the phone—about friends, about music, about picking a college or breaking up with a boyfriend—and Diana would think of the babies that she'd never have, or she'd glimpse a mother and daughter, in the supermarket or on the beach, sometimes squabbling, sometimes just sitting on the sand together, and the sadness would descend like a crushing weight until she could barely breathe.

When that happened, she would go to Michael, and let him hold her, letting his love, and his body, anchor her and keep her in place as she tried to concentrate on something real: the feeling of the sheets against her bare feet. The smell of the cottage: woodsmoke and salt air. The sound of Pedro, on his dog bed in the corner, licking sand from his paws after a walk on the beach.

Those instances became less frequent as the years went by, and they didn't hurt as much. Diana could have spent the rest of her life content, with just those episodes, and those questions, to remind her of what she'd survived and what she'd done. She could have lived like Eve in the garden, ignoring the snake, avoiding the apple tree. And then, one day, the apple tree found her.

She supposed, looking back, it had been building all spring and summer, the months of #MeToo, as more and more men, increasingly prominent, were accused of crimes against women. A movie producer was said to have forced actresses to perform sexual acts. A newscaster was accused of rape, and another one of exposing himself to young female colleagues, calling them to his house and then greeting them naked. Editors and authors, musicians and politicians, the great and the good, one after another after another as the months went on. Diana watched it all, wondering if the boys who'd harmed her—men now—were watching, if they felt guilt or complicity, if they even recognized that they'd done anything wrong.

And then came a bright October Saturday. Michael was closing up clients' houses for the winter, and Diana, dressed in a pair of paint-spattered overalls and a boiled-wool jacket, had tagged along. She wandered through the kitchens and the living rooms and powder rooms of the Springer house and the Killian house, until they arrived at Michael's last stop, a house where Diana had never been, a modern, boxy, cedar-shingled place on the top of a dune. Michael was in the master bedroom, making sure that all the sliding doors were locked. Diana went across the hall, to a guest room decorated in a nautical theme. The two twin beds were covered in duvets with a sailboat print; a framed woodcut of a blue whale hung on the wall. Beneath it was a bookcase full of John Grisham paperbacks and collections of crossword puzzles. On top of it was a framed photograph, a middle-aged man squinting into the sunshine, with one arm around a woman's waist and the other slung over a young girl's shoulders.

Diana glanced at the picture, turned away, then turned back and felt her heart stop beating. She picked it up and looked more closely, ignoring the girl and the woman, her eyes only on the man. His brown hair was graying, but it was still curly. The shape of his nose and his jaw were all familiar. She recognized his smile, as he grinned into the sun, a man without a care in the world.

Diana felt like she'd been dropped from a great height. She collapsed backward onto the bed like a pricked balloon, holding the picture facedown in her lap. She was still sitting there when Michael found her.

"Hey, what's wrong? Didn't you hear me?"

She looked up at him wordlessly and handed him the picture. "This guy," she said, in a toneless voice that didn't sound like her own.

"What? What about him?"

Diana got to her feet. "That's Poe," she said. "That's the guy from that summer. The guy who raped me."

Michael stared at her, face slack and startled, hands hanging by his sides. "That's him!" Diana screamed. She jumped to her feet, stalking toward her husband. "Whose house is this? Do you know his name? Did you know that he's been here this whole entire time?"

She felt Michael's hands on her shoulders; heard his voice coming from what sounded like very far away. When he tried to pull her against him, Diana shoved him back, hard.

"What's his name?" she asked again.

Michael pulled off his baseball cap and raked his hands through his hair. "The man who owns the house is Vernon Shoemaker," he said. His voice was low, and steady, maddeningly reasonable. He pointed at the picture. "I've never met this guy. Never even seen him. My guess is that it's his son. Mr. Shoemaker has two sons, and they both spend part of the summer here, I think.

I really don't know a lot, though. Mr. Shoemaker is the only one I've met. He's the one I deal with. This guy I don't know."

Diana stared at her husband for a long, silent moment, her chest heaving, her hands clenched into fists. Then she shoved her way past him and went stalking down the hall, looking for more pictures, more evidence, a name. After all these years, finally, a name.

In the living room she found two more pictures, one of the man on a sailboat, beside someone who had to be his brother, a slightly older, slightly fatter version of him. The second was a wedding picture, where the man she'd known as Poe seemed to be in his mid-thirties, and his wife, a young woman with wide eyes and dark hair, half-swallowed by an enormous pouf of a white dress. She stared at the two faces, first the man, then the woman, running her fingers over the words monogrammed at the bottom of the picture frame: *Henry and Daisy Shoemaker, June 9, 2001.*

"Diana?" Michael had come up behind her, moving carefully, the way you'd approach a skittish, feral cat.

"I've seen her," she said. Her voice was faint. "Jesus, Michael, I've seen this woman, in the post office, and Jams, and in the Wellfleet Market . . ." A memory was surfacing. She'd been at the market, picking up hot dog buns, and this woman, Daisy, had been right beside her. Diana remembered that her brown hair had been drawn into a loose ponytail, and she'd said something, *Hi,* or *Perfect beach weather, isn't it,* or . . . "Lucky," said Diana. Her voice was hollow. "She said how lucky we were, to be in a place like this." Diana's heart was thumping, her brain spinning. She felt like her windpipe had narrowed, like she couldn't take in enough oxygen. When she shook her head, there was a ringing in her ears. "This guy, the guy who raped me, he comes here every summer, him and his wife and his d-daughter . . ." She swallowed the scream that wanted to escape, and when Michael tried to take her hand, she said, "I can't be in here anymore," and walked, then trotted, down the hall. Right by the front door was a half-moon-shaped table, with more framed pictures, and a glass jar of seashells. Diana picked it up, hoisted it over her head, and sent it smashing down to shatter on the tiled floor before running out the door.

She tried to forget. She tried to put the knowledge of Henry Shoemaker's face, of his presence in Truro, into the farthest reaches of her mind, walling off the new knowledge the way she'd walled off Corn Hill Beach, long ago. *I'm not going to think about it*, she would tell herself, but that promise just turned out to be a guarantee that she was going to think about it, all day long, at work, at home, painting in the shared studio space at the Castle Hill Center for the Arts, where her brushes sat with paint drying on the bristles, and her half-finished canvases were stacked facing the walls. On and on, her brain churned, like a washing machine stuck on "agitate," with one simple phrase, two words, pounding like a drum: *he's here, he's here, he's here.* She resisted, until one day she couldn't stand it anymore, and she did the thing she'd been keeping herself from doing since that Saturday morning with her husband. She went to the Truro library, sat down at one of the public terminals, and typed "Henry Shoemaker" into Google, because she couldn't stand even the idea of typing his name into her own laptop at home.

Two hours later, her eyes were burning, and her neck ached. She'd learned the name of Henry "Hal" Shoemaker's law firm, and where he'd gone to law school and college, and the year he'd made partner. She knew the name of his daughter, and his home address. She'd learned that his wife's real name was not Daisy. It was Diana, and, somehow, that unsettled her almost as badly as finding the picture had. It made her think that she was the rough-draft Diana, the one who got crumpled up and tossed in the trash, while his wife was the final version, the one who was beloved, cherished, marriage material.

Daisy and Hal had one child, a daughter, who was thirteen (if Beatrice Shoemaker was on social media, Diana didn't want to know. Even while gripped by this insanity, she had limits). The Shoemaker clan lived in Gladwyne, Pennsylvania, in a house that she could view on Curbside, and that she knew, thanks to public real-estate records, that Hal had purchased from Vernon Shoemaker in 1998 for one dollar, and that it was now assessed at just over two million dollars. Vernon Shoemaker owned the house in Truro, but his Facebook page informed her that his sons and grandchildren were regular summer guests.

"Can I ask you a question?" Michael had brought home steamed lobsters for dinner, in an attempt to cheer her up. He was cracking a tail enthusiastically. Diana was nibbling, without appetite, at a swimmeret. "You know everything there possibly is to know about this guy except his blood type. What's the endgame? What are you planning to do?"

She didn't answer. She didn't have an answer. What she did was change the subject, then clear the table, and wash the dishes, and climb up to the sleeping loft, willing herself to fall asleep.

She woke in the middle of the night and lay awake, waiting until five o'clock in the morning. She thought about the girl she'd been, and all the girls and women, violated by their bosses and their colleagues, by men whom they'd trusted and admired. She thought about her niece, and her sister's resignation, that this was just the way of the world, that Sunny had no right to expect anything different. She asked herself whether the world could change if she just sat by and did nothing. Just as the sun was rising, she slipped out of bed, careful not to wake her husband or the dog. She propped the note that she'd written the day before against the sugar bowl on the kitchen table, and padded outside, into the predawn dark. Her new car, a Prius, barely made a sound when it started. She turned it on, checking to make sure that the bag she'd packed the day before, while Michael was at work, was on the seat beside her, and went gliding silently through the darkness. She'd be halfway down Route 6 before Michael realized she was gone, on her way to New Hampshire, and the Emlen Academy.

19

Daisy

It had been Hal's idea to host the Melville Upper School spring cocktail party, an undertaking he'd proposed right after they'd gotten Beatrice enrolled. "How can we get involved?" he'd asked, turning his most charming smile on Lynne Parratt, who ran the school's development office, and when she'd said that they were still looking for a venue for their spring cocktail party, he said, without even glancing Daisy's way, "We'd be happy to host." He'd put his hand on Daisy's shoulder and said, "My wife is a wonderful cook."

As soon as they'd gotten in the car, Daisy said, "You could have asked me first, you know."

"It's important for Beatrice that we get to know the school's community. And," he'd said, before Daisy could voice additional objections, "it'll give you a chance to show off. Maybe drum up some new business."

It'll give me a chance to work for three days straight without getting paid anything, Daisy thought, as her husband planted a kiss on her lips. She'd have to clean the house, from top to bottom, dealing with the clutter that seemed to multiply itself exponentially whenever her back was turned, and see if Mireille, the cheerful, competent Frenchwoman she hired when she needed extra hands, would be available. She'd have to rent barware and cocktail chairs and serving pieces; she'd have to order flowers and deal with entertainment, not to mention managing the logistics of the auction itself. Worst of all, she'd have to find something to wear. If there'd been a single benefit to having a kid out of state in boarding school, it was that she got a hiatus from having to squeeze herself into shapewear and make small talk at a school function. Now here she was, less than nine months later, dragging herself to Saks, where being over a size eight meant the sales-ladies would make you feel very, very small.

She gave herself two hours to find a dress and, when her time was up, emerged with a short-sleeved navy-blue jersey dress, knee length, A-line, with cap sleeves. It also had a square neckline, the single feature that would make the new dress distinguishable from the half-dozen other navy-blue and black dresses she already had in her closet, purchased for events just like this one. With the dress draped over the Range Rover's back seat, she drove to New Jersey for the liquor, then returned home to spend over an hour on the phone with the exceedingly chirpy Lynne, who had very specific instructions for how the items were to be described or displayed, and even what kinds of clipboards and pens the Mel-ville community preferred. "And let's make sure we've got some nut-free and vegetarian appetizers. Preferably vegan," she'd said. Daisy had ended the call and had stood in her kitchen, feeling somewhere between infuriated and bemused. She remembered something that Hannah had told her once: *people treat you the way you let them*. Hannah never let herself be treated poorly. She insisted on respect, from her four-year-old students, from waiters, from her husband and daughter, from, once, a jogger who'd spat on the street too close to her feet. "I'm sorry, am I wearing my Cloak of Invisibility?" she'd demanded, and when the guy tried to run past her, Hannah had shouted, "Yo!" so loudly that everyone on the street had turned, and the jogger had been forced to stop and endure Hannah's tirade. Daisy could picture her friend, with two fingers stuck in the air and her other hand on her hip, standing like the Statue of Liberty until her kids settled down, and in Daisy's kitchen, bent over a bubbling cauldron of marinara sauce, asking, "Do you think the steam's good for my pores?" Oh, how Daisy missed her.

On the appointed Saturday in April, Daisy spent the morning getting her hair blown out and her nails manicured. Mireille arrived at three in the afternoon, the florist came at four, and the musicians, a quartet of students who comprised Melville's jazz ensemble, arrived at five o'clock.

At six, Daisy slid the stuffed figs and the pastry-wrapped goat cheese purses into the oven, crammed her feet into a pair of navy-blue high heels, and put a giant straw hat with a navy-blue ribbon on her head. The theme of the party was the Kentucky Derby, even though the Derby itself wasn't until May. At least it had made the menu easy: mint julep punch and bourbon slushies, fried chicken sliders served on biscuits, with hot honey, tea sandwiches with Benedictine spread, bite-sized hot browns, the signature sandwich of Louisville, and miniature Derby pies for dessert.

Mireille fed the jazz kids early and got them set up in the corner, close to a powder room where spit valves could be emptied as needed. "Put on your lipstick," she told Daisy, who was already wearing lipstick. She went upstairs to put on more and to roust Beatrice from her bedroom, just as the first car pulled into the driveway and one of the valets went to park it. Over the weekend, Hal had bought spotlights, which shone on the front of their house, illuminating the half-circle of the driveway and the path to the front door (and, Daisy privately thought, making the place look especially imposing). On Saturday, he'd installed the lights, and he'd spent Sunday pacing around the ground floor, frowning at a spot on the pale-gold and green oriental rug that Lester had scratched, rearranging the ornamental birch logs in the fireplace, and studying the one wall in the kitchen that Daisy had insisted on painting a moody shade of navy blue, a contrast to the rest of the walls, which were tastefully taupe. She'd wanted to hang colorful plates and pieces of pottery over the doors to the pantry, but Hal told her it was "too busy"; she'd wanted to keep her ceramic canisters of flour and sugar and beans on the counter, but he'd said it made the kitchen look cluttered; she'd wanted . . . God, the truth was that Daisy could barely remember what she'd wanted. Only that she'd liked color and coziness, like her navy-blue wall or her row of canisters, and Hal had not.

"Phil! Ellen!" she heard Hal say from the vicinity of the entryway, where there was a delicate pie-crust table (his choice) and, above it, a towering mirror with an ornate gold frame (hers). "Come on in and get comfortable."

Thank God for name tags, Daisy thought, as her house filled up. She plotted a course from one end of the living room all the way to the staircase, stopping to introduce herself and welcome her guests to her home.

"This punch is delicious!" said a woman in a white hat embellished with pink flowers. Her nametag ID'ed her as Eleanor Crane. Her flushed cheeks suggested she was not on her first cup of punch. "What's in it?"

"Muddled mint, bourbon, simple syrup . . ."

"Delicious!" Eleanor Crane repeated, before Daisy could complete the list of ingredients. Peering at Daisy, she said, "You give cooking lessons, right? You'll have to teach me how to do it."

"You can bid on me, if you're interested." Daisy nodded toward the sunroom. She and Hal had moved out all the furniture, massing Daisy's plants in the corner, and set up tables for the auction items, displaying the prizes that were suitable for viewing, posting pictures of the ones that were not. Melville parents and alums had offered stays at vacation homes in Avalon, Ventnor, Martha's Vineyard, and Jackson Hole; tickets to various concerts and sporting events, and various bespoke experiences with, or from, local luminaries (dinner for six with the *Philadelphia Inquirer* food critic; a night behind the scenes with a local TV weatherman; a chance to spend an afternoon with former governor Ed Rendell, or to have your name in a local novelist's next work). There were restaurant gift certificates and boutique gift certificates, personal-trainer sessions and spa days. Daisy herself had donated a three-hour cooking lesson. The last time she'd checked, only one person had bid on her services, and, to make it worse, she'd recognized Hal's handwriting.

"I'll do that!" said Ellie. Daisy thanked her and moved on to the next group, realizing, as she listened in, that everyone had already made summer plans for their children. She'd heard about Mimi Simonton's Shakespeare camp and Marta Wells's lacrosse camp. She found out that Everly Broadnax would be playing tennis in Florida and Charlie O'Day would be doing a language-immersion program in Seville. She sipped her drink and smiled, drifting away before any of the Main Line mommies in their cocktail dresses or the dads in ties could ask how Beatrice was planning to spend her summer, before she'd be forced to say the words "taxidermied mice" out loud. "Beatrice goes to sailing camp near our home in Cape Cod," was the line she planned on using. It sounded fancy as long as she didn't mention that "sailing camp" wasn't even a proper sleepaway camp, but instead just a day camp run out of a single cramped boathouse on Commercial Street, the same place Hal had gone when he'd been Bea's age. She also left out the fact that Beatrice had only consented to go three days a week.

In spite of her best efforts, she found herself at Hal's side, drawn into a conversation with the Byrnes. Mr. Byrne was compact and fit-looking, with silvery hair and a matching goatee. Mrs. Byrne's short, sleeveless, shift-style silk dress revealed a body that suggested many hours spent in the spinning studio. They matched, Daisy thought, and looked at her husband, his body still trim, his hair still mostly dark, his face, with a few more lines and wrinkles and sunspots, still the same handsome, strong-looking face she'd fallen in love with. Did she match him? Probably not. Even in the same kind of dress that they wore (albeit in a larger size), even with her best grooming efforts, she knew she lacked the grace and confidence of these women. She looked, she thought, like she belonged somewhere else, with someone different.

She made herself pay attention to the conversation. The older Byrne boy, Daisy learned, had been accepted to Duke, "ED," which, Daisy had learned, meant "early decision" and not "erectile dysfunction." "So, thank goodness, our spring was pretty tranquil. Now we're gearing up to go it again with Samantha." Mrs. Byrne smiled charmingly at Hal and said, "You did your undergrad at Dartmouth, right?" When Hal acknowledged that this was so, she asked, "Did you like it? Did you feel like Hanover was too small-town?"

"I loved it," Hal said, his voice hearty. "Best four years of my life, aside from prep school."

"But I can't imagine our daughter ending up there. Not unless she has a personality transplant between now and senior year!" Daisy could see her joke landing with a thud. Mr. Byrne chuckled politely. Mrs. Byrne tilted her head. Hal's hand tightened on her arm. She could imagine what he was thinking: *Why are you telling people our daughter's not Dartmouth material?* Which wasn't what she meant, of course. It wasn't that Beatrice wasn't smart enough to get in somewhere good; it was that she wouldn't be happy, a fact that Hal must have realized by now. At least, Daisy hoped that was the case.

"How about you, Daisy? Where did you go to college?"

"I was at Rutgers," said Daisy, feeling her smile tighten her face. It was absolutely, undeniably true. She had been at Rutgers. She'd just never finished.

"That's a great school," said Mr. Byrne, as Hal said, "I think our little artiste is probably going to want someplace smaller."

Daisy smiled and nodded. At the first opportunity, she murmured something about needing to check the punch bowl and escaped to the kitchen. She knew that she shouldn't feel the need to apologize to this roomful of terrifyingly ambitious moms and dads because all her daughter wanted to do was make needle-felted gnomes and elves and miniature replicas of pets, but she did. *You know the summer before junior year is critical*, some mom would say, with the dad beside her nodding his agreement. *It's their last chance to do something big.* As if their lives ended at eighteen if they didn't get into the right kind of school. Which, Daisy realized, these people probably believed.

Daisy replenished the punch bowl. She visited the porch, to see if anyone else had bid on her services (no one had), then went back to the kitchen to check the food. She'd just tied on an apron when she felt Hal come up behind her. "Daisy, come meet the new dean!" In a low voice, he added, "And take off the apron. I don't want you looking like the help."

Then you shouldn't have volunteered me to host, Daisy thought. She untied her apron, wondering, with an unpleasant prickly sensation, if Hal's real problem was not her apron, but the fact that she wasn't like Everly's mother, who was slender and gorgeous and, like Hal, a lawyer, or like Charlie's mom, who had on a pair of red-soled Louboutins and did something important at Comcast. Daisy could never have been one of those women, not even if she'd gotten her college degree and a high-powered job, she thought as she trailed after Hal. She just wasn't that kind of woman. She lacked that level of ambition. She was perfectly happy with her home, her daughter, the business that gave her what Hal referred to, charmingly, as "pin money." She'd been happy, and she thought that Hal had been happy with her—his little bird, with her little job, who made their house a home. Only now, as she saw the appreciative way he looked at the new head of Melville's Upper School, a woman named Krista Dietrich, who was all of thirty-six years old and had degrees from Stanford and Wharton, Daisy wondered if he'd changed his mind, if he wasn't reaching the conclusion that Daisy would never blossom, would never become any more than what she was, and if what he felt was resentment, not satisfaction, with their marriage and with her.

When Ms. Dietrich went off to glad-hand the next couple, Hal took Daisy's arm and leaned in close. "Have you seen our daughter?"

Daisy looked around. Beatrice had clomped down the stairs at the start of the night in a floor-length black crepe dress, Doc Marten boots, and a brooch in the shape of an owl, with ruby-chip eyes, pinned to her chest. "What do you think?" she'd asked, giving them a spin.

"Adorable," said Daisy, just as Hal said, "You look like you're auditioning for a dinner theater production of *Arsenic and Old Lace.*"

Beatrice had glared at him.

"Go upstairs and change," Hal had told her, which Beatrice seemed to have interpreted as "go to your room and don't come back."

Daisy excused herself, went upstairs, slipped off her shoes as soon as she'd rounded the corner that put her out of her guests' view, and knocked on Beatrice's door.

"What?" her daughter snarled.

Daisy eased the door open. Beatrice was flopped down on her bed, still in her dress and her boots. Her eyes were puffy and pink, and there were tear tracks running through her makeup. "Why is Dad always such a jerk to me?" she asked.

"Oh, honey." Daisy sat on the bed and stroked her daughter's back. "He isn't always a jerk. And I think he wants things to go well for you at your new school. He wants to make a good impression."

"He wants me to pretend to be someone I'm not." Her daughter's voice was bitter. "Like Everly and her stupid tennis. Or Mimi and her stupid Shakespeare."

"Stupid Shakespeare," Daisy repeated, in her most teenage-girl tone. "He's totes the worst, right?"

Beatrice sat up, regarding her severely. "Mom," she said, "please don't ever try to talk like a young person."

Daisy stood up and attempted a very bad version of the Backpack. Beatrice groaned, but Daisy thought she detected the very early stages of a smile.

"Okay, but you have to come downstairs."

Beatrice buried her head in her pillows, until only a few tufts of silvery-blue hair were visible.

"Do it," said Daisy, "or I'll get a TikTok."

Beatrice didn't move.

"Okay, how about this? Come downstairs, say hello to three people, get something to eat, let your father see you, and then you can come back and hide."

"Whatever," Beatrice grumbled, but it got her off the bed.

Downstairs, Daisy replenished the tray of deviled eggs (an old-school, dowdy kind of party food, but like the pigs in a blanket, they always got eaten). She picked up a platter and did a quick round, collecting empty cups and discarded plates and crumpled paper napkins, pausing to touch the leaves of her poor schefflera, pushed into a corner of the terra-cotta-floored sunroom along with another half-dozen houseplants because Hal didn't want the place looking like a jungle.

She told the musicians to take a break and brought them glasses of water and lemonade, plus a plate of desserts she'd set aside. That task completed, she checked the time, refilled her drink, and stood in the corner, watching women in six-hundred-dollar shoes and men in thousand-dollar suits talk about which thirty-thousand-dollar summer camp their kids would be attending for the critical summer before junior year.

When she noticed the punch bowl getting low again, she went back to the kitchen. She saw the piles of plates by the sink, the empty crates in which the glasses had arrived stacked in the corner, and Mireille standing with her back against the oven, with Hal in front of her, just inches away. For a moment, Daisy wasn't sure what she'd interrupted. A proposition? A kiss? Then she saw Mireille wasn't just standing, she was cringing; that Hal was too close, his posture menacing.

Daisy hurried closer, in time to see Mireille shake her head. "*Non*—I mean, no, Mr. Shoemaker, I promise, I didn't let anyone into your office."

"Well, then we have a problem," Hal said, biting off each syllable. "I have—or, I should say that I had, five hundred dollars in cash in my desk drawer, and it seems to have grown legs and wandered off."

"Hal." When she touched his back he turned around with such an angry look on his face that Daisy stumbled backward, hitting the counter with the small of her back. *Oh, that's going to leave a mark*, she thought. Immediately, Hal's hands were on her shoulders, and he was the one steadying her, pulling her upright.

"Honey, are you okay?"

"I'm fine," she said, ignoring her throbbing back. "I was in your office. I took the money out of the drawer and brought it upstairs. The kids left their instrument cases in there, and I just thought it'd all be safer somewhere else."

For what felt like a long time, Hal said nothing. His face was pale; his hands were fisted; he looked like a man who wanted to hit someone, and Daisy smelled something so incongruous that at first she didn't recognize it. Scotch, she realized. For the first time since she'd met him, Hal had been drinking. She could feel his anger, could almost see it, like something tightly leashed that was a few frayed strands from breaking free and doing terrible things. Then he relaxed, and she could glimpse her husband again, her kind, thoughtful Hal, who swore he'd remembered her as a girl, who'd left a credit card on her pillow the morning after he'd proposed and said *I want to be your family.*

"Mireille," he said, his voice formal. "I owe you an apology."

"*Ce n'est rien,*" Mireille said faintly.

"No, it's not nothing." He reached into his wallet, and pulled out a bill large enough to make Mireille's eyes widen, and pressed it into her hand. "I'm very sorry."

"It's fine," said Mireille. She gave him a weak smile and went back to the sink, where she was washing wineglasses by hand. When Daisy joined her, holding a dish towel, Mireille bent forward, a sheaf of her hair obscuring her face, and repeated what she'd said to Daisy's husband. "It's fine."

Later, when the party was over, the dishes washed, the punch bowl packed up, and Daisy's plants and potted palms restored to their previous positions, she said, "What's going on?"

"What do you mean?" Hal asked, as if there could be any doubt about what she meant.

"What happened with Mireille?"

"Oh," Hal said, without meeting her eyes. "I guess I overreacted." His hair was tousled, and he was wearing pajamas, the top buttoned and the bottoms ironed. Daisy watched as he stood in front of the bathroom mirror, flossing his teeth. Hal always wore pajamas to bed, he always used the bathroom sink closest to the door, and he always flossed before bedtime. A creature of routine was her husband, which made her wonder what he was like before she met him, if his life had been as messy and chaotic then as it was tidy and regulated now.

"Are you drinking?" she asked, very gently.

He froze, the floss halfway to his mouth. "I had a drink," he said, precisely. "Just one. It's fine."

Daisy didn't answer. She didn't know what to say. She climbed into bed, and, after a moment, Hal got under the duvet and put his arms around her. She could smell his familiar scent: laundry detergent, Colgate toothpaste, dandruff-fighting shampoo. Her familiar husband; everything the same. "I'm sorry," he said. "I've been under the gun at work, and then, with Bubs dying, and Beatrice getting kicked out of Emlen. It's all been . . ." He gave a scoffing laugh. "A lot."

"It's been hard," said Daisy. "I know."

"I just want Beatrice to get off on the right foot. It matters, you know?" He gave her a look, part imploring, part imperious. "But you're right. I shouldn't have raised my voice."

"You scared her," said Daisy. *You scared me*, she thought.

"I know," said Hal. His voice was tight. "I feel terrible about it. I gave her a tip—"

"I know," Daisy said. "I saw."

"But I'll send her a note tomorrow."

"I think that's a good idea."

He gave her a perfunctory kiss, said, "Sleep tight, birdie." Then he rolled onto his side and was instantly asleep. Daisy lay awake beside him, knowing she wouldn't sleep. As the hours ticked by, she thought of the cleaning she'd have to do in the morning; about the silent auction bids to tally and the clipboards to return, about being the only woman in the room without either a college degree or a notable job; trying not to think about what Hannah, or Diana, would have made of the night's events, if Hannah had been alive or if Diana had been invited, or about a saying she'd heard more and more these days: *When someone tells you who they are, believe them.*

20

Beatrice

Beatrice was walking toward the school's front door when she heard a car's horn beep behind her. She jumped, turned around, and saw Cade Langley behind the wheel of a sporty black sedan.

"Hey, Beebee!"

That was what Cade had started calling her, him and his friends. Beatrice still wasn't sure if she liked it, if Beebee was the kind of cutesy nickname you'd give a little girl, or if, instead, it called to mind a BB gun.

She waved. Cade rolled up alongside her, keeping pace with her as she walked.

"You're going to be late," she told him.

"I've got a free." Cade was a junior, and upperclassmen at Melville were allowed to spend two periods each week off campus, with their parents' permission. Most of them, as far as Beatrice could tell, only went to the Starbucks directly across the street from campus. The really daring ones made it all the way to the burrito place next door.

"Hey," said Cade, "I like your outfit."

Beatrice smiled. She was especially proud of her day's look. She'd found an honest-to-God 1950s housedress at a thrift store in Philadelphia. It was blue cotton, with shiny black buttons and a round Peter Pan collar and a tie at the waist. She'd hand-washed the dress, stitched up a rip under the armpit, and ironed it before confirming the perfect fit that she'd seen in the dressing-room mirror, twirling around to make the skirt swish, thinking that she looked like Lucille Ball. She'd tied a pink-and-white polka-dotted kerchief over her hair, and instead of her Doc Martens she'd found a pair of black canvas Chuck Taylors that she thought looked just fine.

"I like your car."

Cade grinned and patted the dashboard. His hair had gotten longer in the few weeks Beatrice had been at Melville. It stuck up from his head in a way that reminded her of a poodle. His cheeks wore their usual flush, and his teeth looked very white beneath them. "My sixteenth birthday present."

"Lucky you. Happy birthday."

"It was in December. Don't worry. I didn't not invite you to my party."

"I wasn't concerned."

"Just in case you were."

This was how it went with Cade. He'd banter and tease her, always, it seemed, finding ways to let her know that she was the new girl, that he knew more than she did—more people, more teachers, more about Melville, more about everything.

"You want to go for a ride?"

She stared at him. "I've got Latin."

"*Amo, amas, amat,*" Cade recited. "Come on. It's only five de-merits if it's your first cut."

Beatrice bit her lip. "Yeah, but I've already gotten three de-merits for dress code violations." Evidently wearing Doc Mar-tens in gym class was demerit-worthy, which, in her opinion, was ridiculous. The girl who sat beside her in Earth Sciences spent most of her time making TikToks; the boy next to her in Advisory wore a T-shirt with the Confederate flag on it, completely visible through his button-down; and she was the one getting in trouble.

"Come on," Cade said. "Don't be like the rest of the sheep!" His *baaa*-ing noise made Beatrice giggle. She looked up at the door. The bell was ringing, and unless she sprinted and risked disarranging her hair, she'd be tardy. If she was already in trouble, she decided, it might as well be for something fun.

She climbed into the passenger's seat, pulled her seat belt in place, and said, "Where are we going?"

Cade seemed a little startled by her assent, but he made a smooth recovery. "Uh, my place?"

Beatrice rolled her eyes. "Uh, no?"

She wondered if this was a plan to get her up to his bedroom and out of her clothes. The night she'd met him at the movies, Cade had held her hand, for a few minutes, when Beatrice was sure none of the other kids were looking. There'd been three other people in the car when he'd driven her home, and he'd walked her to the door but hadn't tried to kiss her. When she sat with him at lunch, he asked her lots of questions, and she'd caught him staring at her a time or two in class, but lots of kids stared at her at Melville. What did Cade Langley want with her now?

"Are you bringing me to your house so you can have your way with me?" she asked.

"Have my way with you?" he repeated. "Do you always talk like you're in a book?"

Beatrice smiled. She was remembering a recent talk she'd had with her mother, about how she should never change herself, or dumb herself down, for some boy's benefit. Beatrice assumed her mother had gotten the speech from some article or expert, given the fact that she herself had dropped out of college and moved to Pennsylvania for some boy—namely Beatrice's father. But Beatrice had decided not to say so.

"Where do you want to go?" he asked.

She thought for a minute, leaned forward, and punched an address into the mapping app on her phone. "Follow my directions," she said, and pointed toward the road.

Twenty minutes later, they pulled up in front of a large, sober-looking brick building that took up the better part of the block on Twenty-Second Street. It would be a test, she'd decided as they drove. If Cade laughed, or told her it was weird, or refused to go inside with her, she'd have nothing more to do with him. But if he could appreciate it, or even just keep an open mind, then he had potential.

She led Cade through the wrought-iron fence, up the stairs, and right to the entrance of one of her favorite places in all of Philadelphia. By then, he'd figured out where they were.

"The Mutter Museum?"

"Moo-ter," she said, correcting his pronunciation. "There's an umlaut. Have you ever been?"

He shook his head. "It's, um, medical oddities, right?"

"The only place in America where you can see the preserved skeleton of conjoined twins," she said happily. "And a cross section of Albert Einstein's brain!" Beatrice bounded inside, flashing her card at the guard at the front desk.

"You're a member?" Cade asked, then, shrugging, answered his own question. "Of course you are."

Beatrice grinned at him. Her sneakers squeaked on the marble floor. This was one of her happy places. Her mother had brought her here when she was a toddler, with her friend Zoe and Zoe's mom, Hannah, so the girls could run around the big upstairs ballroom on rainy days. As Beatrice had gotten older, she'd become more interested in the actual museum, the exhibits of bodies and brains, tumors in jars and the rows of 139 skulls, collected by a single Viennese doctor when phrenology was all the rage. "Come on," she said. "Let's go see some dead things."

She grabbed Cade by the hand and half-walked, half-dragged him into the atrium, which was sunny, and empty, and had a kind of indefinably museum-ish smell. To their right was an exhibit of the history of spinal surgery, complete with spines. To the left, up the stairs, was the Soap Lady, a woman whose body was exhumed in Philadelphia in 1875 and whose remains were encased, per the sign by her glass coffin, in a fatty substance called adipocere. That, she decided, was a good place to start.

Beatrice and Cade stood, shoulder to shoulder, looking down at her: a vaguely female shape that appeared to have been turned not to soap but to stone. Her torso was a mottled brown and white; her mouth was a gaping, dark hole. Hanks of hair still hung from her scalp.

"This must've given you nightmares when you were a kid." Cade leaned forward. He had a few blemishes on his forehead, and bony wrists protruding past his cuffs, like he'd gotten taller overnight. Not perfect, in other words, which made her glad. She wouldn't have been able to tease him if he'd been too good-looking.

"Actually," Beatrice said, "I thought it was kind of cool."

Cade looked down at the woman, then sideways, at Beatrice. "Cool? She looks like the Crypt Keeper."

Beatrice rocked from her heels to her toes, trying to think of how she could explain. "I guess I liked the idea that you could be dead but still interesting. That people would come and look at you."

Cade put his hands in his pockets. "I don't know," he said. "If you want people to care about you after you die, you could write a song, or a book. You could invent something."

"True. But don't you think that dying in just the right place for just the right set of circumstances to turn your body into soap is a lot easier?"

"You might be onto something there." He was smiling, looking at her like she delighted him, was more interesting than anything in the museum.

"Want to see the collection of inhaled and swallowed objects?" she asked.

"You're kidding, right?"

She made her eyes wide. "Oh, I never kid about inhaled and swallowed objects."

"Okay, then," he said, and tucked her arm into his.

"You probably think I'm a weirdo," she said, as they took their seats in a booth at the Silk City Diner on Spring Garden Street. Her original plan had been to ask him to bring her back to school by lunch, but they'd ended up spending the whole morning in the museum. Cade had been fascinated by the replica of conjoined twins Chang and Eng, and Beatrice had asked if he'd read the novel about them, which led to a discussion of their favorite books, with Beatrice passionately insisting that *The Magicians* was much better on the page than it was on TV, and Cade telling her about Neil Gaiman's Lucifer graphic novels.

"No," said Cade, straight-faced. "I think you're a perfectly normal teenage girl."

Beatrice laughed as the waitress slapped menus down on the Formica. When she looked up from her menu, Cade was staring at her again.

"What?" she said, hoping that she didn't have something on her face or stuck between her teeth.

"I'm just trying to figure you out."

"Well, you can't," she said. "I'm a mystery wrapped in an enigma. What do you want to know? How I got to be so stylish?" She batted her eyes. "So fascinating?"

He paused, looking down. With his eyes on his menu. "Brave," he said quietly. Beatrice felt her face flush with pleasure, but before she could fully absorb the compliment, he said, "Like, you don't care that nobody else dresses the way you do, or looks the way you do, or likes the same kind of music, or whatever." He looked at her earnestly. "Everyone else I know, especially the girls, all they want is to be the same as everybody else. Even the stuff they do to be bad, or stand out, it's all the same."

"Stuff like what?"

Cade shrugged. "Julia vapes. And Emma's got a tattoo. But even stuff like that, it's like . . ." He picked up his fork, held it between his thumb and forefinger, and tilted it back and forth. ". . . like they googled 'how to be a rebellious teenager,' and just did whatever popped up." He looked at Beatrice. "All of our parents say the same stuff to us—how you can do anything you want, be anything you want. You're the only person I've ever met who acts like she believes it."

She stared at him, not saying a word, thinking that this was, by far, the best compliment she'd ever been paid, the nicest thing that anyone, boy or girl or parent, had ever said to her.

"You two ready?" asked the waitress.

Beatrice got her favorite fig and pear salad. Cade got the turkey BLT. "And I'm definitely getting a milkshake for dessert," Beatrice said.

"Will you share?" he asked.

"I will if you share your fries. So what's your favorite museum?" she asked. Cade admitted that he didn't have one.

"I used to like the Franklin Institute," he said. "Have you been in the giant heart?"

She shook her head a little at his cluelessness. "Everyone's been in the giant heart. Have you ever been to the Edgar Allan Poe house?"

He told her that he hadn't, but that he had read "The Tell-Tale Heart." They talked about horror stories until the food came. After a few bites of salad, Beatrice asked, "What about you?"

Cade knew what she was asking and answered with a self-deprecating gesture that encompassed his blue polo shirt and khakis.

"Okay, but that's just your clothes. What do you think about? What music do you like? What do you want to do after high school?"

He inhaled, shoulders rising, then shook his head. "I always thought I wanted to get into a good college, and play lacrosse, and go to law school, like my father. But I never thought about it much."

"How about when you were little?" she asked. "Did you want to be a fireman? Or a vet? A ballet dancer?"

He ate a few French fries and said, with a smile of surpassing sweetness, "I wanted to be a taxi driver."

"Really!" said Beatrice.

When he nodded, a tuft of hair bounced against his forehead. She wondered what it would be like to touch it, how it would feel between her fingers. "We went to New York once. I don't even re-member where we were going, but we were late, and my dad said he'd give the guy a twenty-dollar tip if he could get us where we were going in under ten minutes. And this cabdriver, he just . . ." Cade was smiling, eyes bright, lost in the memory. "It was like being on a rocket ship, the way the guy drove. He made every light. He'd use every lane, moving around the slower cars. It was like . . ." He paused, waving his fork again, looking for a word. "Like a dance," he said. His smile faded. "I told my dad that's what I wanted to do, and he said, 'Oh, you want to be a race car driver,' and I said, no, I wanted to drive a taxi, in New York." He looked down at his plate unhappily. "That was not what my dad wanted to hear." He picked up another wedge of his sandwich, devouring it in three quick bites. Beatrice nibbled a slice of pear. She thought he'd ask what she wanted to do with her life, and she'd tell him how she wanted to go to school for art or drama if she went at all, and live in New York, and make things with her hands. She'd tell him that if her Etsy store was earning enough, she'd just do that full-time, living at home, if she had to, until she had enough money saved to move to New York City.

Instead, Cade said, "Did you really get kicked out of boarding school? I mean, I know you said that's what happened."

"Do you think I was lying?"

"No!" He lowered his voice. "I'm just wondering if it happened how you said it did." He was looking at her carefully, brows knitted, eyes intent.

Beatrice nodded. "I had a friend. She'd hooked up with this guy a few times. One night he showed up at our dorm. She didn't want him there. She didn't want anything to do with him. But he wouldn't leave her alone. He wouldn't take no for an answer."

"And the school? The dean, or whatever? They didn't believe her?"

"She wouldn't tell." Beatrice could still remember how Tricia had cried, whispering, *No one's going to believe me, because I slept with him before.* Beatrice and a few other girls in the dorm had tried to convince her that people would listen, that she should tell, but Tricia couldn't be persuaded. She had stayed in bed for the rest of the weekend, crying. On Monday morning in chapel, Colin, the guy who'd done it, sat right beside her, even putting his arm around her. He'd had the nerve to look perplexed, then disappointed, when she stood up and walked away.

"He kept bothering her," Beatrice said. "After it happened, when she was crying and telling him to leave. He just acted like there was nothing wrong."

"Do you think maybe he was . . . I don't know, confused?" Cade asked.

Beatrice glared at him. "Do you think 'no' means something else in New Hampshire?"

Cade shook his head. "It sounds like he was getting mixed messages."

Beatrice huffed out a sigh. "Look, just because a girl agrees to something once doesn't mean she's signed, like, a permanent permission slip. That isn't how it works. We're allowed to change our minds."

Cade reached across the table and took her hand. "Hey," he said. "Don't be mad at me. I'm just trying to understand." His hand was warm; his eyes were locked on her face. She wished that there wasn't a table between them; that she was on his side of the bench and could lean against him. She bet he smelled good, and wondered if, at some point soon, she'd have a chance to find out.

21

Diana

Diana had come to dinner on Friday night, just like they'd planned, on a night when Hal had stayed in town, having his monthly dinner with the partners. Diana had arrived with wine and chocolates. She'd admired Daisy's home, unerringly zeroing in on the kitchen, and the fireplace and the skylight as the most beautiful parts of the room, and had praised Beatrice's jewelry, a beetle with brilliant green wings that hung in a glass pendant that dangled from her neck. "Where did you find it?" Diana had asked, and Beatrice had explained that she did all her shopping on Etsy, that she never gave money to corporations if she could help it, but instead supported her fellow creators, the same way they supported her. Daisy had worried about how her daughter would behave, but Beatrice had seemed impressed with Diana, actually volunteering information about school, and her crafts, and the kids she'd met in class.

Over the past four weeks, Daisy and Diana had gotten in the habit of cooking on Tuesdays, at Diana's apartment, and meeting, on Friday afternoons, for a walk along Forbidden Drive, one of Daisy's favorite places in the city, a spot she'd been eager to show off for her new friend. She'd offered to meet Diana after work, even if it meant fighting rush-hour traffic, but Diana explained that being a consultant gave her the flexibility to set her own hours.

On those walks, they'd talked about everything from Diana's boyfriend, to Daisy's father, to how Daisy felt about being a mother and why Diana had chosen not to become one. The fourth Friday was a gorgeous afternoon, the spring air mild and fresh, the sun shining and the trees dressed in fresh, pale green, but Daisy was struggling to appreciate it. She was still bewildered by what had happened at the cocktail party the weekend before, the way Hal had threatened Mireille, and how he'd been drinking. Her husband's mood had not been improved by the latest #MeToo casualty of another, this one a prominent local politician who'd gotten in trouble for salacious emails sent to his subordinates. All through dinner the night before, Hal had muttered that the women were only trying to leverage notoriety into money, or better jobs, which segued into a complaint about the mandatory sexual harassment training his firm had recently held.

"Half the people in the firm have dated each other," he'd said. "I can name three different guys, and one woman, who've married summer associates. And now you can get in trouble for—wait, let me get this right." He'd rummaged through his briefcase, pulling out a sheaf of papers and flipped through them until he'd landed, triumphantly, on the phrase "Unwelcome sexual advances to colleagues or subordinates." "Do you know what that means? Flirting."

"Well," Daisy had ventured, "maybe not everyone wants to be flirted with at the office."

"It's ridiculous," Hal had told her. When Daisy related the story to Diana, the other woman had shaken her head, a thin smile on her face. "I've met a lot of men who feel that way."

A trio of runners blew past them, young men in skimpy

shorts, their pale legs flashing. They watched them go, and Diana said, "I bet a lot of guys feel like the rug's been pulled out from under them."

"What do you mean?"

"Oh," said Diana, whose sleek, high-tech exercise gear made Daisy, in sweatpants and an ancient T-shirt, feel especially frumpy, "just that the world was one way, and now, all the stuff they could get away with, all the stuff nobody even noticed, now it's all, as they say, problematic." Diana looked sideways at Daisy. "Do you ever worry about Beatrice?"

"Only all the time." Daisy sighed. "Sometimes I think that all these rules are going to take all the romance and the mystery out of sex. Like, if she's with a guy and he's asking for permission for every single thing he's doing, that doesn't seem very exciting. But then I think about her being with a guy who wouldn't ask permission, or who wouldn't take no for an answer . . ." Her voice trailed off, and Diana didn't pick up the ball that Daisy had dropped. She just kept walking, quickening her pace as a woman running alongside a gray pit bull made her way past them.

At the top of the trail, at a wide spot in the Wissahickon, there were ducks you could feed, and a restaurant with a snack bar. Daisy had come here with Beatrice, and Hal, when Beatrice was a toddler. Daisy felt disheartened as she counted backward, the months, then years, since she'd been on a walk with her husband.

She could hear the river's burble, and could see sunshine glinting off its surface, dappling the ground as it filtered through the trees. Diana stretched her arms over her head, then grasped one elbow and pulled her arm behind her neck.

"You know," she finally said, "I told you about meeting Michael at a kind of low point in my life." Daisy nodded. She hadn't wanted to push Diana for details about the boyfriend she hardly ever mentioned, but, at their last lesson, Diana had talked about feeling adrift when she was younger, not sure about where she wanted to live or what she wanted to do.

With her back toward Daisy, her feet planted on the grassy ground, Diana said, in a low, dull voice, "It was a little more than just being confused about my choices, actually. I'd been raped."

"Oh my God!" Daisy said. "Oh, that's awful." She reached out, almost blindly, wanting to touch the other woman's shoulder or her arm. Somehow, she wound up grabbing Diana's hand. For an instant, there was nothing. She felt a flare of panic, wondering if she'd gone too far, and then Diana squeezed back. "I'm so sorry."

Diana nodded, releasing Daisy's hand, turning away as she shook her hair loose and tied it back again. "It was a long time ago."

"But still . . ." Daisy felt a clenching around her heart; a tightening in her throat. She hated the thought of her friend being hurt even as it thrilled her that Diana trusted her enough to tell her. "I don't think that's the kind of thing you ever get over."

"It changes you," Diana said. "Here, let's sit." She led Daisy over to a bench, with a view of the ducks dipping their heads into the water as toddlers tossed handfuls of bread at them. "It took me a long time to trust anyone. A long time," she repeated. "There were years when I couldn't. I didn't let anyone get close. I didn't tell anyone what had happened. Not even my mom and dad."

"That must have been hard."

Nodding, Diana said, "I was very lonely."

Daisy could barely breathe. *I've been lonely, too*, she thought. But Diana had survived a sexual assault. What was Daisy's excuse? Getting married too soon? Missing Hannah?

With her gaze on the water, Diana said, "I tried not to think about it for a long time, after it happened. Michael figured it out, and eventually I told him the whole story. He was the first one I'd ever said it out loud to, and I thought he'd run screaming, but he didn't."

"I'm glad you've got someone," Daisy said. She had a million questions—when had this happened to Diana? At work? In college? Had she gone to the police? Had the guy been arrested? How could she, Daisy, keep such a thing from happening to her daughter? But Diana's jaw was set; her gaze looked severe, the lines of her cheekbones and chin etched in the afternoon sunshine. Daisy thought of a painting, from the single art history class she'd taken in college, of Judith slaying Holofernes. Judith had worn the same kind of expression, as she'd held, dangling, the general's severed head.

"Michael sounds terrific," Daisy said, instead of asking additional questions. "I'd love to meet him."

Diana gave a brief nod, and seemed to gather herself. "And I'd like to meet Hal, too, of course."

"Of course!" said Daisy, a little too quickly, in a voice that was a little too loud. Somehow, for reasons she didn't want to consider too carefully, Diana meeting Hal was the last thing she wanted. Hal wouldn't like Diana any more than he'd liked Hannah, or any of the other women Daisy had liked. A great finder of fault and picker of nits was her husband. At first, Daisy had tried to pretend that there wasn't a problem, but Hannah, of course, was not fooled. ("Oh, come on," she'd said when Daisy had tried to protest that Hal liked her fine, "every time I walk into a room, he runs out like his hair's on fire and his ass is catching.") Hannah had argued that Hal was jealous of Daisy's time, that he wanted her all to himself. Once, Daisy had found it flattering. Now . . .

"Daisy." Diana was looking right at her, with an intensity to her gaze that Daisy found unsettling. Diana's hands were on her hips, the light flaring off the reflective strips sewn onto her sleeves. "There's something else I need to tell you. What happened to me that summer . . ."

Before Diana could continue, Daisy's phone trilled, and she saw the Melville School's number on the screen.

"I'm sorry—it's Bea's school—hello?" she said, picking up the call.

"Hi, Daisy? It's Crystal Johnson, calling from Melville."

"Hi, Crystal!" Crystal Johnson was a fellow Melville parent, a stay-at-home mother, and, years ago, another one of Daisy's almost-friends. Daisy had always liked Crystal, who'd been a lawyer before giving it up for volunteer work and managing her four children, who all seemed to play at least two sports and an instrument.

"I'm calling to let you know that Beatrice was absent this morning. We're just checking to see if she's sick? Or if she had an appointment and you forgot to let the front office know?"

"No. She left for school this morning. Are you saying she just never showed up?" Daisy was already poking at her screen, texting her daughter WHERE ARE YOU?, realizing that, once she found her, Beatrice was going to mock her for spelling out all the words.

"She wasn't present for homeroom, and no one's seen her all day," Crystal said.

Daisy felt something cold wrap around her heart. "Let me see if I can find out what's going on."

Daisy ended the call and saw Diana looking down at her, concern on her face.

"Is everything all right?"

"Beatrice isn't at school." Daisy had already punched in Beatrice's number. The phone rang and rang. No one picked up. She ended the call and said, "I have to go. I should go home, in case she's there."

Wordlessly, they hurried down the trail. As they went, Daisy called home, where no one answered. She spoke with Hal, who hadn't heard from their daughter, and called Beatrice again. Maybe there was some kind of explanation. Crossed wires . . . a research project . . . a teacher who'd marked Beatrice absent when she'd really been there.

They were almost back at the parking lot when Daisy's phone rang, and she saw her daughter's picture, purple hair and all, appear on her screen.

"Mom?"

Beatrice's voice was small, and Daisy thought she sounded frightened.

"Beatrice? Oh my God. Where are you?"

"At school."

"Funny, because that wasn't what the school told me."

Beatrice gave a sigh. "I'm here now. Can you come get me?"

"Did something happen? Is something wrong?"

"Just . . . can you please come get me? Please?"

Daisy turned away, shielding the phone with her body. She felt weak with relief that Beatrice was safe, but even in her happiness she was annoyed that of course Beatrice would assume that she was around and available for immediate pickup, that all Daisy did when Beatrice was not at home was cook and clean, or maybe just sit there, frozen, like a powered-down robot, waiting for her family to need something. She lowered her voice. "Maybe this didn't occur to you, but I'm actually doing something. With a friend."

"I'm sorry!" Beatrice actually sounded apologetic. "I know you have a life, Mom. I'm sorry. Can you please just come get me?"

"It'll take a little while. I'm on a walk on Forbidden Drive, and my car's at the house." Diana tapped her shoulder and mouthed, *I'll drive.* "Hang on." Daisy covered the mouthpiece and said, "Are you sure it's no trouble?"

"No trouble at all," Diana said. "And I'd love to see Beatrice again."

"I'm not sure you're going to be seeing her at her best," Daisy said, but she got back on the phone and told her daughter that she and her friend would be there in twenty minutes to pick her up and bring her home.

22

Diana

When Diana finally made it back to her apartment, she shucked off her fancy jacket, toed off her sneakers, and began pacing the length of her living room, back and forth, faster and faster, her bare heels thumping on the hardwood, realizing, with each turn she made, that things had gotten badly out of control.

Once, she'd had a clear objective: find the men who'd hurt her. Look them in the eye. Make them see her, acknowledging that she was a real person, to whom they had done real damage. She'd wanted to hate the men, and everyone connected to them, including the women. Especially the women, all of those enablers, the mothers and the wives who coddled and petted and made excuses.

Diana had never imagined that she would feel anything besides disgust for the Emlen men or anyone in their orbit. She hadn't considered the possibility of befriending one of their wives. She'd certainly never planned on confiding in Daisy about her rape, on even hinting at what had happened to her, lest Daisy, sweet, clueless Daisy, put the pieces together and realize how her husband fit in.

And then there was Beatrice. During the days before her invitation to Daisy's home she'd done her best to prepare herself for the sight of her rapist's daughter, knowing that the girl was a teenager, like her nieces, the age of the daughter Diana and Michael might have had.

It had helped that Beatrice hadn't looked anything like Hal. Her hair was purple, and Diana thought that she favored her mother. Or maybe it was that she'd had more recent acquaintance with Daisy's face, and was more able to see the similarities. Beatrice was petite, with the same large, round eyes and full cheeks as her mother, and clothes that looked like they'd been plucked from a punk revival of *Little House on the Prairie.* That afternoon, Beatrice and Daisy had held a tense-looking, whispered conversation at the base of the school steps while Diana waited behind the wheel. Daisy appeared to be speaking very intensely. Beatrice was shrugging, wearing the universal expression of adolescent disdain. Daisy shrugged and walked up the steps into the school. Beatrice watched her mother before turning, walking to Diana's car, and climbing into the back seat.

"I am a disgrace," she'd announced, and Diana had said, "I'm sure that you'll survive."

Diana had gotten them to Gladwyne as quickly as she could, declining Daisy's offer to come in for coffee or stay for dinner, saying, "Some other time," to Beatrice, who'd offered to show her a mouse she was working on. She'd sped back to Center City with her hands clenched on the wheel. And now here she was, walking in circles around this tiny apartment, wanting desperately to just go home.

She picked up her phone and punched in her husband's name. He answered on the first ring, sounding gruff when he said her name.

"Michael?"

Diana could picture him: his beard, now as much silvery-gray as reddish-brown; the way he'd be in the post-office parking lot, or in a client's driveway, leaning against his truck with his forehead squinched up and the phone pressed against his cheek. "How are you?" he asked. "Is everything okay?"

"Yes. Fine." She sat down. "No. No, actually." When she started laughing, the noise she made was high and wild. She was sure it scared him. She was scaring herself, a little.

"Hey," he said. His voice was still gruff, but less irritated, more patient. "Tell me."

"I just wish . . ." Her voice trailed off, then she blurted, "I wish I didn't like her so much. Her, and her daughter. Beatrice. She's fourteen."

"You don't have to do anything," Michael said. "Or, at least, you don't have to do anything now. You just come home."

"I can't," Diana whispered. But if she gave up now, without confronting Hal Shoemaker, it would all have been for nothing. He would continue to live in a world without consequences, a world where men like him hurt girls like her, then shook them off like they were dust underneath their shoes, and, worse, all the young women, her nieces, his daughter, purple-haired, oddball, blameless Beatrice, would have to live in that world, too. And then, what if Daisy recognized her on the Cape, on Longnook Beach in Truro, or walking around Provincetown? What if Daisy realized that Diana wasn't who she'd pretended to be?

"I can't come back yet," she told Michael. "But soon. Maybe another week. I just . . ." *Just what? Just need to confront Hal, like I'd planned? Just need to make sure that Daisy will be okay when she learns her husband is a rapist? Just need to figure out how to keep Beatrice from being destroyed?*

"Soon," she repeated. "I'll be home soon."

"Well, I'll be here," said Michael. Diana wondered what he was feeling, if he was impatient, if he was angry. But all he said was, "Pedro keeps taking your socks."

She choked out a laugh through a throat thick with tears. Whenever she went away unexpectedly, Pedro would dig one of her socks, or bras, or pairs of underwear, out of the laundry basket. He'd carry it around in his mouth all day, and tuck it into a corner of his bed at night. It reminded her of how Willa would hide food, all those years ago.

"Don't let him chew holes in anything," she said, and hoped he wouldn't hear how unsteady her voice had become.

"I'll do my best," said Michael. Then he said, "Come home, Diana," but she ended the call without answering, telling herself that she still had work to do.

Part
Four

~~~~~~~~~~~~~~~~

This Happy Land

23

Diana

The Emlen Academy sat high on a hill above a small town in New Hampshire, which it seemed to look down upon with lordly disdain. Or maybe that was just Diana's frame of mind. She parked in the visitors' lot and checked her appearance in the rearview mirror. Lipstick bright against her pale face, a skirt and a blouse and a blazer. In her purse, a letter she'd written herself, on Boston University stationery, which she'd made by cutting and pasting the school's letterhead and logo onto a plain piece of paper. *Diana Carmody is researching the history of single-sex boarding schools in New England.* She'd given the English department's phone number and made up a professor's name, hoping that no one would ask for credentials and that, if they did, just the letter itself would be enough.

She got out of the car and began walking up the hill, crossing the snow-covered quad. She knew the names of all the buildings, the location of the library, the history of the school. She'd sent away for application material, and the eight-page glossy brochure had told her everything she could have ever wanted to know about Emlen, from the size of its endowment to its most recent construction projects and capital campaigns to its most prominent alums. Eighteen state governors, United States senators, a Nobel Prize winner, five Supreme Court justices, abolitionists and architects, a smattering of movie stars and NHL players, authors and lyricists, a billionaire tech mogul, and a semi-famous rapper were all Emlen men. George Washington had visited Emlen in 1789, when it was still a seminary and not yet a prep school; John F. Kennedy had given a speech there while campaigning in 1960.

Diana walked uphill, looking around, trying not to stare or do anything that would mark her as an outsider. Some of the kids looked like they'd snuck into their parents' closets and were playing dress-up, in ties or jackets or blazers and pumps. Some already carried themselves with an air of entitlement; nothing so obvious as noses in the air; just a subtle way of walking and holding themselves that telegraphed, *I'm better than you are.* But others were just teenagers, kids like any other kids, with gangly frames or acne-afflicted skin, laughing and horsing around. Diana paused to read a metal plaque on a post outside one of the classroom buildings. *On this ground, the Emlen Academy was founded in 1898 for the purposes of instructing America's most promising young men, teaching them to aspire to knowledge and good works.*

Good works, she thought, and snorted so loudly that a few of the boys turned to look at her, before shrugging and continuing on their way.

She followed a slate path to the Harwich Library, where the librarian barely gave her a glance, and didn't ask to see any paperwork. "The yearbooks and the back issues of the alumni quarterly are in the first sub-basement," he said, and pointed toward a staircase. Twenty minutes later, Diana was ensconced in a wooden carrel, with its own lamp and a pile of alumni magazines, as slick and well-produced as anything on a newsstand. She picked one up, leafing through it. The cover story was a profile of an Emlen graduate who ran a neurobiology lab, illustrated with a shot of the guy in a white lab coat and a confident smile. A "Letter from the Dean" appeared on the front inside page. Letters from alums, short pieces about professors, a long story about the football team, interviews with students for the "On Campus" column. She flipped to the back, where the "Class Notes" section was, and learned that Alfred Cutty of the Class of 1939 had celebrated his ninety-eighth birthday at the Whitechapel Retirement Center, and that Mrs. Elizabeth E. Ferris (wife of the late Stanhope Ferris) was planning on attending Reunions at This Happy Land, which Diana learned was what alumni called Emlen. The line, she learned, came from the school's alma mater:

> *Dearest Emlen, like no other;*
> *On your ground your sons shall stand*
> *With gladdened hearts, to share with brothers*
> *Mem'ries of this happy land*

That ditty was now referred to as the Old Alma Mater, and a new, gender-neutral one was now officially the school's song, but the nickname had stuck.

She put the magazines aside and picked up the book she'd found, a copy of the 1987 *Emlen Emblem*, the school's yearbook. She settled her hands on its embossed leather cover and took a few breaths, grounding herself: her feet on the carpet-covered floor, her bottom in the curved wooden chair, her hands on the pages. She started with Henry Shoemaker, the boy she'd known as Poe. Looking at this senior picture felt like taking an arrow through her heart. Poe looked just like she'd remembered, with his clear eyes and his curly hair. She read through the half-gibberish of the inscription beneath his name, a dozen lines of dates and initials and barely veiled references to beer and pot and parties, FEN-WAY PARK '84 and IS THERE A PROBLEM, OFFICER and BEER PONG OLYMPIAN and I CLIMBED MOUNT KATRINA. CAPE COD HERE WE

COME, one of the lines read, and she'd swallowed hard, briefly dizzy, tasting bile in her throat.

She started at the first name (Stephen Aaronson) and looked at each picture, all the way to Wesley Yu, reading each line of their inscriptions, taking notes on the references and inside jokes they made. After a few hours' perusal, she had a headache that felt like an ice pick being jabbed between her eyes, and the names of her three suspects: Hal, the boy she believed had raped her; Brad Burlingham, the laughing, doll-boy redhead who'd held her down, and Daniel Rosen, the shorter, more slightly built boy, who'd been there, watching.

Diana stepped outside, letting the icy air cool her burning face. She drew it deep in her lungs. Then she went back inside, pulling out her notebook.

I Climbed Mount Katrina. Poe—Hal—had written that. So had Brad. Danny Rosen hadn't, but several of the other boys in the class had made it part of their inscription. She paged through the yearbook, locating pictures of the Spring Fling, and saw one of the boys—Teddy Bloch—beside a tall blonde with feathered hair. She wore a white poufy dress, white flowers in a wrist corsage. *"Ready" Teddy Bloch escorts St. Anne's senior Katrina Detmer to the dance.*

Googling "Katrina Detmer" and "St. Anne's" gave her a Facebook page and a hometown, which, when googled, gave her an address and a telephone number. This time when Diana stepped outside, it had gotten dark, and her stomach was growling—she'd skipped breakfast and lunch. When she pulled out her phone, she saw seven missed calls from Michael. As she stared at the screen, another call came through.

Diana rejected the call, then sent a text. *I'm fine. Just need to take care of something. I'll be home as soon as I can.*

She got in her car and drove into town, found a diner, made herself eat some soup and half of a grilled cheese sandwich. There was a fancy-looking inn at the center of town, the kind of place that looked like it had "Ye Olde" somewhere in its name, where Emlen parents probably came for graduation and well-heeled alums stayed for reunions. She decided she'd prefer sleeping in her car to staying there, but, luckily, there was a Hampton Inn at the edge of town. She got a room, took a long, hot shower, and changed into the clothes she'd packed—her favorite sweatpants and one of Michael's plaid shirts, which was soft against her skin, and smelled like him. Thus fortified, she called Katrina Detmer, who lived in a suburb outside of St. Paul, Minnesota.

All through dinner, all through her shower, she'd tried to come up with a story. *I'm a researcher. I'm a journalist.* Or some version of the truth: *I knew those boys the summer they graduated from Emlen.* In the end, she went with the truth, which she relayed to Katrina Detmer as soon as she got the other woman on the phone.

"My name is Diana Scalzi. I worked on Cape Cod the summer of 1987. I met a bunch of Emlen graduates who were on vacation there."

Katrina's voice was low and husky, polite, but not especially warm. "Yes?"

Diana curled her toes into the hotel-room floor. "One of the boys assaulted me at a party on the beach."

Diana could hear her blood pounding in her ears, in her temples. There was what felt like a very long pause. Then, angrily, Katrina said, "How did you get my name?"

"From their yearbook."

"Excuse me?" Katrina's voice had gotten louder.

"The boy who—the boy who raped me—his name is Henry Shoemaker."

"Poe," Katrina said immediately. "I never knew why they called him that. They all had those names. Raven and Bubs and Griff."

"I read Henry's yearbook entry, and he mentioned you by name. And so did a few of the other boys in the class," Diana said.

"What did they write?"

Diana swallowed hard. "It isn't—it's not very nice."

"You don't say." The other woman's voice was hard-edged and scornful. "Look, either you tell me or I figure out how to get my hands on their yearbook."

Diana swallowed hard. "They all wrote 'I climbed Mount Katrina.'"

Silence. Then Katrina demanded, "How many of them wrote that? And which ones?" Before Diana could answer, Katrina said, "How'd you find me, anyhow? Who are you again?"

Diana told her. "I saw the 1987 yearbook. You went to a dance with a boy named Teddy Bloch. There was a picture of the two of you, and your full name was in the caption. I just guessed that you were the Katrina in the . . ." Diana swallowed hard. ". . . other references."

"Jesus," said Katrina, in a more muted voice. "Teddy was my boyfriend, for my whole senior year," she said. "He came to see me almost every weekend. I knew all those boys. Not biblically, of course, which certainly seems to be the implication there, but I knew them." Through the receiver, Diana heard her swallow. "I thought they were my friends."

"I understand," Diana said. "The summer I knew Poe, I thought he liked me. That he wanted me to be his girlfriend." Even now, her naivete burned at her, like a throatful of acid. "And that's why I'm calling. I wanted to ask someone who knew him, back then."

"But that's the thing. I barely knew Poe. I mean, I knew him as one of Teddy's friends, but I didn't really know him." Katrina's voice was becoming increasingly higher, more distressed. "I certainly didn't realize that I was a joke to them."

"I'm sorry," said Diana, and listened as the woman breathed.

When Katrina spoke again, her voice was clipped, angry and direct.

"So what, then?" Before Diana could answer, Katrina said, "You want to know if Poe's capable of raping someone. Because that's what happened, right?"

Diana shut her eyes. "Yes."

Katrina gave a mirthless laugh. "I guess anyone's capable of anything, right? That's our lesson for this evening. And I know it's not your fault, but to tell you the truth, I wish you hadn't called me. I could have probably died happy not knowing what they'd said." There was a beep, letting Diana know that the call had been ended.

Diana sat back on the bed and opened her notebook. The Mount Katrina joke had made her furious, but, still, nothing had upset her as much as the news of Hal Shoemaker's wedding, to the other Diana. Especially not after it turned out that the other Diana, twelve years Hal's junior, was also one of his classmates' sister. She flipped to the page where she'd written it, word for word:

Your faithful correspondent is delighted to report that late bloomer Hal Shoemaker, aka the Last Man Standing, has finally tied the knot! Hal got hitched at the Four Seasons in Center City, Philadelphia, where he practices law, to Diana "Daisy" Rosen, a college student, and little sister to none other than our classmate Daniel Rosen. Danny played inadvertent matchmaker when he recommended Daisy's services as a cooking instructor to Hal, who was looking for help for his father, Vernon Shoemaker (Emlen Class of 1963). Other Emlen classmates in attendance at the wedding included Danny's brother, David (Class of 1985), Gerald Justin, Bryan Tavistock, Crosby Wolf, Richard Rutledge, and Brad Burlingham.

"She's his sister?" Diana had blurted, drawing stares from a few nearby students. She'd gotten up to take a turn around the library, attempting to make sense of it. Danny had witnessed her rape. He'd known about it and kept quiet. And then he'd served his sister up, on a platter, to the boy who'd done it. It didn't make sense.

Diana paced and fretted, mumbling to herself (out of earshot of the students), then dove back into her research. By the end of the afternoon, she knew that Daniel Rosen was married to a man. He and his husband lived in a small, artsy-looking town in New Jersey, across the river from New Hope, Pennsylvania, and he worked as a school counselor in Trenton.

Bradley Telford Burlingham, the one who'd held her wrists and laughed, lived in Baltimore. He'd matriculated at Trinity College, but Diana couldn't find any evidence of his having graduated. He'd gotten married in his late twenties, in Baltimore, his hometown, and he and his wife had started a family. There'd been a daughter, Lila, and a son, Austin. He'd popped up at the class's tenth reunion, and again in 2003, having lost most of his hair and gained at least thirty pounds, in a picture with five Emlen men on a fishing boat, each of them holding a giant fish by its jaws. Hal Shoemaker was one of the other men, which meant he and Brad had stayed friends. *How touching*, Diana thought. Google had filled in some of the blanks, and LinkedIn had helped, too. Brad had held almost a dozen different jobs, mostly in marketing, in all kinds of different businesses. His current address was a not-especially-impressive-looking two-bedroom apartment in a neighborhood called Roland Park.

She would start with him, Diana decided, and work her way up to Hal. She would pay Brad a visit, look him in the eye, let him see what he'd done; let him live with that knowledge, and the knowledge of the world his daughter would eventually inherit, the world he'd made for her, and the rest of the girls and women.

The next morning, at six o'clock, she was driving down the street where Brad Burlingham lived. She found a parking spot with a view of the modest-looking development with two-story build-ings clad in white stucco. At nine o'clock, a middle-aged man emerged from a second-story front door and locked it behind him. He made his way down two flights of steps, his breath steaming in a cloud in front of him. Brad's red hair was mostly gone, his round, doll-like face had gotten broader, but it was still him. There was the snub nose; there was the smirk.

Diana swallowed hard, feeling breathless, almost hearing her heart thump. The guy climbed behind the wheel of an undistin-guished Honda, rolling down the window and lighting a cigarette before pulling out of his spot. Keeping a prudent distance, Diana trailed him as he drove down Roland Avenue. Less than a mile from home, he turned, without signaling, onto Deepdene Road, and then into the Starbucks parking lot. *Coffee run*, Diana fig-ured, but changed her mind after he got out of the car holding a crumpled mass of green fabric in his hands.

She drove once around the block, slowly, then pulled into the parking lot of the Enoch Pratt Library across the street from the coffee shop. It was a crisp, clear February morning, the skies a cloudless blue, the temperature in the low forties. The trees were still bare, stretching their branches like claws into the sky. Dingy, patchy snow lined the lawns and the sides of the roads. Diana waited for an hour, watching as the morning rush swelled and dispersed. Then she put on some lipstick, slung her purse over her shoulder, and walked across the street.

Brad was wearing his apron, standing with his shoulders slumped, behind the glass case of baked goods. He looked to be a

solid twenty-five years older than the young people busily froth-
ing milk or heating up croissants. The years had not been kind to
him. His eyes were sunken, ringed with dark circles; his nose and
cheeks were a constellation of burst capillaries.

"Help you?" he asked, when Diana approached the counter.

"I'd like a venti latte, please."

"Whole milk okay?"

"Sure."

"Can I get a name?"

"Katrina."

She watched to see if he'd flinch, or twitch, or run screaming
at the name, but all he did was speak to the barista, reach for a
black marker, and misspell the name—*Catrina*—on the cup. He
looked as if a resigned sigh had assumed human form, his every
move telegraphing weariness and distaste. She wondered what
the story was. Surely this wasn't the glorious future an Emlen
education was meant to assure, and, even if his marketing jobs
hadn't been especially impressive, they'd been several cuts above
serving coffee. Had he fallen so far that his family couldn't help;
had he run through all their money; had he exhausted every favor
he could have called in, every classmate he could have tapped
for help?

She sipped her drink, watching Brad noodling behind the
counter, ignoring his coworkers, using the absolute minimal
amount of energy to take orders and make change. When her
latte was gone, she tossed the cup, left the shop, crossed the street,
and spent the next seven hours with only a single bathroom break
watching Brad's car.

At four o'clock, he emerged from the back door, with his
apron balled up in his hands. He got behind the wheel of his car
and started driving along Roland Avenue, in the opposite direction of his parents' house. After another mile or so, he pulled into
the lot of a restaurant. HAPPY HOUR 4–7. DOLLAR BEERS, TWO-
DOLLAR WELL DRINKS, DOLLAR WINGS.

Diana watched him through the restaurant's windows as he said something to the hostess, and parked himself on a barstool. The bartender seemed to know him: there was a beer on a coaster waiting almost before he'd settled onto the stool. For the next two hours, Diana sat in the parking lot as Brad drank, head down, shoulders hunched, working his way through at least six beers, ignoring the basket of nuts at his elbow, and the other patrons and the help. When his glass was empty he'd jerk his chin toward it, and another beer would appear. At seven o'clock he put a bill down on the counter, dismounted his barstool, and, weaving slightly, made his way to his car.

Is he going to drive like that? Diana wondered. It seemed that he was. He got behind the wheel and pulled out onto the street, crossing the yellow line as he did it. The car in the opposite lane honked. Brad jerked the car back and drove down Roland Avenue, crossing over the yellow line at least half a dozen times during the five-minute ride back home.

She watched him go plodding back up to his apartment. Then she drove back to the bar. By the time she walked through the door, Brad's seat had been taken by a young woman deep in conversation with her date. It took Diana a few minutes, and a prominently displayed twenty-dollar bill, to attract the young female bartender's attention. When she said, "Help you?" Diana pointed to Brad's seat.

"The guy who was sitting there a little while ago. The bald one. Do you know his name?"

The bartender was dressed in a white button-down shirt and suspenders. She gave Diana a shrug. "I know he's told me. Brad? Bart? Some name like that."

"Is he a good customer?" The bar was crowded by then, hot and noisy, and Diana had to shout to be heard.

The young woman smirked. "He stays for hours, and that"— she pointed at his seat—"is prime happy-hour real estate. Sits there pounding dollar beers like it's his job. Puts down a ten-dollar bill to cover a seven-dollar-and-twenty-cent tab. Or sometimes it's a twenty, and he'll ask for eleven bucks back." She rolled her eyes, pale blue beneath stubby black lashes. "A real prince."

"Does he ever come in here with anyone else?"

The woman crossed her arms against her chest and stared at Diana with narrowed eyes. "Why? You his wife or something?"

Diana shook her head.

The bartender considered, then gave a shrug. "I've never seen him here with a girl. Or a guy. He doesn't really talk to anyone. He just drinks."

Diana slid the money across the bar in thanks and went to the hotel room she'd rented, paying cash at the front desk, giving the name Julie Christie.

She watched Brad for three weekdays in a row, and every day was the same. At nine or so he'd come shuffling out of the house and drive to work. After work he'd go to the bar. After the bar he'd drive home, and park in the driveway before going inside, head hanging and hands dangling at his sides. By the end of the third night, Diana's rage and loathing had been joined by a pinprick of pity. She stubbed it out fiercely, imagining she was grinding a lit cigarette butt out with her heel. She told herself that she had to act soon, before that ember came back and started a conflagration.

On Saturday, things were different. Nine o'clock came and went without Brad's emergence. At noon, a late-model sedan purred up to his building. The back doors opened, eventually disgorging two kids—either teens or tweens, Diana couldn't tell because of their winter coats and hats. They each wore a back-pack, and each carried an overnight bag. *Lila and Austin, I presume*, Diana thought, but she rolled down her window in time to hear a woman call from the driver's seat: "Eli, Claudia, be good for your dad!"

Eli and Claudia both said, "We will, Mom!" They walked up the stairs, neither one looking especially enthusiastic as they climbed, and disappeared through the front door. The next morning at eleven, Diana was back in place to watch the children, in the same winter coats, leave the building and climb back into their mother's car. She figured the woman to be Brad's second ex-wife; the children, his second ex-family. And she knew she couldn't wait any longer. The restaurant needed her. So did her husband. It was time to go home.

Diana smoothed her hair. She bent down to make sure her sneakers' laces were tied. She'd worn jeans, a dark-blue hooded sweatshirt; unremarkable, anonymous clothes that would let her fade into a crowd and move fast if she had to. She freshened her lipstick, working hard to keep her hand steady, and returned it to her makeup case, which she placed in her purse, right next to the ladies' Colt revolver she'd purchased the week before. She locked her car, walked up the stairs, and stood on the windswept portico, knocking on Brad Burlingham's door.

"Hold on!" she heard him call. A minute later, he was standing in front of her, in a T-shirt, sweatpants, and bare feet. "Yes?"

"Brad Burlingham?"

"Yes?" His forehead furrowed as he squinted at her. "Have we met?" His eyes widened as he leaned backward into the warmth of his apartment. "Are you serving me?"

For a minute, she couldn't make sense of the words. "What?"

"If you're a process server, you have to say so."

She shook her head. "I just want to talk to you."

"Who are you?" he asked, peering at her.

"You don't remember?" She looked at him, waiting for the click; waiting for something to show in his posture or on his face. When nothing did, she said, "Cape Cod. 1987. Corn Hill Beach." Those words, finally, registered. She saw the smallest flare of panic in his eyes, and pushed past him into his apartment, waiting there, until, shoulders slumped, Brad turned to face her and pulled the door shut behind him.

In the living room, she saw the detritus of the children's visit: video-game controllers on the floor, a bowl of potato chips on a coffee table, next to a copy of the AA Big Book.

"Come on in," said Brad, with an ironic, courtly gesture. "Make yourself at home." Diana waited a minute, then took a seat, perched on the edge of an armchair that was one of a matched set, upholstered in a fawn-colored velvet. She wondered if he'd gotten them in the divorce, carted them out of the marital house and brought them here, to this sad-single-dad apartment.

"I recognize you now," he said. "From Starbucks. You came in a few days ago, right?" Before she could answer, he said, "It's a rehab job." He sat down heavily on the couch, which was brown leather, enormous, and out of proportion to the daintier armchairs. "Probably wondering what an Emlen man's doing, steaming lattes." He shrugged. "When you go to rehab, at a twelve-step place, they tell you to get a job like that. In the service industry, or as a custodian. Stocking shelves, mopping floors. We're supposed to be of use and stay humble. And it helps to have somewhere to go in the morning."

Diana couldn't help her gaze shifting to the open beer bottle on the side table, next to the chips. Brad saw her looking, and shrugged. "I'm staying off the hard stuff. They call it harm reduction." Diana thought they could more properly call it *bullshit*, but she kept quiet. "I've been waiting for you," he said.

"What?"

"Oh, sure. What with all this #MeToo stuff in the news . . ." He waved one hand above his head and declaimed, "First they came for Harvey Weinstein, and I kept silent, because I was not a big-deal Jewish movie producer. Then they came for Charlie Rose and Matt Lauer, and I kept silent, because I wasn't on TV. Then they came for Brett Kavanaugh, and I kept silent, because

I'm not a judge. And when they came for me, there was no one left to speak." He turned the bottle in his hand. Speaking quietly, he said, "I've been waiting a long time for this. For you. So." He put down the bottle and clapped his hands together, the bluff, hearty host welcoming a guest to his abode. It reminded her of Reese, except Reese was always sincere, he genuinely wanted to host people, to make them feel welcome, whereas this man only wanted her gone. "Here you are." He picked up his bottle again and raised it in a toast. "What happens next?"

"What?"

"I mean, there's kind of an order to these things now, right? You tell my boss, or the paper, or my ex." She saw his throat give a jerk as he swallowed. "Or my kids."

Diana didn't answer. Knowing that Brad had children, knowing that any revelation would hurt them, too, had been bad enough when the kids were just theoretical. Now that she'd seen them, the knowledge weighed on her even more heavily.

"So what do you want? Money?" He gave a smirk. "Can't help you there. Could have, once. But two divorces and four kids will clean a man out." He looked at her closely. She imagined she could feel his attention, like an insect, something many-footed and loathsome, crawling on her skin. "So what, then? An apology?"

She swallowed, as best she could. "Words are cheap."

Brad Burlingham put his hand on his heart. In a mocking tone, he said, "How about my solemn pledge to never, ever do a terrible thing like that again?"

She looked at him steadily. "It was a terrible thing."

He glared at her for a minute. Then his shoulders slumped. "Yeah," he said. "It was."

They sat for a moment in silence. Diana thought that this wasn't the leering, laughing boy she remembered from that night at the beach. Brad seemed . . . the word "damaged" dropped itself into her mind. She pushed it away, watching as he drank, his

Adam's apple bobbing and jerking with each swallow. *He drinks like it's his job*, Diana remembered the bartender saying.

"You know what I want?" she asked. "How about this. I want to know why. You had to know . . ." She wiped her hands on her legs. "You had to know that what you did to me was going to have consequences. That it was going to hurt me. To the extent that I was real to you at all."

He looked at her, rubbing at his mouth with the back of his hand. "Look," he finally said. "The guy—the one who did it—he wasn't my friend."

"Oh, no? Because you seemed pretty close."

"None of those guys were my friends," he said. His voice cracked. "I thought they were. I wanted them to be. But they weren't."

"So that's why you let Hal Shoemaker rape me? That's why you laughed about sloppy seconds? You were trying to get in with the in-crowd?"

"Yes," he said. His voice was almost inaudible. "I wanted them to like me. And I knew it was wrong . . ." He picked up his bottle, seemed surprised to find it was empty, and held on to it with both hands, clutching it like a life preserver. "Look," he said. "I went to Emlen because my brothers went, and my dad went, and my uncle, and their dad went there, too. And they were all . . ." His voice trailed off. He gestured vaguely with his free hand. "They could handle it there, you know? I couldn't. I wasn't smart, and I wasn't good at sports." He dropped his head, so that his chin almost rested on his chest. "No one liked me."

Diana stared at him in disbelief. "No one *liked* you?" she repeated. Her heart was thumping, and her face was burning, and she wanted to slap him, to claw at his smug face, to pull out what was left of his hair by the handful. "Do you know how I felt when I went home? Do you know what it did to me? I almost flunked out of high school, and I did flunk out of college. It's been all this time, and I still have nightmares. I wake up in the middle of the night because I think that someone's in my house, or in my bed with me, or in the closet. I was a virgin, before that night."

He dropped his gaze and slumped backward like he was trying to merge his body with the couch.

"Do you know what you did to me?" Diana asked him again, leaning forward.

"Yes," he said quietly. "I know."

"No," she said. "You don't." She sat back, waiting for him to say something else. When she realized he wouldn't—that this was all she was going to get from him, that he didn't have the capacity to give her any more—she stood up and picked up her bag.

With his eyes on his lap, Brad said, "I went to rehab the first time when I was twenty-six. I couldn't figure it out, you know? Couldn't hang on to a job when people gave them to me. Couldn't keep a girlfriend. Couldn't make anything work. So I drank. And then I totaled my car, and my wife finally left, and my brothers and my parents did an intervention, and they sent me to Minnesota. Everyone there talked about hitting rock bottom, and how maybe that was mine." Finally, he raised his eyes, which were bloodshot and bleary. His gaze was unfocused and very far away. "But I don't think that they were right. I don't think that was my bottom. I think that maybe the best thing would have been if they'd just let me keep falling."

Diana felt very heavy, as if her limbs, her hands, her heart had all been encased in lead. Was this victory? Not really. She couldn't feel like she'd hurt Brad, or opened his eyes, or injured him. He'd been broken already, broken for years, well before he'd ever seen her face.

"So what now?" he asked with a chilling indifference. "You got a gun in that purse?"

"I don't want you to die," said Diana. "I want you to live with what you've done. Every time you look at your daughters, I want you to think about what you did to me, and think of some guy doing it to them. I want you to suffer."

She stood, without looking to see how he'd react, and struggled against that paralyzing heaviness to make it to the door, taking one step, then another, and then she was in the hall, at the stairs, in her car. She drove straight through the night to Cape Cod, stopping just once for gas. Michael and Pedro were both already awake when she got home just after dawn, sitting side by side on the couch.

"Where did you go?" Michael asked. Diana didn't answer; couldn't answer. Michael looked at her carefully, then stood up and opened his arms. She stepped into his embrace, pressed her face against the soft plaid of his shirt, and let him hold her, rocking her gently against him.

"You could have told me, you know," he said in his soothing rumble. "Whatever you do, I'll support you as best I can. Only don't shut me out."

She sat down with him at the table and told him where she'd been. "I went to Emlen," she said, head down at the small table in the kitchen, with Pedro at her feet. "I learned their names."

Michael nodded calmly. "And that took you a week?"

"The guy who held me down—he lives in Baltimore. I went to see him. I watched him for a while, and then I knocked on his door yesterday morning and told him who I was."

Her husband stared at her, his face dismayed. "Diana. You went there by yourself? Without anyone knowing where you were? Jesus! Did you think about what could have happened?"

"I did," she said, and didn't mention her gun. "But it was okay. We talked. And now he knows. And I feel . . ." She breathed in, trying to find the words to express this new lightness, like she'd taken off a tight piece of clothing, like she'd set down a heavy load.

"Well, good for you, I guess." Michael's expression was still dubious.

"No, it is good," she said. "I think that this is what I needed. Just to see him, and have him see me."

"You deserve more than that," Michael rumbled.

"Yes," she said. "But I'll take what I can get." She stood up, and he stood, too, and Diana stepped into his arms, resting her cheek against his chest, hearing the familiar rhythm of his heart.

"Don't do that again," he said. "Don't leave me like that."

"I won't," she said. "I promise."

She'd thought that things were getting better, as the days went by . . . but she'd forgotten that she still had a Google Alert set up for Brad's name, the same as she'd set one for Henry, and for Danny. Six days after her return, her phone chimed with a story about Brad. Diana felt her pulse trilling as she clicked the link, which led to what turned out to be Brad Burlingham's obituary.

> *Bradley Telford Burlingham, 51, died at his home Saturday afternoon. Burlingham, a son of Bradley Burlingham Senior and Tessa (White) Burlingham, was a graduate of the Emlen Academy, and attended Trinity College. Survivors include his parents, two brothers, Davis and Stuart, daughters Lila and Claudia, sons Austin and Eli . . .*

Diana set down her phone and shoved her chair back from the table where she stood, breathing hard, her hands fisted at her sides. *Maybe he had a heart attack*, she thought. *Maybe he'd been sick.* But she knew the truth, even before she found the courage to go back to her laptop and do some digging. The *Baltimore Sun* had been circumspect, but the city's alt-weekly website had all the facts.

> *Scion of Prominent Baltimore Family a Suicide. A police source has revealed exclusively to the* Weekly *that Bradley Burlingham III, the 51-year-old youngest son of city titan Bradley Burlingham Senior, killed himself in his Roland Park apartment Saturday night.*

A few minutes later, Diana found herself outside, on her deck, with Pedro at her feet and no memory of how she'd come to be there.

"Diana?" Michael said, but all she could do was shake her head and wordlessly hand him her phone with the story still on its screen, the evidence of her guilt, a burden she'd have to carry until the end of her days, the knowledge that she'd killed Brad Burlingham, as surely as if she'd put a gun to his head and pulled the trigger.

24

Daisy

Ten minutes after Diana dropped them off, Daisy saw her husband's car swing into the driveway. She felt her heart sink. Hal wasn't due home for another hour, which meant he'd left work early. Beatrice's face looked frightened beneath her purple bangs. Daisy straightened her shoulders and opened the door.

"Well, well," he said, as soon as he saw Beatrice. "The prodigal daughter returns." He swept Daisy and Beatrice with his gaze and asked, "Which one of you wants to tell me what happened?"

"I cut school," Beatrice said, without meeting his eyes. "I went into Center City with a friend."

Hal looked at her coolly. "Why?"

Beatrice shrugged. "I don't know. It seemed like a good idea at the time?"

Hal walked right up to her, so close the lapels of his coat brushed her shoulders. "Do you think this is a joke? You think you can just throw your opportunities away? I work my ass off to pay for private school . . ."

"I never asked to go to private school!" Beatrice shouted. And then they were off, yelling at each other, *You always* and *You never*; *I'm disappointed* and *I'm sorry I'm not who you want me to be.*

Daisy had known that her husband would be furious about Beatrice's dereliction. Her plan had been to nod along, calmly agreeing with whatever points he wanted to make, while praying her daughter wouldn't provoke him. She should have known better. Provoking her parents was pretty much Beatrice's job description at this point.

"If you get kicked out of another school, how's that going to look on your college applications?" Hal demanded. "You've already got one strike against you. Why are you going for two?"

"I don't even want to go to college," Beatrice replied. With her chin jutting out and her brows drawn down, Daisy thought she looked exactly like her father, a small, female, purple-haired version of Hal Shoemaker. "I keep telling you guys! I tell you and I tell you and I tell you and you don't listen."

"Don't be ridiculous," Hal said. "Of course you're going to college."

"Why?" Beatrice demanded. "I don't need college for what I want to do."

"And what's that again?" He threw his arms wide, appealing to an invisible jury. "Sit around poking a needle into a bunch of fluff? You think you're really going to support yourself that way?"

"I won't know until I try." Which, Daisy thought, sounded pretty reasonable. Clearly, Hal disagreed.

"You can do whatever you want with your life," he said, his voice low and dangerous. "After you go to college."

"Not everyone needs college!" Beatrice howled. *Don't say it,* Daisy prayed, but of course Beatrice couldn't hear her. "Mom never graduated, and she's doing fine!"

"Mom is doing fine," Hal said, through clenched teeth, "because I am supporting her."

Daisy's head snapped around. "Excuse me?" She hadn't meant to say anything, but that was just too much.

Hal kept talking, as if Daisy hadn't spoken. "Do you think that you'd be living in this house, in this neighborhood, going to an excellent school, if I hadn't gone to college? Maybe I should've just decided to sit around and knit or make muffins." His lip curled as he said "muffins." Daisy felt his scorn like a slap. And then she asked herself, what would Hannah have said to this, if she'd heard? What would Diana say, if she was listening?

"Hal," said Daisy. Her voice was cool, and hardly sounded like her own. "That's enough."

Hal, red-faced, muttered something about "ungrateful" and "disrespect." "That's enough," Daisy said again, and, finally, he subsided.

Daisy turned to her daughter. "Beatrice," she said. "All your father and I want is for you to have options. If you decide you want to make a living doing crafts, that's your choice, but a college degree opens a lot more doors than a high-school diploma does. And maybe you can get an arts degree."

"Not on my dime," Hal muttered, but at least he'd stopped shouting.

"My point," Daisy continued doggedly, "is that we don't need to decide any of that right now." She pulled in a breath. "But you can't cut school. You can't get into any more trouble. You need to follow the rules."

"Fine," Beatrice muttered. She gave her father an insolent look, handed her mother her phone without being asked, and sauntered up the stairs, with floral skirts swishing around her legs and her carpet bag banging against her hip.

Daisy turned to her husband, but Hal was already on his feet.

"Hey," she said, in a sharper tone than the one she normally used to address him.

Hal turned, and on his face was an expression of such cold

fury that Daisy found herself breathless. "What?" he asked, but Daisy could barely speak. The way he was looking at her, it was like he was trying to decide whether to talk to her or just pick up one of the steak knives and throw it at her heart.

"Just . . . do you think that denigrating the work I do is going to make Beatrice want to go to college?" She used the word "denigrating" on purpose and hoped that she'd pronounced it correctly. "Because I don't."

"I'm sorry," he said. He didn't sound sorry at all. "But maybe you don't understand the reality of the situation any more than she does. There's no way you'd be living in this house, if you were trying to pay the mortgage with what you earn giving cooking lessons."

"Well," said Daisy, struggling to sound pleasant, "I also might not have decided to live in Lower Merion. I might not have thought I needed a four-bedroom house for three people. There're all kinds of places to live in the world. All kinds of ways to live."

"I never knew you had a problem with our life." Hal's voice had taken on a distinctly sarcastic edge.

Daisy threw up her hands. "I don't have a problem with it, Hal. I'm happy here. I'm very happy. I'm just saying . . ." God, what was she saying? What was even the point?

"I know what you're saying," Hal replied. Unbelievably, he had picked up a stack of mail from the table by the door and was going through it, as if Daisy only required half of his attention. "And I'm glad you have your little business."

My little business? But of course that's how Hal would see it. He earned many, many times what Daisy brought into the family coffers. Maybe she could have earned more, if she'd rented space and opened a school, if she'd advertised or solicited clients more actively, but her current arrangement allowed her to be home every morning and every night, endlessly available for whatever the two of them might need.

Hal put down the mail. He opened his arms, waiting, with a patient, avuncular look, until Daisy stepped against him and let him hold her.

"You know, the feminists can say whatever they want, about women making money and men staying home," Hal said into her hair. "But in my opinion, this is the way it's supposed to work."

"And what do you mean by 'this,' exactly?" Daisy's voice was faint. Hal didn't seem to notice.

"I've got the job. You keep the house. You cook us wonderful meals. You take care of Beatrice." He kissed the tip of her nose, then her forehead. "You make our house a home."

"Yes, but . . ."

"And you're happy, aren't you?"

"I am, except . . ."

"Then good." He put his lips against hers; a hard, dry kiss that made her feel more like a document being stamped than a woman being appreciated. "I just want my little birds to be happy in their nest." Hal hooked his suit coat over his finger and went upstairs. Daisy sighed. She felt exhausted, utterly drained, but she still had to get dinner on the table. She went to the kitchen to pull steaks out of the refrigerator and snip a few stalks of rosemary from the pot. She was reaching for the cast-iron pan when she heard a voice.

"You know where that's from, don't you?"

Daisy gave a startled screech. When she looked up, Beatrice was hanging over the balcony, staring down.

"What?"

"Little bird."

Daisy was surprised that her daughter had even noticed the endearment, given how determined she seemed to ignore everything about her parents in general and Daisy specifically. "I don't know. That song? The Bob Marley one?"

"No," said Beatrice. "You're thinking of 'Three Little Birds.'

'Little bird' was what Torvald called Nora in *A Doll's House*. 'Little squirrel.' 'Little skylark.' 'My pretty little pet.'" Beatrice smirked, then turned and went back to her bedroom. Daisy heard her door close, very gently.

"Well, I'll bet I would have known it if I'd graduated from college!" Daisy yelled. *There*, she thought. *A teachable moment.*

She seared the steaks, and finished them with a sauce of rosemary and red wine, and served them with mashed potatoes and broccoli with lemon zest. She set the table, then cleared it, scraping the leftovers into the trash can. Then, leaving the rest of the dishes on the table and, unwashed, in the sink, Daisy went to the living room, where she sat on the edge of the fireplace, feeling the cold stone underneath her. She wasn't unfamiliar with feeling inadequate or unlettered, in a world where all the men and almost all the women she'd met had finished college, and most of them had earned advanced degrees, but this was the first time she'd thought about Beatrice seeing her that way. She wondered if, someday, her daughter would treat her with that same faintly patronizing air she'd gotten used to in her years as Hal Shoemaker's wife.

Daisy pulled her phone out of her pocket and started googling. *The play begins at Christmastime as Nora Helmer enters her home carrying many packages. Torvald, her husband, playfully teases her for spending so much money, calling her his "little squirrel."*

Daisy grimaced and slipped her phone in her pocket. Upstairs, the door to the bedroom that she and Hal shared was half-open, and she could hear the sound of the television, the voices of the sportscasters on ESPN. Hal would be lying on the bed, shoes off, feet up, maybe scrolling through some documents on his iPad, half paying attention to what was on TV. Beatrice's door was closed, but Daisy could hear music—Enya, she thought, or maybe Conan Lee Gray—coming from her daughter's bedroom, and could picture Beatrice in her rocker, furiously needle-felting, her face red as she jabbed her needle into the wool. She stood for a moment, undecided, then turned and went to the guest bedroom, which was empty for most of the year. No matter how she pleaded with Danny and Jesse to come for a weekend, or even a night, they were always busy, or off to someplace better: Fire Island or Florence or San Francisco. She didn't bother to turn on the light when she lay on top of the comforter. Lester followed her into the room and heaved himself up onto the bed on his second attempt. Daisy downloaded the entire play, scrolling through it, faster and faster, skimming, then reading closely when she neared the end.

"Then I passed over from father's hands into yours," Nora said. *"You settled everything according to your taste; or I did only what you liked; I don't exactly know. I think it was both ways, first one and then the other. When I look back on it now it seems to me as if I had been living here like a poor man, only from hand to mouth. I lived by performing tricks for you, Torvald. But you would have it so. You and father have sinned greatly against me."*

Daisy stared at the screen as if it had slapped her. She knew that her father had loved her. Hal loved her, too. He didn't treat her like a child, just like . . . *someone less than him*, her mind whispered. Someone who wasn't as smart or as important, someone whose opinion barely registered, and whose voice didn't matter much. At least, not as much as his did.

She put her phone in her pocket and walked down the hall to knock on her daughter's door. When Beatrice opened it, she said, "I need some help with the dishes."

Beatrice looked startled. Usually, all Daisy asked was that Beatrice set the table and clear her own plate. The kitchen was Daisy's domain, which made everything that happened there Daisy's job. Hal had his work, and Beatrice had school, and she had pots and pans to scrub, floors to sweep, countertops to wipe. A home to make, for the two of them.

"So, Nora leaves him in the end," she said, as they walked down the stairs.

"What?"

"In the play. *A Doll's House*."

"That's right." Beatrice went to the sink. "She says she can't be anyone's wife or anyone's mother until she knows who she is. She walks out of their house and closes the door behind. It's this iconic moment. At least, that's what our teacher said."

"That's very interesting." Daisy's voice was brittle. She bent over the dishwasher, feeling a great pressure on her chest, something bearing down on her, making it hard to breathe. "You're growing up to be a very impressive young lady."

Beatrice looked troubled. "Mom," she said. "Why didn't you finish college?"

Daisy thought she knew what Beatrice was fishing for: affirmation that her life would be fine with just a high-school diploma; permission to ignore Hal's wishes. Even if Daisy agreed—and she wasn't sure she did—she knew better than to say so. Hal would be furious.

"It was a long time ago," she said. "And things were different."

They finished cleaning the kitchen in silence. When Beatrice asked for permission to go back to her room and finish her homework, Daisy nodded. She turned off all the lights downstairs, making sure that the windows were latched and the doors were locked. In her bedroom, Hal had fallen asleep, with the television on and the remote on the bed beside him. Daisy turned off the TV. She put on her nightgown, washed her face, brushed her teeth, then went to the bed, where she lay on her back with her eyes open, as the clock ticked down the hours until morning.

Something is changing, she thought, as the sky beyond the window went from black to faintly gray. The house was quiet, except for Lester's noisy snores and Hal's quieter ones. Was it her? Was it Hal? Was it the world?

She lay awake on the bed, staring up at the ceiling, until it was six o'clock and her husband got up, quietly, to put on his running clothes, feigning sleep until she heard the front door open, and close. Then she lay there for another hour, wondering if she could continue to live like this, and, if not, what she was supposed to do next.

25

Beatrice

Normally, Beatrice hated it when her parents had dinner parties. She disliked the way they'd show her off, parading her around, introducing her to the guests, making her talk to strangers about her school or her soccer team or what books she was reading. She hated how her mom would get stressed and screechy, and how her dad would send Beatrice back upstairs to change her clothes if he disapproved of Beatrice's outfit, saying, "You can express yourself three hundred and sixty days of the year, but for five days I get to pick."

But what her mother had planned for Saturday night wasn't exactly a dinner party; it was relatives: Beatrice's grandfather and his lady friend, her grandmother and her grandma's gentleman caller, her uncles Danny and Jesse, with just one new person coming over. And the new person was actually someone Beatrice liked—her mother's new friend, Diana.

A few days after she'd cut school with Cade, she'd come home from school to find Diana and her mother cooking in the kitchen. They'd looked like birds: her mother, a plump brown wren, flitting and twittering around, picking up a pinch of this and a bit of that as she built her nest. Diana, meanwhile, looked like an eagle, imperious and watchful, hovering on the currents, peering at the scurrying rodents and rabbits below her, waiting to strike. Beatrice prepared for awkward questions about why she'd missed school and where she'd been, but instead, Diana looked her over appreciatively and said, "I love your hat. And your pin! It's perfect."

The hat had been a black cloche, with a tiny bit of veil over her left eye. The pin was one of Beatrice's treasures, an Art Deco tiger, in a prowling pose, with bits of topaz for the eyes. She'd bought it for twenty dollars at a store on South Street.

"That is quite a look," Diana had said. Beatrice knew when she was being humored, and could tell that Diana was sincere. "Are you interested in fashion as a career?"

Beatrice had shrugged. But then, instead of asking the predictable follow-up question—"Well, what are you interested in?"—which, of course, would segue into what most of her parents' friends really wanted to know, which was "Where are you thinking about going to college?" Diana had said, "You'll have to tell me where the good vintage stores in Philadelphia are."

"Oh, Beatrice knows them all," said her mother, who of course had to jump into every conversation to prove how well she knew her daughter, and how great a mother she was.

"Do you like vintage clothes?" Beatrice had asked Diana. Nothing from the other woman's appearance hinted at her tastes inclining in that direction. Diana was wearing dark-rinse jeans, a silk blouse, and no accessories except for the gold cuff on her wrist and diamond stud earrings. Her shoes were plain velvet flats, but probably designer—Tory Burch or even Chanel.

"I like vintage textiles and prints. Vintage postcards," Diana had answered. And she'd looked almost shy when she'd said, "I decoupage seashells with them. And I've been learning how to embroider."

"Beatrice makes shadowboxes. And she does taxidermy!" said

her mom, and actually managed to sound proud about it, even though Beatrice knew for a fact that she wasn't proud, at all.

Ignoring her mother, Beatrice had asked Diana, "Do you have any pictures?"

Diana had pulled out her phone, flicked at her screen, and showed Beatrice a shot of six oyster shells, edged in gold, decoupaged with fleur-de-lis or patterns of lobsters or starfish or bits of paisley print, and then samplers, squares of plain white linen embroidered with birds and flowers and, in one case, the word BULLSHIT in elaborate cursive. "I lived near the beach for a while, and I picked up seashells when I walked, and I was looking for something to do with them."

"Have you ever seen John Derian's stuff?" Beatrice asked.

Diana had smiled. "I've actually met him a few times."

Beatrice immediately abandoned any pretensions of being cool. "No way. Really?"

"Really." Diana looked delighted by Beatrice's pleasure. "Maybe someday, you guys will come visit me, and I'll take you to his shop." Diana had turned to Beatrice's mother. "Do you know his work?"

Beatrice's mother looked thoughtful. "He's got a shop in Provincetown. I've been there a few times." She was probably delighted that Beatrice was being "pleasant," as she'd probably put it, to one of her friends. "Have you ever been there?"

Beatrice thought she saw Diana stiffen. "To Provincetown? Not recently." Then Diana turned back to Beatrice, saying, "I would love to see your taxidermy," and Beatrice had led her upstairs. Before she'd left, her mother had invited her to the dinner party, and as soon as Diana had gotten in the car her mom had started planning the meal.

Cooking was her mother's business, and her mom hosted a number of parties every year as a way of attracting new business and showing off her skills. There was Thanksgiving, where everyone from both sides of the family came. Her mom roasted ducks and ordered a smoked goose from some place in North Dakota. In December, there was a Christmas cookie exchange. Her mother would bake for weeks, and invite everyone from the neighborhood over, and send them all home with a specially printed tin that had her name and the address of her website on a sticker on the front. There were the parties on the long weekends that bracketed summer: the Memorial Day barbecue, and the Labor Day Goodbye to the Cape clambake—and then the May Day dinner, which celebrated Grandma Judy's birthday, and her dad's.

Beatrice had already decided what she'd wear on Saturday night—a black tulle dress with crinolines, fitted at the bodice, flared at the hips, that she'd found at Goodwill for eight dollars. She would wear sparkly gold heels with it, and her black hat. Her mom was making one of her favorites, the coq au vin that took hours to prepare, and the dish her mom only served to her very favorite people.

Saturday, the day of the party, started off gray and cool. Her mother began cooking at lunchtime, reducing the wine and chicken stock, frying the lardons, then the onions and carrots, browning the chicken and putting everything into a big, deep pan. She added tomato paste, flambéed the brandy, and let the dish simmer. The smell reminded Beatrice of being a little girl, the first time she'd sat at the table, surveying the guests from her booster seat and feeling like a queen.

Beatrice set the table ("and I only had to ask her once," she heard her mom marvel to her dad), using her favorite blue-and-yellow patterned tablecloth, pale gold napkins, and her mother's good china, which had a red-and-gold pattern and gold leaf around the rim. On the counter in the kitchen was the red leaf salad with toasted hazelnuts, which would be dressed with a sesame vinaigrette at the last minute and served with warmed baguettes and unsalted butter. There would be warm spiced nuts and

Beatrice's very favorite treat, olives, wrapped in a cheesy dough and deep-fried. As irritating as Beatrice found her mom, as much as she pitied her, she could still recognize her culinary skills, and acknowledge that the fried breaded olives were the most delicious thing in the world.

It had started to rain when Diana arrived. Her pale-gray trench coat was spattered with raindrops, and the wind had tumbled her hair. "Beatrice!" she said, smiling and touching Beatrice's crinoline-puffed skirt. "What a fabulous outfit. Is it okay if I give you a hug?"

Beatrice decided that it was, and Diana enfolded her in her warmth and her perfume. Under her chic, belted coat, she was wearing wide-legged black pants, black leather boots, and a black cashmere wrap that looked like a cross between a cape and a blanket.

"I know," Diana said, like she was reading Beatrice's mind. "It's basically a Snuggie."

Beatrice didn't know what a Snuggie was, but she loved the sweater. "It's so soft," she said, touching Diana's sleeve.

"It's cashmere," said Diana. "I found it at this shop in—oh, Lord, Atlanta, I think. It was on clearance, probably because not many women want to walk around wearing blankets. I bought it in every color they had. Pink, pale gray, this kind of plum color, and black." She gave Beatrice an assessing look. "You know, the pink never really suited me. But I bet you'd look fabulous in it."

Beatrice's heart felt strangely swoopy. "Really?"

"Really. I'll box it up and put it in the mail the minute I'm home."

Beatrice's mom came out of the kitchen, wiping her hands on her apron. Next to Diana, in her green flowered apron and black leggings and bare feet, with her hair in a scrunchie, her mom looked ridiculous, and very young. The two women hugged each other warmly, and Diana kissed her mom's cheek before turning to Beatrice. "You know, your mother is saving my life."

"Oh, that's an exaggeration," said her mom, looking pleased nonetheless.

"It's true!" said Diana. "Thanks to your mom, I'm going to eat well for the rest of my life." Her mother was beaming when Beatrice's father came down the stairs.

"Hello, ladies!" The women didn't exactly spring apart, but Diana stepped back and her mom looked down. Her dad wore a button-down shirt and khakis, instead of the jeans he'd normally have on for a Saturday night at home. If her mom was a wren, and Diana was an eagle, what was her father, swooping in to eat as soon as the meal was prepared? Maybe a vulture, Beatrice thought, and turned away to hide her smile. Her dad kissed Diana on the cheek, and Beatrice saw, or thought she saw, the other woman stiffen, very briefly, the same way she had at the mention of Provincetown.

Beatrice knew that her father hadn't wanted Diana at the dinner party. "I'm glad you have a new friend. But I don't want to have to make conversation with a stranger."

"Diana is my friend," her mom had said, her tone unexpectedly sharp. She'd dropped her voice, but Beatrice could imagine what she was saying: *after everything I do around here, after everything I do for you.*

From her bedroom, Beatrice heard the low sound of her dad's voice, probably agreeing. Giving her mother permission to include her friend, the same way he'd give Beatrice permission to go to a sleepover. Her dad was so much older than her mom, sometimes listening to the two of them was like listening to a parent with a child, not a husband with a wife. Beatrice hadn't noticed it until recently—probably right around when they'd read *A Doll's House*, back at Emlen—but now, she could see that her dad was the one making decisions, about where they'd go on vacations, about where Beatrice went to school, probably about things that had been decided before she'd even been born, like where they would live, in which house and in which town. Usually, her mom went along with the program and seemed happy enough. But lately, Beatrice had noticed changes, small acts of resistance, barely notable—or at least, they would have been barely notable in other families. A few days ago, her mom had been in Center City, with Diana, and she'd called to say they'd decided to go out to dinner. "Well, what are we supposed to do?" her dad had asked, and her mom said, "Get a pizza!" so loudly that Beatrice heard her, even though she wasn't on speaker.

Before Beatrice could figure out whether Diana had actually pulled away from her father, and what it meant, Grandma Judy and Arnold Mishkin arrived. Beatrice received a kiss on the cheek from her grandmother, who was short and plump, with silvery-blonde bobbed hair, and probably looked exactly the way Beatrice's mother would in forty years. She watched from the foyer as the adults made small talk. "Where are you based?" Arnold asked Diana.

"New York," Diana said. "But I'm hardly ever there. I have an apartment, but it's really just a place to unpack my suitcase, and pack it again."

Arnold nodded. "It's a hard life, with all that travel."

"And such an expensive city to live in!" said Grandma Judy. "I hope your clients pay you well."

"Oh, there are definitely compensations," Diana said, with a kind of tucked-in, ironic smile that hinted at another meaning to the words. Beatrice wondered what it was. Something about sex, maybe. In her experience, whenever adults hinted, instead of coming out and saying what they meant, sex was usually the reason why. Personally, she thought that Diana was lucky, and that traveling all the time sounded glamorous, and exciting. No home meant no kids, no husband, nobody nagging you or needing you or dragging you down.

She was just about to say something along those lines when the doorbell rang again. Her mom detached herself to greet Beatrice's Pop-Pop, and Evelyn, his lady friend, whom Beatrice knew her father didn't like.

"Hello, dear," said Pop-Pop, giving Beatrice a hug, and a full dose of his denture breath. Her grandfather didn't have much use for girls. His favorite was Scott, Beatrice's cousin, her father's brother Jeremy's son. Scott was nineteen and in college now. When he was in elementary school and junior high he'd played baseball on some special select team that practiced year-round and traveled all over New Jersey. He'd gotten to skip out on half of the family functions because he had games, or practice, and leave the rest of them early. Beatrice had envied him desperately . . . just not desperately enough to take up a sport.

"Trixie!" said Evelyn. Beatrice gave her partial credit for at least remembering what Beatrice used to be called and not resorting to "dear" the way Pop-Pop did. Evelyn was slender and elegant, with close-cropped white hair and dramatic, penciled-in eyebrows. She wore lots of rings, with colorful stones, and bright silk scarves that she could tie in all kinds of shapes around her neck. Evelyn loved Broadway and travel, and had been to every big city in Europe, as well as Iceland and Moscow. Pop-Pop hated musicals—"all those people singing instead of talking"—and saw no reason to travel any farther than Augusta, Georgia, where he'd once golfed on the course where the Masters was played. Beatrice could not understand why they were together. It was easy enough to see what Pop-Pop was getting out of their arrangement: three hot meals a day, a well-ventilated garage for his collection of vintage comic books, and an extra-large flat-screen TV on which he could watch the Yankees and the Giants. Evelyn, meanwhile, had gotten a man with a pulse and a driver's license. Beatrice knew Pop-Pop had been living by himself, in an apartment, before he'd met Evelyn, and had moved into Evelyn's four-bedroom house in Fort Lee after they'd been dating for six months.

"Evelyn's generation was raised to believe that a woman needed a man," Beatrice's mom had said. Beatrice had wanted to ask her mom what her generation believed, but knew that any conversation that could involve love or marriage was just two or three perilous steps away from a reprise of the dreaded masturbation talk, so she'd just nodded and gone to her room.

In the foyer, Pop-Pop removed his coat, helped Evelyn off with hers, handed both coats to Beatrice's mom, and said, "What's for dinner, dear?"

"Chicken," her mother said. The one time she'd said *coq au vin* to her father-in-law, he'd spent the entire night saying every French word he could think of—*Croissant! Escargot!*—in an exaggerated French accent and demanding to know what was wrong with American food. Now her mom just called it chicken, or chicken stew, or, sometimes, *that chicken you like.*

"I'll take a Scotch," Pop-Pop said, before her mom had even asked what he wanted to drink. Her mom looked to her father for help, but Beatrice's dad was already talking to his father about the baseball game the night before.

Beatrice saw Diana, standing by the staircase, watching the other guests. Diana's expression was thoughtful, her dark eyes following her mom on her way to the coat closet. Beatrice wondered what Diana made of it all: their small suburban lives. She couldn't imagine Diana carrying coats and fetching drinks. Probably, she had people who did that for her. An assistant. Maybe more than one.

Another knock on the door came. Lester bayed his basset-hound howl, alerting them to the presence of newcomers, and Beatrice went to welcome Uncle Danny and Uncle Jesse. Uncle Jesse was handsome as ever, with his white teeth and his glossy curls, but his smile looked strained. Uncle Danny, meanwhile, looked terrible. He'd always been round-faced and cheerful, like a Jewish Santa with a brown beard instead of a white one. Now his face looked baggy and droopy. There were dark smudges under his eyes, and gray in his beard. Beatrice gave him an extra-long hug, her heart already fluttering in her chest as she wondered if he was sick, and if the adults would tell her the truth. Already, she could hear Grandma Judy's voice, high and nasal and anxious. "Danneleh, you look terrible! Are you eating? What's going on?" and Uncle Jesse's voice, lower and soothing, saying they'd been taking care of a baby, that the baby hadn't slept, and neither had they.

Beatrice knew how the evening would go. First, the guests would spend a half hour or so in the living room, where her dad had laid a fire, nibbling nuts and olives and crackers. Evelyn and Grandma Judy would ask about her grades and her field hockey team (that was back in middle school, when she'd been forced to take a sport); her uncles would ask about her crafts. Pop-Pop would ask if she'd met any nice young men. All the adults would sneak sideways glances at her clothes and her hair, and Uncle Jesse's would be the only look that was approving.

Then it would be time for dinner. At the table, Pop-Pop would talk about sports with—or, really, at—whoever would listen. Grandma Judy and Arnold would describe the latest trip they'd taken, and the next one they'd planned, while Evelyn would look envious, and Uncle Danny and Uncle Jesse, who'd also been all over the world, would offer tips, or stories of their own. Pop-Pop would look at Uncle Danny and Uncle Jesse with his lip curled when he thought no one was watching. A few years ago, Beatrice had noticed that he wouldn't take food that either of them had passed or served him. When she'd asked her dad why, he'd looked startled, then said, "Older people have a lot of weird superstitions." Then he'd pretended he had to make a phone call, and it wasn't until she'd asked her cousin Scott, who'd said, "He thinks they'll give him AIDS, probably," and turned back to his video game, that she'd understood.

When everyone was finished, her mom, who'd probably barely even sat down and might not have eaten more than a few bites, would clear the table, with Evelyn and Grandma Judy's help, and make coffee, and get the dishes started as whatever she'd made for dessert came to room temperature or warmed up in the oven. Uncle Danny and Uncle Jesse would help wash dishes, and Grandma Judy would keep them company in the kitchen while her dad and his father and Arnold adjourned to the den to watch TV. Coffee and dessert would be taken back in the living room. Her grandfather would tell them the same handful of jokes, her dad would look at his watch and say, "It's getting late," and everyone would get their coats and leave.

But this dinner party was different.

26

Diana

"What do you do, dear?" Evelyn asked Diana, as they all took their seats in the living room.

Diana smiled the smile she'd practiced in the mirror as she'd gotten dressed that afternoon, in all that black. The cashmere sweater was lovely, one of the nicest things she owned, one of the few pieces that could successfully be worn by the woman she was and the one she was pretending to be, but everything else was Rent the Runway–provided, or a drag queen loaner, including the gold cuff. She'd applied her makeup carefully, coating her face with concealer and foundation, wishing she had an actual mask to wear, one that would keep her real feelings hidden when she saw, for the first time since that summer, the man who'd raped her, and the man who'd watched.

Hal Shoemaker looked much the same as he had on the Cape. Older now, with lines on his face and gray at the temples of his dark hair, but essentially unchanged, with a confidence that was almost cockiness, an attitude suggesting that it was the world's job to lay its riches at his feet, and that the world had, for the most part, complied. He addressed his wife with the same hearty, almost condescending good humor with which he spoke to his daughter. When he'd kissed her cheek, Diana struggled to keep her hands loose at her sides when they wanted to curl into fists. She'd had to excuse herself to go to the powder room and run cold water over her wrists. She'd wanted to rinse her face, but knew she couldn't risk ruining her makeup.

Daniel Rosen looked terrible. Stricken, almost ill, his face pale and jowly, his eyes haunted. She wondered what was behind that, if word of Brad Burlingham's suicide had reached him, or if something else was responsible for his appearance.

"I'm a consultant," she answered. "And Daisy's been giving me cooking lessons."

"You don't cook?" Evelyn asked, cocking her head.

"I do now. Thanks to Daisy," Diana said, and Beatrice's mom had beamed. Diana felt the other woman's pleasure like a thumbtack piercing some soft part of her. The poor woman got so little praise, so little gratitude. "But I never really learned."

"Your mother didn't teach you?"

Diana shook her head. "My father was actually the cook in our house."

At that, Vernon Shoemaker made a show of incredulity. "What kind of consulting do you do?" he asked Diana.

"I work with pharmaceutical companies." When she told him she was there working with Quaker, Vernon's expression became respectful. "You must be good at what you do. They're, what, a hundred-billion-dollar business?"

"And still growing, with the genetic screening kits they've launched."

Vernon looked at her hands. "So no family? No husband?"

Diana shook her head, with her smile still in place, and quickly glanced at Hal, and Danny, to see if they were paying her any special attention.

Vernon, meanwhile, nodded as if she'd confirmed something. "That's how it goes for women," he said to Beatrice. "It's either a big job or a husband and kids. You can't have both."

Jesse put his hand on Danny's shoulder as Beatrice asked, "Why not?"

All three of the adults turned to look at her. Beatrice stood up straight. "I mean, Dad's got a big job and a family."

"Your father's got a wife," Vernon said, with heavy good humor.

"Well, maybe I'll grow up and have a wife. Or a husband who wants to stay home. And I'll be the one with the big career."

Her grandfather laughed. Or, really, he spoke the syllables *Ha, ha, ha.* "I wish you a lot of luck," he said. "Good luck finding a man who wants to stay home while you're out hunting and gathering."

"You don't think that there are men who want to stay home?" Beatrice asked indignantly. Again, Diana wanted to look, to see how Hal was reacting to this, as Daisy jumped in to ask who was ready for another drink.

"Another Scotch, sweetie," Vernon said, and Daisy hurried to get it.

Beatrice plopped on the couch, looking disconsolate, and helped herself to a fistful of cheese-dough-wrapped olives. Diana couldn't help herself. She sat down beside the girl and said, quietly, "Don't let them discourage you. You can do anything you want. The world is changing."

Beatrice nodded, then looked at Diana. "Did you ever want a family?" she asked. "Like, do you feel like you missed out?"

Diana's heart gave a terrible wrench. She hadn't longed for a baby, or a toddler, or a house in the suburbs, hadn't cared about cars or clothes or jewelry, but she would have loved to have a ten- or twelve- or fourteen-year-old daughter, a smart, spirited girl like Beatrice. She pressed her lips together, then said, "I wanted a lot of things when I was your age."

Beatrice looked unhappy at that answer. Diana wondered what she was thinking, if she was coming to the conclusion that adulthood was just one long process of settling for what you'd gotten, whether or not it was what you'd wanted.

"But, listen, you have plenty of time to decide what you want to do, and what your life will be like."

"I don't know," said Beatrice, as Daisy came to the living room entrance. "Dinner's ready," she said, and everyone went to the dining room. Diana was seated with Daisy on one side and Beatrice on the other, across from Danny and Jesse. "Let me help you," she said to Daisy, as Hal spread his napkin on his lap. Daisy, flustered, said, "No, no, you're my guest."

"You can show me how you plate the food," said Diana. She didn't trust herself to stay at the table with Hal and Danny. All she wanted to do was grab Beatrice, and maybe Daisy, too, and throw them in her car and drive away, maybe all the way back to Cape Cod, so that she and Daisy could keep Beatrice there until she was old enough to move safely through the world. In other words, Diana thought, forever.

She watched in the kitchen, with her trembling hands in her pockets, as Daisy put a scoop of mashed potatoes on the bottom of each shallow bowl and spooned chicken and sauce on top. "Can you grab me the slotted spoon?" she asked, and Diana handed it over. "Vernon doesn't eat mushrooms," she explained, straining the sauce for his portion. Diana didn't comment as she helped Daisy carry the food to the table. When everyone was served, Diana picked up her fork. She was wondering how to proceed when Beatrice did her job for her.

"So," she said, "what do you all think will happen with Huey Sanders?" Huey Sanders was a twenty-one-year-old pitcher who'd been signed by the Phillies for a contract worth six million dollars for his first year. A few days ago some social-media sleuth had discovered tweets and Reddit posts he'd made when he was fourteen using the n-word and calling his friends faggots. Huey had issued a version of the statement most athletes released in similar circumstances, saying that the words did not reflect the man he'd become, saying that he'd been wrong and that he was sorry. He'd asked for forgiveness and had promised to do better.

So far, the Phillies hadn't said anything about whether they intended to ignore the incident, cut him loose, or find some middle ground.

"I hope the Phillies get rid of him," Beatrice said.

Daisy looked proud. Hal pressed his lips together. Vernon Shoemaker swung his head around to peer at his granddaughter. "Oh, really?" he said. "You want to punish a young man for stupid things he said when he was younger than you are right now?"

"Fourteen is still old enough to know what hate speech is," Beatrice said.

"I agree," said Jesse, and, beside him, Danny nodded his assent.

"Maybe you're old enough to know," said Hal, in a patronizing tone. "You've had the benefit of a fine education. We don't know anything about how this young man was brought up."

"And why should one mistake mean he loses his chance to play for the Phillies?" Vernon asked Beatrice. "More chicken, please, dear," he said to Daisy, who'd just pulled out her chair to sit.

"I'll get it," said Evelyn, standing up and taking his dish.

"It's all being blown out of proportion," Vernon scoffed. "I mean, a few twits, or tweets, or whatever it is he did." He picked up his water glass, his thumb leaving a smear of chicken grease on its side. "Poor kid's not the only one to have done something stupid when he was young." He grinned at Beatrice's father. "I mean, if they'd had Tweeter when you were a kid, you probably would've never gotten into Dartmouth."

"Dad," Hal said sharply. But Vernon kept talking. "Remember that party in—oh, where was it, Newport? One of your friends' families had a place. And you and your buddies went there for the weekend." He used his knife to point at Danny. "You were there, weren't you?"

Danny gave a nod, his pale face looking even paler. Jesse frowned and said something quietly. Danny picked up his water glass in a hand that seemed to shake.

Ignoring that byplay, Vernon turned back to the table and picked up the story. "It's the middle of the night, and I get a call from the police, because they'd gotten a call from the neighbors, because . . ."

"Dad."

". . . my sons, both of them, got drunk, and decided to go skinny-dipping at two in the morning . . ."

"Dad."

". . . and then run naked through the neighbors' backyard."

Diana saw Daisy glaring at her father-in-law. She saw Jesse take his husband's hand. She saw Hal sitting, enraged and frozen, as Vernon kept talking, oblivious to everyone's discomfort, or maybe just enjoying the spotlight. "One of the boys had driven his car right onto the next-door neighbors' backyard and through their screened porch, and passed out, naked as a jaybird, on the hood. The police couldn't identify him because, obviously, he didn't have his wallet. So they called the homeowners, who called all the boys' parents. Including me." He wiped his eyes and said to his son, "It's a good thing your mother didn't pick up the phone that night!"

Hal's face was stony. Daisy looked desperately embarrassed. Danny gave a faint, protesting moan. "Excuse us," said Jesse, standing up and taking Danny by the shoulder, practically hauling him out of the dining room.

"Did Dad get in trouble?" Beatrice asked. Diana could feel the tension in the room as she waited for Vernon to answer.

"Oh, I'm sure we punished him somehow," Vernon said, with a conspiratorial wink at his son. "But there was no internet, is my point. The stupid things you did when you were young never made headlines. Which, in the case of your father, Beatrice, was a very good thing."

"Boys will be boys." Diana had meant to sound teasing and agreeable, but her voice sounded flat and cold. Hal had narrowed his eyes in a way that made her heart briefly stop beating. Vernon, meanwhile, thought she was agreeing with him.

"That's it. That's right. Boys will be boys. Boys have always been boys. And nothing—not political correctness, not all of this 'Me Too' stuff, not feminism—none of it will ever change that. It's their nature." Having concluded his speech, Vernon went back to attacking his mushroom-free chicken. Hal was still glaring at him, white around the lips, one hand fisted around his fork.

"And what if it was a girl who'd done what Dad did?" Beatrice asked.

"A girl wouldn't," Vernon said. "That's my point."

"Oh, I don't know," said Evelyn. "Some of the girls these days are pretty wild. Just as bad as the boys are, from what I hear."

Vernon shook his head. "Everything's upside down these days. And everyone's so damn sensitive! Women acting like a man paying her a compliment is some kind of assault. People getting up in arms if you get their pronouns wrong. All these rules about what you can and can't do in the office. You know," he said to Beatrice, "that your grandmother Margie was my office gal."

"No," said Beatrice.

"It's nonsense," he said, as he began wiping his plate with a chunk of bread.

"I disagree," said Daisy. She'd drawn herself up tall, and her face looked flushed above the same blue necklace she'd worn to New York City, the first time Diana had met her.

Vernon looked at her sharply. So did Hal. Daisy's gaze was steady.

"I don't think the new rules are bad," said Daisy. "I mean, obviously, you can't stop people from being attracted to their co-workers. But sometimes there's a power differential, and I don't think it's wrong to make people aware of that."

"You can't have bosses chasing secretaries around the desk." Evelyn looked like she was remembering something unpleasant.

"Hear, hear," said Judy. Diana wondered how many desks the two of them had been chased around in their day, how much bad behavior they'd had to endure.

"I'll bet boys today are afraid to even look at a girl," Vernon said, shaking his head. His jowls wobbled, but his comb-over remained motionless.

"Poor boys," Diana said. She said it very softly, but Hal, who'd been looking at his plate, jerked his head up. For a long, silent moment, their eyes met across the table. Diana forced herself to hold his gaze, even though she wanted desperately to get up from the table and run. *I see you,* she thought . . . and imagined that she could hear Hal saying, *I see you,* too. She was going to ask him something, to poke at him again, but Beatrice got there first.

"Dad, what do you think?" she asked.

Diana could see red spots, high on Hal's cheeks. His voice was tight. "Do I think that some of the women are making mountains out of molehills? Yes."

"Damn right," Vernon muttered.

"Do I think there's kind of a one-size-fits-all mentality to the punishment, where a guy who hits on a subordinate is treated the exact same way a violent rapist is treated?" Hal continued doggedly. "Yes. Do I think there should be some way for men to make amends and rejoin polite society? Yes. And on the whole . . ." He looked around the table, his gaze touching on each woman's face, first Judy's, then Evelyn's, then his daughter's, then his wife's, before his gaze found its way to Diana. "I think this country is long overdue for a reckoning."

"I agree," said Daisy, getting quickly to her feet. "Now, who's ready for dessert?"

Diana watched, and waited, hoping there'd be an opening, a moment where Hal was alone. She waited until Vernon and Evelyn departed, and Danny and Jesse were saying that they should be going home, too; that Danny had the early shift at the soup kitchen in the morning. *Now or never*, she thought.

"Hal, can I ask you a question?"

He looked at her. "Of course," he said, his voice cool and polite. His shirt still looked perfectly pressed, not a hair on his head disarranged.

"And Danny, you too." Danny's eyes were very wide, and his sweater had come untucked. "It's a question about Emlen. You're both Emlen men, right?"

Diana led the men as far away from the group as she could, to the very edge of the room. She could hear Daisy in the kitchen, the small, domestic sounds of running water, the clink of silverware and the clatter of dishes. Lester the basset hound was standing with his front paws on the dishwasher's open door, gazing adoringly at his mistress as she scrubbed and rinsed, pausing only to swipe his tongue over each dish placed into the machine. Diana thought about how men made messes and women cleaned them up; how this was the way of the world.

"What can we do for you?" asked Hal, and crossed his arms over his chest.

"Well," said Diana. "For starters, you can tell me if you remember me."

Danny gave a small, pained noise. Hal just stared.

"It was a long time ago, right after you'd finished high school. Do you remember a party on the beach? A bonfire?" she asked. She saw Hal's shoulders stiffen as his eyes narrowed to a squint.

In a low, impressively level voice, he said, "You need to leave." His hands were steady, but she saw the way he'd gone white around his lips.

Diana arched her eyebrow. "You don't want me in your house? It's a terrible feeling, isn't it, having someone where you don't want them? Acting like your wishes don't matter?"

"I'm sorry," Danny whispered. And then Jesse was there, as if drawn by his husband's distress, glaring at Diana.

"Danny?" he said. "Is everything all right here?"

"Everything's fine," said Diana, and smiled, showing her teeth. "Turns out, Danny and Hal and I all knew each other, a long time ago. We were just getting reacquainted." She could read Hal's thoughts, evident in the lines of his body, his tensed shoulders and narrowed eyes: *I will hurt you.* And she smiled even more widely, knowing that he couldn't. For once, finally, she was the one with the power, the knowledge, the upper hand. His life was an oyster, dropped from a great height onto a rocky shore. Now his shell had been cracked open and the soft, defenseless meat had been exposed. Hal couldn't protect himself. Not from this. The only question left was how much damage she would do.

"To be continued. Good night, for now," she said very softly. "Thank you for having me." And she leaned forward to gently press a kiss on Hal's cheek.

27

Beatrice

That night, after the party, the line of light beneath her parents' door stayed lit for hours. Beatrice could hear their voices in their bedroom, rising and falling in a way that suggested an argument. She lingered in the hallway, hoping to hear what they were saying, but all she could make out once was the sound of her name.

On Sunday morning, she decided to start a new project. Her dad had left early for his office, saying something about a deposition he needed to review, and her mom had decided to clean out the pantry, which, Beatrice knew, was a task she reserved for moments of greatest unease. Neither one of them seemed to have any inclination to spend time with her, or ask her opinion of Saturday night's festivities. That was fine with her.

She began by retrieving one of her frozen mice from way back behind the quarts of chicken and beef stock, where she'd stashed her latest haul. By then, eviscerating a frozen mouse was a matter of minutes, a few quick steps. She picked up her scalpel and sliced down the spine, from the mouse's shoulder to hips, slipping in her fingertip and gradually, gently, separating the pelt from the flesh. When it was free, she stuffed the skin with the cotton and wire form she'd made, sewed the skin shut, and used straight pins to keep the feet and mouth in place. She snipped the gold clasp off an eight-by-twelve envelope and bent it into a cuff, and used a bit of red silk for a cape. She adjusted her pins to give the mouse's head an arrogant tilt, and worked at the wires to pose it, just so. Maybe Diana needed an intern, or a housesitter. Maybe she would just take Beatrice under her wing and introduce her to her famous, stylish friends, and teach Beatrice all her secrets, so that Beatrice could grow up and be just like her, glamorous and confident and unbothered and brave.

She left her art to dry overnight and turned to her homework: a problem set for math class, two chapters of history to read, and an English essay to rewrite. For dinner, her mother served left-over chicken, with a fresh loaf of sourdough bread. Her father was still at the office, and when the meal concluded, her mom didn't ask Beatrice to play Scrabble with her, or at least sit in the den and watch TV. She just trudged off to her bedroom. Which gave Beatrice the perfect opportunity to color her hair, a silvery lavender that she was quite pleased with in the end.

On Monday morning, Beatrice was on her way to homeroom when Cade Langley called her name.

"I need to talk to you."

"I can't be tardy." Beatrice had barely spoken to Cade since their trip to the Mütter Museum. After he'd brought her back to school she'd gone to English class and, from there, straight to the office, where the high-school dean asked where she'd been, then called her mom and dad. Since then, Cade and his friends had been ignoring her in the cafeteria, and Cade had barely even looked at her in class, or when they'd passed in the halls. And, of course, her parents had taken her phone away, so she had no way of getting in touch with him.

Cade took her hand and pulled her into a dark nook under

the staircase. Beatrice could hear the pounding of feet overhead as kids made their way to class.

Beatrice waited. Cade didn't say anything.

"Hey," she said, "I really need to go to class."

Cade reached into his backpack and pulled out a small, wrapped package, a light rectangle that felt like a book. "I got you a present."

She looked at him curiously.

"Open it."

Shrugging, she ripped the paper and saw a copy of Edward Gorey's *The Gashlycrumb Tinies*. "Ooh!" She already had a copy, but figured everyone could use a spare. Opening the book at random, she read, "M is for Maud who was swept out to sea. N is for Neville who died of ennui." She closed it and looked up at Cade.

"Thank you," she said. "What's the occasion?"

Cade fidgeted, putting his hands in his pockets, then taking them out. His cheeks looked especially red, like he'd been running, or outside in the wind. "I thought you'd like it. It made me think of you."

"Because it's dark and weird?"

"Pretty much."

"Okay," said Beatrice. "So what's going on?"

"What do you mean?"

"You ignore me for a week, and then you give me a present. I'm confused."

Cade made an agonized sound, and practically groaned the words, "I like you!" Then he grabbed his hair in both hands and pulled, as if the confession made his head hurt.

"I feel," said Beatrice, "like I'm missing something here."

Cade gave another pained noise. Without meeting her eyes, he said, "I need to tell you something, but you can't be mad."

Beatrice raised her eyebrows, up toward her newly purple bangs. "I can be anything I want. Remember?"

Cade squeezed his eyes shut. "Right," he muttered. "Okay. So. Um. At first—when I asked you to sit with us at lunch—that was, uh, not entirely sincere."

Beatrice waited.

"They dared me to do it," Cade said, with his eyes still shut.

She wasn't surprised. Still, she felt the icy, electric shock of shame crawl over her skin. "Who did?"

"Ian and Ezra. They thought it would be funny, because you're . . ." He made a formless gesture with his hands, something that Beatrice guessed was meant to communicate *weird* or *strange* or even just *purple hair.*

"That's why you asked me to go with you last week." Beatrice felt like she was watching this happen to someone else, some other girl, the spunky heroine of the kind of movie her mother liked, who'd get her heart broken halfway through and find true love in the end.

"Yeah," said Cade. He gave a noisy sigh. "They said they'd pay me a hundred bucks if I spent the day with you. And more, if we . . ." His voice trailed off. Which was a good thing. Beatrice was wearing her Doc Martens. If she decided to kick him, it would hurt. "But I like you." Cade's voice was pained, and when he opened his eyes and looked at her, his expression seemed sincere. He took her hand. "Can I call you?"

Beatrice gave him a long look. Then she pulled her hand away.

"How many other girls have you guys done this to?"

"What?"

"You and Ezra and Ian. Is this, like, a regular thing? Like, choose some weirdo and bet each other a hundred bucks to take her out, or kiss her?"

Cade squirmed and finally muttered, "We don't do it a lot."

"Why, though? Why would you do it at all?"

He wriggled around, tugging at his hair, looking like he was trying to climb out of his skin. Beatrice did not relent.

"Why would you hurt people who haven't done anything to hurt you?"

"I don't know," he said. "I don't know why."

Beatrice could feel herself getting angry, a heated flush rising from the pit of her stomach up over her chest and her neck. "Well. Thank you for the gift. Thank you for telling me the truth." She turned on her heel. Cade grabbed her shoulder.

"Beatrice . . ."

"Just leave me alone, okay?" She found that she was almost crying, and it made her even more angry and ashamed. Angry at him, for what he'd done; ashamed of herself, for being susceptible to his charms.

"Wait!" Cade pulled her back into the alcove, looking a question into her eyes. She didn't say anything, but she didn't pull away as he bent down and pressed his lips against hers. For a few seconds, just long enough to think *What's all the fuss about?*, she felt nothing. Then he cupped the back of her neck, and her mouth opened, seemingly on its own. His tongue touched hers, then slid into her mouth, a shockingly intimate invasion. Beatrice's arms found their way around his shoulders, and she found her hips tilting toward him like she'd been magnetized. *Oh*, she thought. *Oh*.

Cade let her go. His pupils looked very dark; his lips looked slightly swollen. "Sorry—I—was that okay?" His voice was hoarse, and when Beatrice thought, *I made him sound that way*, she felt pleasure wash through her.

She tried to sound nonchalant as she smoothed her hair. "It wasn't terrible."

He smiled at her, looking grateful.

"Does this mean you're my boyfriend?" Beatrice asked sweetly, and she almost laughed out loud when she saw the expressions moving across his face—panic, terror, grim resignation, then something that looked like Cade's idea of nobility and courage. "Or are we only going to do this when no one can see?"

His throat jerked as he swallowed. She gave him a few seconds to say something. Anything. When he didn't, she said, "Come find me when you figure it out," and walked off toward her first class, not knowing how to feel.

At lunchtime, she took her food outside and sat on a bench, waiting for him to come find her. She felt like her body had turned into a lighthouse, flashing out his name. She touched her lips, remembering, in spite of herself, the speech her mom had given her, about how powerful sex was, about how it was hard not to give your heart to someone who'd already had access to your body. If this was how a single kiss could make her feel, what would actual intercourse do to her poor heart?

She waited, thinking that Cade had to be feeling some version of what she was experiencing, that he wanted to see her as much as she wanted to see him. All through lunch, and the rest of the day, Beatrice waited for him to approach her again, to hand her a note, to pull her back into the alcove and kiss her again. But he never came.

28

Daisy

Who?" asked the doorman.

"Diana Starling," Daisy said, and shifted the container of coq au vin from her left arm to her right, feeling its contents shift and slosh.

The doorman—a man Daisy hadn't seen on any of her previous visits—shook his head. "Nobody here by that name."

"It's apartment 1402," said Daisy. She hadn't made plans to see Diana, but she'd been in the city to pick up a lamp she'd had rewired, and had impulsively decided to drop off some of the leftover chicken, which was actually better the day after it was cooked.

"Apartment 1402," she repeated. The man shook his head. "I've been there with her."

Speaking slowly and loudly, as if Daisy didn't understand English, the man said, "1402 is the model apartment. Nobody lives there. We keep it to show renters."

Daisy felt herself staring. "She's a consultant for Quaker Pharmaceuticals. She told me they rent the place. Can you check again? Maybe I'm confused."

"Look," said the doorman. He beckoned Daisy around the desk and pointed to his laptop screen. "This is the directory of every single person who lives at 15 Rittenhouse. There are two companies that keep units for long-term stays, but Quaker isn't one of them."

Daisy scanned the list of names. No Diana Starling. In fact, no Dianas at all.

"Maybe it's a different building?" the doorman said. "There's a lot of apartment buildings around here, and a lot of them have lobbies that look alike."

Daisy thanked him. She left the building with her chicken still under her arm, feeling baffled. After two laps around the perimeter of Rittenhouse Square Park, dodging joggers and strollers, she landed on a plan.

The Center City office for Quaker Pharmaceuticals was on Market Street, two blocks west of Hal's office. Not that she had any intention of going there. *There's something wrong with that woman*, Hal had told her, the night after the party. Daisy had to admit that Diana's behavior had been a little strange, her remarks abrupt and her expressions hard to read. She'd also left without saying goodbye. "What?" Daisy had asked. "What's wrong with her? Tell me what!" Hal hadn't. "Just listen to me," he'd said, and Daisy hadn't answered, but she'd thought, *I've listened to you without thinking for too long*, and she'd barely said another word to Hal since then.

Daisy forced herself to put on her brightest smile as she approached the woman at the front desk.

"Hi there. I'm looking for Diana Starling. She's a consultant who's been working here for the past few months."

Click click click went the woman's long, silvery nails. "No one here by that name."

"She's a consultant. So maybe she's not in your directory."

In a bored voice, the woman said, "Every single person who

comes in here has to be in our system. Either they've been assigned a permanent ID card, or they have to leave identification at the desk so we can issue a temporary pass. If this woman's consulting here, she'd have a permanent ID. If she visited, she'd still be in our system. And I don't have any record of anyone by that name."

Daisy thanked the woman and walked outside before sitting heavily down on a bench in the courtyard. Her head was churning. If Diana wasn't really a consultant, if she didn't really live at 15 Rittenhouse or work at Quaker Pharmaceuticals, who was she? Why was she in Philadelphia? And what did she want with Daisy? *There's something wrong with that woman*, she thought, and then pushed the memory of Hal's voice away.

She walked back toward the park, thinking back to the first misdirected email she'd gotten, and checked her phone, grateful, for once, that she never remembered to delete things. Hal preached the gospel of the empty in-box. Meanwhile, Daisy's in-box was a morass of coupons and spam and notices from Beatrice's school that she never got rid of. The first DianaS/Diana.S email she'd gotten had arrived four months ago. Coinciding with . . . what, exactly? Six months ago was before Beatrice had gotten kicked out of Emlen. Before Hal's classmate's suicide, before the cocktail party, before he'd started drinking, and before her brother had started acting, and looking, so strained and drawn and sad. But not too far before. Were any of these things connected?

Daisy thought and got nowhere. Finally, because she couldn't think of what else to do, she pulled out her phone and called Diana.

"Daisy!" Diana's voice was warm and pleased, not at all furtive or guilty. "Thank you again for Saturday night. I had a wonderful time, and I'm sorry I had to leave in such a hurry. I've been meaning to call you. What's up?"

"I was in town, running errands, and I thought I'd bring you some leftover chicken."

There was the tiniest pause. "That's so nice of you. Unfortunately, I'm a little snowed under right now. Maybe we can—"

"I went to your apartment building," Daisy said.

The next pause was longer. "Oh," Diana finally said. Still not furtive, still not guilty. Just calm, and patient. Waiting.

"They told me that 1402 is the model apartment. And that no one's living there, and no one ever does. And no one at Quaker Pharmaceutical's ever heard of you."

She waited for excuses, for an *I can explain*. When Diana didn't say anything, Daisy said, "What's going on? Is this some kind of . . ." Game? Joke? Trick?

"Where are you?" Diana finally asked.

"Rittenhouse Square."

"Can you meet me at Ants Pants on South Street in ten minutes?"

Daisy found herself absurdly relieved, thinking, *At least she's actually in Philadelphia. At least she didn't lie to me about that.* "Fine."

"Okay. Thanks. I'll see you there."

Daisy didn't even realize she'd left the chicken on a park bench until she was a block away from the restaurant. Her heart was booming like a bass drum, her brain serving up a buffet of awful possibilities, each one worse than the last. *She's a scammer. She's trying to steal my identity. She's having an affair with Hal*, Daisy thought. Maybe the dinner party had been a kind of audition, with Hal watching to see how the other Diana, Diana 2.0, did with his daughter and his dad. Maybe the two of them wanted to rub her nose in it. Maybe they'd been laughing at how gullible she was, how stupid, how they'd probably have to have sex right on her kitchen's island for her to notice, and how, if they did, she'd probably just want to make sure they didn't damage the countertops.

Diana had beaten her to the restaurant. Instead of one of her sleek dresses or her high-tech, fitted athleisurewear, she wore jeans, sneakers, and a fleece pullover. Her hair was up in a ponytail; her face was makeup-free. Daisy saw lines, age spots, a few freckles on her cheeks and nose. Her expression was anxious; her eyes wary.

"Let's sit down," Diana said, and held the door so that Daisy could precede her inside.

They found a table for two in the back. The restaurant was empty except for them, and a table of four moms with toddlers, whose strollers were lined up against the wall. A waiter handed them menus.

"Anything to drink?"

"Just water for now," said Daisy. Then she changed her mind. "Actually, can I get an egg cream?" If her marriage was ending and her life going down in flames, if she was seconds away from being replaced as a wife and a mother and exposed as the biggest dope on the entire Main Line, chocolate would help.

Diana said, "That sounds good. One for me, too."

When the waiter departed, Daisy looked across the table, bracing herself. Diana sighed.

"I don't know where to start."

Daisy just stared. Diana pulled a paper napkin out of the dispenser, smoothed it on the table, and said, "My name really is Diana. It's Diana Scalzi Carmody. And I really am living in Philadelphia, just not at 15 Rittenhouse Place. I've got a very nice Airbnb on South Twentieth Street." She sighed. "The boyfriend I told you about is actually my husband. His name is Michael. And I'm not a consultant. I work at a restaurant on Cape Cod."

Daisy shook her head, which felt muddy, and her tongue felt thick. "I don't understand," she said.

Diana started to talk, then closed her mouth as the waiter approached and set their drinks in front of them. She tore the paper off her straw, then wrapped it around her index finger. "I started to tell you about it, that day we went for a walk."

For a few seconds, Daisy couldn't think of what Diana meant. "About being raped?"

Diana nodded. "The summer I was fifteen, I was working as a mother's helper on Cape Cod, in Truro. At the end of the summer, I went to a party on the beach. That was where it happened."

Daisy felt her skin go cold. She heard the words tolling like bells: "Truro" and "fifteen" and "raped."

Diana kept talking. "That summer, there were a lot of boys in town. They had just graduated from prep school, and they were celebrating before they all went off to college." She looked Daisy in the eye. "They had all gone to the same place. The Emlen Academy."

Daisy couldn't move, couldn't breathe. She wanted to get up from the table, to walk out of the restaurant, to leave without looking back, but she couldn't make her legs listen to her brain. Every part of her felt frozen—her lips, her tongue, her hands, her heart. Meanwhile, Diana was looking at her steadily, her words coming, relentlessly, hammering against Daisy like hail. "It was dark, and I'd been drinking. I went off into the dunes, to lie down. I must have passed out, and when I opened my eyes there was one boy on top of me, and one boy holding me down, and another boy watching."

Daisy found that she was shaking her head, back and forth, back and forth, like that gesture could somehow undo what had happened, or, barring that, make Diana stop talking. "Oh, no."

"I thought the boys had only been there for the summer. That's why I was able to go back, and get a job, and make a life there. I never thought I'd see any of them ever again. I had no idea that Hal spent his summers there, that his family had a place, but my husband's a caretaker . . ."

A piece of the puzzle clicked into place. "Carmody. Your name—your husband's Michael Carmody?" Diana nodded, and

Daisy, recognizing the name of the caretaker of Vernon's place in Truro, felt her head begin to throb. This was bad, she realized. This was very, very bad. As awful as it would have been to learn that Hal was cheating on her, she knew that the truth, when she finally heard it, was going to be much, much worse.

"Michael was at your house—or your father-in-law's house, I guess. And I saw a picture of you and Hal."

Daisy winced. She could guess which picture Diana had seen, a shot of her and Hal on their wedding day. She'd always loved the picture. Hal looked so handsome in his crisp tuxedo with his dark curls, and she'd felt beautiful, and serene, and so hopeful, a beloved princess with her whole life ahead of her and the biggest hurdle—*who will I marry? Will anyone love me enough to want to be with me forever?*—already cleared.

"I thought I'd made my peace with it." Diana's voice was soft, her tone almost musing. "So much time had passed. I'm not the girl I was that summer. But then I saw that picture, and I found out that Hal had been there, on the Cape, every summer, for all those years." Diana sighed, and lifted her chin, looking Daisy in the eyes. "I found out about you. And that he had a daughter. And that the boy—the one who was watching—"

Daisy shook her head. She felt as breathless as if she'd been punched, all the air forced out of her lungs. "No," she said, an instant before Diana said, "was your brother."

"No," Daisy said again, but her voice was barely a whisper. "No, I don't—I can't believe that. He would never—Danny's the kindest person I know!"

"Maybe." Diana's voice was grave. "Maybe he's a good guy now. But, that summer, he saw what was happening, and he didn't stop it."

"Oh, God." Daisy shook her head, back and forth, again and again, and finally managed to open her eyes. "Why are you here?" she whispered. "What do you want?"

"I used to know." Diana's voice was troubled. "I can tell you why I found you, and why I came, and what I wanted, and what I planned on doing." She steepled her fingers on the table. "Except. Well." A smile flashed across her face before vanishing as quickly as it had appeared. "I wasn't expecting to like you so much. Or Beatrice."

Daisy's chair made a terrible screech as she shoved it back. The mommies at the next table stopped talking and looked their way. She wasn't sure if Diana would get up, too, if she'd grab her by the arm or the shoulder, if she'd demand that Daisy sit back down or at least hand over her cell phone. But Diana didn't say a word. She sat, composed and still, her face calm, her eyes watchful.

Somehow, Daisy got herself to the back of the restaurant, and found the ladies' room. She made sure the bathroom door was locked, and then she slumped back against the cool, tiled wall. She thought of the man who'd carried Beatrice on his shoulders when she was small. Who'd taught Beatrice how to ice-skate by gliding along behind her, gripping her under her armpits, holding her up as she wobbled around the rink. She thought about her Danny, who used to give her five dollars, sometimes, when he came home from school, and walk her to the 7-Eleven on Bloomfield Avenue and let her buy whatever she wanted, Danny, whose home felt like a sanctuary, Danny who'd done nothing but good with his life.

She couldn't imagine her brother watching a girl get raped. She couldn't imagine Hal being a rapist. Yes, he had a temper; yes, he could get angry. But not rape. Not that.

Except, even as she tried to convince herself that it had never happened, at least not the way Diana said, her mind replayed a snippet of what Vernon had told Beatrice on Saturday night. *Your dad was a wild one.* But "wild" didn't mean he'd raped a girl. Wild could have just meant drunk, or pulling pranks, vandalism and troublemaking. If Hal had been at a party, if he had known a girl—a girl exactly their daughter's age—was being hurt, he would have stopped it, he would have stepped in and stopped it, and made sure the transgressors were punished.

But was that the truth, or only what Daisy wanted to be true?

Daisy gave her head a shake, and drew herself upright. At the sink, she splashed cold water on her cheeks and let it run over her wrists. She took a few deep breaths, and then unlocked the door. The table that she and Diana had occupied was empty. There were just two egg creams, a ten-dollar bill, and a note, scribbled on a paper napkin. *I'm sorry*, it read. Diana herself was gone.

Part
Five

~~~~~~~~~~

The Downward Path

29

<center>~~~~~~</center>

Daisy

When Diana Suzanne Rosen met Henry Albert Shoemaker, the summer before her senior year at Rutgers, she'd just completed three months of rigorous dieting. She wanted to be as confident as possible by the time the university spat her out into the world, and "confident," of course, meant "thin." So in May she'd signed herself up for Weight Watchers—again—and began tracking points, cutting out breads, desserts, and almost everything else she loved.

She'd moved back home for the summer, back to the apartment in West Orange. She slept on the pullout couch, while her mother took the bedroom. She'd wanted to be in New York City, sharing a summer sublet with roommates, with an internship, maybe at one of the food magazines, but she needed to earn money for her books and clothes and other incidentals. Instead, she lived at home, rent-free, and waitressed at a place called the Fox and the Hen, where she tried to avoid the older waiters, especially the one who liked to back her into dark corners and grind himself against her, pressing his mouth moistly against her ear and muttering things he wanted to do to her.

Her dream was to graduate and find a job at a magazine like *Gourmet* or *Saveur* or *Bon Appétit*, or at a newspaper's features section, where she could write about food. Not restaurant reviews, but stories about trends, different kinds of cuisine, and, of course, recipes. She could solicit them, edit them, test them, suggest substitutions to make dishes healthier, meatless, safe for diners with allergies. She'd taken some photography courses, and had been practicing taking pictures and videos of the cooking process, breaking the recipes down, step by step, and staging scenes of the completed dishes. She knew it wouldn't be easy to get the kind of job she wanted, but she was determined. She worked five nights a week, from four in the afternoon until two in the morning. On her mornings and afternoons off, she'd give cooking lessons to anyone who'd hire her, and when she wasn't working, she would shop, and cook, preparing the same dish four or five or six times, adjusting the seasonings or the oven temperature, refining her technique, dreaming of the day when she could live on her own and do the work she loved; picturing every part of the life she longed for: a beautiful apartment in New York City, a glamorous job at a big-name publication. Money in the bank, money that she'd earned; a husband who adored her, and children, upon whom they could lavish their combined attention and love.

All of that meant that Daisy was exhausted the night that Hal picked her up for dinner, sleep-deprived and footsore. Not to mention starving. For the past three months, she'd been sticking rigorously to her diet. She ate an apple and a spoonful of peanut butter for breakfast, a salad with grilled chicken breast for lunch, and a Lean Cuisine for dinner. At work, she avoided the carb-heavy staff meals. One of the sous-chefs was always happy to roast her some chicken breast or salmon. She'd chew spearmint gum while she cooked, and allow herself just a taste of even her favorite dishes. At bedtime, after her mom had gone to bed, she would sneak into the kitchen to slug down a shot of the vodka that she kept in the freezer, with a squeeze of fresh lime. Without that final step, she faced a night lying in bed, listening to her mom snuffling and sighing and sometimes weeping through the thin bedroom door, tormented by thoughts of everything she wanted to eat, when she started eating again: brownies with caramel swirled on top, and a sprinkling of flaky sea salt on top of that. Spicy chicken wings; garlic with pea shoots; spicy tofu in sesame honey sauce, curried goat—from the Jamaican place she'd discovered—over rice cooked with saffron. Vanilla custard in a cake cone, topped with a shower of rainbow sprinkles; eclairs; sugar cookies dusted with green and red; and hot chocolate drunk in front of a fire.

Hal lived in Philadelphia, but when she'd offered to meet him halfway, he'd said, "Absolutely not. What's your favorite kind of food?"

"Oh, I eat everything."

"What's your favorite?"

She'd bitten her lip, then mentally shrugged and told him what she'd been craving, which was ramen. One giant bowl of perfectly cooked ramen in rich, golden pork broth, densely packed with noodles and with an egg, boiled to just the right degree of softness, perched on top, beneath a sprinkling of bright, crunchy green scallions. She could almost taste it, and feel it in her mouth, the rich glide of egg yolk, the chewy, toothsome tangle of noodles, the sharp bite of scallion, and the comforting warmth of the broth, as salty as the ocean.

It wasn't until Hal asked, "Are your folks in the same house?" that she realized he thought she was living in the same place he'd visited as Danny's classmate, all those years ago. She filled him in as briefly as she could—dad dead, house sold, brothers living elsewhere, she and her mom in West Orange, in a small, dingy apartment (she left out the "small" and "dingy" part). "I've been staying with my mom this summer," she'd said brightly, hoping her tone would suggest a lighthearted college girl who'd gone to a state university instead of the kind of liberal arts college her brothers had attended because she'd wanted a school with a reputable football team and a big Greek scene, and was living with her mother out of kindness and not necessity.

Judy Rosen had been thrilled when Daisy gave her the news. Before Hal arrived she looked her daughter over with a critical eye, smoothing a lock of hair, which was shoulder-length that year, cut to feather around her face. She adjusted the straps of the dress Daisy wore with a cap-sleeved white T-shirt, frowned at her black suede sandals with their chunky platform soles, and said, "I hope you have a wonderful time."

At six o'clock, Hal had arrived. Her mom had opened the door, revealing a compact, well-built, dark-haired man, in a navy-blue suit and a red silk tie. He looked very mature to Daisy, a world away from the college boys in Birkenstocks and cargo shorts.

"Hal Shoemaker," Daisy's mother said. She'd touched his face and kissed his cheek and then, just as Daisy had feared she would, started to get a little sniffly. Hal represented a better time, a lost Eden, a golden-hued era when her sons had been boys; when home had been a near-mansion in Montclair and not an apartment in West Orange, when she'd been a mom, and not a single mom. He was everything she'd loved that had been so cruelly taken away, in a five-foot-nine-inch package.

He'd brought tulips, and as Judy wiped her eyes, he held them out to her, stiffly, his expression bewildered.

Quickly, Daisy swooped in. She took the flowers, put them in a water glass, and ushered Hal to the living room while her mother went to the bathroom to freshen up, and probably take a Valium.

"Sorry about that," Daisy said. "She still gets upset by . . . well. Pretty much everything."

"It's okay. You two must have been through a lot." He looked around the apartment, then at her.

"Danny's little sister. Look at you, all grown up."

"Well, it's been a while," she said. She'd been just six years old when Danny, a high-school senior, brought his friends home, and she had only the vaguest memories of a loud collection of large, clumsy male bodies descending on her mother's kitchen like an invading horde.

Hal said, "I think I remember seeing you, sitting on the staircase. You had a blue-and-white nightgown with flowers, right?"

She nodded, remembering the flannel Lanz of Vienna, with a ruffled yoke and lace trim at the sleeves, a birthday gift from her parents. She'd loved that nightgown.

Judy came back to the living room, giving Hal a watery smile.

"And, of course, I remember Thanksgiving dinner, Mrs. Rosen. Your sweet potatoes were the best I've ever had."

"Thank you," Judy had said. *Dad and I probably made those sweet potatoes*, Daisy thought but did not say. Even as a girl, she'd helped out in the kitchen. She'd had a stepstool, and she'd stood next to her father as he'd help her measure and sift and pour, show her how to crack eggs, and separate them, and fold stiff egg whites into a batter—"gently, be gentle, you don't want to break up the foam!"

Hal got to his feet, looking eager to be on their way. Daisy realized, with a sinking heart, that his spot on the sofa gave him a clear view of the kitchen and the fly strip dangling from the ceiling, with a few dead flies ornamenting its curls. He held out his hand. "Shall we?"

Hal had made a reservation at the ramen place Daisy had recommended, and the hostess led them to a table in the corner. They sat down, and both began talking at once.

"So tell me about—"

"So is it weird—"

They'd laughed, and he'd gestured at her, saying, "Please."

"I was going to ask you to tell me about being a lawyer."

"Oh, you don't really want to hear about that," he said. "I'd rather hear about you."

So they'd talked. She told him charming stories about taking over the family cooking, emphasizing how much she enjoyed it, not telling him that, for years, her mom had been too exhausted and sad to put dinner on the table. Hal told her stories about his summers on Cape Cod, tales she suspected had been significantly bowdlerized, especially since she'd heard some of the unexpurgated details from Danny. He drank water with his meal, but he ordered an expensive bottle of plum sake and kept her cup full, and his eyes on her face, perfectly attentive and solicitous even when the buxom waitress dipped her knees and bent over to set down their dishes or clear them away. Daisy had enjoyed herself . . . or, looking back, maybe she'd just enjoyed the idea of the night, a handsome older man treating her with such thoughtfulness and care. She basked in his attention, going a glass of sake past her usual first-date two-drink limit, and then letting him order her Irish coffee with the mochi they got for dessert. When they walked outside at the end of the meal. Daisy's body felt warm and loose, her gestures expansive and her voice perhaps a touch too loud.

"That was fun," she'd said, when she'd gotten into the passenger's seat. She fumbled with her seat belt, realizing she was more drunk than she'd thought. Then she held perfectly still as Hal reached over, took the buckle from her hand, and slid it into place with a final-sounding *click*. She rested her head against the back of her seat, and she must have dozed off. When she opened her eyes, they were back in the parking lot in front of the apartment. Daisy yawned enormously, then, embarrassed, put her hand over her mouth, hoping she hadn't snored, or drooled, or otherwise managed to embarrass herself.

"Sorry," she said. "This is a pretty late night for me."

"I understand." Hal slid his hand over hers, and squeezed. "You're a peach," he said.

A peach, she thought. It made sense at the moment, when her thoughts were all fuzzy. And she liked the idea of being round and juicy, sweet and delicately furred. Well, maybe not that, she thought, and giggled.

"I'd like to see you again," he said, and Daisy, who was used to guys who waited two or three days or even a week before deigning to call again, flushed with surprised pleasure.

"Okay."

"But I should tell you," Hal continued. He squeezed her fingers again. "I'm not interested in playing games. I want something serious. If you aren't ready for that, I understand. I know you've got another year of college, and maybe you're not ready to settle down. I just want you to tell me now, so we don't waste each other's time."

And there it was, Daisy thought dreamily. The difference between being in your twenties and your thirties; the difference between Hal Shoemaker and all the boys she'd been wasting her time with. Here was a man, an actual, in-the-flesh man, stable and employed and interested in her. It seemed almost too good to be true, and even though she hadn't planned on getting married that young, hadn't imagined she'd meet a likely candidate for years, it seemed that the world had set one in her lap, and who was she to turn away such a gift? Daisy could hear her mother's voice: *Don't let this one get away.* She gave Hal a slightly woozy smile. "I'd like that."

"Good." He walked her to the door and insisted on taking the elevator back upstairs. In front of her mother's door, he cupped the back of her neck and pressed his lips briefly against hers.

"Oh, come on," she whispered. "I bet you can do better than that." *If you want me, show me*, she thought. She stood on her tiptoes, and he'd pulled her close and kissed her, slowly and thoroughly, a long, dreamy kiss that left her flushed and breathless and completely on board with whatever Hal had planned for their future.

"There's just one thing," he said.

"What's that?"

"You're going to think it's silly."

"What is it?" He was rubbing gently at the back of her neck, slowly and tenderly. Daisy felt like she was melting, her body slowly transforming from solid to liquid. He leaned close and whispered in her ear, "Can I call you something else?"

Daisy drew back, staring at him. She wasn't sure what she'd been expecting, but it hadn't been that. "Don't you like 'Diana'?"

"I knew another Diana, once. I'd rather call you something different. Something that's special, just for you."

Like a secret, she thought. *He'll give me a secret name. And when he names me, I'll be his.* She giggled, realizing that she was still very drunk. When she stopped laughing, Hal was still looking at her, still cupping the back of her head, waiting for her answer.

"My middle name is Suzanne. Diana Suzanne. My grandma used to call me Daisy. But she's been dead—"

"Daisy," he interrupted. He raised his hand and settled it in her hair, stroking her cheek with his thumb. "My pretty little flower. That's perfect."

30

Daisy

Daisy parked her car, unlocked her front door, walked inside, and stood in her beautiful kitchen, still as a pillar of salt while Lester whined at her feet.

She'd managed to stay calm as she'd made the drive home, replaying the conversation over and over again, listing the facts: Diana did not live at the apartment where Daisy had cooked with her; Diana did not work at the company where Daisy believed she spent her busy days. Diana was not a consultant. Diana was not anything that Daisy had believed. Diana lived in a cottage on Cape Cod, in the same town where Daisy had spent every one of the last eighteen summers, the town where, as a teenager, Diana had been assaulted by an Emlen Class of 1987 graduate, a white man with curly dark hair. Diana believed that Hal had raped her, and that Danny had watched. And now Diana had disappeared, and Daisy had no idea of what to do with any of that information. She had no plan, no clue, nothing except a muddied jumble of thoughts and a frantic, overarching need to run. Run from whom? Run to where? She didn't know.

One part of her mind was screaming the particulars of Diana's revelations: *Not who she said she was! Not living where you thought she'd lived! Everything she told you was a lie!* Another part was trying to insist that maybe Diana was wrong. Maybe it hadn't been an Emlen boy who'd raped her, or, if it had, maybe not from the class of 1987, and, if it was a boy from that class, maybe it hadn't been Hal, and a third part was saying, *You knew. You knew it was something bad. You've always known.*

Head down, hands squeezed into fists, nails pressing at the flesh of her palms, Daisy walked in circles around her beautiful, airy kitchen. Lester trailed after her, his tail drooping, making worried grumbles in the back of his throat as Daisy walked from the apron-fronted farmhouse sink, around the marble and butcher block island, past the built-in benches of the dining nook and the bump-out bay window, past the rows of cabinets and countertops and specially designed drawers for her utensils and her spices. "Whatever you want," Hal had told her. "Whatever makes my little bird happy."

Daisy walked. She thought about Hal, the man she'd lived with for almost twenty years, the man she'd slept beside almost every night. She remembered a famous optical illusion; a drawing that could be either a beautiful young woman or an ugly old hag, depending on how you saw it. For almost twenty years, she'd seen only the good—a loving, kind, generous husband; a beautiful house; a beloved, cherished daughter. But for the past weeks and months, things had been changing. It felt like she had finally seen the witch, after years of only seeing the young woman, and now she couldn't un-see. *I lived by performing tricks for you, Torvald. But you would have it so.*

Daisy's breaths were coming in painful gasps. Her chest felt tight, her guts clenched, and she had to race to the bathroom, barely making it in time. The instant she made contact with the toilet seat it felt like everything inside of her came flooding out in a horrible, scalding gush. She moaned, leaning forward with her elbows on her thighs, burying her hot face in her hands.

What was she going to do? And what about her brother? Had he actually watched Hal rape a young woman, then let Daisy marry him, without even a word of warning? If Danny knew what Hal was, surely that was the reason Daisy and Hal and Danny and Jesse hardly ever spent time together as a foursome, the reason she almost always saw them by herself. Daisy's mind lurched back to the days before her wedding, when both of her brothers had come home; David with his wife and children, Danny, by himself, from New York City. Danny had been distant the week of the festivities, so quiet that she'd asked Hal if something had happened at the bachelor party. Once she and Hal had said their vows, her brother had given her a quick kiss, said, "Good luck, Di," and left the party early.

Daisy moaned again. Her mouth was very dry, and her stomach was still twisting. She was remembering that morning in the fall; Hal in his running clothes, his spinach drink untouched, staring at his iPad, telling her that Bubs had committed suicide. Had he been involved? Had Diana tracked him down, the same way she'd done with Hal and Danny? Had Brad Burlingham's death actually been a suicide, or had it maybe been a murder? She had never asked Hal any more questions. She'd never followed up. The incident had flown right out of her mind, in the whirl of handling Beatrice's return, managing her business, running the house. *My little scatterbrain*, Hal would say, smiling affectionately when Daisy misplaced her car keys or her phone. He'd rest his hand on her hair. *You'd lose your head if it weren't attached, wouldn't you?*

Daisy's laptop sat beside the bed. She pulled it out and plugged Brad Burlingham's name into Google, which obligingly spat out a pageful of headlines. The first was an obituary from the *Baltimore Sun. Bradley Telford Burlingham, 51, died at his home Saturday.* The second story, from a Baltimore news and gossip blog, was more helpful: *Prominent Baltimore Family Mourns Its Son.*

On Sunday evening, the body of Brad Burlingham, youngest son of the Baltimore Burlinghams, real-estate magnates and political kingmakers, was found at his apartment, a mile away from his parents' mansion on Deepdene Drive. Like his brothers, his father, his uncles, his grandfather, and his great-uncles, Burlingham was a graduate of the Emlen Academy in New Hampshire and attended Trinity College. Friends and relatives acknowledged that Burlingham's life was troubled. He was arrested three times in two different states for driving under the influence, and eventually had his license revoked. He married Marianne Conover in 1996. They had two children and divorced in 2005, and Conover was awarded full custody of the children. A second marriage, to Elspeth Dryer in 2009, lasted only four years. Burlingham held various marketing jobs for institutions including the Baltimore Sun *and the University of Maryland Medical Center.*

"Brad was the black sheep," said a longtime observer of Baltimore's upper crust, a friend of the family who requested anonymity in order to speak freely about the deceased. "Every big, rich family's got one, and the Burlinghams had Brad. He didn't have an easy life. I hope wherever he is, he's found peace."

Friends describe a man who'd made numerous attempts at getting sober. Prior to his death, Burlingham had been working at Starbucks, a job his AA sponsor recommended, according to Corby Kincaid, a college classmate of Burlingham's.

"He tried very hard to clean up his act, and be a father to

his children," Kincaid said. "He had demons, though, and I guess in the end they won."

"Brad was a loyal friend, a devoted son, and a loyal member of the Emlen community," Dr. G. Baptiste, dean of Emlen, said in an interview. "This is an unfathomable loss for all of us."

Daisy looked at her phone. It was just past four thirty. Beatrice would be home in fifteen minutes. Hal would be home in an hour. She stood, washed her hands, then picked up her phone and punched in her brother's name.

"Hello? Di? Is that you?"

"It's me." Her voice sounded faint, like it was coming from the bottom of a well. "I need to ask you about something."

"Oh? What's that?"

"The summer after you graduated from Emlen, you went to the Cape. There was a party there. The last party of the summer. I need you to tell me what happened that night."

There was a pause, so long it felt endless. Then, finally, Danny began to speak. "You have to understand, this was a long, long time ago," he said, his voice low and rough. "People's understanding about consent and—and things like that—has changed in the last thirty years."

"Danny," said Daisy. "Can you cut the bullshit? Please? Just tell me what happened!"

Her brother sighed. "Hal had been talking to a girl for most of the time we were there. A townie, or an au pair. Something like that. And yes, there was a party on the beach, and everyone had a lot to drink, and I saw—what I saw—" Danny's voice was getting higher, more hesitant.

"Just spit it out," Daisy said. "Just tell me."

"Hal was having sex with the girl."

"And was another boy holding her down?"

"I—I can't—" She could picture her brother, the way his neck would get flushed when he was upset, the way he'd pace, the same way she did. Maybe he'd be walking the tiled floor of his tiny office at the high school, with its walls covered, floor to ceiling, with college brochures meant to inspire the students, or in the gym at the Boys & Girls Club, or in his kitchen, with a visiting baby in his arms. "It was a long time ago, Di. And I was a different person. Things were hard for me. I'm not making excuses . . ."

"Yes, you are," Daisy said.

Danny's voice was mournful. "Every time I think about it, I think I should have done more, that I could have done more. But I was . . ." His voice trailed off. "I had a crush on Hal. I thought I was in love with him, and I was terrified about what would happen if he found out about me. When he took me into the dunes . . ." He sighed again, and, against her will, Daisy found herself imagining it—Hal's hands on Danny's shoulders, both of them drunk and stumbling, Hal urging Danny on and Danny going willingly, maybe hoping that Hal felt the same way he did, not seeing until it was too late, where Hal was leading him.

"It was a long time ago," Danny said bleakly.

"But it wasn't," said Daisy. "Not for the woman Hal did this to. Diana has to live with what he did to her, every day of her life. And she was fifteen years old, and she was passed-out drunk!" Daisy found that she was shouting. "Jesus. How would you like it if someone did that to Beatrice? Did you ever try to find the woman, and tell her you should have done more? Did you ever feel anything about what you'd done? Does Jesse know?" *I'll tell him*, she thought, the idea sizzling like acid, hot and spiteful in her mind. *I'll tell Jesse, and Jesse will leave Danny, and Danny will have his heart broken, which is what he deserves.*

"Yes," Danny said heavily. "Yes, Jesse knows. I spent years trying to figure out who the woman was, but I never could. And yes, I feel awful, and yes"—his voice was rising—"I've felt awful about it for years, and I have tried to do better, to be better, because I know exactly how lucky and how privileged I am, and I know how we h-hurt her." His voice cracked. "Every day of my life," he said, speaking each word distinctly through his tears, "I have tried to be a better man than I was that night."

Daisy's mouth was dry, and her eyes were, too, at the enormity of everything that Danny had done, or not done; the terrible things he'd allowed to happen. "You let me marry him," she whispered. Her voice was anguished. She could feel tears squeeze out of the corners of her eyes and fall onto her shirt. "You didn't tell me about him," she said. "Why didn't you tell me?"

"I tried to." Danny's voice was plaintive. "Don't you remember?"

"No! No, I do not! And I'm pretty sure I would have remembered anyone, at any point, taking me aside and saying, 'Hey, guess what, the man who wants to marry you is a rapist!'"

"I promise you, I tried to tell you about Hal," Danny said.

"When?" Daisy snapped.

"Right after you called to say you'd gotten engaged."

Daisy put her fisted hand against her lips. She and Hal had had a whirlwind courtship—three months of dating, a proposal, a wedding six months after that. She remembered making phone calls to her mom, her brothers, her grandma Rose. She remembered calling David and his wife, and she remembered calling Danny. He'd congratulated her, and he'd asked her to put Hal on the phone so he could say hello to the groom. A minute later, Hal had handed the cordless phone back to her, and they'd continued going down their list.

And then, she remembered, the next morning, Danny had called back. "Diana, are you sure about this?"

"Sure I'm sure!" she'd said. The two-carat square-cut diamond Hal had given her was sparkling on her finger, sending rainbow spangles against the wall as it caught the light. She couldn't stop looking at it.

"It's just . . . you're still a baby. And Hal was . . ." His voice had trailed off. "Hal's got kind of a history."

"I know. He told me. He quit drinking when he turned thirty, though. I don't think I have anything to worry about."

No, you're wrong, Danny could have said. He could have told her the whole ugly truth, could have explained what he'd meant by *kind of a history*. Instead, he'd said something like *I just want what's best for you*, and *If you're happy, then I'm happy*, and Daisy had ended the call, eager to get back to work on her registry, to tear out pages featuring possible dresses from the bridal magazines she'd bought and plan the menu for her wedding-night dinner.

"You told me he had a history," Daisy said. "Isn't that right?" Danny had barely mumbled his confirmation when Daisy continued. "Did you ever think that maybe you could have been a little more explicit? Like, maybe said, 'Oh, by the way, he raped a girl when he was eighteen'?"

"Would you have listened?" Danny asked heavily.

"Of course! Of course I would have listened!" Daisy shouted. "My God, Danny. What would Dad think of you? He would have been so disappointed. He wouldn't have cared that you're gay, he would have loved you, no matter what, but if he found out that you didn't look out for me, that you let this happen to me . . ."

"You didn't want to hear it. You made that very clear. And anyhow, that wasn't the end of it. I kept trying."

"No, you didn't!" Daisy was trembling with fury. She wanted to tear her clothes, she wanted to scream, she wanted to hit something. She'd never in her life imagined feeling so furious, so betrayed. "You never said another word about it!"

"No," Danny said, very quietly. "Not to you. To Mom."

. . .

Daisy's legs felt like planks of wood, solid and unbending. Somehow, she got them to carry her into the bedroom. Lester stared at her unhappily as she pulled her suitcase out from its shelf in the closet and began to fill it with what she'd need for the weekend, pulling out handfuls of underwear and stacks of T-shirts without even a glance. She found a duffel bag for Beatrice. Then she took out her phone and punched in a number from her contact list.

"The Melville School. This is Crystal Johnson. How can I help you?"

"Crystal? It's Daisy Shoemaker."

"Daisy!" Crystal said cheerfully. "Everything okay?"

"I need to take Beatrice out of school for the rest of the week." Lowering her voice, even though the house was still empty, Daisy said, "My mom hasn't been well. We're going to head up to New Jersey to see her."

"Oh, I'm sorry to hear that! Well, it's no problem." Crystal laughed. "I swear, it's like a ghost town here already. Half the kids took off early for Memorial Day. A bunch of the teachers, too. But I'll be sure to let her advisor know."

"Thank you. And, listen, this is a little delicate. But if Hal calls, looking for Bea, can you just tell him she's with me? And that we'll see him on the Cape this weekend?" The lies were flying out of her mouth, one after another, like a flock of birds she'd kept penned up behind her lips. "It's kind of a mess. Hal thinks I've been doing too much for my mom, and that my brothers aren't pitching in enough, and I promised him the next time she asked, I'd tell her no, and I did, but then my mom called me herself, and she was pretty insistent that I'm the one who has to help. So we'll swing by her place on our way up, and Hal doesn't need to know."

"I gotcha." The warmth in Crystal's voice made Daisy's eyes sting. "Family drama. Believe me, I completely understand. If he calls, I'll just let him know that Beatrice is with you."

"Thank you," she murmured. She imagined that Hannah was with her, watching, following along as she made one last pass through the bathroom, gathering sunscreen, toothpaste, and soap. She called the pet hotel where Lester occasionally stayed, and made a reservation for a week, with some extra daily one-on-one time, because she felt terrible about leaving him.

Glad you're looking after the dog, she imagined Hannah saying. *But what about you? What about Beatrice?*

She stood by the door, waiting. When her daughter arrived, carpetbag looped daintily over her forearm, Daisy shoved the duffel bag into her arms. "Go upstairs and get enough clothes for the weekend. Bring your homework, and a sweatshirt and shoes you can walk in. Quick as you can, okay? I'll explain everything once we're in the car."

For once, thank God, Beatrice didn't argue, or roll her eyes or do any of her usual teenager tricks. "What's going on? Where are we going?"

"Grandma's place first."

Beatrice's eyes were very wide. "What about Daddy?"

Daisy hadn't heard Beatrice call her father "Daddy" in as long as she could remember. *Don't tell her*, she thought. *Hal is still her father, no matter what he's done, he's still her dad.* And there was another voice, the one that could see the bones of Beatrice's face, the outline of the woman she was becoming. It was that voice that Daisy spoke with. "Honey, it's complicated. I promise I'll tell you as much as I can. But, for right now, I need to ask you not to tell Dad where we're going. No phone calls, no texts, no emails."

"I can't call anyone. You've got my phone, remember?"

"Oh. Right."

"Mom." Her daughter's face was troubled. "What happened? What's going on?"

"I can't tell you any more right now, but I promise that I'm going to keep you safe. Nothing bad is going to happen to you. I swear, I'm going to keep you safe, no matter what."

31

Diana

After what had happened in Baltimore, with Brad, Diana swore that she was done. She'd learned her tormentor's name. She had hunted him down. She had called him to account for what he'd done, made him look at her, made him see her, and the damage that he'd done. Now he was dead.

Had he belatedly developed a conscience? Was it that Diana pulled the veil from his eyes, showing him who he was and what he'd done, and had he been unable to live for even another day with the knowledge? Or had she found a troubled, broken man; a man truly trying to do better, and pushed him over the edge, depriving his children of their father, his parents of their son?

She didn't know. And when she tried to think it through, the facts that she laid out so reasonably kept sliding away, replaced by an image of Brad's children, Claudia and Eli, trudging up the stairs with their backpacks and their unsuspecting faces. Those children, and their half-siblings, would all grow up without a father. And that was her fault.

For the first time in a long time, Diana started having trouble sleeping. *Menopause*, suggested her doctor, and Hazel, her therapist, had looked her over carefully with eyes that saw too much and asked, *Why don't you tell me what's on your mind?* Diana hadn't been able to do it, because what would Hazel say if Diana told her the truth?

Every night, Michael would sleep by her side, and Pedro would sleep at her feet, and Diana would lie awake, staring out into the blackness. On moonless nights, it was impossible to tell where the sky became land, and where the land became water. *I am going to forget about this*, she told herself. I am going to forget about Henry Shoemaker and Daniel Rosen. I'm not going to think about what happened to me, all those years ago. I am going to get on with my happy life.

She might have been able to do it, if she'd been better rested, or if the entire country was not in the midst of facing the wreckage of decades of sexual harassment and sexual assault, if the news had not been full of stories of the terrible things that some man or another had done, and how many women he'd done them to.

Diana would read the stories and think about Hal, and her hands would clench, and she'd think, *He should suffer. He should pay.* Then she'd remember what had happened with Brad, and think how much worse it would be, because Daniel Rosen had a husband and Henry Shoemaker had a wife and a daughter, a daughter who was almost exactly the age Diana had been that summer, a daughter the age that her nieces were now. *I can't do anything*, she would think . . . and then, an instant later, she'd think, *but I can't do nothing*.

"See the paper?" Michael asked one morning in June, tossing the *Cape Cod Times* down on the table.

"Who is it this time?" Diana asked without looking. So far, there'd been the famous movie producer, the morning news anchor, the conductor of a prominent orchestra, the editor of a famous literary magazine. Actors, athletes, NFL owners, one by one by one, they'd been exposed.

Michael poured himself a cup of coffee, and made Diana her tea. Then, instead of sitting at the table, he'd gone to the couch and patted the space beside him. There was gray in his reddish beard now, to go with the gray in her hair. He wore orthotic inserts in his shoes, and did stretches for his back before he went to bed at night.

He held a section of the paper, turning it so that she could see. A RECKONING, read the headline.

"I don't want to tell you what to do," he began.

"I think you do," she said, her voice sharp.

Michael shook his head. "Look, all I'm saying ..." He'd stopped talking, then nodded at the newspaper. "This is a moment. It's a chance."

"For what?" she'd asked. Not justice. She'd given up on justice a long time ago.

"You don't have to go to the police and demand a trial. I'm not saying you call WGBH, or call the guy's boss."

"I don't think he has a boss," said Diana.

Michael had continued doggedly. "I'm just saying that this is maybe a chance to get some closure. To find this guy and tell him that he hurt a real person."

"Because that went so well the last time," Diana said bitterly.

"What happened the last time was not your fault," Michael said, the way he'd said the same words to her a thousand times already. Diana didn't answer. For a moment, they sat in silence. Then Michael said, "What if he did it to other women? Did you ever think about that?"

Diana buried her face in her hands, because, as Michael undoubtedly suspected, the answer was *all the time*. It was her biggest fear—that her rapist hadn't stopped with her, that, to the contrary, she'd been the first, in a line, maybe a long one. She'd spent many of her recent sleepless nights wondering what her obligation was to that possibility, what she owed those girls and women.

Michael touched her back, then the nape of her neck, until he was cupping her head in his big, warm hand.

"I was reading an essay online. It said this was a whaddayacal-lit. An inflection point. Things are changing." After all their years together, she could hear what he wasn't saying. *Things are changing if there are people brave enough to come forward, to stand up and say enough is enough.*

"I tried," she said, her voice quavering. "I tried to do the right thing, and look how that turned out!"

"Okay, okay," said Michael, holding up his hands. "It's up to you. Completely up to you. It's just—I know you aren't sleeping. I feel like you're suffering. I just want you to be able to find some peace. And I wonder—I wonder if maybe . . ."

Diana shook her head. Her mind had been made up, and she'd been firm in her convictions. *Leave it alone*, she told herself. *Live your happy life, run your restaurant, be with the people you love, and leave it alone.* But Hal's existence nagged at her, tugged at her, like a hangnail or a loose thread. What if he did it to other women? *This is a reckoning*, she'd think. *And if I sit here and do nothing, I'm just as bad, just as complicit, as he is.*

She would spend hours convincing herself to live her life, her happy, peaceful life, and do nothing. Then, at night, awake in the dark, she'd remember what had happened with the judge, a man about her age with an Ivy League education and impeccable credentials, who'd been on the fast track for confirmation to the Supreme Court, when a woman came forward and said that he'd assaulted her at a party when they'd both been teenagers.

The man had denied everything, had called the woman a liar, part of a political plot to take him down. The woman had testi-fied, telling her story in a calm, clear voice, telling the world what the boys had done. *Indelible upon the hippocampus is the laughter*, she'd said. She'd gone on to become a professor of neuroscience, an expert in how the brain processes trauma, a fact that only amplified Diana's shame at her own life having been so thoroughly derailed.

Diana had watched every second of the hearings. She'd sat, riveted, holding out hope that the judge, who'd seemed so mild-mannered, would confess to his actions and apologize. Maybe he would say that he was drunk and immature and stupid and that he was sorry, that he'd never treated another woman like that since and certainly never would again; that he loved his daughters and did not want them living in a world where men could harm them without consequences. Instead, the judge, red-faced and furious, spewing indignation and spittle, had denied everything. He'd insisted—before anyone had asked—that he'd earned all of his achievements by working his tail off, that he had no connections or extra help ("I guess parents who paid for prep school and a grandfather who went to Yale don't count," Michael said). He bullied the female senators who asked about his drinking. "I like beer. Do you like beer?" he'd asked one of them, the daughter of an alcoholic, who'd gently asked about the possibility of blackouts. "What do you like to drink? Do you have a drinking problem?" Diana kept watching, paralyzed and wordless in her fury, power-less to look away as the judge blustered and brayed, red-faced and wet-eyed with rage, convinced that he was the real victim.

The man became a Supreme Court justice. The woman went into hiding. And every day, every night, Diana Carmody, who'd once been a fifteen-year-old girl, running over the sand on the beach on a warm summer night, would think about him, and about Hal Shoemaker, about all the men who'd harmed women and who'd sailed on with lives continued, unimpaired. She would think about her nieces, and all the girls and young women she knew, growing up in a world where every day was dangerous, and she knew she couldn't give herself the luxury of inaction.

This time, she decided, she would do it differently. This time, instead of going straight for the men, she'd approach the problem sideways and come at the women. Or, really, just one woman: Daisy Shoemaker, wife of her rapist, sister of the boy who'd watched. She would be much more careful, making sure that her actions did not cause children to suffer, or that at least she did whatever she could to minimize their suffering. Awake at night, she laid her traps, claiming an email address that was close to the other Diana's, constructing a fake website and a bogus Facebook page, finding blogs and books about consultants, so she'd get the lingo down, seeding the ground for the day she would meet Daisy Shoemaker, the main connection between the two living men who'd harmed her, the wife of one, the sister of the other. She would look this other Diana in the eyes and then she'd decide what she would do, how she could confront Hal without hurting some poor blameless woman, in a world where being born female meant spending years of your life at risk, and the rest of it invisible, existing as prey or barely existing at all.

32

Daisy

"Why are we going to Grandma's?" Beatrice asked, after they'd dropped off poor, sad-looking Lester and gotten on the highway.

"I need to speak with her."

"And you can't just call?"

"I need to speak with her in person," Daisy said. Once she'd gotten behind the wheel, a strange coolness had descended over her. She felt as if she was enclosed in a bubble where she could be reasonable and calm. The bubble would pop at some point, and all the terrible truths would come flooding in to assault her, but, for now, she could listen, and reason, and think.

"Mom," said Beatrice. "What's going on? You have to tell me something." Daisy could hear the anxiety in her daughter's voice, and knew that Beatrice was right. She had to say something. She just didn't know what that should be.

"I need to ask my mother some questions about what happened when Danny was a teenager."

"What do you mean? What happened?" Beatrice demanded. She was putting the pieces together, much more quickly than

Daisy had hoped she would. "Did this happen at Emlen? Was Dad involved?"

"It didn't happen at Emlen. It involved Emlen students." *Careful*, Daisy told herself. *You need to be careful now.* She would have given years of her life to be able to tell her daughter that Hal wasn't involved. But she couldn't. "I don't want to say any more until I know for sure."

Beatrice shifted in her seat. "What happened?" she asked. "Did someone die?"

"No one died," she said quietly. "And I can't tell you anything else. I promise, when I know the facts, I'll tell you. But right now, I can't."

She was picturing Hal as he'd been when she'd first met him, handsome and solid and mature. She could still hear what he had told her, on their very first date: *I used to be wild. I drank a lot. I don't want to be that person anymore.* She'd been able to intuit what he wasn't telling her: that, if they proceeded, it would be her job to prevent him from backsliding. That, in becoming her husband and a father, he would be turning himself into something other than what he had been; a butterfly emerging from a cocoon, with a loyal, loving wife by his side. She would be an integral part of his transformation, even if that meant putting her own dreams to the side. She'd be his guardrails, his early-warning system; she'd keep him from going over the edge. She'd done her part, Daisy thought. And if he'd made good on that promise, if he'd truly become someone other than who he'd been, if he'd been a good husband and father, if he'd done good with his life, how much could she hold him accountable for his actions when he was eighteen? How much punishment was the right amount? What did Hal deserve?

"Mom." Beatrice's voice was tiny. "How bad is this? What's going to happen? Is Dad in trouble?"

And again, Daisy gave her daughter as much of the truth as she could. "I don't know."

. . .

Just over three hours after they'd left Lower Merion, Daisy pulled into the parking lot of her mother's apartment building. "Stay here," she told Beatrice.

"No! I'm coming with you."

Daisy made her voice firm. "Stay in the car. I'll be back soon." Daisy climbed out quickly and walked across the parking lot and into the lobby, locking her legs to keep her knees from shaking as she rode the elevator up to the eighteenth floor. She lifted the brass knocker, feeling its cold weight in her hand, and let it fall, once, then again.

A minute later, there was Arnold, in neatly pressed pants, a button-down shirt, and slippers. "Daisy," he said, beaming. "What an unexpected surprise!" When she didn't return his smile, he said, "Is everything all right?"

"Everything's fine," Daisy said, through cold lips. "But I need to speak to my mom for a minute."

"Of course." After a worried glance at her face, he said, "I'll get Judy," and hurried down the hall in his slippered feet.

Daisy went to the kitchen. The black marble countertops, white cabinets, and clear glass subway-tile backsplash had all been the height of decorating style in the early 2000s. Now they were starting to look a bit dated. Arnold's wife had cooked for him, and Judy had never been much of a cook and hadn't cared enough to redecorate. She and Arnold ate most of their meals out.

"Daisy?" Judy Rosen wore loose-fitting velour pants, a fine-gauge cashmere sweater, and her usual full face of makeup. "Is everything all right?"

Daisy stood on the other side of the breakfast bar and set her hands on the counter, leaning forward. "I need to ask you something."

"All right," her mom said, her voice hesitant, her expression suddenly wary.

"Did Danny ever tell you anything about Hal? About things Hal had done in high school?"

Judy just stared. Daisy tried again. "Did he ever tell you about a party on the Cape, the summer after they graduated from Emlen?"

"I'm not sure what you're talking about," Judy said, but Daisy saw the way her mother's eyes flickered briefly to the left, like she couldn't quite hold Daisy's gaze.

"Hal raped a girl."

"Oh, Daisy." Her mother clasped her hands and looked at Daisy with disapproval. "What a terrible thing to say."

For a moment, Daisy was sure she must have heard incorrectly. "A terrible thing to say?" she repeated. "How about a terrible thing to do?"

"Let me get you something to drink." Her mother turned away, and Daisy followed her, staying right on her heels.

"I don't want anything to drink. I want to know what Danny told you about that party."

Her mother sighed, shaking her head. "What Danny told me," she repeated. "What Danny told me was that a girl at the party had gotten very drunk, and that he'd heard that something might have happened to her, and that Hal might have been involved. Your brother was concerned for you. But, Daisy, he didn't have any reason to worry. Whatever happened when Hal was in high school happened almost fifteen years before you two met. He was a different person by then."

Daisy shook her head, hearing nothing but mealy-mouthed "mights" and "somethings," and "that girl." "My friend Diana. The woman who came to dinner on Saturday. The consultant. She's the one who says Hal raped her."

Judy cocked her head, looking quizzical. "The other Diana?"

As soon as her mother spoke, Daisy realized that she should have known. The truth was right there, that it had been there all along, if she'd only been willing to see it. "You know that Hal was the one who started calling me Daisy, right? He said he wanted to give me a name that was special. He said . . ." She took a breath and tried to remember. ". . . he said he'd known another Diana, once." Her mouth felt dry, her body numb, as if it had been packed with snow, as she remembered. "And you knew. You knew what he was. Danny told you."

Judy Rosen raised her chin. "What Danny told me was that something might have happened when Hal was eighteen. Even if he'd done something terrible, even if it wasn't just a case of too much alcohol and mixed signals, Daisy, it was so long ago!"

"What if he'd done it to me?" Daisy asked. "What if some boy did that to Beatrice? Would it matter, how long ago it had happened? Would you be okay if he said, *Oh, sorry, we were both drinking and I guess I got mixed signals?*"

For some endless span of time, her mother didn't speak. "Hal's a good man," Judy finally managed. "He loved you very much. And you loved him! I really don't see the point in stirring up all of this old mess." Her lips curled in distaste, and Daisy wanted to grab her by the shoulders and shake her.

"You know what I think?" Her voice was strident, her hands were balled into fists. "I think Danny told you exactly what Hal was. I think you didn't care. And you know what else I think?" She could see Arnold Mishkin in the darkened hallway, his pale face glimmering, ghostlike, as he listened, but Daisy didn't stop. "I think you were done being a mother. I think that, after Daddy died, you didn't have anything left for me. I think you were glad for me to be someone else's responsibility."

"Daisy, that's not true! All I wanted was for you to be happy!" her mother said. "Happy, and safe, and secure, so you'd never have to worry about your whole life falling apart!" Her voice was getting louder. "Hal was a good man, he had a good job, he had a house, he had plenty of money, and he was generous . . ."

"He pulled me out of college," said Daisy, half to herself, remembering what Hal had told her: *There's a lot of great schools in Philadelphia. You can finish your degree. But, right now, I need your help getting the house together.*

"No, Daisy, that's not true. He wanted you to finish!"

"Well, he certainly never pushed for me to go back." She thought of what Diana had said, the first night that they'd met in New York City: *You were a child bride.* She'd laughed it off, but now she saw herself as a newlywed, wide-eyed and innocent, happy to let Hal guide her, happy to surrender her power, her agency, her voice. Everything. She'd given him everything. Even her name.

She turned for the door, feeling hollowed out and exhausted. "I'm leaving," she said, and began walking toward the door. "I'm done."

"Daisy!" her mother called.

Daisy turned around. "What's wrong with you?" she shouted at her mother. "I wasn't that much older than Beatrice, and I'd die to keep anything bad from happening to her, and you! You let me marry a *criminal*," she hissed.

Her mother was crying, shaking her head. "People change," she said. "Hal is a good man. I know he is. And if some silly girl got drunk at a party and showed up, all these years later, to make crazy accusations about Hal raping her, it doesn't change anything. It doesn't change what the two of you have."

Daisy shook her head and kept walking. Her mother called after her.

"What are you going to do?"

When Daisy didn't turn around, her mother ran after her, putting her hand on Daisy's shoulder. "He's still Beatrice's father," she whispered.

"Do you think I don't know that?" Daisy shouted. Crying, her mother retreated to the kitchen. Then Arnold was there, touching her arm gently. Daisy whirled around to glare at him. "Did you know about this?"

He shook his head. "I can't imagine how you must feel."

"Not good!" said Daisy, with a harsh, barking laugh. Arnold nodded sadly.

"Your mother only wanted what was best for you. She wanted you to be happy, and safe, and well taken care of. I'm sure you know how hard it was after your father died."

"I could have taken care of myself," Daisy said. "I could have gotten my degree, and gotten a job."

"Of course," Arnold said. "But Judy didn't see it that way. It was different for her generation. She didn't want you to struggle, as she had. I know it doesn't seem like it now, but I know your mother, and all she's ever wanted for any of her children was that you be safe, and comfortable, and happy."

Daisy looked over his shoulder at her mother, a small, slump-shouldered figure, weeping softly.

"And she's right," Arnold continued, his voice gentle. "You have a daughter. You need to think about her."

Daisy's chest felt tight, and the air felt thin. "I need to make a phone call," she said.

Arnold led her to his office, where a framed wedding portrait of Daisy and Hal stood on the desk, the same one that Diana must have seen in Vernon's Cape house. Daisy looked at it: her twenty-year-old self, in a frothy confection of white lace and tulle, a fairy-tale princess dressed for her happily-ever-after.

She flipped the picture facedown on the desk and sat in Arnold's creaking leather chair. Steeling herself, she found her phone in her purse and called Diana.

The phone rang once. Again. Again. Then she heard Diana's voice.

"Daisy."

Daisy didn't say a word.

"Are you there?"

"I'm here," Daisy said.

"I owe you an apology." Diana's voice was quiet. "I lied to you, and I'm sorry. What I told you . . . it must be a hard thing to hear about someone you love."

"You shouldn't have lied to me," said Daisy.

"You're right. But what would have happened if I'd been honest? Or if I'd tried to confront Hal?"

"You didn't have to . . ." Daisy's throat was thick, and it was hard to speak. "You didn't have to involve me," she finally whispered.

On the other end of the line, she heard Diana sigh. "You are involved, though," she said. "You, and Beatrice, too. I wish it was different, but it's not."

Daisy felt an icy hand take hold of her heart, and she didn't speak, couldn't speak.

"Where are you?" asked Diana.

"At my mom's." Daisy knew what she wanted to say, but she wasn't ready to say it out loud, how maybe a part of her had always suspected the truth about her husband; that, with her family's complicity and her own willingness, she'd kept her eyes shut for a long, long time.

She cleared her throat. "Where are you?"

"I'm home," Diana said. "In Truro. I live in a cottage at the very end of Knowles Heights Road."

"Send me your address." Even as she spoke, a plan was forming in Daisy's mind. "I'm driving up tonight, and I want to see you, in person. Tomorrow, first thing in the morning."

"Okay," said Diana. "And, Daisy? I'm sorry. I can't tell you how sorry I am that you and Beatrice are involved in all of this. I'm sorry for everything."

Daisy didn't answer. She ended the call, set the phone down, walked to the powder room, used the toilet, and washed her hands without meeting her own eyes in the mirror. Back in Arnold's office, she picked up her phone again. She had one more call to make before she started driving.

The phone barely rang before Hal's voice was in her ear. "Daisy? Where are you? Where's Beatrice? What's going on?"

Daisy sat up very straight. She licked her lips. "Hello, Hal. We need to talk," she said.

33

<u>∿∿∿</u>

Hal

They were eighteen years old, and the world was theirs, laid out before them like a banquet before kings.

All summer long, they'd kept tallies in Magic Marker on the cottage walls. Who'd kicked a keg. Who'd booted and rallied. Who'd gotten into the Squealing Pig or the A House or the Dory Bar, who'd gotten a blow job, who'd gotten laid. Writing on the wall probably meant that Crosby's parents would lose their security deposit, but none of them cared. It was their last summer together, one last, epic summer for the Class of 1987, and Hal Shoemaker, class president, had appointed himself Vice Admiral. "Leave no man behind" was the motto they'd adopted, and, as the last beach bonfire approached, Hal was worried about Daniel Rosen. Diesel Dan, Dan the Man, whose nickname had been lengthened to Manfred, then shortened to Freddie. (Hal had gotten his own nickname after a mixer at Miss Porter's, when there had been an unfortunate encounter with a girl who'd just started her period. Bryan Tavistock had made a joke about the Masque of the Red Death, and, thus, Hal became Poe.)

Twenty-three boys out of the fifty-eight members of their graduating class had come to the Cape for August. They spent their days drinking on the bayside beach in front of the cottage named Begonia, where four guys were staying. Hal was at his folks' place a few miles away, hosting three more classmates there. Other members of the class were roughing it on the KOA campgrounds near the Head of the Meadow Beach.

Hal considered Dan, lying on his belly on a towel, motionless except for the slow expansion and collapse of his rib cage. He poked at the other boy's shoulder with the handle of a plastic shovel. Dan sat up, squinting into the sun.

"Hey," said Hal. "Any luck last night?"

Instead of answering, Dan just muttered, "I gotta take a leak," and hauled himself unsteadily upright. Hal sighed. Dan was short and skinny, the perfect build for a coxswain but less than ideal, Hal guessed, for attracting the ladies. There was also something dainty, something almost girlish in the cast of Dan's features, the round, long-lashed eyes that turned up at the corners, and his ears, which came to points at their tips. Of course, his looks wouldn't have held him back, if he'd had any confidence. Bryan Tavistock, for example, whose nickname was Whale and who always smelled faintly of salami, scored almost as much as Hal himself, because Bryan was confident and funny and, perhaps most of all, extremely persistent. He told every girl he met that she was the most beautiful woman he'd ever seen, and he never took no for an answer. *No*, Bryan liked to say, *is just the opening in the negotiations.*

"Just piss in the ocean!" Hal urged, but Danny was already halfway to the cottage door. Hal got up and followed him. Once he was inside, he stood for a moment, letting his eyes adjust to the dimness, breathing in the smell of sun-warmed garbage and sour spilled beer. The place was getting seriously rank. *Oh, well*, he thought. They'd be leaving on Sunday, and it would be someone else's job to clean up once they were gone.

He waited until he heard the toilet flush, then positioned himself outside the bathroom door. When it opened, he grabbed Danny in a bear hug, lifting him off his feet, and wrestled him onto one of the unmade beds.

"Dan the Man!" he shouted, lying on top of him as Danny wriggled and kicked, finally working himself free. "So what's the count?"

Danny shrugged. Hal didn't even try to conceal his disappointment.

"Blow jobs?" he asked, and thumped Dan's bony shoulder. "Come on. Tell me you've gotten at least a few of these townies to gobble your knob."

"Three?" Danny said, with a question in his voice. When Hal stared at him, Danny dropped his gaze. "I remember two of them for sure. That night we all went to the Boatslip?"

Hal nodded. Dan had been talking to a girl at the bar, and they'd slipped out together, and Danny had come back grinning, which they'd all assumed meant that he'd gotten some. That was good, but not enough.

Hal shoved Dan back on the bed and straddled him, planting one knee on either side of his chest.

"Have you gotten laid this summer?" he asked. "Don't even think about lying to me."

Danny shoved at him, struggling to buck Hal off, but Hal had at least fifty pounds, plus gravity, on his side.

"Have you?" Hal demanded, and Danny looked away.

"The girls here are pigs. I'm not really into any of them."

Hal shook his head. "Danny," he said. "Danny, Dan, Dan." The girls were not pigs. More to the point, there was one for every taste, petite freckled redheads, dark-eyed, sultry brunettes, or busty blondes, his personal favorites. Some guys said that anything more than a handful was wasted, but Hal thought those guys were full of shit. He loved nothing more than motorboating a girl, putting his mouth on her chest and wrapping her boobs around his ears, like sex earmuffs.

Sex earmuffs. He tucked the phrase away, hoping to remember it later. Meanwhile, Danny had squirmed out from underneath him and was sitting on the edge of the bed, picking at a scab on his knee. "Look," Dan muttered. "Maybe it's okay if I just—you know—don't."

"Are you a homo?" Hal demanded.

"Fuck you," said Danny, and shoved him with both hands, which was the minimum acceptable response to such a query. Hal didn't actually think Danny was a homo. He wasn't sure what Dan's story was, if he was shy, or just picky or what, but it didn't matter. Hal was the class president, he was Vice Admiral, and if he had to personally drag each one of his men between some girl's spread legs, like a lieutenant hauling his wounded soldiers off the beaches of Normandy, he'd do it.

"Okay, then," he said. "Tonight's your night. You know that girl I've been talking to? Little chickie from the beach?"

Danny looked queasy, which Hal ascribed to either the afternoon's beer or the epic amounts of Fireball whiskey they'd consumed the night before. Maybe both. "Isn't she your . . ." Danny's eyelashes, absurdly long for a boy, fluttered as he groped for a word, knowing that nothing like "girlfriend" could apply. Not to a local, a townie they'd met a few weeks ago.

Hal thumped Danny's shoulders, grinning. "Lucky for you, I don't mind sharing." Hal had been flirting with her, chatting her up, cultivating the girl, like a farmer tending his fields, for just this purpose. She wasn't his type, but she was *a* type: young for her age, and starry-eyed, a girl who'd be honored that these prep-school gods, these future masters of the universe, were even paying attention to her. A girl who'd do anything, with a little fifty-proof inducement. A break-glass-in-case-of-emergency girl, and Dan was an emergency, if ever there'd been one. Hal clapped him on the back, the way his own father had frequently clapped him on the back. It was the single gesture of affection Vernon Shoemaker was capable of deploying with his boys.

"Get ready, soldier. Tonight's your night."

Most of the other girls at the bonfire wore cutoffs and college sweatshirts and practical ponytails to keep the wind from whipping their hair in their faces, but the girl from the beach was floating around in a stupid white dress, like the angel on top of a Christmas tree, with her hair down around her shoulders. Worse, she was clinging to him, like a barnacle stuck to a ship's bottom. Hal knew he'd have to get things going—obviously Danny was not going to take the lead—so he gave her his most charming smile and handed her a cup of punch, which was mostly vodka, with just enough juice mixed in to hide the taste. "Here you go, beautiful," he said. "Bottoms up." She gave him a shy smile, and drank. For the next hour he kept her cup full, being his most charming, solicitous self, even though he had his eye on a blonde who was filling out her cutoffs and her UMass sweatshirt in a way this girl never would.

She touched his arm. "I need to go for a li'l walk," she whispered. Hal mentally kicked himself, wondering if he'd given her too much to drink, if she'd puke while Danny was fucking her. He'd had that happen a few times, plus one girl had gotten so drunk that she'd peed in his bed when they'd finished. Not fun.

Hal watched as she stumbled off into the dunes. When the girl had disappeared from view, he summoned Brad Burlingham, aka "Bubs," to keep an eye on her. "You got it, chief," said Bubs, and giggled his creepy giggle. Hal ignored him and went to find Danny, who was standing at the water's edge, chucking shells into the waves, without even a beer or a flask to hand.

"Come on, fella," he said, and recited the unofficial class motto. "No man left behind."

Except Danny couldn't do it. With Bubs watching, giggling, holding the girl's wrists, and calling out encouragement, Danny kissed her neck and her chest and worked at removing her bra. He was pawing clumsily at the clasp when the girl woke up enough to slur out the words "I love you." That had been the end of Danny. He'd backed away as if the girl was on fire, and crouched on his heels in the sand, looking sick.

"I . . . no. I can't, man."

"Come on," Hal said, his voice impatient. "She wants it!"

Danny shook his head. "I'm not feeling so good." He didn't look very good, Hal had to admit. His face looked pale and sweaty, his eyes wide, the irises ringed with white.

"You want me to go first?" Hal asked, looking down at the girl. When the girl didn't answer, he sighed, bidding a mental farewell to Miss Junk in the Trunk. "Fine." He reached into his pocket for a condom, ripping the package open with his teeth, thinking about that old song, about how if you can't be with the one you love, you've got to love the one you're with. "Let me show you how it's done." Danny sat on the edge of the dune, watching, and Bubs held on to the girl's arms as Hal bent to the task.

1992

"It catches up with you," said the older man.

"What's that?" asked Hal. The words came out sounding more like *wass'at*? His tongue tended to get mushy after his eighth or ninth beer, and his eighth and ninth beer had both been some time ago.

It was a beautiful night in New Hampshire, the first night of Emlen's three-day-long reunions, and there were tents set up all along the quad, one for every class celebrating a reunion, all the way back to the Class of 1940. The sounds of a cover band playing "She Loves You" for the Class of 1960 competed with the DJ spinning "Push It" for the newest graduates in the Class of 1990. The spring air smelled of lilacs. The darkness softened the hard edges of the marble and granite buildings, and the trees were clothed in fresh, young green.

All afternoon and into the night, Hal had been reliving his glory days with his Emlen brothers. *Remember that road trip to Foxwoods? Remember the R.E.M. concert? Remember that summer at the Cape?* Some of the guys had brought girlfriends, and one, Dennis Hsiu, had even brought a wife, but as the night had progressed the women had peeled off, retreating back to the dorm rooms or to hotels in town.

At the sound of the other man's sigh, Hal turned around. The alum—Hal thought he had to be forty-five, maybe even fifty— looked wistful as he peered out over the campus, and Hal remembered what he'd said. "What catches up?" he asked, taking time to form each word with care.

"Time," said the man. He'd given the beer in his hand a rueful look. "And booze." He'd drained the bottle and set it down. "All through college, all through law school, it was nothing but wine and lots of women. Monday mornings—and sometimes Tuesdays, and sometimes Fridays—I'd wake up, stick my finger down my throat, chew up a few breath mints, have a shot of vodka to keep my hands steady, and drive in to the office."

Hal nodded. He'd had a few mornings like that himself since starting law school. Maybe more than a few.

"Then, one Monday morning, I'm at work. I'm on my knees in the corporate bathroom, praying to the porcelain god, and my boss walks in. He sees me, and says, 'Walker, it's time to put away childish things.' Then he turns around and walks out the door."

"Huh." Hal wondered if Walker was going to give him some

Alcoholics Anonymous–style speech, and tell him that the first step toward solving his problem was admitting he had one. "I don't have a problem," he said, aware that the slurred, sloppy sound of the words made him sound like a liar.

Walker shook his head, giving Hal a good-natured smile. "You're still young. You can take it. But like I said, it catches up. Eventually, you have to find something to keep you grounded. Something to send you home before last call some of the time, or stay in instead of going out every once in a while. An anchor."

Hal looked and saw the gold wedding band on the other man's hand. So this wasn't a pitch for AA; it was a pitch for marriage. He wondered if the man had a sister he was trying to unload, or maybe a sister-in-law.

"Wha' 'appans . . ." Hal shut his mouth, wiped his lips with the back of his hand, and started again. "What happens if you don't wanna?"

The man picked up his bottle and began picking at the corner of the label with his thumbnail. In the distance, Hal could hear the men of Emlen singing the alma mater, "This Happy Land."

"There were fifty-four men in my class," Walker said. "This is our twentieth, and we're already down five." He lifted a finger for each cause of death he named. "Liver cancer. Car accident. AIDS."

Hal opened his mouth. He had a few things to say about that last one, but before he could get them out, Walker added, "And two suicides. One guy used a gun. The other one drank himself to death. Booze and cocaine. Took longer, but it got him to the same place." The man had a half-smile on his face. Hal couldn't see his eyes. "I wish there'd been someone to talk to me—to all of us—the way I'm talking to you. To tell us that's what women are for. They ground us. They keep us in line." He clapped Hal on the shoulder and said, "Find yourself a good woman. Go get yourself grounded." And then, whistling the tune of "This Happy Land," he walked off into the night.

1997

"Do you ever think about it?" asked Danny Rosen.

"Think about what?" asked Hal. It was Saturday night or, technically, Sunday morning, and Hal's class had been assigned the school's boathouse for the celebration of their tenth reunion. Hal and five or six others had taken cigars out to the dock, which wobbled slightly as Danny approached and came to sit beside him. Danny had put on a few pounds since his coxswain days, and he'd grown a beard, probably to compensate for his disappearing jawline. He no longer looked elfin. Now he looked like a hobbit. One of the old ones. Bilbo Baggins, or someone like that.

In the distance, Hal could hear Brad Burlingham, telling some joke. Voices carried, out here, over the water, and he could hear ". . . and she says, 'That's what the stick is for!'" followed by Brad's loud, braying laugh. Brad sounded drunk. Brad always sounded drunk these days. Whenever Hal saw him, at reunions or at one of their summer weekends, he was always at least half in the bag, and he never made a move without a hip flask. It was getting to the point that Hal was starting to wonder if Brad had a problem. Hal himself had stopped drinking except for Friday and Saturday nights, and, even then, he tried to limit himself, stopping before he got to a point that would leave him impaired on Monday mornings.

He turned back to Danny Rosen. "Think about what?" he asked again.

"That summer," said Danny. Hal looked at him, puzzled. "The party," Danny prompted, and lowered his voice. "The girl. The one you . . ." His voice trailed off.

Hal still had no idea what Danny was talking about, but he could see that Dan the Man looked wretched. There were circles under his eyes, and Hal had noticed earlier that his fingernails were bitten to bloody nubs.

"There was a girl. A townie. A babysitter or an au pair or something. The last night, we had a party on the beach."

"Oh, yeah!" The memory was cutting through the fog of Hal's drunkenness. "She was s'posed to be for you!" Shit. What had her name been? Dana? Delores? "But then you couldn't, so I did!"

"Hal, I'm gay."

Hal blinked a few times. He peered at Danny, waiting for the punch line, as more laughter came drifting over the water. "Huh?"

"I'm gay," Danny repeated. "I'm—I'm in a relationship. With a man. I'm in love."

"Oh." Hal blinked a few more times and rubbed his eyes. If Danny had dropped this bomb back when they'd been roommates at Emlen, Hal would have had a different response. At eighteen, there was no way he'd have been comfortable with some ass bandit sleeping six feet away, but now? "Good for you," he said, a little dubiously. "If you're happy, I'm happy." Hal looked around. Cy Coffey and Eric Feinberg were sitting on the far edge of the dock, and, back on the land, four or five more guys were playing quarters.

As for Danny, he didn't look happy, or like a man in love. He looked awful, Hal thought. Haunted. Miserable.

"Do people know?" he asked. "Your folks?"

"Not yet," Danny said shortly. "And that's not what I want to talk about. I want to talk about what happened with that girl, that summer."

Hal's brain felt very foggy, like every thought required extra amounts of effort. "Okay."

"Hal . . ." Danny rubbed the side of his face. "I think you raped her."

Hal stared, trying to make sense of the words, trying to fit them into his memories of the night, before shaking his head. "Nah."

"She was passed out! And Bubs was . . ." He lowered his voice, looking over his shoulder to make sure that Brad wasn't listening. "Bubs was holding her down."

"Nah," Hal said again, even as he wondered if that was right, and exactly what had happened. The night in question, and the girl in question, had been many nights and many girls ago. "She was drunk. We all were drunk. But I didn't force her to do anything. She didn't tell me to stop."

"I don't think she could have told you anything," Danny said, his voice cold. "I don't think she could talk."

Hal shook his head, trying to clear it. "Okay," he said. "Say you're right. Say I raped her. What'm I supposed to do about it now?"

"I don't know!" Danny sounded anguished. "Do you know her name? Do you know how we can find her?"

Hal felt a trill of alarm at Danny's "we." Did Danny think they were in this together? Was Danny proposing some kind of joint confession? "I'm not sure I knew her name." Except, just then, it popped up into his mind. Not Dana. Not Delores. *Diana.* But he was absolutely not sharing that particular factoid with Danny. "I know she worked as a mother's helper . . ." Hal could picture the girl, though: her hair, long and brown, the silly sundress she'd worn. He felt another unfamiliar jolt of fear as he considered whether Danny was contemplating anything as stupid as going to the authorities.

"So what're you going to do?" Hal asked.

"I don't know," said Danny, sounding hopeless. "I don't know if there's anything we can do. We've just got to live with it, I guess."

Hal shrugged. If Dan wanted to eat himself up with guilt over something that had happened a decade ago, Hal wasn't going to stop him. He supposed it explained Dan's life. Working in that shitty public school in Trenton, taking in foster kids and stray puppies, all of it made sense. Dan's entire life had been atonement, one long act of contrition. The same way, maybe, that Brad Burlingham, now coming off his second stint in rehab, at present trying to drown himself in whiskey, had turned his whole life into an attempt at escape. Which begged the question: What was Hal's life going to be?

Hal clapped Danny on the shoulder and used the other man's body to lever himself upright. "You know what we can do? We can clean up our acts. Go forth and sin no more," he said, his voice loud and confident. As he spoke, he heard an echo of the man he'd met at his fifth reunion. *It catches up with you.* You need things to keep you on the straight and narrow. A wife, a family. Anchors. It's time, Hal decided. Time to go forth and sin no more. Time to find some anchors and get his house in order, and claim the glorious future that he deserved.

2019

Hal had been expecting the call ever since Saturday night, and when, at ten in the morning the Monday after the party, his administrative assistant (you couldn't call them secretaries anymore) said, "I have your brother-in-law on the line," Hal sighed, mentally spat on his fists, and said, "Put him through."

Danny sounded just as hysterical as Hal had imagined he would; just as panicked and dismayed. "What are we going to do?"

"About what?" Hal asked.

"About Diana!" Danny shouted. "About the fact that she thinks you raped her, and that I watched, and she's found us!"

"True. But what can she do?" Hal asked. "Even if she's got a case about being assaulted—which, legally speaking, is dubious— the statute of limitations in Massachusetts expired years ago. It would be her word against ours."

"Have you not been reading the news for the last year and a half?" Danny's voice was shrill. He sounded, Hal thought, like his sister at her most infuriated, and he could feel a headache forming, like a cap tightening around his skull. "People believe women. They believe them more than men."

"Not every time," Hal said, but Danny talked right over him.

"What if she told someone? Or kept a diary? What if she had bruises, and took pictures? Jesus, what if she got pregnant?"

"Would you stop?" With two fingers, Hal pinched the bridge of his nose and ignored the prickles of sweat under his arms and above his lip. "If she wants to try to come forward, if she thinks she's got a story, the first chapter involves her wandering down to the beach and getting shit-faced. How does that make her look?"

"You raped her, and Bubs held her down, and I watched. How does that make us look?" Danny countered. "She was fifteen years old, Hal. She was basically Beatrice's age. Don't you feel anything about this? Don't you feel the tiniest little bit of remorse?"

Hal didn't answer. He was remembering the speech his father had given him the morning they were set to depart for his first year at Emlen. Vernon had thumped him on the back, then reached into his pocket and tossed a box of condoms on top of the duffel bag on his bed.

"There's going to be a lot of young ladies who are going to be looking to trap you as you get older," his dad said. "So be good." He'd topped off his speech with a broad wink. "And if you can't be good, be careful." Hal wondered if Diana's mother had given her a speech, about not drinking, or going to parties alone, or throwing herself at boys. Or if maybe Diana had gotten a different kind of speech. Maybe she'd been given that yellow bikini the same way Hal had been given the condoms. Maybe, instead of *Be careful*, her mom had said, *Be smart. There're a lot of rich boys on the Cape in the summer, and maybe you'll be able to get your hooks into one of them.*

He shook his head. "She isn't going to do anything. She just wants to scare us. I promise. You're worrying about nothing. This is going to blow over, and everything's going to be fine." Which was what he'd believed, with all his heart, until that night, when he had come home and found Daisy and Beatrice gone.

"Honey?" he called, hearing the house echo. None of the familiar sounds that said "home" came to his ears; nor could he catch a whiff of any of the smells. No chicken roasting in the oven; no green pork chili, made with tomatillos specially purchased from one of the markets on Ninth Street, simmering on the stove. The countertops were bare; the table was empty; the dog did not come running to greet him. He checked his phone for recent texts or calls from his daughter or his wife, but there were none. When he called Daisy's number, it just rang and rang. He texted the words CALL ME, then put his phone away, trying to ignore the voice in his head that was speaking up, more and more insistently: *she knows.*

He went to the bedroom, taking the stairs two at a time. His plan was to check for missing luggage or clothes, but he quickly realized that he had no idea where Daisy kept their suitcases, or if he'd be able to discern if any of her clothes or toiletries had been moved or taken. Everything seemed to be in order. The perfume he liked, that he'd bought to replace the perfume he didn't, was still in its spot on the dresser. Her good earrings and her pearl necklace were still in the jewelry box . . . but if she'd packed some clothes and a toothbrush, he wouldn't necessarily notice they were gone. He didn't even try looking in Beatrice's room, knowing that would be futile.

Instead, he stood in the center of their bedroom, forcing his mind to go blank. *Ladybug, ladybug,* he thought. Daisy had flown off, somewhere. His little songbird, out of her cage. Where had she gone? Was she alone, or was she with Diana, to soak up more of her new friend's poison?

His phone buzzed in his pocket. Hal jumped, pressed his lips together, and looked down to see his wife's face flashing on the screen.

"Daisy?"

"Hello, Hal." Her voice sounded different. Cool, and faraway.

"Where are you, sweetheart? Where's Beatrice? What's going on?"

Instead of answering, Daisy said, "Is there anything you want to tell me?"

A lesser man, a non-lawyer, might have fallen into that trap. Hal knew better. "Where are you?" he asked again. When she didn't answer, he bit back the words that wanted to escape: *Tell me where you went! Tell me where you took my car and my daughter!* Struggling for calm, he said, "If there's anything we need to discuss, we can do it face-to-face. But I need to know where you are. I just want to make sure you're all right."

He heard Daisy sigh. It was a familiar sound and, in it, Hal heard what he wanted to hear—capitulation. *That's my girl*, he thought.

"Beatrice and I are on the Cape."

Hal forced himself to smile. Making that shape with his mouth would change the sound of his voice. He would sound calm, and Daisy would hear that, and she wouldn't panic, or do anything rash. That was how it was with women. You could fool them; you could lead them. It was what they required. Without someone to impose order, some man to run the show, it would just be twittering hysteria all the time, flocks of chirping birds flapping their wings pointlessly, going nowhere, accomplishing nothing. "Stay right there," he told his wife.

"Meet me tomorrow morning at Diana's house. I'll text you the address. I think that we should talk. The three of us."

"Fine," said Hal. "I look forward to it." Even if the other Diana had gotten hold of his wife, filled her head with lies and exaggerations, ensorcelled her, somehow, Hal would find the words to break the spell. He'd plead his case, he'd tell Daisy his side of things, and he'd win, because he was, in the end, a winner. "Tell Beatrice I love her, and that I'm on my way."

34

~~~~~

Daisy

At six in the morning, as the sun was coming up, Daisy steered her car up the driveway and parked it beside the small, cedar-shingled cottage that stood on the edge of the dune. Diana was sitting on the edge of a wooden deck. A short-legged, chunky dog with shaggy brown fur frolicked around her legs.

"That's Pedro," said Diana, as she got to her feet. "Pedro, behave."

Daisy walked toward the deck. The air was thick with the promise of rain, weighty with humidity. She could see rafts of gray clouds rolling in from Provincetown. She felt unreality nagging at her, like the ground beneath her feet was going to crumble, like the cottage would slide into the sea, and everything she'd known or seen or believed in would disappear.

"Do you want some coffee?" Diana asked.

Daisy stared at her. Of all the things she'd been expecting, nothing as prosaic as coffee had made the list. She imagined sitting, her hands wrapped around a warm mug, the simple comfort of it. "Sure."

Diana led her into the cottage. Daisy took it in: the white-painted walls, the ledge lined with brightly patterned decoupaged seashells and dried starfish, framed postcards hung from bright bits of ribbon, paintings of flowers and landscapes in frames made from driftwood. She saw the piles of books, the white voile curtains, and the narrow refectory table with the easel and the guitar in the corner. "God," she said, "Beatrice would love it here."

"She's always welcome," said Diana, and led Daisy to the galley kitchen, which was separated from the living space by a half-height wall. Daisy looked around at the well-worn utensils in their ceramic container, the copper pots, the rows of spices in glass jars, the blue ceramic bowl full of clementines.

Daisy went back to the living space. She let her hand brush Pedro's leash, hanging on a peg by the door. She touched the rocking chair, then the white chenille throw, and went straight to the framed wedding photograph of Diana and Michael that stood on her bedside table.

"This is your husband?"

Diana nodded. Daisy picked up the photograph and studied it in the light. Diana wore a simple white dress, and there were white blossoms in her hair. The man by her side was big and burly, with rounded shoulders and tree-trunk thighs and a broad chest. Diana looked radiant, and the man looked ecstatic, almost delirious with joy, his eyes barely slits above his cheeks, his smile as wide as his face.

Diana sounded almost shy. "He was the caretaker for the cottage, when I moved in."

"Do you have children?"

Diana shook her head.

"I don't know anything about you. Not one true thing," Daisy said as she watched the other woman moving in the kitchen, her hands deft and her movements economical as she measured coffee and poured water into her machine. "Jesus, did you even need cooking lessons?"

Diana looked rueful. "Well, I can't cook like you do, but I'm not quite as pathetic as I pretended to be. I own a restaurant in Provincetown. The Abbey?"

"Oh my God," said Daisy. "We've been there."

"I own it now, but I was a waitress there, for a long time. For the first few years I lived here I would go back to Boston in the summertime. I couldn't stand to be here in July or August. Everything I saw, or heard, or smelled, it all reminded me of what happened." Diana poured coffee into a mug, adding sugar and cream, because by then she knew how Daisy took her coffee.

"Is Beatrice here?" Diana asked.

"She's back at the house. Vernon's house. The one where you found our picture."

Diana nodded. "And Hal?"

Daisy swallowed. It felt like her heart had taken up residence in her throat and was sitting there, quivering. "On his way. I told him that we needed to talk to him. I left him a note, so he'd know where to come."

Diana nodded again. After she'd poured a cup of coffee for herself, she held the door, and Daisy followed her back outside, out to the beach stairs at the top of the dune. A pair of wooden benches were built into the platform at the top of the six flights, a comfortable spot for people to sit and catch their breath and brush the sand off their shoes, with views of the bay to both sides.

"Careful," Diana said, as Daisy grasped the lintel on the top of the post, which wobbled alarmingly under her hand. "That post is loose. Michael's been meaning to fix that forever," she said. "It's like the joke about the cobbler's children with no shoes, right? Nothing around here gets fixed as fast as it should."

They sat on the benches, facing each other, as more clouds rolled in and the wind picked up, blowing the patchy grass almost flat. Daisy waited for Diana to say something, to offer an apology or an explanation. When Diana didn't speak, Daisy decided to begin.

"I told you how when I met Hal, he was an older man. A lawyer. A partner in a big firm, with a big house. And I was twenty years old. My dad had died, my mom had no money, I was thirty thousand dollars in debt, and . . . well." She looked down at the water. "I was dazzled by him. For a lot of reasons. He swept me off my feet. He was everything I thought I'd ever wanted, and would never get. You know? The answer to all my prayers."

"I can imagine how appealing that must have been." Diana's voice was dry. "A man who comes along and looks like he can give you anything you want."

Daisy sighed. "Back then, I thought I was fat. Hideous. I wasn't—not really. Sometimes I look at pictures of myself, back then, and I get angry that I ever felt bad about myself. But, at the time, it felt like my friends, my roommates, they were always the ones guys paid attention to. So I had no self-esteem, and a dead father, and a mother who was falling apart . . ." She swallowed, realizing that it still hurt to talk about that part of her life. Realizing, too, how self-indulgent and whiny she must sound, to someone who'd survived what Diana had survived. "Hal wanted me. More than that. He needed me. He made that clear. And I liked being needed. I liked feeling important to someone." She sipped her coffee, then set her mug down. "I think he tried to be honest with me, in his way. He said that he'd been wild when he was younger. That he used to drink. He gave me the idea that there were things that he'd done, things he wasn't proud of."

"But he didn't say what they were?"

Daisy shook her head. "He never said. And I never asked. But I understood the deal. I would . . . I don't know. I'd be a civilizing influence, and I wouldn't ask questions. I'd make a home for him. Have babies. Well," she said, and smiled sadly. "That was the plan, anyhow, even though it ended up being baby, singular. I would cook . . ." She looked up, meeting Diana's eyes. "I was happy. You know?" Diana nodded. Daisy sniffled, and swiped at her cheeks with her sleeve. "That's the shitty part. I'm trying to help Beatrice to grow up and be a strong woman. I'm trying to be a role model. And I thought—I mean, I had a business, and I volunteered, and I thought . . ." Her voice trailed off. "I thought that I was doing fine. That I was happy, and that I had the kind of life I wanted. That I wasn't dependent, the way my mother was. And sure, there were things that happened that I don't think about, or didn't, until all of this stuff in the news . . ." Daisy waved her hands, a gesture she hoped encompassed her history, and current events, the damage that had been done to her; the same kind of damage it seemed like every woman who'd ever drawn breath had endured. "And now all I see is what he did to me—to us. That I was dependent. That I could have been more, and done more. That Hal hurt people. He hurt you. And he kept my world very small."

"Hey." Gently, Diana put her hand on Daisy's forearm. "Beatrice is great. You've done a good job with her."

Daisy was crying in earnest by then, tears rolling off her chin to plop on her lap. She waved away the compliment. "Please. You hardly know her."

"I can tell. She's confident and curious and smart. Smart enough to figure out what I was doing, anyhow. I think she's terrific."

"She makes clothes for dead mice." Now Daisy was crying and laughing at the same time.

"She does. And she's got blue hair, and old-lady clothes. It's fine. She's one hundred percent herself. And she wouldn't be that strong, she wouldn't have the courage of her convictions, if she didn't have a mom like you."

Daisy made herself breathe deeply, and sat up straight, squaring her shoulders, feeling the wind coming off the water. "Are you going to tell the police?"

Diana shook her head. "If that had been my plan, I would have had to tell a long time ago."

"So what, then? Do you want him to say he's sorry?" As soon as Daisy spoke the words she heard how insipid they sounded, how meaningless, and she wished she could take them back. "No. Never mind. Do you think—if he actually did something to make it right . . ."

Diana was looking at her curiously. "What would that be?"

"I don't know," Daisy said. "Like, if he took a leave from his job and went back to Emlen. If he volunteered there, and told the boys there what he'd done, and worked with them, and the teachers, so none of them would ever do a thing like that?"

Diana cocked her head. "Would he do it?"

"I don't know," said Daisy. She was remembering what Hal had said, at the dinner party, that rainy night; about how there had to be a way back for the transgressors; about how famous broadcasters and athletes couldn't just be canceled forever. She thought about Danny, who at least had been trying to do better, as opposed to her husband, who, she thought, simply wanted to put the events of that summer behind him, to stick them in a folder labeled CHILD-HOOD and never think of them again. "I don't know what atone-ment looks like. I don't know how a man makes this right. Or even if it's possible." She bent her head and cleared her throat. Staring down at her hands, she said, "I'm not much of an adult, I think. I never finished college, and I barely have any friends."

Diana looked at her, waiting.

"I always thought that it was me. That I was selfish, or self-involved, or boring, or stupid, or silly." Daisy heard Hal's voice in her head. *My little songbird. Happy in her cage.* "I thought people didn't like me, or that I wasn't as smart as they were, or at least, not as educated. And maybe I am unlikable. I'm not discounting that possibility, but Hal . . ." She touched her lips. "I think that Hal wanted me all to himself, so he kept other people away. I could sense some of that, at least some of the time. But I thought . . ." She looked down. Her heart was so heavy. The world seemed bleak and gray and sunless, and like it would be that way forever. "It felt like love," she said.

Diana nodded. For a moment they sat in silence, before the rumble of distant thunder made Diana cast a practiced glance upward.

"Looks like we're going to get a thunderstorm."

"This was always my favorite thing about being on the Cape," said Daisy. "Sitting in the living room, in front of the windows, and watching the storms roll in." If Diana noted Daisy's use of the past tense, she didn't say anything. Daisy took a deep breath and made herself ask the question.

"So tell me," said Daisy. "Tell me what happened."

Diana looked out toward the water. The wind blew her hair away from her face. "I was fifteen," she began. "It was the summer after my sophomore year in high school. I played soccer, and I loved reading. My parents and my older sisters and I lived in South Boston. My mom was a secretary for the English department at Boston University, and that's where she met Dr. Levy."

Diana told Daisy everything. She told Daisy about convincing her father to let her take the job and how happy her parents had been when Dr. Levy had offered her the job. She told her what happened that summer, and about the lost years that followed, and how Dr. Levy had given her the cottage and Diana had come to live in it, alone. She talked about getting her job at the Abbey, and all the people she'd met there; she talked about adopting Willa, and meeting Michael Carmody, her caretaker. She told her about her marriage, her happy years painting and crafting and working at the Abbey. She told her about finding Daisy's wedding picture, about creating the email address and the fake profile page as a way of getting close to Daisy.

"I just couldn't believe that he'd married someone else named

408 · Jennifer Weiner

Diana. It was so weird. It felt like he was rubbing it in, somehow." She smoothed back her hair. "Like, you were the Diana he married, and I was the Diana that he ... well. You know."

Daisy's face burned, and she had to force the words out of her mouth. "After our first date, he told me he'd known another Diana. That's when he started calling me Daisy." She shook her head, thinking of the girl she'd been then, trusting and hopeful and naive. "I should have known that something was wrong."

"No," said Diana. "Don't blame yourself. You couldn't have known something like that."

Daisy nodded reluctantly. Then, with every muscle tensed, she asked, "What happens now?"

"I don't know," said Diana. "I thought I knew. I thought that I just wanted to look him in the eye and let him see me, and tell him that he'd hurt me."

"Do you think that's going to be enough?" Diana's expression was hard to read, and Daisy felt herself shudder. *He's still Beatrice's father*, she heard her mother saying. What would it do to her daughter if Hal was put on trial, if he was convicted and sent to jail? And then she asked herself the same question she'd asked her brother, and her mom: What if this had happened to Beatrice? What would justice look like then?

She knew that there had to be more to it than just mouthing an apology; there had to be deeds, in addition to words. Maybe Hal could go take a leave of absence from the law firm, and go to Emlen and talk to the boys there. Maybe he could work with a therapist, and he could figure out why he'd done what he'd done, and what to say to other rich, privileged young men to keep them from inflicting similar harm. That would be something, but Daisy knew that it still wouldn't be enough. And part of her, a cool, removed part whose existence she'd never previously suspected, was saying, *Not my problem*. Because, no matter what happened, it seemed like a part of her had decided that Hal wasn't going to be her problem for much longer.

She snorted. Diana looked at her quizzically.

"I was just thinking, I read once, in India there's a tradition where if you want to end your marriage, you just say 'I divorce thee' three times." She shrugged. "And then I was thinking about Michael Scott on *The Office*, and how he tried to declare bankruptcy by just yelling . . ."

"'I declare bankruptcy!'" Diana said.

"Yeah, that's it," said Daisy. She rubbed her face. She'd been awake all night, first driving, then lying, sleepless, in the bed she'd once shared with Hal, playing and replaying the history of their marriage, running her mind along its seams the way she'd run her fingers over a pie crust, looking for rips, for holes, for anything that might have indicated trouble. "I should have known," she said again.

Diana's voice was gentle. "You can't blame yourself."

"Who should I blame, then?"

Diana shrugged. "I don't think it's about blame. It's about what happens next." She bent down to pick up an oyster shell. "It's about Beatrice. And all the girls who come after us."

"I know, I know. You're right. I'm just so sorry."

Diana nodded. They were silent for a moment, and then Diana spoke again. "Whatever happens, I'm glad that I met you. And Beatrice. I'm glad you were my friend."

Daisy made a noise, a kind of sobbing, hiccupy laugh. Diana took Daisy's hand and squeezed it. And after that, it seemed like there was nothing else to say. They sat, in silence, until Pedro started barking at the sound of a car coming up the driveway. Both women got to their feet, watching, as Hal parked the car and got out.

"Daisy," he said, and had the nerve to smile. He'd worn khakis and a crisp button-down shirt, and looked like he was ready to host a barbecue, or attend a cocktail party. "There you are!" Daisy thought that he sounded indulgent and amused; a parent whose toddler had put her favorite teddy bear in a shopping bag and run away from home, only to be spotted and scooped up at the end of the driveway.

Daisy heard the rain begin, pattering on the water. A moment later, she felt the first raindrops splashing on her cheeks and in her hair.

Hal stopped a few feet away from the benches. "Excuse us, please," he said to Diana. "I need a moment with my wife."

"No. Stay," said Daisy.

"It's fine," Diana murmured. "You could go for a walk on the beach." She leaned forward as she got to her feet and, in a voice meant for Daisy's ears alone, she said, "Just be careful. The deck gets slippery. And you want to watch out for that wobbly post." Then, head down, she hurried across the deck. Pedro gave Hal a baleful look and followed his mistress inside.

Daisy stood up, resting her hands on the railing, looking out over the water. The wind had whipped the ripples into white-capped waves. She heard thunder again, and she could feel the presence of her husband behind her.

Hal's voice was still jolly and indulgent. "You always did love a storm."

Daisy didn't turn. "Do you know who she is?" Before he could answer, she told him. "You raped her," she said.

Hal sighed. "It was a party. Everyone was drunk. And it was a long, long time ago."

She turned, looking Hal full in the face. "Did you ever think about it? About her?"

Hal reached for her. Daisy jerked away.

"Daisy, listen to me."

"No," she said. "No. I don't have to listen to you anymore."

"I want to tell you that I'm sorry. I owe you an apology."

"I'm not the one who is owed an apology," she said.

Hal kept talking in that low, soothing voice. "But you're absolutely right. I should have told you." He put his hands in his pockets and gave a shrug, and suddenly she was furious, angrier at him than she'd ever been angry at anyone in her life.

"But you didn't," she said. "Because when did I ever deserve your honesty? Or your respect? When did you ever see me as a partner? Or even an actual adult?" She stalked toward him, sticking her finger in his chest. "You decided where we'd live. You decided who we would see. You decided where we'd go on vacation, and what kind of car I would drive, and where Beatrice would go to school. You controlled me."

"Daisy, I never—"

"Stop lying!" she yelled. "For once in this pathetic excuse for a marriage, be honest with me! Tell me the truth!"

"All I did was love you!" Hal roared.

Daisy stared at him, mouth hanging open.

"Everything I did, everything I kept to myself, every decision I made for us, it was all because I wanted to keep us safe."

"Oh, please." She could see his chest heaving underneath his blue button-down shirt. She knew that shirt. She'd bought it for him at Bloomingdale's; she'd pulled it from the hamper (or sometimes picked it up from the bedroom floor) a hundred times. She'd taken it to the dry cleaner and back again and hung it in his closet. His little bird.

"I know how men are," Hal was saying. "I know how the world is. And yes, I knew how I was. I wanted a home, I needed a wife, I needed a family. And you," he said, jabbing his finger at his chest, "needed me."

"No," Daisy said. "Maybe you thought so. Maybe you made me think it, too. But it's not true."

"I took care of you! I loved you!"

"You controlled me," Daisy said. "Being your wife meant that I couldn't have a real business, and I barely had friends. You didn't ever let me go anywhere, or see anyone, or do anything."

"What would you have done?" he demanded, with a sneer supplanting his easygoing smile. His voice was low and mean. "What do you think you would have become?" He shook his head. "You think I kept you off the cover of *Bon Appétit*? That you were going to be Martha Stewart?"

Daisy turned so that her back was toward the water. She braced her feet and raised her chin as the wind whipped at her hair. "You're a criminal," she said. "You knew if you told me the truth, and if I told anyone else, you could lose your law license."

"And then where would you be?" he taunted. "No big house in the suburbs. No private school for Beatrice. No Lexus to drive around."

"You think I care about that?" she screamed. "You lied to me!" With that, the rain arrived in earnest. Icy raindrops sheeted down, plastering her hair to her head and her clothes to her body. "I want a divorce," she shouted, feeling hot, salty tears join the rain on her face. "I want you gone when I get home. I want you to stay away from Beatrice. I never want to see you again."

Through the rain, she saw something flare in his eyes. Alarm at her threat to leave him, fear that he'd lose the house, or his daughter, or maybe, worst of all, his reputation. "I gave you everything," Hal shouted.

"No, you took everything!" she yelled back. "You took my name away!"

Hal looked as bewildered as if she'd slapped him. Then his jolly, reasonable look was back, the mask once again in place.

"Daisy," he said, his voice calm.

"That's not my name!" she shrieked.

He reached out to put his hands on her shoulders, as he'd done so many times before, to hold her still, to instruct her, and in her head she ducked and saw Hal stumbling forward, grabbing for the wobbly post, the one that had never been repaired. She saw his feet skid on the slick surface of the deck, saw his arms pinwheeling, hands groping, reaching for her, for help that wouldn't come. She saw him fall, thudding down one, two, three, four, five, six flights of stairs, to lie, broken and motionless, on the sand, limbs twisted, eyes open to the rain. She saw herself look down at him, seeing nothing but a male body around a man-shaped void.

Not a man at all, but a creature with cold, flat eyes, a monster with instincts for self-preservation and a species of low cunning, but not a man, not a person who had loved her, or anyone.

Hal had looked like what she was supposed to want—the body, the name, the degrees and the job and the money that he earned. She had taken those facts and built a man around them; had taken a collection of gestures and phrases and called them love. She'd willed a husband into existence, because Hal had said he'd give her the life she'd wanted, because he'd caught her at a moment of weakness and unfurled his promises like a banner. *You'll never be lonely. You'll never be afraid. You'll never worry about money or worry that no one wants you.* She remembered her mother's face when she'd come home with the news, how Judy had grabbed her hand and kissed the diamond of her ring. She remembered Hal lifting their newborn daughter into his arms, with pride and adoration on his face. But had that been real, or again, just a projection, a mirage, her mind showing her what she wanted to see? He'd taught Beatrice how to ice-skate and swim and ride a bike; he'd coached her T-ball team, he'd taken her to every father-daughter dance. Daisy had thought that, too, was love, but now she thought it was closer to camouflage; the protective actions of a man who knew how he had to behave if he wanted the world to count him as one of the good guys. Hal, she thought, had only gone through the motions, doing what was required to get the life he wanted, the life that he thought he deserved.

All of those thoughts flashed through her head in an instant as the wind howled and the rain poured down. *I could end it all, right now*, she thought. I wouldn't even have to do anything. Just duck. But, as much as the idea pleased her, she wouldn't let him fall. Death would be too easy. Death would let him off the hook. Life, though, life with the knowledge that Daisy knew what he'd done and who he was . . . that would be close to intolerable for a man as proud as Hal Shoemaker. Let him live, like a parachutist with his straps cut, tumbling down and down, forever. Let him live, with his every moment a torment, every hour burning.

Through the rain, Daisy could see another life, a life where she lived out here full-time, with Beatrice, and Diana nearby. Where she could walk her dog on the beach every morning, with her friend, and spend her days cooking in a restaurant. Where Diana could spend time with Beatrice, where Beatrice could go to public school and figure out for herself who she wanted to be, if she wanted to go to college or not. Maybe Daisy could even help at the restaurant and give Diana and her husband time to travel, to see the world. Maybe she had gifts she could give them, ways to repair the damage, and stitch up what had been torn. The only thing she knew for sure was that there was no way forward with Hal, not knowing what she knew about what he'd done. Her life as his wife, as Daisy Shoemaker, was over. *I divorce thee.*

And so, instead of ducking, Daisy stood still. When she felt Hal's hands on her shoulders, she said, "We're done, you and I," and waited until she saw that knowledge land in his eyes, before she turned and walked away with the rain scouring her skin, wishing only for a door to close, quietly but firmly, behind her.

Coda

On a hot August afternoon, a girl in a yellow bikini stood on a paddleboard and made her way across the glassy, blue-green waters of Cape Cod Bay. A breeze lifted the spill of shiny silvery hair that fell halfway down her back; the sun warmed her face and shoulders. She still didn't know everything that her parents had discussed, in long conversations with their bedroom door locked, or how, precisely, her uncle Danny and her mother's friend Diana fit into the story. Her mind shied away from the worst of the possibilities, like a little kid's fingers from a hot stove. All she knew was that things had been tense with Uncle Danny and Diana, but, over the past weeks, there'd been a thawing.

As for her parents, Beatrice still wasn't sure. Her father had ceded his father's house to her and her mom for the entire summer and beyond. Her mom had told her they'd stay through the school year, that Beatrice would go to the public high school in Orleans—at least for the next year.

Her father had been coming up every other weekend, renting a cottage in North Truro instead of staying with them. He brought presents for her mother—bouquets of hydrangeas, fancy chocolates, expensive sea salts, once, a whole bag full of spices and rubs from the Atlantic Spice Company—and he didn't bring his laptop, giving Beatrice his entire attention and hours of his time. One weekend, they'd ridden their bikes all the way from Wellfleet to Orleans and back again; once, they'd spent an entire afternoon on the beach. When Beatrice asked her father, "Are you and Mom getting divorced?" he'd said, "It's not what I want. But it's not up to me." When Beatrice asked her mom, her mom said, "Can we talk about this later? I have to get to work." Her mother had a job now, cooking at the restaurant that Diana owned, and Diana herself was spending a lot of time at their house. She'd shown Beatrice how to turn an old book into a birdhouse using balsa wood and glue; Beatrice had shown her how to preserve insects in resin. Beatrice had met Diana's husband, who was, it turned out, the caretaker for the house, and he was teaching Beatrice how to surf cast. It would have been the perfect summer, minus the uncertainty, and the unhappy looks she saw her dad sending in her mom's direction, and the way her mom's shoulders would stiffen every time Beatrice's father touched her, or said her name.

"Hey!"

Beatrice turned at the sound of a voice calling across the water, and saw a guy, maybe a few years older than she was, paddling toward her. Beatrice angled her board until they were floating, side by side, facing the beach, where a volleyball game was in progress. Beatrice could hear the smack of palms against leather, the good-natured trash talk as a girl leapt up high and spiked the ball down on the sand.

"Great day for it," said the guy. He wore dark-blue board shorts and a red Red Sox cap.

Beatrice nodded. "It's perfect," she said.

"You here on vacation?" the guy asked.

"I actually live here," Beatrice said.

"Lucky you," said the guy, his eyes widened in approval.

"That's right," she said. Her tone was friendly, but her expres-

sion was thoughtful and even a little sad. "Lucky me." A motor-
boat zoomed past them. Beatrice gripped the base of her board
with her feet, letting her body sway with the motion, instead of
resisting. "We used to just come for the summers. But this year
we're going to be washashores."

The guy considered. "I'll bet it gets lonely out here in the
winter."

Beatrice gave a little shrug. "I don't mind being by myself.
And we've got lots of company. My uncle Danny and his husband were here for a few weeks. And my mom's best friend lives
right up there." With her paddle, she pointed at a little cottage,
shingled in silvery cedar, perched high on the dune. "She's got
two nieces about my age, and they come up on the weekends, so
I've got some friends."

"Sweet," said the guy.

"Sweet," Beatrice agreed. "My mom's friend owns a restaurant
in P-town. My mom cooks. I bus tables on the weekends."

"What's it called?"

"The Abbey. Ever been?"

"I know I've walked past it."

"You should go," Beatrice told him. "Get the crabmeat-stuffed
cod. It's the best thing my mom makes."

"Sounds great. I love seafood." The guy turned his paddle in
his hands, gathering himself. "You, uh, want to come to the beach
for a while and hang out?"

Beatrice thought it over, balanced lightly on her board, sway-
ing with the waves that advanced and retreated beneath her.

"Maybe later," she said. "But right now, I'm just getting
started." She gave him a little wave before she turned her board,
bracing her feet, digging her paddle deeply into the water, propel-
ling herself out toward the fullness of the sun.

Acknowledgments

Writing a novel is an adventure. Even after all these books, and all these years, every time still feels like the first time when I head into undiscovered country with only my imagination to guide me. Writing a book during a pandemic presents a special set of challenges. I am very grateful to everyone on my publishing team for all their help and support through these difficult days.

Libby McGuire kept a steady hand on the wheel as she guided this book to publication. I'm grateful to her and to Simon & Schuster CEO Jon Karp.

This is the second book I've written with Lindsay Sagnette, whose smart, thoughtful suggestions improved the plot and the characters immensely.

Ariele Fredman is a genius publicist. She works hard, she's funny, she's good company, and she is mother to one of the most charming little girls you'll ever meet.

Dana Trocker is a marketing wizard, and every writer should be lucky enough to work with someone with her energy and smarts.

I'm grateful to everyone on the Atria team: Maudee Genao and Karlyn Hixson in the marketing department and Suzanne

Donahue and Nicole Bond, who handle my backlist and world-wide sales. In the art department, my thanks to James Iacobelli, who always makes my books look good, and to designer and illustrator Olga Grlic.

Thanks to Chris Lynch, Sarah Lieberman, and Elisa Shokoff in the audio department.

Big, big thanks to the assistants, who are unfailingly helpful and smart and will be in charge of everything someday: Libby's assistant, Kitt Reckord-Mabicki; Lindsay's assistant, Fiora Elbers-Tibbitts; and Joanna's assistant, Opal Theodossi.

Dhonielle Clayton did her usual perceptive job of editing this book, and her suggestions made it stronger.

I'm grateful to my agent, Joanna Pulcini, for all her hard work, on this book and on all my books.

Thanks, as always, to my assistant, Meghan Burnett, whose indefatigable good nature and good cheer made the isolation feel less lonely, and who, in addition to her stellar work handling all aspects of my working world, has become one of my trusted first readers.

Sarah Christensen Fu keeps my website spiffy and my newsletter on schedule.

Out in Hollywood, I'm grateful for the help of Michelle Weiner (no relation) and to my brothers, Jake and Joe Weiner (relations). And, on a very practical level, I'm grateful to everyone at the UPS Store on Fourth and Bainbridge, who acted as a miniature warehouse/shipping center/office during the pandemic and were unfailingly helpful, whether they were printing manuscripts or shipping books or towels or Girl Scout cookies. Thanks to Scott Vradelis and to Dennis Jardel, Ben Quach, Victor Rivera, Alix Fequiere, and Henry Vradelis.

I am grateful to all of the librarians and the booksellers who have hosted me for events, who've recommended my books to readers and recommended other people's books to me. Thank you for loving stories and for treating readers and writers with such generosity and kindness.

Of all the characters I've written, Beatrice Shoemaker is one of my favorites, and she's very much inspired by my own girls. I'm grateful to my daughter Phoebe, who is sweet and caring, who asks me "How was your day?" and actually cares about the answer, and especially to my daughter Lucy, who is funny and opinionated, for her help in explaining teen culture and social media, for occasionally letting me look at her Finsta, and for not being as difficult IRL as Beatrice was in fiction. It's true what they say: the hours can feel long, but the years go by fast. Lucy's gone from being a baby to a little girl to an almost-adult playwright/ director/stage manager in training, on her way to college, and it has been such a privilege to be her mom. The world is imperfect and there's still a lot of work to be done, but my daughters and their friends give me faith that the kids are going to save us all.

I am grateful to Bill Syken, husband and first reader, for his love and support, for being calm when I'm not, for his wonderful cooking and for laughing at (most of) my jokes. There's no one I'd rather quarantine with. And, of course, my dog, Moochie, is a loyal muse and a faithful companion.

My mom, Fran Weiner, and her partner, Clair Kaplan, probably love and appreciate Cape Cod more than anyone. I am grateful to my mother for introducing me to the Cape, and to Clair for teaching me and my daughters how to clam. And, of course, I am grateful to you, my readers, for your willingness to come sit beside me and let me tell you a story.

Finally, Carolyn Reidy, who died unexpectedly in 2020, was a force in the world of publishing. She was the president and CEO of Simon & Schuster and one of the very first people to believe in me as a writer. She published my first book, and every book since then, and was a tremendous advocate and a brilliant editor. When I was stuck, her suggestions would be pithy and direct, and pretty much always right. When I was done, she'd read an early version and send me a long, beautifully written letter about specific scenes she liked or lines of dialogue she appreciated. I was always grateful for her contributions to my books and for her advocacy of me and of women in publishing. Carolyn was one of the smartest and best-read people I've ever met. She understood how fiction worked, and, maybe more important, she understood how writers work. She was a pioneer who opened doors for the generations of women who came behind her. I was lucky to have worked with her and proud to have been one of her authors.

That
Summer

~~~~~~~~~~~~~~~~~~~~~~~~

Jennifer
Weiner

This reading group guide for That Summer *includes an introduction, discussion questions, and ideas for enhancing your book club. The suggested questions are intended to help your reading group find new and interesting angles and topics for your discussion. We hope that these ideas will enrich your conversation and increase your enjoyment of the book.*

Introduction

From the #1 *New York Times* bestselling author of *Big Summer* comes another timely and deliciously twisty novel of intrigue, secrets, and the transformative power of female friendship.

Topics & Questions
for Discussion

1. Daisy and Diana are originally framed as opposites—Daisy as the timid housewife and Diana as the woman about town. However, the two end up having more in common than they could have ever imagined. Compare and contrast these characters and what they learn from each other.

2. From *That Summer*'s onset, Weiner draws a connection between appearance, status, and perception; Diana even calls her executive getup "drag" (p. 96). What are some other ways that characters signal their status? Across the book, do you think clothes are used more as a form of personal expression or as performance? In particular, you might think about Beatrice's style and how it differs from her mom's or Diana's.

3. Our two main characters first meet as the result of a name mix-up. What is the importance of other names in this novel? In what ways do they serve as protective shields, or possibly burdens?

4. Various characters struggle with society's suffocatingly narrow definition of success. In high school, Beatrice observes that "all the kids bragged about how little sleep they'd gotten and how much coffee they'd consumed" (p. 44). Daisy creates her own dichotomy of better/worse life outcomes ("Instead of a college graduate, she'd become a mom" [p. 32]). Does this novel argue that success should be equated with happiness? Which character is ultimately presented as the most "successful"?

5. Diana still thinks about what her life would have been like if she'd never been raped; "sometimes, the sorrow of the road not taken would overwhelm her" (p. 240). How are other characters haunted by the past, and how do they struggle to retain control of their lives and decisions? Does the novel ultimately offer hope for how to move forward?

6. How is social class portrayed in this novel? What is the effect of having characters in relationships with people of different backgrounds? What is meant to be our takeaway about the concept of an "institution"?

7. Age is a major theme in *That Summer*: Diana was robbed of her youthful innocence, while Daisy was slotted into a maternal role usually inhabited by older women. Hal's horrific actions are mostly dismissed under the guise of his "manly needs" (p. 28), and Beatrice's actions are rejected due to teen stereotypes ("'Teenage girls. They get emotional. As I'm sure you know'" [p. 41]). How do gender and age intersect here? What is Beatrice's role in the novel, given that she is almost the same age that Diana was when she was raped?

8. Why do you think the author chose to set the novel on Cape Cod? What are some other important locations that inform or reflect these characters? Consider their homes, as well. How does Weiner evoke the power of both nostalgia and trauma in her descriptions? Is there a home you would want to live in?

9. Diana has had decades to imagine what she will do upon seeing her attacker. After she meets Brad she concludes, "'I think that this is what I needed. Just to see him, and have him see me'" (p. 301). What exactly does this mean? Did your feelings about Diana's quest change after Brad's death?

10. Diana describes a "world where being born female meant spending years of your life at risk, and the rest of it invisible, existing as prey or barely existing at all" (p. 375). Do you think that Beatrice's short-lived flirtation with Cade is proof that this principle still holds true, or is this a more generational concept? How do the women in the novel defy this idea? How does Michael fit into this viewpoint?

11. What is the effect of the novel's different points of view? What do we learn about Beatrice and Daisy in being able to see the two from each other's perspectives? How about Daisy and Diana? What did you think about Hal's final section, and did it change your opinion of him?

12. *That Summer* asks complex questions about who needs to be held responsible for assaults, and what it means to be a bystander. According to the book, what actions are considered irredeemable, and how has the Internet affected the answer to this question? Do you agree with Katrina, Teddy's high school girlfriend, when she says, "'I guess anyone's capable of any-

thing, right?'" (p. 289). How does this idea play into your idea of how severely actions should be punished, or whether they should be forgiven? Does the novel offer a definitive conclusion about who should be punished? How do the characters of Brad, Danny, and Daisy further complicate this question?

Enhance Your Book Club

1. *That Summer* is filled with mouthwatering food descriptions. Visit www.jenniferweiner.com/bookclubs to download the book club kit for recipe suggestions.

2. If your group hasn't already read Jennifer Weiner's novel *Big Summer*, consider reading it together and comparing its themes of complicated and enduring friendship with those of *That Summer*. What similarities do you notice between the women in these two novels? What ideas and feelings does Jennifer Weiner explore in both?

3. Consider donating to or volunteering with RAINN, the Rape, Abuse & Incest National Network, the nation's largest anti–sexual violence organization.

4. Beatrice loves making her beloved mouse crafts; Diana decoupages shells. Together with your book club, create a craft featured in the novel, garnering inspiration from creations on Etsy and Pinterest.